IF I COULD FLOAT ON A CLOUD, WHERE WOULD I GO?

SECOND EDITION

JENNIFER DAWN DECONINCK SMITH

authorHOUSE

AuthorHouse™
1663 Liberty Drive
Bloomington, IN 47403
www.authorhouse.com
Phone: 1 (800) 839-8640

© 2019 Jennifer Dawn deConinck Smith. All rights reserved.

No part of this book may be reproduced, stored in a retrieval system, or transmitted by any means without the written permission of the author.

Published by AuthorHouse 11/22/2019

ISBN: 978-1-7283-3405-9 (sc)
ISBN: 978-1-7283-3406-6 (hc)
ISBN: 978-1-7283-3404-2 (e)

Library of Congress Control Number: 2019917799

Scripture quotations marked NIV are taken from the Holy Bible, New International Version®. NIV®. Copyright © 1973, 1978, 1984 by International Bible Society. Used by permission of Zondervan. All rights reserved. [Biblica]

Print information available on the last page.

Any people depicted in stock imagery provided by Getty Images are models, and such images are being used for illustrative purposes only.
Certain stock imagery © Getty Images.

This book is printed on acid-free paper.

Because of the dynamic nature of the Internet, any web addresses or links contained in this book may have changed since publication and may no longer be valid. The views expressed in this work are solely those of the author and do not necessarily reflect the views of the publisher, and the publisher hereby disclaims any responsibility for them.

CONTENTS

A Special Thank You To ix
Acknowledgements xi
What God's Love Is xvii
Mini-Autobiography xix
Full Armour Of God.. xliii
Painting With Words xlvi
Inspiration For Writing This Story xlix
Introduction... liii

Chapter 1	Here I Go! 1
Chapter 2	Even In A Storm, There Is Light 41
Chapter 3	Was This A Miracle?.. 74
Chapter 4	Head In The Clouds 98
Chapter 5	Friendship Is Forever.. 129
Chapter 6	Something To Smile About................................. 159
Chapter 7	Papa's Forged Lamb Or Inferno's Puppet 199
Chapter 8	The Greatest Gifts, Money Cannot Buy 206
Chapter 9	It Is Time, To Come Home 218

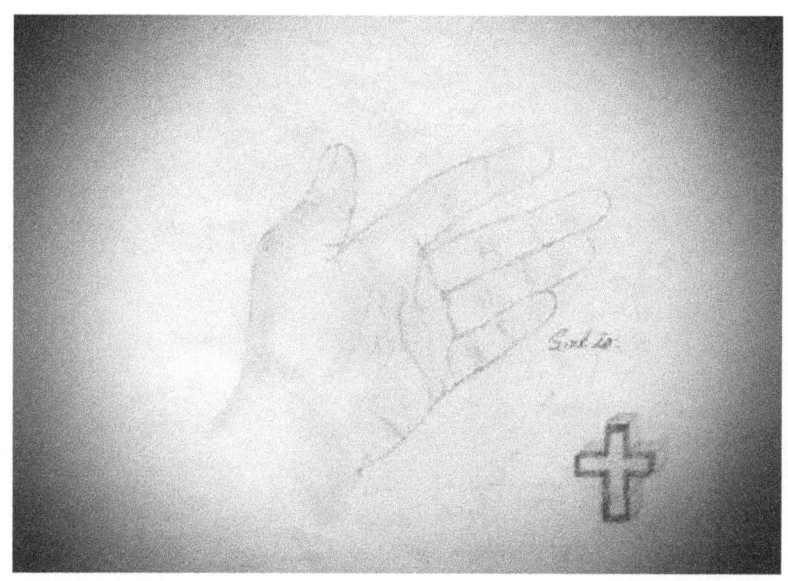

Pencil Artwork drawing of Papa's Hand entitled, "God Is" by Kipper

A SPECIAL THANK YOU TO

With all of my love and continued prayers,
I wish to give a special thank you & dedicate this
Second Edition, to the most special people in my life.
To the most wonderful, supportive & loving children
God has blessed me with, C., D. & C.
To the Best Friend & Companion in whom I get to walk this
journey with, during this temporary camping trip, Darcy M.
To the earthly spiritual parents whom I can call
Mom&Dad, C. & G.
To the many other wonderful people not mentioned
here that I also hold dear to my heart and lean on a lot
for support and prayer, you all know who you are!
And most of all, to God, my Papa in Heaven and
for His Gracious and Everlasting Love and
For Blessing our lives so abundantly, even with and
during the chaos of the highs and lows of life—
In sharing with me the privilege to live this life, <u>together</u>!
Thank you to all of you, for the continuing of persistent prayers,
genuinely loving support and for your faithful encouragement!

May God Bless you all abundantly! God is good!

Pencil Artwork drawing entitled, "Lynx in Winter" by Kipper

ACKNOWLEDGEMENTS

My strength and courage have abundantly been under fire throughout my entire life. Although we forget as humans and get down from time to time, I am learning that it is important to try to remember to be, consistently giving the credit to where credit is due—to learn to praise God not just during the victories in life but also during the storms. I now call God, my Papa, for He is my Brave...the Strength that I do not have on my own...the Courage that thrives deep within my spirit...He is Love, like no other...the Key to my Purpose in Life...My Hope is in Jesus, my Big Brother whom Rescued me and Set me Free...Papa is my Brave... my Teacher...and my Best Friend; my EVERYTHING. I thank you Papa, for your Endless, Unconditional, Everlasting and Eternal Love. THANK YOU! I love you Papa!

My three wonderful children, have always been my biggest supporters in my life and I cannot possibly convey just how incredibly humble in gratitude I am, for their constant, determined and unconditional loving support, as well! We have been through so much together and I wouldn't want it any other way, what a journey that this has been so far! Thank you to my precious babies, for all of the many memories that we have created together and shared, through the hardships and trials, to the victories and joy—for going through it, with you. I am grateful to have you all in my life, always. No regrets! THANK YOU, to my precious growing babies! You are such blessings to anyone and everyone, whom has the privilege to be apart of your lives. Never forget that you are, so loved and valued beyond measure! I love you always!

By God's own hand, it was an incredible miracle performed, in which I am truly grateful for. My children and I were delivered and given a place of protection and love...cared for, by someone I had least expected, for God to send our way. Words cannot fully express, my endless and humbling gratitude, to my Heaven-sent Best Friend and Companion—in whom I am to be able to spend my life with, both in fellowship and live freely in the spirit. My many thanks, go out to Darcy M., whom has sacrificed and flipped his entire life around—in order to provide for my three children and I. It is so cool, to be able to live in a loving and Christ-filled place where we can truly call, home. For me, I really feel that this is a second chance at life for us. Words cannot truly, fully express how grateful I am to you, Darcy M. THANK YOU from the bottom of my heart! No matter what, I will love you forever!

I am also very grateful, for the Christ-loving support and wisdom given by a growing number of wonderful Christian people, in whom continue to pour out their hearts, on a daily basis for others—both openly and relentlessly. God is so good. We really need to keep reminding ourselves of this truth because the way of the world's methods and ways of life, are always trying to bog us down and distract us from our Heavenly Father's peace and love. It is true, God really is, so very good to us!

To a wonderful married couple of many years, whom have constantly, kept me in their thoughts and prayers—loving me regardless of my faults and keeping it real through the heart of Jesus—these two have blessed my life and embraced me, adopting me as though I was one of their own daughters and taking me in under their wings. They continue to teach me to learn to soar through life without fear while persistently and always continuing, to point my eyes back to Jesus again and again—reminding me and encouraging me to look to Jesus daily and remember where my help comes from. To the spiritual parents in whom, I can now call Mom and Dad, C. and G. Thank you for loving me unconditionally, without condemnation, nor ridicule and for keeping us, both humbly in prayer and encouragement. Thank you for loving us and for your supportive wisdom given. I very much appreciate that you have always been willing to be a listening ear and a shoulder for me, to lean on when I need it but especially for always pointing me back to God and reminding me, of His everlasting and stable Love. Thank you for your hugs that embrace me, your smiles to encourage me, and hearts of fellowship shared with the Holy Spirit—with my heart and with my growing family. THANK YOU! I am very grateful for you both! I love you Mom and Dad!

"A new command I give you: Love one another. As I have loved you, so you must love one another. By this everyone will know that you are my disciples, if you love one another." —John 12:34-35

Papa, THANK YOU for loving me!

Pencil Artwork drawing of a tree losing its leaves entitled, "Autumn" by Kipper

Pencil Artwork drawing in progress entitled,
"Tiger In The Grass" by Kipper

WHAT GOD'S LOVE IS

"Love is patient, love is kind.
It does not envy, it does not boast,
It is not proud.
It does not dishonour others,
It is not self-seeking,
It is not easily angered,
It keeps no record of wrongs.
Love does not delight in evil
But rejoices with the truth.
It always protects, always trusts,
Always hopes, always perseveres,
Love never fails.
But where there are prophecies.
They will cease;
Where there are tongues,
They will be stilled;
Where there is knowledge,
It will pass away."

— 1 Corinthians 13:4-8

"I have been crucified with Christ. It is no longer
I who live, but Christ who lives in me.
And the life I now live in the flesh I love by faith in the Son of God,
Who loved me and gave himself for me."

— Galatians 2:20

"Be completely humble and gentle; be patient, bearing with one another in love. Make every effort to keep the unity of the Spirit through the bond of peace. There is no body and one Spirit, just as you were called to one hope when you were called; one Lord, one faith, one baptism; one God and Father of all, who is over all and through all and in all. But to each one of us grace has been given as Christ apportioned it."

— Ephesians 4:2-6

"As for you, you were dead in your transgressions and sins, in which you used to live when you followed the ways of this world and of the ruler of the kingdom of the air, the spirit who is now at work in those who are disobedient. All of us also lived among them at one time, gratifying the cravings of our flesh and following its desires and thoughts. Like the rest, we were by nature deserving of wrath. But because of his great love for us, God, who is rich in mercy, made us alive with Christ even when we were dead in transgressions—it is by grace you have been saved. And God raised us up with Christ and seated us with him in the heavenly realms in Christ Jesus, in order that in the coming ages he might show the incomparable riches of his grace, expressed in his kindness to us in Christ Jesus. For it is by grace you have been saved, through faith—and this is not from yourselves, it is the gift of God—not by works, so that no one can boast. For we are God's handiwork, created in Christ Jesus to do good works, which God prepared in advance for us to do."

— Ephesians 2:1-10

MINI-AUTOBIOGRAPHY

This mini-autobiography, is the shortened-version story of a young survivor, whom when faced with so many mind-blowing tribulations that were so rare and complicated—that not even professional specialists in the medical and dental field, could even fathom in how to help diagnose, ease or cure my suffering.

I did not have much of a physical immune system at all. Most of my experiences were quite harsh and unbearably painful and exhausting, with the symptoms and lab-rat testing throughout the processes. Despite where others were mentally and physically in their own lives—I had to withstand the tests of time through many such trials for the most part, braving them on my own.

I was born and raised in Alberta, Canada until I was nine years old, but then I moved to British Columbia, following my ninth birthday and lived there for four years. I then moved back to Alberta, where I completed my high school diploma in grade twelve, went to college following graduation and then moved to Saskatchewan the year after, where I was eventually married and gave birth to my three beautiful children. After many years later, through unresolvable matters—divorce was the healthiest choice that I had to make for my family. So my children and I then moved back to Alberta, where we now officially, call home.

So, to break it up a little bit and explain further, it is clear that I moved around a fair bit while growing up and later, into my adult years. I home-schooled for ten out of twelve years and then attended college at age eighteen, right out of high school and studied Child Psychology—successfully receiving Certification, in Early Childhood Development.

I survived many trials and tribulations throughout my upbringing, with more than enough excruciatingly and 'most painful known to man' sort of health complications and more which were due to far too many involuntary, afflicted stresses brought into my life. Many people would not have been able to hardly even bear, such trauma. I would not ever wish such pain on anyone else to have to endure. Throughout my life's testimony of nearly almost thirty-seven years to this very day, are amplified in number. I pray that if anything, other than my own personal learning through such forging in my life—that it may perhaps in hopes, be encouraging to others, to not to give up the fight.

I am a survivor of many trials, including the old 'Butterfly' Open-Heart Surgery method which was performed back in the nineteen eighties—which I had endured for Atrial-Septal Defect, at age four. I was born with a hole in my heart that did not close and the clean blood was mixing with the bad blood which had made me very sick.

This surgery was unfortunately followed by further, life-altering complications caused by an accident during the surgery—a severed sinus node complication had caused an irregular slow heart beat called, Bradycardia. This was then accompanied by an extended stay for me, in the ICU—the Intensive Care Unit, for an additional eighteen or so more days—on top of however long I had already been in the hospital prior, during and following my surgery...I remember being told on a regular daily basis that I could possibly go home soon but found myself just having to wait and wait—as yet another day, week and so forth had passed on by. I would not even eat my breakfast, until one of my parents would even show up.

The damage caused during my Open-Heart surgery as a result, had led to plenty of endurance testing at age five where I had to try and prove that I didn't need a pacemaker implant—which at the time, they were supposedly the size of a VHS video tape—remember those? Ha, ha! Well, many of you may not but they were the old original versions of movie slides.

Anyhow, as far as I have been told, these large pacemaker devices could have only been implanted, within the stomach region in children at the time. By doing so, this would have prevented me from many activities as a child whom lived out of town on an acreage, with brothers and we hunted and so on. I would have essentially had to be in a wheelchair, as even leaning over a railing or getting bumped by a ball while playing, would offset the implanted device and would have to then be removed, reprogrammed and so forth. I was so scrawny and sick for the majority of my childhood as it was.

During the process, I underwent a gruelling series of physical testing in preparation for a large meeting endurance test that would soon come, when I was five years old—about six months following my surgery. It would be to prove to those doctors, that I did not need one of those large pacemaker devices, implanted into my stomach for the Bradycardia that they had caused. I was told that supposedly, this would be a way they could cover their butts for the incident but who knows?

This was during the time when every doctor and nurse, to even the walls in a hospital, were pretty much all white and it had just felt so intimidating and unfriendly to me, as a young child. It was a time, when patients were even treated as numbers on a clipboard. I had the good, the bad and the ugly of medical experiences and doctors, throughout my life. Why do you think that now-a-days, many walls are different colours and even nurses wear a variety in vibrant colours and patterns, so that it is more friendly and less scary to that of children? Now you know.

The nerve wracking test day, had eventually arrived—it was time to face the music. I remember it like it was yesterday, as much of the memories are still very vivid within my mind. I walked into this fairly small, testing room in the hospital. There was a treadmill which I called a 'dread-mill,' an examining bed table, and some cabinetry and counters with a sink. I do not even think that there was a single window in sight. My biological parents and brothers were there with me and I felt okay I suppose, while I waited for my big moment at age five. In walked a nurse to prepare me for the biggest, medical endurance test of my life. There I stood on this dread-mill, wearing nothing but running shoes, light grey sweatpants, and a lot of wires attached with sticky things from my chest to machines. Then they arrived.

In walked white coats, one after the other. You see, it was considered 'non-orthodox' to perform such a test, to prove that I 'did not need' such an implantation at the time. I was told that my biological parents had to fight legally and in verbal communications, through multiple meetings and phone calls with both the cardiology department in the hospital and the pacemaker company itself—so that I could actually, have this test done to prevent undergoing the large pacemaker implant procedure at all. As little as I could understand at such a young age, I did what was asked of me.

The doctors entered the small room and literally, filled in the space behind and off to the right of me, as I could see them in the corner of my eye. I don't even recall, just how many had attended this meeting but there were many. I stood there on this machine, facing forward with no person in front of me, just the front of this machine and cabinet to my left. It is possible there was a small window up high to my left above the cabinet, however I do not remember that detail very much at all.

The room was quiet and then I heard chatter among the doctors, literally speaking out loud, just enough for my biological family to hear it—not even caring enough to realize that I could hear them too—Comments such as, "I got to see this" or, "she's not going to make it" along with laughs, had filled the room. I was five years old and this I will tell you, truly had tested my faith. I needed a miracle, for I could never get my heart rate up to anywhere nearly enough, for any test prior. My normal heart rate's rhythm was around forty-five beats per minute.

Another prior detail that I feel God wants for me to share with you, is about a week or so after my Open-Heart surgery but while still in recovery in the ICU—before I was released out of the ICU to go to another hospital room, an older male, head doctor, had come in. I was told that this particular doctor, did not believe that children could feel pain. Instead of a safe, routinely performed procedure to remove a handful bundle of wire cables that were sticking out of my chest, he grabbed ahold of it with one hand as I looked up at him while wide awake and then he pulled—ripping the wire cables, right straight out of my body! It had been so traumatic that I don't even remember, the part about me screaming—to before waking up some time later, with a breathing mask on my face and a black and white cartoon was playing on a tiny television set, in the ICU with me slightly propped up. I had no interest in watching it though… It had been explained to me, that the most horrifying screams could be heard which had echoed right through the walls, through those doors and down the hallway.

Sadly yes, it really did happen. I still have some of the physical scarring, even now. Prior to my hospital stay experience, I had wanted to be a nurse, we I enjoy caring for others but unfortunately following it, I had no desire to even try to become one because of the things patients went through and in how staff were at times. As a nurse, I would not have even been able to withstand seeing children, back then—endure being, just another number to the old-school doctors—as I had been. Fortunately, times have changed and have gotten better.

Back to my endurance test. As the treadmill machine was turned on, while facing forward, the belt began to move and I began to walk with its pace. I could hear some cheering from my older brother saying, "You can do it Jenny!" The machine sped up and to make it even more difficult on me, the doctors ordered that I was not allowed to hold onto nothing—not even onto the rails of the machine. I had to keep myself upright on my own, as I was now speed walking. The machine picked up its pace. I was now running and trying to grasp for air, as I normally would breathe quite shallow compared to others as it was, with longer pauses in between breaths. I literally, ran for my life. By this time, I could only hear the machine, as it was so loud and it drowned out any voices that may have been behind me. I ran and I ran, and I ran and I ran. I do not even know, just how long I was on that machine for, as it felt endless.

I remember no longer thinking about anyone else in the room, not even of the monitor screens, showing the speed and heart rate which I was not allowed to actually see anything, as it was blocked from my view on purpose—yet another discouragement, ordered by the doctors. I am crying, while I am telling you this story. I remember it as though it were just yesterday. It was so hard and even now, it is hard to even fathom that that child, was me—I needed, a miracle. Please, someone help me, I had thought to myself as I ran. I was supposed to get my heart rate up to one-hundred and two BPM—beats per minute. My heart rate average was around forty-five to fifty or even lower—for beats per minute and if I did any physical activity, my chest would just pound harder but not faster.

I recalled that the room was in an eery silence, no one even said a word. Then the timer rang and I was told that I could stop and so I collapsed and I fell. Just before I could hit the floor, someone or something had scooped me up in their arms and carried me to the examining bed table. I heard my older brother say, "Good job Jenny, you did it"…yet, I was so faintly exhausted that even my view was more of a fuzzy tunnel vision sort of way, as I could not see much beyond a couple feet passed my own eyes—only a narrow view of the motion was all that I could see, as I was being carried from the 'dread-mill', to the examining bed table. While wanting to know if I had been successful or not, I was then barely able to see the ceiling. As I lay down to rest, I wondered…did I make it? Then the last thing that I had remembered was, a doctor saying out loud, "Well, she will have to come back in six months, to do it again." A final let out of breath as I had exhaled in disappointment—I failed, I had thought to myself while so discouraged and then, I passed out.

Ever since that endurance test, I have found that throughout my life, when confronted with trials or times of pain that seem to want to push me to my limits—I had the tendency to go beyond them. I ended up overdoing it and pushing myself so hard that my body after a while, would be so drained and need a few days to recover afterwards. I would even get sick and then end up requiring even more time, just to recover. I have a habit of taking on physical pain harder and for a much longer period of time, that I just have to learn to remember that I do not have to go it alone. God is always with me and I am learning to lean into Him and focus on Him when in suffering. I find that by putting on praise music during a storm in life—during a trial of any kind, this method really helps.

Time had gone by and I was not even told, on what had happened that day until many years later. I know that I did not show up for a second endurance test, such as my first but I was not told anything. It had been kept from me and forgotten on purpose. Why? Why was I made to believe that I had failed, for all of those years? I could not understand as to why. Perhaps it didn't matter? Did I make it? I would often wonder to myself, on what my results actually were in the end. I would spend Sunday after Sunday, watching World Vision on television following church. My heart would ache for those children, as my desire grew more and more to want to help them. When I was six years old, I wanted to ask Jesus into my heart. I became a Christian in my biological parent's living room, though I did not know much about Jesus or of being a Christian, until much later in life.

So, what had happened on that day that I was tested, by the medical field, of 'old-school' doctors? Decades later, I was finally told. Not only did my heart rate reach the requirements of one-hundred and two beats per minute (BPM)—it was apparently a very traumatizing miracle not by man's strength nor credibility at all, but by God's own hand such that a miracle had happened. My heart rate, went up to two-hundred and four, beats per minute! It doubled everyone's own human expectations! Just amazing! For God sure had shown everyone that day, even if they did not, believe. No one in that room could take such credit in this miracle, because I had asked for help and received it by believing not in man but in God. My God, you do love me! A real Father that I did not even know yet, had rescued me—a big brother, called Jesus, that not even mankind could love me this way. What a miracle, to have survived through! Father, thank you. That was quite a miracle that everyone had witnessed that day, that perhaps the reason why no one would talk about it afterwards to me, for so many years, may have to do with the fact that not even my biological family could take credit for my Father's divine rescue. When we choose to believe with all of our heart and our mind, miracles do happen. Just, wow.... I believe.

All throughout my childhood, I had been sick quite a lot. My stamina was minuscule in comparison, to other children my age and among the children that I was around from the age of four, right into my adolescent years. Many did not want to spend much time playing with me—I often ended up visiting with my 'friend's' parents, most of the time. I was so scrawny and white in complexion, but was kept home for most of my years, to homeschool instead. I tended to disappear into my bedroom to either draw pictures or write poetry or music, or go outside and explore. I did not feel welcome to be at home among my biological family.

Over time, I had wondered the motive behind why, I was not allowed to have the implant, after the damage which was caused during my Open-Heart surgery. Was the endurance test necessary and led by God? Or was it led by self-righteousness through man and in turn putting me, through the fire as a punishment, caused by the enemy's scheming lies fed to man, to convince someone else's saviour chance to be 'the hero'? That may have been most likely but we are human and we make mistakes—as we were born into a fallen world, since Adam and Eve had first sinned. Yet through faith, even as little as I had—God used my bad experiences and made something good, from out of them. This is so that He can use these situations for the good of His glory so that one day, I could use them as a testimony of faith—along with the weapon of truth of God's word, in whom became flesh, Jesus the Son of God and so that His Holy Spirit, may live through me and shine—with forgiveness and in love, in the hopes to encourage others, down the road…

I had many thoughts and questions that had not yet been answered until much, much later in life. I am grateful, not about having had to suffer and bear the physical scarring throughout life, but to have healed by Grace, from the mental, emotional and spiritual scarring—through the strength and perseverance through faith, following the tribulations of my life, and into triumph from out of testimony, to show others not to give up the fight. God wants everyone to make it home. He loves everyone so much more than we could ever fathom possible because, **God *IS* Love**.

Over time as I got older, the ways of the world, in pushing people into become robotic-like, by distracting them from all of the goodness God is and wants for us—like making work, money, stuff, and self-righteousness to perform and serve self—even, 'be the hero' …has become priority to many. Truthfully, I don't even think that many people even knew of this taking place, within their own lives, or especially, within themselves. Even among my own biological family, the rollercoaster relationships with them, had seem to have fallen short over time—becoming less of a priority through much of our time spent together that eventually, was lost. Despite the fact that I truly, wholeheartedly loved and still love them to this day, our fallout and differences won't stop me from praying and wishing the best for them—to even now. Growing up, I especially adored my brothers and often looked up to my older brother, whom often on purpose, would get me into trouble…funny enough, I still looked up to him. I personally choose, not to hold onto grudges—so whatever he would try to do to me, I never let it come between us. It likely angered him, even more I suppose.

It seemed that the old way of mental, emotional and physical punishment fed by anger, had ahold of our biological dad's ways—in taking it as his preferred method towards his children, much more than showing compassion and God's loving merciful way instead; such as his own biological dad had similarly done to him as a child. So it was the only way that he had known. We cannot teach what we do not know and just as mercy, compassion, patience, love and so forth—we cannot give what we do not have, for such things if not learned lovingly through Christ's eyes, often become confused and performed in negative ways via the devil's lies. I still forgave him and chose to love him anyway. That is how I have chosen to raise my children, to this very day…to forgive right way and to love anyway. If I am to be a Christian, a Christ-follower—then I better act like one.

Finding out many years later, as a young adult now with children of my own—I had learned that my older brother had actually really hated me and I honestly, had no idea that he had felt this way all those years. I could not understand why. I would even help him out financially and with a roof over his head from time to time, when he was in a bind. I loved him like the best, big brother that any little sister thought they could ever have—I learned the hard way instead. For a brief moment, he told me that he actually, saw me as his hero, after all that I had gone through—he said that he looked up to me instead but had grown so envious and filled with a hate for me that he actually, wanted me gone and out of the way since I was born—once he was no longer the only child, as the first born. I could never understand this, as I did not have any positive, special treatment from our biological parents, like he had thought. He was envious and filled with hatred which then, when we choose to own the devil's thoughts that do not belong to us, we become filled with the emery's dark lies that overtake our thinking, cloud our judgement and end up darkening our hearts, toward others. It turned out to be the exact opposite actually, as it seemed that no one in the 'family' really wanted me around much, ever since my Open-Heart surgery. Though I could not understand why, because I lived forgiving and loving anyway, unconditionally—regardless how I was treated, or mistreated—it was never enough. I was really whole hearted towards people, I have a sensitivity for their pain—even in their own suffering.

Sadly overtime, immediately following my marital separation and seeking help from a mutually wonderful, old friend—my older biological bother had cut ties with each one of us and we had grown a part, as many lies had been spread about me, by the enemy's lies. I know this because of a confession that was made prior to my departure, right to my face that had never been withdrawn, to make things right. Their views on how I chose to go about my separation and divorce to be as fair as humanly possible, had angered them but it was not their business to make such decisions nor was it their place, to dictate how it was to go. I grew up in a house where everything seems to come with strings and with that, condemnation should you even dare to partake. I find it hard to even bring myself to ask for help from people because many just seem to go through the enemy's lies that which they took in, as false truth. I learned at an early age in how to be humble. I have learned that by to press in and hold onto faith, that God will, lead hearts by His hands, in His Ways and in His timing. Just being able to talk it out, with genuinely non-judgemental and caring people, is such a blessing. Everyone's experiences are different, for no two are alike. I have also learned that you have to be aware and be careful in whom you place your trust in, when it is in people in this world. Not everyone will be happy for you and your victories in life. Some people just like to be miserable and don't know any other way. It is also important to not lose heart when you have accepted something beautiful from someone, even a gift or anything that someone else had given you—that the enemy can and will try to use those things against you whenever he can. I have learned the hard way but I have also learned that it was not my fault. It was their own personal battle, they had yet to go through and to learn from. Through my separation and divorce, I had chosen to follow, only what God was telling me, because I chose to trust in Him alone, to guide me through—for I knew that He would not fail me. God knows all and so I knew that I had to trust Him, through that as well. It was a true test of faith, as many around me were of no healthy support—only going about it, by their own views or enemy-fed fears. The chances for any real relationship with my biologically immediate family, were no more. It was no longer healthy to be, together. I had to listen to my Father in Heaven, no matter what others thought, said or threatened. The truth of the matter of fact is that they never really knew me. Think about it, if all you hear is negatives and reminders of your own mistakes by those who think they are doing good for you but keep pounding your head in with condemnation, then they do not know you, nor can they be of a sound shoulder to lean on. Why? Well, this is because they are listening to the enemy's thoughts and lies a lot more than God's own truth and the enemy then will lash outwardly as he strikes inwardly, as well. This is why learning about the Full Armour of God, is so important and praying in the Spirit is listed last because it is the most important key to help make the full Armour, complete. When praying in the Spirit, we cannot dictate how the prayer will go. It is God's own prayer and only He, needs to understand the words being said. We are to trust in the Lord with all our heart and not lean on our own understanding. Right? In all your ways acknowledge Him and HE will make your paths straight. This means that only God can help and only He, will heal and restore you and your life—Not money, not circumstances, not accolades or entertainment, not idols or false gods in this world—not even, people. We are not to follow people, we are meant to follow Jesus. Only God will set you free and help you through, everything. God is a very patient Father, He is so loving with us and it is up to us, in how long we want to take to learn through our trials. People may not know me, nor accept me for who I am, or from where I came from, no matter how trivial or noteworthy of a life we have lived…God will accept us for who we are, when we accept, His Son.

If you could actually be able to divide the thoughts of God's own heart, from the fears and lies of the enemy—would it not be powerful to have the gift of discernment, to be able to literally, put your fears and the enemy's lies out of the picture, but honing in and focusing your determination through life, on Jesus and allow for our Father's righteous right hand to carry you, no matter what the enemy throws at you? That is powerful and that is possible—yet, even if it feels or appears to be impossible, we have to remember that God is a God of the impossible.

Let us be honest with ourselves—believers are in a spiritual war and we should not be ignorant of the enemy's tactics. When he attacks, are you aware of how he moves and slithers, of his own choice of weapons of war that war against you? A negative spoken word or thought, are very powerful and deadly—they come as a crippling heavy weighted fear, disguised in many forms and entertaining such thoughts or words, will harm you and others, much more than you realize. Take heart and be cautious of your words, before they exit your mouth, or fingers in a text message or email—negative thoughts are toxic.

Throughout my life, other's souls of all ages always seemed magnetized to mine—feeling that they could talk to me about their problems. That my shoulders were strong enough, or even experienced enough to bear their sorrow and for my ears to be mature enough to listen and understand—even comfort. I could not say no, for God gave me a kind and caring soul. I still am always wanting to help comfort others and not condemn them, nor run away for self.

I have been very ill on and off throughout most of my life. It was as though, I was often thrown into the fire on purpose by those, whom chose to hate or have a hate out for me while they listened to the devil's lies—a lot more often than anyone else that I had ever met or heard of, that would go through such affliction, one right after the other—yet, I remained able through God, to stand back up and try again. Just to name a few of my personal health battles throughout my life; I have had full trigeminal neuralgia nerve attacks on both sides of my head and face, numerous trips to the ER and stays in the hospital—my tonsils removed with complications, severe rare infections in the sinus facial area, and countless extremes that were beyond unfathomable to many and incapable to resolve by man. It took most of my life, that I had to gain such pain tolerance to withstand and bear such physically unbearable pain that would bring a grown man down to his knees in tears—and the mistreatment I had received by the many specialists over the years, would make you sick to your stomach. It was truly, only by my faith in God which has helped me through life.

Many years later, following mowing the lawn with a push mower one day at age seventeen—I had not been feeling too well, as though something had just gone terribly wrong and I didn't feel right. So I took a break and went back inside the house to my bedroom and laid down to rest. My heartbeat would be heavy enough to count beats, but slow enough to notice even more so, as it dropped suddenly to twenty-two beats per minute! I could not even move, nor call for help. I was so weak.

Fortunately by that time, technology had greatly improved and the size of a Dual-Lead Pacemaker, was about the size of two and a half to three pennies thick and only about two inches across in diameter. The funny thing when I had first went into see my old Paediatric Cardiologist, prior to my initial pacemaker implantation which I had undergone, to receive a Dual-Lead Pacemaker implant at age eighteen—the doctor, whom still practices there to this day, he had actually remembered me, after fourteen years! Wow! I couldn't believe it, that was amazing! He was so kind. I would go to him as a child for tests and check-ups. He had said that I was an 'Antique' as fourteen years later, the 'Butterfly' Open-Heart Surgery method, was no longer in existence. It was now a Day Surgery where they use microscopic technology. They put a plug in and you return home, the same day!Amazing!

Unfortunately, I would not have been able to wait that long for my surgery, as I was very ill and so I was in great need for the surgery at the time but I am very grateful and I thank the staff whom helped me—all along the way. I forgave those who caused harm and asked God to forgive them, for they know now what they have done or do—it was not their fault, accidents happen. My life has shaped me into who I am, scars and all. I choose to not live in regret, nor anger. I am grateful for what my Father in Heaven has relentlessly in love, forged me and made me to become—to whom, I am today. There is no other way to be, regardless what the way of the world says, or tries to do to me. We are to be the light, so the others can see Jesus in us and want to go to the Father through Him, and come home.

I had received additional Pacemaker implant replacements, roughly every five to seven years, depending upon battery use and routine testing programming performed annually. Thankfully, now with further changes and through learning what works best for my own heart and lifestyle—we managed to extend the battery life to much longer which will be much more beneficial in the long run.

Along with the multiple health trials throughout my life, I have had many stays in various hospitals that were both hellish ordeals and few, that were not so severe at times. While visiting with quite a number of roommates and other hospital in-patients and visitors throughout the years—despite dreading being there, I learned to appreciate the help and the company given. I have met many different people and I actually can remember most of them that from time to time, I think about them and send a prayer their way. Recalling a fair bit of detail, from the many medical memories that I have experienced, they are rather difficult to forget, as I have a very vivid memory and we humans, have the tendency to remember the bad memories, more so than the good ones—via the hands of the devil's ruthless determination, as he feeds his lies and negativity into our mind, relentlessly. What makes this a critical task to master successfully, is in how we rise from it—even learning to deflect his lying, no-good flaming arrows, so that they don't even have any chance to fester—let alone manifest and be entertained within our own minds. Just say, 'in Jesus' name, no'.

While dealing with a lot of the stresses of the highs and lows and negativity, in and out of the home growing up, I had eventually suffered from depression during my pre-teen, teenager, and even into my young adult years. I was bullied so much in a 'Christian' school during grades six and seven, by music teachers whom had their pupil favourites and wouldn't let me sing or take a solo role, as I so desired to and I could actually sing in tune. I was also bullied by a classroom of severely misbehaved fake Christian students, whom was classified as 'the worst group of students' in the school's history in the entire school, for two years! Daily, I was bullied on the bus by random children of all ages and at the bus stop by a group of three brothers—for which, not for many years until I was in my adult years, had I finally found out that it was because of something that my older brother had done—not me. I was treated like an outsider for two years, as it seemed as though, the whole valley was related, or had some kind of incapability for anything or anyone, new that it was like they had some kind of a hate out for me. I could never fathom as to why. I was kind to everyone. I tried to be everyone's friend, even turning the other cheek when others acted poorly towards me—while putting others first again and again, I still got beaten down, repeatedly. I was so hurt inside for years how could one possibly feel valued, even loved? Thankfully, I have learned from a wonderful friend, that God loves me completely and unconditionally and He deems me far too valuable to Him, to not be wasted. I was even bullied in church of all places, by a Sunday School teacher—none of them would even apologize to me—and I was bullied at home. I had such a low self-esteem and therefore, I overly put others first—often, at my own expense. I could not understand either side of it all, as 'Christians' behaved like non-believers, but preached the talk that they did not walk—nor did they behave as they should have. I was so confused, as to who was who and what was what. This could not have been Christianity, at all. Why did such things keep happening to me, I had wondered about this for many years! How could people, who would actually claim that they were 'Christian' choose to behave in such a shaded and twisted way? Now, I know that no one is immune to the enemy's lies and dark-minded, negative behaviour but by choice.

I was bit of a loner, I had little choice but had to kept my troubles to myself, as I didn't want to add to the many stresses that others, most likely already had on their plate. I went about it on my own though, God was always there with me, even when I was weak in my faith, throughout it. God never leaves our side, ever. I have many self-taught talents that I have gained over my life, as I used my imagination and creativity as an outlet which helped keep my sanity, through the many hardships that I had to patiently endured learn through.

Although things in life don't always go how we want them to, God has us in more realistic plans of His own. So no matter what happens in life, we must remember that we are always looked after. No matter how much we run and try to do everything ourselves, thinking that we don't need Him, when in actuality, we do need Him—He never leaves our side. Our lives are simply, not in our control. The devil wants us badly, but God wants us more. It is only through God's hands, done in His way and in His timing—only then, can we be right, where we actually belong. Only then, can we even begin to live in His Kingdom on earth, as it is in Heaven.

For most of my life, I had always tried to be close to my biological parents and brothers, even though we differed from one another's point of views, beliefs and choices made throughout life—not being on the same plate since childhood. Much has happened, to cause us to go adrift from one another but it has been healthier in ways, for both sides of the spectrum of life. It was apparent that I was not going to be able to grow in my relationship with God, had I stayed. Different values, goals and beliefs, greatly alter one's path in life and divides His flock but that just goes to show, the determination God has to persistently pursue us, His lost sheep—now doesn't it? I think that that is pretty amazing.

So, despite the hardships and the very different priorities, I still forgive them, I still love them, and I want for them to know that they are often thought of and prayed for, to this very day—regardless. I have no ill feelings towards them and I want the best for them, as I always have and that my friend, is the truth.

Just imagine what this world would be like, if we all chose to forgive and love anyway—and through faith in Christ, chose to believe? Imagine what this world could be, if God's children were not divided by denominations and the world could then actually see, the love of Jesus, through each and every one of us, as Christians. I purpose a challenge for all Christians out there, to walk in real faith—a lot more willingly and selflessly, and then see just how great, God's love for everyone, will shine through.

Through all of this you have read, it is obvious that I have an incredibly high tolerance for physical pain and have been through a relentless count of heartache and torment—but please don't think for a second that I don't feel anything, for I have a sensitive heart as well. I hurt when others are hurting. When in sensing their feelings, I try to let the Holy Spirit lead me in how to approach with proper, deep thought and caring caution, when their soul or God, asks for me to. My experiences vary in a vastly colourful and not-so colourful array, of highs and extreme lows. Surviving many spiritual, emotional and physical abusive and life-altering ordeals—which as a side-effect, had caused suffering in a great lack of emotional and loving support by both kin and false friendships that were clearly hurting too, from their own battles in life and didn't really truly know it, themselves. We are to come to the end of ourselves, to see that it is not about us but about God and letting Him, be God of all. We CAN DO, all things through Christ Jesus—when we choose, daily, to believe. We have to want, what our Father wants for us and that takes total submission to Him.

God is good. Thankfully, I am now in a place where I can mutually be free, from further non-Christlike ways of living which caused such affliction and neglect, to both sides of the picture…yet, I see that even those around me at the time, still were unaware of what they were doing or lack there of. Everyone is going through some kind of battle, some a little more noticeable and traumatic than others—some, still caught in the process to learn yet. I had never been all for divorce but it was by God's guidance to provide my children and I, with the more important necessities and values of life, that it was absolutely necessary and time to be able to move forward for us—making it one of the best decisions that we have ever made and I do not regret it. I am so grateful for my best friend and companion, whom has been of great support in our prosperous, spiritual growth in that of my children's lives and in our growing faith family.

The enemy is clever to deceive and confuse us with his many lies, fed to our minds that cloud our hearts. No human is immune to his lies. We are all human. Only Jesus was and is perfect—for there is no such Christian here on earth that has not fallen short on believing through God's gift of faith and made mistakes that was a misleading by the enemy, himself. But God is greater—surely we must get to a point of, actively believing this truth, beyond the shadow of a doubt? I have forgiven each and every one of those that I have crossed paths with in my life and I keep them in my prayers, as well. God wants everyone to make it because He loves everyone—so there is no need for me, to not do the same.

"As for those who were held in high esteem—whatever they were makes no difference to me; God does not show favouritism—they added nothing to my message." — Galatians 2:6

"For God does not show favouritism." — Romans 2:11

I am a God fearing woman—a Christian filled with a faith like no other that I have ever known before until recently, when I reunited with old friends, of various ages in whom I can share my testimony and both the highs and the lows with, companionship with kindred hearts through faith, honesty and love—without judgement, condemnation, nor ridicule. I now have a second chance in life, where I can continue to pursue my love of writing freely and creatively—to raise my children up right as best as I can and to continue to work hard in everything that God leads me to do.

The best thing to do for any bully, no matter how big or small they are—is to pray for them and tell God that you can't but He can and to simply, ignore the souring whine maker part. They know not what they do. The less attention you choose to give to a bully, the sooner they begin to lose interest, as they eventually will leave you alone. I have learned about spiritual discernment and am learning to be more aware of what God, my Papa—Jesus' Holy Spirit says and what the enemy says to try and ruin my day, for the most part. I am still in the learning, as we all are. In knowing the difference between both and that not all thoughts are our own, we can become much more of what God wants for us to be—through His eyes and not our own.

After nearly thirty-seven years, my passions in life have always remained, strong pursuits within my heart. From the ever-growing relationship in my faith and putting Christ first, at the centre of everything—to raising my three wonderful children, as a very strong believer, in putting both my faith and family, as top priority in life—and in that order. Being a parent, is such a privilege in life. I am learning so much, as they grow older and discover life in different ways, it is so cool to be apart of! I have always been very creative throughout my life as well—a hobbyist at heart. Even using it as an outlet, when times got tough. I enjoy motherhood, friendships, writing, photography, crocheting, music, singing, drawing, cooking, baking, crafting, traveling, hiking, mowing lawn, going for walks, watching movies, helping others, visiting with people and trying my hand at anything crafty and challenging—but always with Christ at the centre, of it all. I have always been a daydreamer and without it, I just simply, wouldn't be myself. I thank God everyday for everything wonderful that He has done for my children, for myself, and for those I hold dearly to my heart. I have nothing to complain about—only loving gratitude.

"Blessed is the man who perseveres under trial, because when he has stood the test, he will receive the crown of life that God has promised to those who love him." —James 1:12

"Whoever lives in love lives in God, and God in Him. In this way, love is made complete among us so that we will have confidence on the day of judgement, because in this world we are like him". — 1 John 4:17

— <u>*As is Jesus, so are we, in this world*</u>. —

Despite life's unexpected surprises, whether they are new illnesses or any kind of trial yet to come, everything happens for a reason—they are like hidden blessings, intricately woven in disguise, to teach us in our own personal stretching and forging, as we grow to be who we were always meant to become.

I have a highly greater appreciation for life and a much further along and clearer understanding, with a more positive and encouraging Christ-like attitude to go with it. What a joy it is to have a real relationship with my Papa in Heaven that I hold dear to my heart while pressing in, to remain in constant conversation in the Spirit with Him. God has richly blessed my life and I am both humble and grateful in faith.

You may ask, how did I get through it all? I was once told by a very good friend, that we can always learn something from everyone, even if they are doing it wrong. Everything is a part of our growing, even through the scares and the memories, to the blessings and amplified truth that God literally is here for us and loves us unconditionally! Everything happens for a reason in our forging, to become a beautiful new creation in Christ Jesus—a diamond in the rough—to become a well, sharpened and skillfully and wonderfully made, forged blade in the sword of the Spirit and lead God's people, home.

Thankfully, God does not show favouritism, we are equal in His eyes because of what Jesus did for us. When God the Father looks at you, He no longer sees sin nor death, no ill-thought feeling whatsoever. God sees us, robed in His righteousness and He wants to make good from out of our bad situations, as the loving Father that He truly is—if we just let Him in, to do that for us. God blessed me with people whom cared enough, whom delighted in Him, with the heart of Papa at the centre and reached out to help me get through—no matter how hard it became, I was not alone. Even though life has brought many challenges and tough ones at that, it would not be right to say that it wasn't worth it. I am grateful for the family that Papa has surrounded me with, for sticking it out with me, when the times got tough. We are to praise Him in both the storms and the victories.

My faith has certainly been shaky throughout my life, as I never truly knew much about the truth, between being religious and actually being a Christian. For I have learned a lot in that, the way of the world misuses such a position and privilege, when following Christ. No one is perfect, we all make mistakes—how else may we learn, right?

I have learned more over the last few years, through other's wisdom and knowledge, that Christianity is not a religion, it is a lifestyle—a daily choice to walk in faith, while putting all of your trust and hope into Jesus, regardless what the world is telling you, or pushing you to do. I would much rather be ready and know where I am going and share with others that in hope, they are encouraged—during such times as these. Truly, the most valuable thing that we do not want to lose, in all of this world, is our faith in believing what Jesus did for us—that is the most important treasure to hold onto, may we never forget that.

I do believe that children deserve to know the truth about what is actually important in life and to be aware of Heaven and Hell, because those two places are very real—they are not fantasy. So much truth is sheltered from children these days, while too much inappropriate things through 'the way of the world', has been overloaded onto children through public school teachings, to swearing, drugs, drinking and lust being exploited through catchy music—all a part of the devil's lies, to make people become accepting of it, without thinking twice. We have to remind them and ourselves, that he is here to seek, kill and destroy anything and everything to do, with God's plans for us—His children, from making it—and before it is too late for the unsaved. People are dying everyday. Heaven and Hell are very much real, so what are you waiting around for? When is it going to be time, to talk truth? If you truthfully care about someone and they are not saved, then what are you doing about it? It is something to think about anyhow.

We have Freewill—the power and privilege of choice, where good versus evil, is not just in the movies or in television shows, with fake super heroes. We already have a hero in whom has saved mankind and His name is Jesus Christ—and His work was finished on the cross, at Calvary. There is only one Saviour in this life and it is He. God is a gentleman. If we do not want a life with Him in it, then we will get a life, without Him in it. If we want a life with Him in it, then we will get a life, with Him in it. Remembering that the battle is a spiritual battle—about good versus evil and the enemy, Satan, the devil, Lucifer, Legion, however you choose to refer to him—he has been permanently cut off from Heaven. This is when God came to earth as flesh and chose, to come down to our level to become, just a man in the flesh—the Son of God called Jesus Christ, whom carried all of mankind's cross, was beaten and nailed to it. He took on all sin of man and asked for God to forgive us all, for we know not, what we do. Then, He died, so that we through Him, once He rose from the grave and in giving us His powerful Holy Spirit, that we may have eternal life and reign with God, forever—just amazing…it humbles me with emotion, in just thinking about it and I then once again, thank Jesus for His most, passionate, pure loving sacrifice—the greatest gift given, of all!

So back up here—the fact of the matter here is, that the devil whom is Satan and his demon minions, wants to prevent as much of the world, from being saved and join him in an eternity of an endless death in Hell… It is true, that the Christian life is not easy because believers are the very threat now, to the enemy—he is freaking out and angry, crude and jealous, and he hates every single one of us. Is this not enough for Christians, to want to save non-believers? We are no better than them, for if we got what we each deserved, we would all be going to hell. If Jesus did not do what He did, for every single human being on this planet, then we would not have the gift of hope and the gift of faith to believe in life, after this world. God is good.

In truth—Here is a thought, if one isn't really having any life-changing struggles in life, by actually being selfless and doing things for others that are good things and isn't saved as a believer, with Jesus in their heart—then we know, that they are not much of a threat to the enemy because well, they are already hell-bound and are not on the winning side. But if the person is a believer and is pressing into being selfless and helping others, and they are getting hammered with struggles that seem to try and throw them off—then they must be doing something right. If you are trying to please everyone, you will be miserable. If you have chosen to do good with your life and believe in Jesus and want to reach out to others to help—then you will meet resistance via the enemy's doing. But my friend, take heart and know that God loves you, no matter what trials come your way—lean into God and don't give up.

The enemy, the devil—he will attack through the mind and through circumstances, and even use people around you, from the medical field and science, to politicians and governments, to even those closest to you—to try and make your life a living hell—which is hardly a fraction of what Hell really, actually is like. God is so good. He is not the angry and mean Father that the way of the world has made Him out to be. That was Old Testament, we live in the New Testament, after Jesus died and sent His Holy Spirit to come and fill us with His Hope, His Holy Spirit and His power, to reign over the enemy's lies—for the battle is not against flesh and blood. We must learn how to deflect the flaming arrows of the evil one and realize, the truth—That Satan and his demons, cannot hurt us—he will relentlessly push to try and scheme and feed our minds, lie after lie but only, until we learn to push back hard through Christ and know that the devil is lies, all lies and a thief—and that we are not to own, such self-harming and toxic non-Christlike thoughts—ever again… **W.W.J.D?** Remember this? **What Would Jesus Do?** If when faced with a question that puts your morals on the stand, as yourself this. Ask yourself, **What Would Jesus Do?**—The next time that you are faced with an unkind, or untruthful and testing thought. That, 'inner voice' or 'let your conscious be your guide' is just the way of the world's way in masking the truth—for it is the One, whom speaks good and pours out His holy and pure love, not anger nor lust—that is God's Holy Spirit, trying to reach out to you with wide open arms my friend and He keeps on pursuing you because He loves you oh, so very much—and He wants for you, to make it too. Is that not, amazing? Is it not, finally time to rise up and put on, the full armour of God?

These are very confusing and troubling times. I pray for you, to have the clarity of truth and become aware with God's Spiritual discernment through Jesus, to come to the knowledge that is of the truth of Jesus Christ and the confusion in lies that which is caused by the enemy, the devil. In Jesus' awesome and holy, holy name… Amen!

I hope that you will at least, think about it. **GOD IS, L-O-V-E!** He died and rose again, for you, as Jesus Christ. I love you because God loves you. There is no condemnation, as a Christian when we have Jesus in our hearts. God is so good and truly loves everyone, regardless what they have done, or who you are. He knows all. It is not about what we have done but about what Jesus did for us—and that my friend, is so awesome!

This beauty of truth—it sets us free!—Free from the snares of the enemy's grasp and gives us life and hope again. May God Bless you, abundantly!

Life is a journey and our challenge, awaiting for us to test ourselves and to learn from our mistakes, so that we can better ourselves, in the preparation for other mistakes that we or others, may face down the road—because we are not perfect, we are human. This life, it is all about Jesus and the greatest sacrifice of all time!—And in us, for God's children, to prepare as many fellow humans possible, in the readying, to come home. We cannot graduate from the school of learning called life, until we have completed, what we were put here by God, to learn. Through all of the experiences in my life, I have learned one of many, very important things and that is—you should never doubt, what you can do, when you have the Living God on your side. God Bless you!

~ Instead of thinking outside the box…Think like, *there is no box.* **The sky is not the limit,** *the mind is.* **~**

Thank you for reading!

FULL ARMOUR OF GOD

"Finally, be strong in the Lord and in his mighty power.
Put on the full armour of God, so that you can
take your stand against the devil's schemes.
For our struggle is not against flesh and blood, but
against the rulers, against the authorities,
Against the powers of this dark world and against the spiritual
forces of evil in the heavenly realms. Therefore put on the
full armour of God, so that when the day of evil comes,
You may be able to stand your ground, and after
you have done everything, to stand.
Stand firm then, with the belt of truth buckled around your waist,
With the breastplate of righteousness in place,
And with your feet fitted with the readiness
that comes from the gospel of peace.
In addition to all this, take up the shield of faith,
With which you can extinguish all the flaming arrows of the evil one.
Take the helmet of salvation and the sword of
the Spirit, which is the word of God.
And pray in the Spirit on all occasions with
all kinds of prayers and requests.
With this in mind, be alert and always keep
on praying for all the Lord's people.
Pray also for me, that whenever I speak,
Words may be given me so that I will fearlessly
make known the mystery of the gospel,
For which I am an ambassador in chains.
Pray that I may declare it fearlessly, as I should."

— Ephesians 6:10-20

Pencil Artwork drawing of some wild looking clouds entitled, "Imagination Beyond" by Kipper

This is an incredibly rare find—a genuine double-blossomed, wild daisy that I had discovered during the summer of 2019! So instead of a four-leaf clover, may this truly unique beauty, bless you and bring you new beginnings—filled with nothing less than pure joy, in abundance! May God Bless you abundantly and know, that Jesus loves you!

— Jennifer Dawn deConinck Smith

PAINTING WITH WORDS

"Let Me Try
To Paint A Story
For You
With Words...
So That You
May Take
This Journey,
With Me!"

— Jennifer Dawn deConinck Smith

This Original First Edition Novel, was Self-Published in the fall of 2010. It was then recognized in the spring of 2019, to receive a Hollywood Coverage Synopses over the summer. Through this process, this novel has received an amazing review by professionals—catered to producing fine published work and production.

As the author, I was highly encouraged to expand and add more content to my novel—for a feature-length adaptation possibility! Following this very exciting and incredible news which I received at the end of the summer of 2019, I felt so blessed that I immediately began writing my Second Edition of, "If I Could Float On A Cloud, Where Would I Go?"

Throughout the writing of this story, I truly felt inspired by God—my Papa and so, it is with my hope and His grace, that this Second Edition novel, both encourages and blesses you abundantly!

— Jennifer Dawn deConinck Smith

INSPIRATION FOR WRITING THIS STORY

I was inspired to write this story from my own dreams and from both my personal and others' experiences throughout life itself—God's gifts come in many ways, shapes and forms. I enjoy allowing for His words, to flow from my imagination to paper, making it meaningful to write something that we can creatively express—together. I cannot imagine without Him, so all good-hearted creativity, is from Him.

Now, obviously I am not a boy and I have never experienced a life, with terminal cancer. However, I have personally gone through so much heartache, abuse and severe pain. I may be young but I have witnessed and observed so much in my short, fast approaching thirty-seven years—much of which, I would not even wish on anyone. It would be foolish for me to be ignorant to the world's many fears, for the truth to be revealed—why should I allow the enemy to silence me from telling my story, so that it can be heard, when God is on my side? We have nothing to fear, when we believe in the One. I believe, that we all have a story worth being heard—testimonies of weakness and that of strength. You are worth everything good because God made you. Remember that.

I was encouraged to expand and revise the original first edition of this story which I had created nearly twelve years ago and self-published back in 2010.

Experience, in this expanded version Second Edition of, "If I Could Float On A Cloud, Where Would I Go?" —As a view written from a young suffer's eyes, it is with my hope, in helping others through this book—to try and see life in another view, other than their own.

Our true challenge in life is to learn, for we never graduate from the school of learning called life, until it is gone—as we are here to grow from what we learn while we are still here. I fully believe that there is a reason to why things happen—a reason for everything, as they are all apart of our learning and growing.

Some say that it is our destiny, some say that it is fate, we can call it whatever we like, but no matter how many angles we look at it from or how many extra steps that it can take for others to get there—we all see one purpose, one goal, one finish line. If we do not experience, then we do not learn, therefore we cannot grow—we then become a broken record, going around and around in circles and getting no where.

Suffering is not something anyone should feel, but it is a part of our journey—making it another lesson in life. It is not about the end of our journey but about the ride, how we get there, how we decide to wake up in the morning, who will I be today, what will I strive to learn for tomorrow…through all of these and so much more, we can work together and build up life, instead of shorten it, belittling what it truly is about.

It does not matter what nationality, race, colour, or if you are religious or not, whether you speak one or a thousand languages, or where you come from—we are all alike, we are all human and we are all here to learn and to grow.

So instead of trashing one another, politically, religiously or not, different whether of disability or of different colour, height, weight, look, etc.; let us stop it, for we cannot grow from this.

No one said that life would be easy, they said that it would be worth it. Put your best foot forward and keep trying and when life gets too hard to stand, kneel. There is hope in the midst—keep looking. If you put your hope in Jesus, you can move mountains.

<u>*Change your heart and you will change the world. Life is worth living—just don't give up.*</u>

Pencil Artwork drawing of a fiercely wild skyline
entitled, "Fear Not" by Kipper

INTRODUCTION

In this story—*Experience a world of unique and creative imagination, through the eyes of a young boy,* whom is *living with cancer and is bed stricken*.

Connect with him through his personal adventures while *traveling on a cloud* and *through his incredible strength, in his cancer struggle.*

Uncover this epic journey beyond your own imagination—Explore a world of beauty, play, curiosity, wonder and *peace.*

Each child's illness in this story, is for you to contemplate—to *figure out*, what he or she may have; *for you as the reader*, must *read from cover to cover, to reveal the truth* inside.

Discover, for your own inner being, what an incredible strength through faith and strong-will can be—to persevere through anything!

Read, the Second Edition of, *"If I Could Float On A Cloud, Where Would I Go?" and decide for yourself, the true meaning to life*, itself.

<u>*Enjoy!*</u>

Pencil Artwork drawing entitled, "Yawning Jaguar" by Kipper

This is Kipper's "Self-Portrait" Pencil Artwork drawing entitled, "Me"
...And this is his story. Blessings and enjoy!

CHAPTER ONE

HERE I GO!

It was the bedtime calling coming from the hallway, as the late-evening shift nurse, had walked by my room in the ICU where I had been staying for some time now. ICU means Intensive Care Unit—this is where patients, who are in need of a very critical, specialty care, are cared for. I had so many surgeries since I was a baby that I honestly, cannot even remember just how many I have had—let alone, what each one was actually for. I don't think that I was ever really told about them before.

Generally, this place is for those who had just undergone a big surgery of some kind, or just need critical care and need to remain in this part of the hospital—for any given amount of time that is needed for them to recover. It is until then, once they have recovered to a stable condition, to the point of being able to be transferred from here—they are then relocated into a different part of the hospital, into a room where they will either stay until they can go home, or they are then relocated to an extended care wing of the hospital. This is where they don't go back to their home from where they came from and continue to actually live in the hospital, until the end of their time on earth.

Just being honest here—sometimes patients do get better and can go to a shorter term type of hospital room but also, sometimes patients do not recover and are transferred to the Long Term Ward which is where you are sent, when you are expected to stay a while longer—or until you get to go home but to Heaven. There is a separate Long Term Ward, one each for adults and one for children.

There is always the possibility that I might be here for a while longer—but who is to say? I just try to take one day at a time because that is all I can do. So why would I bother, in wanting to worry about tomorrow, when it hasn't even happened yet? Ha, ha…I would like to consider myself fairly, carefree in a way—I don't like to worry because it doesn't make me feel too good—so I choose not to.

I think that I would consider myself to be, well, probably a very artistic child, ha, ha! I seem to have such a big, gigantic imagination that I just have to let it out, or I might explode! Ha, ha, ha! I mean, I am practically always drawing something, even if it was a really small doodle, on the corner of a binder or a notepad—I would still be drawing, something… and sometimes, I would just be doodling and I wouldn't even be really thinking about it and then, after however long the time was that had just passed—to me, I suddenly would have a work of art, right there in front of me! Ha, ha!

My mind, it would like a volcano that is filled with a huge collection of creativity that just stirs and heats up, until it becomes beyond, a cool-down boil-over and turns into such a seriously, determined habit that is just so excited and going crazy inside and cannot help but explode words and drawings, onto paper with pencil and crayons!—And I just cannot help but let it rip! Ha, ha! That means, to let it fly or sail and shoot for the moon—to get it done! Ha, ha…

I think, as far as the imagination part goes…that if it is not used, to as grand and as wide of a scale, as it could possibly be—then it is kind of like a waste, don't you think so? What with my, unbound-less imagination that it is! Ha, ha! You can't keep my brain in a box, ha, ha! I like to think of it as, instead of 'thinking outside of the box'…*imagine*, there is no box. The sky is not the limit, *the mind is*. Kipper holds his closed hands into fists, up to each side of his head and then motions outwardly, opening them as though, making an explosion with a mind-blowing expression and sound effects, to go with it.

You can't catch me, ha, ha! When I daydream on my clouds or draw—I am free! Let me loose, I will show you the world in how, I see it! Ha, ha! I will plow through the blockades that try to stopple me down—they will not take me hostage! I command them to flee! Ha, ha! I will not give room to the enemy's deceptive lies that he so cleverly tries, to scheme upon me. No! Ha, ha! I, this brave young warrior of the ICU, shalt not give way to allow the enemy, to bring me to ruin. I have little time to waste to prevent myself from joy. I try to detail a picture, as well as one could be, with what little strength that I physically have…by painting a picture with words—but I obviously, do actually have a lot more strength mentally and spiritually as you see, than that of, physically.

You see…I cannot…um, how do I explain it… I am told that I am bed stricken, like, I have been told that it means, that I cannot get out of this hospital bed—let alone, out of any bed. I don't really know why but I guess it is because I was born this way. I have never walked before, in all of my life—or crawled, or sat up by myself, or even ran…I-I don't know why but I, well I just deal with it, this is my life and I just have to then use my imagination, as my outlet—my escape, you know?

When I cannot see a cloud in the sky and it does happen—there has definitely been days and days, and even more days that would go by, day after day, where I would go without seeing even one single, teeny, tiny cloud—not even one…it's just a deep and bright blue colour, all across the sky! I mean, don't get me wrong, that is nice and many people really love it but, if you ask me—it is kind of boring. Not to complain or anything but I just wanted to be honest. Fortunately, I have some strength in my hands and arms and so I like to read and draw, on those days.

There are so many good stories out there, written by others, each with a big imagination too! It is on such days as those, that if I am feeling well enough, to hold up a pencil and stare at the paper—I work on my drawings…it definitely helps pass the time and is relaxing for me. Don't you think? Do you like to draw and if so, what do you like to create on paper while using your imagination, as well? I guess there are many things one can do, especially when they can be mobile and use their legs and upper part of their body. What would you do with your time, if it was limited or delayed? I like to hear other people's stories—they are always good to read about, in helping pass the time as well.

I was never really interested in going to sleep at night. Well, not even during the daytime, if I could help it that is—as that is when I would dream of terrible and very strange things and much of what I did dream of while asleep—well, none of it made any sense and I don't like that so much. Do you get that too? I don't really like the feeling of, umm—in not being able to actually, actively use my own imagination, during nighttime dreaming because I don't have the ability during sleep, to have the 'privilege of choice' and to just be—well, myself.

I like being awake during the daytime because I get to gaze out of the window and just imagine, something beyond amazing, as I look out and beyond my current circumstances…even others just didn't always seem too thrilled to see me, or come visit me because they always came across as awkward-like—as if they were more embarrassed for my situation, appearance and lack of mobility, than me ever feeling that way, about myself towards them… It seems weird to me and kind of unfair, don't you think? It is not my fault that I look and live this way though—this is who I am, so I figured, why not embrace it, right?

I would often wonder of where the clouds came from but mostly, of where they would go. When using my imagination, I could see so many amazing shapes—they would turn into great, big adventures, above and beyond what I could make!

This is a collage, featuring some of Kipper's "Picture Journal Collection" Pencil Artwork drawings.

IF I COULD FLOAT ON A CLOUD, WHERE WOULD I GO?

I would then try to draw pictures on paper, drawing as much detail as I could, from what I had remembered—like telling a story but with pictures. I call it my "Picture Journal". I actually don't know how to write with words but I can draw and if I add detailing and try to be creative with my art, then you can hopefully be able to read my pictures but with your eyes. My Picture Journal, also helps me remember my dreams, my adventures. I would keep them in my own personal art binder that I had next to my bed, on my end table which was all of the time—it never left my side.

I also like to draw portrait pictures, of the many different roommates that I have had over the years. This way, it helps me remember them—from their faces to what they like, to even their smiles…that sort of thing. Pictures that I like to keep, well they are like a dose of medicine, that of smiles and laughter—they were friendly reminders, of happy memories. So when we take note of the happy ones and not of the sad ones that frustrate us, they can help brighten our day when we are feeling blue. I think everyone would really feel better, if they started trying that too.

Completed Pencil Artwork drawing entitled,
"Tiger In The Grass" by Kipper

Why remind ourselves of the hard times that just end up, making us upset or sad? I would much rather, remember a happy one but especially, when I am feeling down—that is then, what I like to do, when I pull out my art binder and look through the pictures. It is much healthier medicine, if you ask me. They would often remind me of the joy and laughter that brought tears to my eyes and would even make me burst out laughing, once again. It is so, totally worth it! You should try it! I am sure that it won't disappoint you but rather, uplift you instead!

While looking out the window from my hospital bed, I could see fluffy, white clouds and there were rainy, grey and blue clouds that often passed by during a storm—it was as though God had turned on the sprinklers of Heaven. To me, it looked as though the heavens had opened up, as the sky flooded with flickering flashes—hidden within the clouds as the rain began to fall. The raindrops fell sporadically, a little at a time and then it just came down steadily, as the thunder clouds rolled in.

Have you ever imagined God or the Angels, bowling? You know, bowling—the game where you wear those weird, clown-looking shoes and throw big, heavy marble-looking balls down a waxed surface, just to try and knock over those juggling pins? Or at least I think that is what they look like, I have only read about them...hmm...

Okay, okay, so it is kind of a weird question...but what do you think? Here is what I have been thinking... I wonder, if they have bowling up in Heaven? The reason I wonder that, is because of when a thunderstorm comes roaring through the city, over the hospital and passed my window—the thunder sounds like Heaven started a game of bowling. Ha, ha!

...And you know what? I would like to think, that if God in Heaven is bowling—well, He probably would get a strike, each time we would see the lightning bolts, crackle all across and through the storm-darkened, rumbling and flashing sky—and that the sound just travels differently, so we end up seeing the lightning first and then the thunder strikes, when the bowling ball hits the alley and knocks over the pins—then returns the ball... That's how I imagine it, anyhow...

IF I COULD FLOAT ON A CLOUD, WHERE WOULD I GO?

Pencil Artwork drawing entitled, "The Powerful Hands Of God" by Kipper

What do you think? The next time you hear thunder rumbling in the sky, let me know if you imagine God and His Angels, enjoying a game of bowling—together. Would you let me know? I would really love to hear your story! It could be so creative that you just may decide, to even write your own story, too! Wouldn't that be so cool?

Morning broke and the sun was shining in the clear and brilliantly, bright blue sky—even though, there wasn't a cloud in sight quite yet, I hoped and just knew that they would come by soon. They always do, eventually. I just have to be patient…which is something that I definitely need to work on—well, that we all probably need to work on, ha, ha! Perhaps we all could use a lot more, than just a little more practice on that one. Ha, ha... There are of course, plenty of days when the clouds do not even show up but I just then, try and focus on drawing my pictures instead—in the meantime.

What sort of things do you like to do, in your spare time? Another thing for you to try and remember, is that if you find that you do not have spare time, then that is a sign that you can and should, make the time...*just a thought*! Life is short and we may only have a little to spare, so it is critical to prepare for what is ahead—to know where you are going, for when this temporary camping trip's departure, has arrived. I would prefer, to have more of an idea of the timeline but I know that it doesn't work that way, or we wouldn't rely on God to lead us through life, with His powerful Holy Spirit, right? Or that is at least, what I have read about.

The daily routine began for me, as the nurses checked my vitals—they tested my blood pressure, poked and prodded me, took my temperature, listened to my heart, told me that I had to eat all of my porridge and drink up all of my milk... and they would ask me so many questions, as they would always do. You see...I was also hooked up to an IV which is called intravenous, I think? Yeah, um...I think that is what it is called. I am told that it is for fluids and medications, and stuff like that that the doctor would put me on, or rather put in me...ha, ha... I don't really know the names of them, so I will just leave that up to your own imagination.

Yet, all I really could think of was...as I sighed quietly to myself—of where the clouds were and how soon they would come back again soon... hoping sooner rather than later of course, as always. Ha, ha! Some days though, well they just can feel so, very, very long without them. I guess I am, fairly patient but, I don't like waiting for when I don't have a window, to try and look out of—to imagine. Do you know what I mean?

Another thing is, that I actually struggle with trying to keep up, on my fluids intake—so they were able to help me with that too—through the IV. I practically, was permanently attached to the thing that I guess I just, got used to it. Also, I wear a tube thingy that has little, tiny tubes that go right straight into both of my bear caves. Ha, ha!

IF I COULD FLOAT ON A CLOUD, WHERE WOULD I GO?

Pencil Artwork drawing entitled, "Bear In A Cave, Picking His Nose" by Kipper

Oh, you've never heard of that term before? Ha, ha! I call my nose holes or nostrils, bear caves, so that when I admittedly, ha, ha—need to dig in there for a moment, to clean one or two of them out, I actually pretend that I am digging in a bear's cave, to get the bear! Ha, ha, ha! "I'm going on a bear hunt…I'm going on a bear hunt. I'm not scared…I'm not scared…" that's the song that I think of, when I am trying to dig for a bear, ha, ha, ha! Pretty funny, huh? Ha, ha! It makes me laugh so much, ha, ha! Hey, I'm a kid—what do you except from me? Ha, ha! It's funny! I'd like to think so anyway, ha, ha!

Finally! At last, I could see a cloud—a blanket of white fluff afloat, gliding ever so gracefully, right across the sky—just in time, to come see me! Yay! Ha, ha! I laughed so much, every time I saw one! Ha, ha! I was just so excited! I would focus so hard through the window, staring really hard at one little cloud, as it moved by very slowly. It was my magic carpet ride, just ready to take me away! Ha, ha!

I closed my eyes tightly—allowing for my super, hyperactive imagination to take ahold of me, now. …While facing towards the warm and Heaven-sent, embracing sunshine that gleamed, ever so boldly and bright…oh but did I ever picture it—well, it was like I had become, this true and humble, noble royalty, striding to a different tune and that it was, of my sworn momentous, bequeathed duty—while picturing, breathing in the outdoor's fresh air, deep into my lungs through my nose—I then exhaled, as I smile with a great satisfaction—I was now sitting on the cloud and off I was, to leave this place and explore! Woohoo! Ha, ha, ha!

"Here I go!" Ha, ha! I called out, as loud as I could, for this was my reality that I forever wished to believe—it was so freeing for me, to be able to be outside in a curious, yet wondrous, daydream world-way, that just needed to be explored! Higher! Faster! I yelled! Ha, ha!

Hey, I'm whispering to you, yeah you, that is reading this…come with me and explore! Ha, ha! Woo-hoo! I was just so truly, very grateful…do you feel it? Just imagine it with me…*feel* that freedom! I am just so happy that I get to see such things that I, while sick in my hospital bed, don't get to actually ever see. So, come and imagine—dream with me. Yes, I guess I really do like big words, ha, ha! But a big imagination, need not be wasted, nor waste such awesome words! Ha, ha! I hope that you don't mind but you just have to admit that sometimes, there are designated moments in life that just, *scream* 'Big Words' and that they, just need to be said! Ha, ha!…And this, was one of those times, for sure! Ha, ha, ha!

IF I COULD FLOAT ON A CLOUD, WHERE WOULD I GO?

Pencil Artwork drawing of Kipper, floating on a cloud entitled, "Free Rein" by Kipper

"Faster, FASTER" I yelled and the fluffy, white cloud picked up its pace even more and just soared through the heavens so incredibly, whopping fast! Ha, ha, ha! Woo-hoo! I laughed out loud, as my cloud manoeuvred through, in and out and all around, what was an extensively spread out, skyline of heaven-sent rolling and puffed up blooming clouds—down and around, I went! Ha, ha!

While I was on my knees on the cloud, I leaned forward even more, as I held onto the cloud from out in front of me. I then darted even faster through tree tops—swerving and dodging in and out, above and under, and all throughout anything and everything that you could possibly imagine, of where a cloud could go—I went there! It was the most astonishingly, adventurous flight, indeed! Ha, ha, ha!

I just couldn't help but laugh out loud even more and tell it to go, even faster! Ha, ha! Yes, higher, HIGHER! I yelled! Ha, ha! I was so in my element, for this was my therapy escape, my evermore world—my earthly cosmos.

Suddenly below, in a valley blanketed with a wide variety of vegetation, of colourful wildflowers, green shrubs and both small and this, huge timber—among many different kinds of healthy, flourishing leafy and needle loaded trees. I then spotted a younger child than I— running to meet me, in bare feet and waving to flag me down. It was a boy, with wavy, thick chin-length and strawberry-blond hair. He was wearing knee-length, tan coloured cargo shorts and a white t-shirt. It was a little boy named Pete, he was ill too with something long term, just as I. We had met some time ago here, so we had remained good friends.

It was now time to make my landing—so I swooped around and downwards, to begin my descent, where I could go to meet my buddy, Pete. Hovering just a few inches off the ground's slowly, wavy wind-blown, tall grass—I had reached down my hand, to help Pete up onto my cloud and it wasn't long that we were then, ascending back up into the sky, gaining speed now and accelerating faster and faster we went—taking off to my place of peace. Woo-hoo! We both shouted, in a complete wonder and animation! We were just so excited and in our element—laughing a lot, as the cloud soared and dashed through the other clouds and around, through the mountainous forest. It was so awesome. What a thrill!

The meadow curved around a rock face, on a mountainous valley that was so stunning and filled with an abundance of life. Wildlife such as, a variety in breeds of deer, red stag, gazelle, antelope, red, blonde and even silver fox breeds—beavers, lemmings, chipmunks and squirrels, black and white pandas, and even red pandas too! It was outstanding! There were lynx, racoons, bush rabbits and longhairs, zebras, koala bears, donkeys and wild horses, gentle lions, tigers, bears of all kinds, noble wolves and friendly coyotes, cougars, tigers, leopards and jaguars—they were all gentle and purred like a kitten. There was no aggression at all, from any of them! It was crazy cool!

I could even see ferrets and mink, caribou, elk, moose and buffalo—big and tall elephants, giraffes and kangaroos. I could see just about every kind of animal that you ever knew and yet, some that I didn't even know had existed and yet, they all lived here in harmony—roaming the vast valleys, rolling hills, forest and climbing the mountainous rock face. The scenery really was breathtaking and very peaceful.

There was no shortage in aliveness—it was truly an animation of constant movement and thrill. Wow! From as far as the eye could see, it had taken my breath away, when I had first seen everything and then, again each time after that! Ha, ha! It was so cool!

Various Pencil Artwork drawings of Canada's mammals entitled, "Cool Wildlife" by Kipper

JENNIFER DAWN DECONINCK SMITH

Pencil Artwork drawing of the safe haven in one of Kipper's cloud adventures entitled, "My Place Of Peace" by Kipper

A variety of green moss species had grown and scattered the rock face and ground, in different hues of yellows, reds, greens, whites and blues—even pinks and orange. There was an abundance of life-filled ponds that were teamed with all kinds of fish and every water-dwelling creature possible—per each, according to their required size, of water body…wow!

There was a lively, flowing winding creek that was just down through the dip, in the valleys mountainous, rolling hills…and oh wow, were there ever, so many beautiful wildflowers! It was so enchanting, as I sighed in awe and wonder…looking at all of the many different kinds, colours and sizes of floral fascination that had blanketed the plains and in among the trees—the masterfully colourful birds of many, raised their precious young—even cool, very unique looking wild mushrooms of many, had dwelled there and in such an array of colours, textures, shapes and sizes. It was just, wow!

I especially loved, the incredibly fast and colourful humming birds—buzzing back and forth, at a highly rated speed from flower to flower. Oh and all of the different and very brightly, colourful tree frogs! They were so cool! Woooow! Nothing was poisonous here, for every living creature literally, got along and prospered—not one living thing here, was harmful at all. Just imagine!

Oh and you should see the hundreds of thousands, even by the millions—of hard working, little yellow and orange-golden coloured honey bees! They built incredible masses of honeycomb, in crevasses that were really deep within gaps, inside the mountain rock face walls! It was oh, so, so delicious and m-m good! You just have to try it! They are just so, amazing! Don't you think? And it is truly only honey bees, all across this planet, who are the only creatures who make all of the honey in the world! Wow! Ha, ha! Such, bizzz-zzzy, hard workers, they are! Ha, ha! Can't argue with that, that's for sure! Just, amazing! I solute the bees! Long live, the honey bees of the world! Ha, ha!

Varieties of richly filled berry bushes and trees, bared sweet and succulent fruit of many. Every kind of fruit tree possible stood there, just waiting for you to eat its harvest! Birds sang their songs of life and gave off a rhythmic harmony that brought a soothing calm to the soul, as it entered one ear and out the other—moving you as you took it all in, which caused you to move to it and tap your foot or hand in some way. It was surely, a most heavenly, graced venue to soak up, don't you think? I like to read the dictionary and thesaurus, can you tell? Ha, ha! I like trying to be creative with words and I definitely, love to learn new ones! Ha, ha! I would love to spend hours, just watching honey bees while they worked—from the fields during the pollinating, to the harvesting and making honeycomb, in their hives. I bet that, would be something really cool to see.

There were so many breathtaking, endless-flowing waterfalls that flowed down from the rock face, from up above—and as the sunshine glistened through the valley, a rainbow dazzled a luring beauty, across the waterfall's, graceful cascades. The view was so breathtaking to the eye and awe-inspiring to the soul. A heartfelt, toasty-warm feeling—it was just radiating from the warmth, of the sun's blissful rays which was inspiring a great depth of inner peace. To me, this was Heaven.

It was endlessly, thriving and breathing of life and to no end, with its countless beauty and prosperous, harmonious life that was just so, awesome and unfathomable to behold! Yet, it could very possibly have been, Heaven itself. What do you think? In your own words, how would you describe Heaven? It just had to be, I had thought to myself.

This is a variety of Pencil Artwork drawings, featuring some of nature's many wonders, captured on paper entitled, "Wondrous Nature" by Kipper.

IF I COULD FLOAT ON A CLOUD, WHERE WOULD I GO?

Pencil Artwork drawings of cascading waterfalls entitled,
"The Father's Overflowing Heart" by Kipper

I listened carefully at the sounds in the air...I could hear birds chirping, a wide range of enchanting melodies, as they flew by and landed on branches and all around near the creek—among where children by the hundreds, were laughing and playing throughout the valleys meadow greens. Children were even dancing to the many birds' glorious tunes. This nature's orchestration of Heavenly music was so riveting, it sounded like it could have even been, Heaven's welcoming song of Grace.

It was there, where Pete and I had finally landed, at our greatest destination...we hopped off the cloud and joined with other young children—all playing in the lush green meadow, running around and dancing in their bare feet, with arms reaching up into the sky, as some spun, twirled and ran around—in a relaxed comfort wear medley. Everyone was filled with nothing short, of an inner sheer joy. The collaboration of both nature's copious collection of sounds, when paired up with the children's joyful laughter—it could not possibly match anything else, more breathtaking and serene! Don't you think?

Then, as though in the background but from behind me, I faintly heard, "Kipper!" I then heard it again but it was a lot more pronounced and closer, "Kipper!" Oh yeah—that is me by the way—that is the name I was given, since as young as I could remember. I am not really sure in how I got it but I think that I like it…it's unique and well, I am unique too. As with my imagination, combined with the many adventures that I am so passionate about and with every chance I get—through the many worlds traveled on a cloud through the skies…they were always the highlight of my life. So yes, I think that I like my name very much, as I thought with a distinct satisfied smile on my face.

"Kipper!" My name was repeated and I snapped back into the present. Pete and I hopped off the cloud and it floated back up into the sky. It was another friend of mine, a boy named Nicolas, whom had called out my name. "Kipper, where have you been, buddy? We're ready to race sailboats in the creek!" my friend Nicolas had stated. "Awesome!" I replied. Nicolas, Pete and I had joined up with the others, who were over by the creek.

There were so many children here of all ages! I did not know many of them personally, but it didn't really matter much because we all just got along and well, we were all just, genuinely happy—running around and playing together, without conflict at all—just being here, was of satisfactory. We had met here so many times before that everyone was just comfortable. All boys and girls of many ages, none of the worldly confusion of genders, nor of any such dispute over race. We were of many and in many colours of skin—besides, racism is not born, it is taught… and we have no desire to learn such irrational unfairness here, ever. We all just roamed around and played in the meadows, the forests, the mountainous rocky hills and in the deeps of the waters that which spread across the lands.

"Kipper, do you want to know the poem I wrote?" Asked a girl from the valley side, her name was Roselyn. "Sure" I replied. "Okay, it goes like this" she stated…

"A Heart We Hold

What is this heart that we hold,
Given in time, as we grow old?
It can be touched and held with care,
But can be broken with words unfair.

IF I COULD FLOAT ON A CLOUD, WHERE WOULD I GO?

Giving it all the love it needs,
It builds up strong as we want it to be.
Some prefer it as cold as night,
But I prefer it as bold and bright.
In order to change a weakened heart,
You must first be tender and look afar.
Seek the problem that lies within,
Then piece it gentle together again.
In order to change a stone cold heart,
You just sometimes must break it apart.
To make it new and drain the pain within,
And then inside a new one will begin.
Life is indeed the world's pinnacle,
And friendship is truly a gift we hold.
For as one we are a miracle,
Together love is like a pot of gold.

What do you think, Kipper?" Roselyn asked. "It was very nice." I replied. "Thank you Kipper!" She had stated and then skipped along passed us. Another girl came over and had a poem as well. They had a group that worked on poems together and I guess they were finished writing them and wanted to show their work. Poems can definitely tell a story too, if one is listening. Another poem read like this:

"On Your Graduation Day

Today is a joyous day,
…And you knew that it would come.
You parents cry with joy and tears,
…For your child years have passed and gone.
Today is your great day,
…And the future says welcome.
Sometimes words are hard to find,
…But Jesus says, "Well done".

This next one was by a girl that hunted in the real world…

JENNIFER DAWN DECONINCK SMITH

"The Big Ones

While walking through the bush, the air got cold and bleak.
Thinking that I'd find the one, so I'd have a story to keep.
The sun was going down, and the end of the season drew near.
So we headed back towards the road, then we spotted two little dear.
My dad and I looked at each other, knowing that it was a little late.
So we passed them by and hopped in the truck, and said…that's okay.
As we turned the truck around, with the headlights turned on;
There was the big guy standing broadside, and we sat there in awe.
Little time passed but continued on, as we sat there and stared.
This massive buck had muscles, even a coat
rack and so we asked ourselves…dare?
With frantic breathing and questions of confusion,
we're waiting to make our guns dance.
That big old buck never looked at us, he just
watched those two little deer prance.
Oh brother, leap'n leopard frogs… really what can you do?
You'll know when man gets desperate, when
someone almost shoots you.
Now it's after dark and all of the deer came out to play.
The Hunting Season's now over, you know
the deer get smarter by the day.
So you know that there are deer around,
some even with large coat racks!
Trying to have patience though, this is something that hunters lack.
But just remember, all of you hunters out
there—be careful with your guns!
Those are wise old critters, living up their days
and they're identified as, 'The Big Ones'"

Wow! Now that was quite a poem I had to say. I hadn't heard one quite like that one before…. "Good job, Jenny!" I commended her on her efforts. "Nice job, girls! Ha, ha, that was awesome. Now, we can head down to the creek. It is race time!" Nicolas stated. "Woohoo!" Cried out Pete. "Let's go!" I replied and we continued towards the

IF I COULD FLOAT ON A CLOUD, WHERE WOULD I GO?

creek, which was not more than about fifteen feet away, from us to where the sailboat crew that had gathered. A crowd of spectators had grown too. The temperature had been always quite perfect here each time. Many children even floated on their own hand-built, two-person handmade rafts—right across the ponds, which were just down the valley side. Others would even swim all around the ponds, splashing and laughing—just having a blast! We also really enjoyed climbing the huge, massively gigantic, monstrous trees that grew here! They were epic cool! We would climb up the winding and very thick branches, of these trees which were the biggest trees in the forest! They were so incredibly huge, that you could build a home inside of their trunks or could have a seriously cool treehouse, built way up high in their huge branches and live in them! Now, wouldn't that be cool or what? Ha, ha!

Pencil Artwork drawing, featuring children climbing a big tree, on one of Kipper's cloud adventures entitled, "Continue The Climb" by Kipper

Pencil Artwork drawing of the view of the flowing, winding creek through the dip in the valley's mountainous, rolling hills entitled, "Serene River" by Kipper.

Among the dozens of children who were here, there were about ten of us kids, including myself, who had been working on a project for some time—can you guess what it was? Sailboats! Everyone who joined up, had to create their very own sailboat, right from scratch! We used materials that came right from nature—you know, natural stuff like sticks, twigs, leaves, bark, grass, flowers, vines, willow, reeds, feathers, shells, rocks, moss, mud and clay.

Practically anything that you could get your hands on, we tried building with! It was so much fun! Ha, ha! The great outdoors was our craft room! We could design it in however way that we wanted—making a sailboat out of just about anything from the earth that we could find. Then we all each gave our sailboat a name. It was an awesome project challenge!

IF I COULD FLOAT ON A CLOUD, WHERE WOULD I GO?

Pencil Artwork drawings featuring sandy beaches with white waves, crashing inland across the shore entitled, "God, You Are My Anchor" by Kipper

Today, was finally the day when we could put our final projects, right into action and just have fun with it! Everyone was just so excited! Out of the 10 children and me as you already know, as one of them—there are nine more children in the group that I will tell you more about. So, stay tuned! Ha, ha!

The ten handmade sailboats that are in the sailboat race!

JENNIFER DAWN DECONINCK SMITH

Pencil Artwork drawing of Pete's handmade sailboat
entitled, 'Slick Frogger' by Kipper

Pete, whom you met recently—he was about six and a half years old, with white skin and strawberry blonde hair. He made his sailboat out of a reddish-orange clay and banana leaves, for both the sail and the waterproofed exterior part, of his clay boat. He then used sticks, to hold the sail up and made it look like a frog shape, with shells for eyes and called it 'Slick Frogger'. Ha, ha—pretty ribbit cool, hey? Ha, ha!

IF I COULD FLOAT ON A CLOUD, WHERE WOULD I GO?

Pencil Artwork drawing of Kelly's handmade sailboat entitled, 'Commando' by Kipper

Kelly had just turned twelve years old. He had red hair, brown eyes and had to wear glasses in order to be able to see properly. He wore a horizontal, long sleeve royal blue and white striped polo style shirt, with dark khaki corduroy shorts on—but his sleeves were pushed up to his elbows. He built his sailboat from bamboo tree stalks. It was really inventive in how he used them—making it look like a raft, with a sail built from various waxy leaves that he had gathered and then attached them with grape tree vine. He named his sailboat 'Commando'. With a chunk of black coal, Kelly drew on the sail. It was a picture of a stickman with a captain's hat and he was saluting. It looked pretty cool, if you ask me.

Pencil Artwork drawing of Nicolas' handmade
sailboat entitled, 'Racer' by Kipper

Nicolas was almost ten years old. He was Asian with black hair and very dark brown eyes. He wore a dark red t-shirt and black pants. Nicolas had built his sailboat with a halved coconut shell, as the boat—carving it, to give it a point at the front and then built a little bit of a tent-like sail for it, which he used corn maze husk leaves for the sail and the stringy stuff that comes from the outside of the ear of the corn, to tie it all together. Nicolas named his sailboat, 'Racer'. Drawing an image onto the sail, he smeared on a reddish-orange clay, to make it look like lightning bolts. It was really unique looking!

IF I COULD FLOAT ON A CLOUD, WHERE WOULD I GO?

Pencil Artwork drawing of Sandy's handmade
sailboat entitled, 'Saint Peers' by Kipper

Sandy was eight years old and he was really dark skinned in colour. He had no hair and very dark brown, almost black in colour, eyes. He wore denim overalls with a yellow and green striped short sleeve polo shirt. Sandy decided to build the boat part of his sailboat, from carving out a really wide, fat stick. It actually had that similar look, much like a simple fisherman's wooden boat—it was pretty cool. He then used leaves for the sail and strawberry runner vines, to tie it all together. He named his sailboat 'Saint Peers' and then weaved a cross shape, out of thin, red willow tree branches and attached it to the very top of the sail's mast.

Sandy had said that it reminded him of a small countryside, nondenominational church that he attended before he had gotten too sick to be out of the hospital. He added that many people come from afar, just to be a part of the loving and very joyful atmosphere, where Jesus's heart, just loves on everyone—gracefully. It sounded amazing and I must say that his sailboat, was pretty impressive! I also wondered about the church he mentioned, as it had really sounded very nice. I have never been to a church before…it must have been amazing, considering that many people actually had wanted to be there and that the environment, was that of a genuinely Godly loving nature.

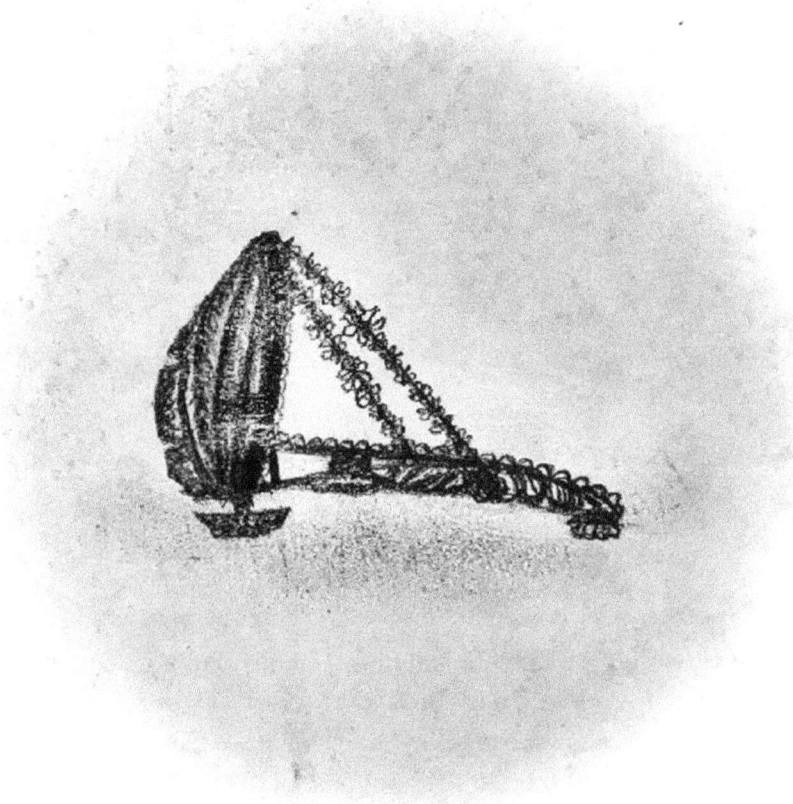

Pencil Artwork drawing of Marcy's handmade
sailboat entitled, 'Princess Missy' by Kipper

Marcy had two French braids—I think that's what she had called them—anyway, she had this light brown hair but with many natural blonde streaks of highlights that were mixed throughout…I guess you might call it a dark blonde or something like that? She had really unique and stunningly big, blue eyes a natural beauty for sure. Okay, okay—I may, have a little crush on her...but she is really sweet and pretty. Kipper sighs. Oh and her smile, she has some dimples that really come to life, every time when she smiles. Kipper pauses with another sigh, then continues—she makes my heart smile in return, even though I may have, a goofy look on my face, at the same time. Ha, ha, I don't really know...ha, ha...

Marcy was a little older than I. I think she was about ten and a half years old. She had a healthy-light tan and white skin complexion, with freckles across her nose from one cheek, to the other. Marcy wore a white summer dress that had white puff, short sleeves, with light yellow and salmon pink flowers and green leaves on the rest of her dress. Marcy also had matching ribbons tied into bows, at the ends of her braids. And then there was this handmade crown of flowers that she had worn on the top of her head—just around the top half of her forehead. She had made it from a variety of wildflowers that she had picked from the meadow greens. It looked really pretty on her. She just always had this really great, dreamlike quality about her, that was mesmerizing.

I will admit that I am a little shy when she is around because I don't really know what to say or how to talk to her... Do you know what I mean? I kind of just go into like a stare and after a little while, I forget that I am still staring at her—as though the world just slows down and everything goes into a pause, each time that I lose focus and think about her while I stare. I eventually manage to snap out of this trance she has me in, but only when someone, such as Pete walks by and kind of bumps his fist into my shoulder—just enough to wake me up. Oh my and her eyes... I have never seen anyone with such intoxicatingly beautiful, big, deep, bright blue eyes like hers.... *(cough, cough)*... Oh, uh right, where was I? Kipper's cheeks begin to blush...

Marcy created her sailboat, from a variety of different colourful duck feathers, some grey clay, shells, banana leaves, wildflowers, strawberry runner vines and real freshwater pearls. It was really fancy and decked out! Wow! I was really impressed! I managed to make a remark, on how really, fancy nice it was, but I think I may have stumbled my words. Ha, oops... She named her sailboat 'Princess Missy'. Awe, it was a perfect name for it, as she really did look like a princess...

Pencil Artwork drawing of Sally's handmade sailboat entitled, 'Rainbow Puff' by Kipper

Sally was eight years old. She had very white skin in colour. I think she was from Japan. Her eyes were a dark, hazel brown in colour and she had medium-length, shiny black hair that she wore in a ponytail, with a matching ribbon that was tied into a bow at the top of her ponytail. She had a light blue, summery-type of dress on, with very short sleeves and white lace around the trim.

You could tell that Sally was really into making crafty things because she used a lot of different natural materials to build her sailboat and she really made it, extremely colourful! She was very creative! Sally made her sailboat with a bird's nest for the boat part. She then wrapped it with waxy leaves for waterproofing, for both the inside and outside. For the mast, she used sticks to hold up her sail, just right. The sail was made out of a lot of very colourful feathers that she had gathered. Sally named her sailboat 'Rainbow Puff'. It was a very good name for it, I had thought to myself because it was very colourful and the feathers were very puffy—like a cloud.

IF I COULD FLOAT ON A CLOUD, WHERE WOULD I GO?

Pencil Artwork drawing of Marco's handmade
sailboat entitled, 'Bumbo' by Kipper

Next was Marco, whom was Mexican. He was seven years old and had a medium black coloured skin tone, dark brown eyes, reddish-brown, shiny black hair and he wore a light brown t-shirt, with dark blue jeans.

Marco made his sailboat, out of weaving together very green, bush tree roots that were like a weaved braid vine-look. It sure looked pretty cool in how he did it! He definitely had some skills. Marco then filled the holes in with a little bit of clay and mounted his sail, made with a nicely curved, delayered rectangular birch bark slab—and then to finish it off, he tied it down with thin but very strong, cattail reeds. He named his sailboat 'Bumbo'. He said that he really loved shrimp gumbo, which was his favourite food—so he rhymed with gumbo, to find a name for his sailboat and found, "Bumbo". Now that, was pretty inventive, I had thought. Marco then used a chunk of black coal, to draw a shrimp on the sail. It made me hungry! Ha, ha!

Pencil Artwork drawing of Andy's handmade
sailboat entitled, 'Silly Ship' by Kipper

Andy was six years old. He had special thick eye glasses on to see. His hair was like a bleached white blonde colour. Andy's eyes were a very bright blue and he had pinkish-white skin in colour. He wore a green t-shirt with navy blue pants.

Andy had built his sailboat in a very different way than that of the others. His sailboat looked like one of those, cool surf racing boats. You know, the ones that have two floats that were separated by a connecting seat in the middle and a very tall, big sail mounted in the middle towards the back—with a smaller narrower, pointy sail right in front of it, towards the front of the sailboat. It was just a real genius build, I think. He was really smart and could build all kinds of cool things, with moving parts and stuff—a real child prodigy of his time and at such an early age too.

He used, hollowed out bamboo shoots for both floats—carved and

IF I COULD FLOAT ON A CLOUD, WHERE WOULD I GO?

shaped just right, at both end tips for speed and to cut through the water current. Andy had then sealed the ends off with clay, so that no water could enter, from any angle. He used sticks for the masts, to hold up his two different-sized triangular sails, which were made from a grass weave that he had made and sliced to the right precision of both shape and size.

Andy had then decided to use a thin slab of wood, for the connection in the middle of both floats. He added some weight near the back end of it, using shells and put a little in the middle as well. Andy said that it would help keep his sailboat steady and that it would help it glide through the water much easier. He also Had made little fins, with pieces of wood that went through the bottom of each float, just underneath at the back ends.

Andy named his sailboat, 'Silly Ship' which I think, is definitely a very silly name, for something that is a genius build and is really actually, very cool! Ha, ha! Silly Ship…Kipper shakes his head, as he walked by with a smile…. Ha, ha!

Pencil Artwork drawing of Billy's handmade
sailboat entitled, 'Liberty' by Kipper

Billy was a big, broad shouldered kid. He was I think, eleven or twelve years old—actually, he may have even been more like, maybe fourteen years old. He could be a football player, at his size and with his strength capabilities because he could lift big rocks and carry much larger stacks of branches, than most of us. He had medium brown coloured skin, very short black hair and unique coloured hazel eyes. He wore a black t-shirt with blue jeans.

Billy built his sailboat using, nicely carved-to-length and pencil-sharpened, pointy end-shaped sticks for both ends. He then strapped them all together well, with a sturdy, thin tree vine that he weaved tightly together. He used some of a banana leaf as the sail, more hand carved sticks to hold it up and then finished it off, by tying it all together with more thin tree vine—fastening the sail to his raft-like sailboat. He named his sailboat 'Liberty' and carved an image of a Liberty Bell, into the sail. I was rather impressed, as it really did look like a small scaled version, of a real life-sized raft with a sail. It was so cool that everyone wished that it was life-size, so that we could all go for a ride on it! Ha, ha! Nice job, Billy!

IF I COULD FLOAT ON A CLOUD, WHERE WOULD I GO?

Pencil Artwork drawing of Kipper, building his handmade Golden Eye sailboat entitled, "Aspiration Assembly" by Kipper

As for myself, Kipper, we have already been introduced a little but you will get to know more about me, yet. I am about six—or is it, seven? Hmm…I think I am, seven… ha, ha! I have auburn colour hair which is short to the back of my neck and dark, deep coloured blue eyes…um, I am very pale in skin colour but that's just because I am really sick and don't get any actual sunlight, ha, ha—being stuck, in my hospital bed and all.

Um…oh yeah, what I am wearing, is not a hospital gown, that's for sure! Ha, ha! I tend to wear different clothes, each time that I journey on my clouds—it basically depends on what kind of an adventure that I am on too. Today, I am wearing a light blue t-shirt, which is my favourite colour because of the sky and clouds—with light, greyish-sand colour cargo shorts. Comfort, is the key ingredient for me! Ha, ha!

Pencil Artwork drawing of Kipper's handmade sailboat entitled, "Golden Eye" by Kipper

I had decided to make my sailboat with the top of the line, top secret, special ingredients…muawahahahahahaaaaa…. Ha, ha! Just kidding! Ha, ha! Okay, okay…so I decided to use Ponderosa Pine Tree bark—carefully and nicely delayered, to a smoother textured surface and handcrafted into the shape of a wide long ship, like a viking warship sailboat shape, from bow to stern.

I wanted to make a really nice and intricately weaved design, so I had made long strips of the delayered bark, braiding it and then sewed along the edging, for further detailing effect. The best way to use this bark, was to boil it in hot water and then it was soft enough, to use and separate layers that could then be manipulated easier while it was still wet and malleable. I had found a natural wax that I then melted and coated the exterior and interior for a waterproofing coating, after I let it dry to harden. This helped keep it watertight from leaks. Yeah, I'd say that I was fairly intelligent myself. Ha, ha!

I then sliced a huge banana leaf, into a big square shape and tied it to a t-shape mast, in the centre of the boat. I then made more braided rope, with thin layers of the tree bark and tethered the tops and bottom corners of the sail, to the back sides and the end of the ship. Finally, I then tethered the very top of the mast, to the front corner of the boat as well. I named my sailboat, 'Golden Eye'. Pretty sweet, hey? Ha, ha! I drew a gold colour eagle on the sail, with a yellowish-golden colour, chalk-like rock. I'm no professional artist but I think that it looked pretty awesome!

The time had finally arrived! Ha, ha! Woohoo! All sailboats were accounted for. There were ten, individually handcrafted sailboats, ready to go! "Let's do this!" I shouted! Every child, carefully placed their handmade sailboat into the creek. While still holding onto them, we all began the countdown together, before letting them go. Calling out loud, we had begun the countdown! "Three…Two…ONE!" and simultaneously, everyone let go of their sailboat! Yay! Woohoo!

The race was on! Look at them go! The sailboats would float, swerve and bump, along the creeks rough edges! They floated across the waters surface and down its centre—going with the flow and the power of the waters force and currents movement. No one could truly guess their direction, as nature took them to wherever it had decided! It was so exciting to watch, as this race unfolded! Ha, ha! Wow! Woohoo! Let's do this! Ha, ha! Everyone cheered out loud for their sailboat, as they set off, to begin the race!

"GO! Golden Eye!" I yelled, as Kelly's Commando, was just passed mine! I saw Pete's Slick Frogger had hit a rock and then suddenly sank to the bottom of the creek, while Nicolas's Racer was well ahead! Sandy Saint Peer's, was going down, "MAYDAY!" He called out, as it had got eaten, by a giant bullfrog! Whoa! Oh no! Ha, ha, oh my goodness! What? Ha, ha! We were not expecting, that! Ha, ha! Sorry buddy! What a rush!

Marcy's Princess Missy had suddenly bumped into Sally's Rainbow Puff! Oh no! Oh but they both thankfully, stayed afloat in the race! Oh my goodness! Fewf! I consistently would hope that Marcy's sailboat would do well. While wanting the best for her, as I would think to myself—I had caught a glimpse of her while she cheered her sailboat on. I'm pretty sure that I began to blush again! Ha, ha! Gosh, she sure was pretty…

Marco's Bumbo then picked up its pace, thanks to a gusty breeze which had managed to swoop down, just in the nick of time to help him on! "Ha, ha, awesome! Yesss," he yelled with excitement! Was it ever an exciting process to behold and be a part of, indeed!

Andy's Silly Ship carried onward down the creek, dodging floating debris along the way. His sailboat then managed to slide, right passed Billy's Liberty and right into first place! Whoa! "Wow, great job Andy!" We shouted! What a whirlwind of adventure! Ha, ha! Woohoo! Keep up the great work everyone! We can do this, I yelled! Then…

The scene suddenly changed from a most beautiful, breathtaking and wondrous place of peace—into a stuffy, small room that was surrounded by many beeping machines and those nauseating cleaning medical smells—I was suddenly back, laying in my hospital bed.

The head doctor was examining me and asking me many questions—though I was still a little out of it, as I slowly woke and heard such sounds and talking, however, I was not completely alert just yet. I had then heard the head doctor, order for me to be moved to a different room—one that was filled with others, just like me… 'Just like me…' I dwelled on those words, rather cautiously. They are going to move me, into the Long Term Children's Ward—this had scared me, as I had thought quietly to myself.

Many thoughts had overcome me, with such big worrisome concerns, as they began to roll right into my mind and all throughout my head, all of a sudden. Will I, b-be next to a-a window? I had thought to myself. Questions were now completely overwhelming my mind and I began to stutter even more while in a panic mode. D-do they even, h-have windows in th-there? Are th-the n-nurses, s-scary? Will, I get a n-new b-bed or d-do I s-stay, on th-this one?

What if, I g-get cold and-and they don't wa-want to p-pay any at-attention, t-to me? I m-might freeze into a g-giant ice cube! B-brrrrr! Ha, ha! Ouch, yikes! I thought to myself, just above a whisper. I am u-usually, p-pretty c-cold as it-it is…. I began to worry myself sick, you know into a fr-frenzy but of sheer and utter panic! MAY-DAY! I was going down! Kipper made a falling sound with a crash into the ocean sort of sound with his mouth. I mean, w-what will I-I do? I asked myself. I was so worried, as I thought to myself—feeling so uncertain of the, potentially inevitable unknown—I was overcome by, fear.

I began to think about those fears that had me cringing, of even the very thought, of change. Where did all of these sudden, fearful panic thoughts, even come from? They felt like they could be mine but I am not usually that, afraid—I was most definitely overcome by a doubtful fear—it was so skeptical for change, that it seemed to even have held me, captive! Held against my will. I was taken as, a prisoner of a mental war! A POMW! What was I to do? I had thought. It was as if I was chained to a cage…well, I did not like it one bit! I was afraid to ask anyone, anything! Even all of the white coats seemed to intimidate me—even more. I was so incredibly leery, of this 'relocation situation,' that's for sure!

I-I, well I guess there is only one w-way t-to find out, is-isn't there? I took a deep breath and then slowly let it out, as I tried to slow down my heart rate and pause long enough to think this through but without panic on my confused little mind… "Okay Kipper…we can do this" I quietly whispered to myself… "be, brave Kipper…be brave…" I took a deep breath and slowly let it out and repeated this, until I felt, a little calmer. It began to work…

I turned my head towards the clouds, staring and wishing to go back—my face had just filled with a grave concern, once again—but just then, the nurses had grabbed me and pulled me back to stay in my hospital bed. So, as I lay in my hospital bed, with my head facing towards the window—I peered through at the clouds that had floated on by… I had my arms on the inside of the bed railing and my right hand was gripping the side railing bar of the bed. Then for a moment of pause, all movement had slowed right down, all around me—to a slow timely motioned fashion. I looked up towards the window, to the outside world, the entrance to my dreamworlds of many—and then, slightly waving with an upward motion with a couple fingers and then slowly back down—to the window and dear clouds, I had to say, "Until we m-meet, again…" The window was covered.

JENNIFER DAWN DECONINCK SMITH

Pencil Artwork drawing entitled, "Even In A Storm, There Is Light" by Kipper

CHAPTER TWO

Even in a Storm, There is Light

It was sometime in the late afternoon, I think—it was hard to tell as I could not look out of the window that was once upon a time, uncovered for my imagination's view. There was a clock on the wall but the minute hand just twitched back and forth, while the hour hand never moved, not even once. It never seemed to work properly, for what I could remember. But even still, when you think of it, even a broken clock is right, two times, every single day… which is rather impressive, for a broken thing. Just imagine, what a human being could do in this world, even when broken?

There were a few nurses that had walked into my ICU room, which if you can remember, means Intensive Care Unit. The nurses had come in with a transport hospital bed and began to carefully unhook various cables from the machines attached to the walls above me, behind my hospital bed. They rerouted lines and power cables, intravenous tubes and such—then reconnected them to the portable machines on the transport hospital bed—that were still hooked up to me, where I lay. I guess they were most likely getting me ready for transport. Once they were ready and had gathered up my own personal things into a bag, they placed the bag on the foot of my hospital bed, on top of my legs—the nurses then transferred me, out of my ICU room. Could I possibly feel, any further in despair?

Well, I sure sat there in despair all right, as I was feeling rather intimidated beyond belief. The feeling was as though I was being, totally ripped away, from something so familiar. My imagination had then taken over, as I was imagining myself standing on a dock, wearing a life jacket that was all fastened up and properly secured, right to my body—but then, all of a sudden, someone had then decided to take it completely off, then forcing me to jump into the water without it—even giving me the push, to fall in! I was feeling so upset and saddened, all at the same time. What an unfair and sorrowful thing, that was charged upon me... I had thought to myself.

Okay, so that maybe was an overdrawn thought—but that's, just how I felt... I was really upset! It was a deep and most desperate despair of disappointment that had led me downward, into a depressed state of mind. I was tremendously uncomfortable being forced away from my window— to give it all up, being ripped entirely from it and against my wishes. What else was I supposed to do?

While on my hospital bed, I was wheeled out of the Intensive Care Unit, down a hallway, into a big elevator, then out of the elevator, and down a long stretch of what seemed to feel like, an endless maze of hallways...oh my goodness! Could this long and dreadful traverse, possibly take any longer, that time felt as though it had abruptly slowed right down and decided to just become very still—making it seem, even more unbearably unpleasant, of a wait?

Are we there yet, I thought to myself? I was beginning to feel dizzy, from staring at all of the lights, lines, vents and signs in the ceilings and walls—as I was wheeled on my hospital bed, while laying down. This was my first majorly big move and I'm not so sure, if I had liked it that much...

Finally, we had arrived at the admitting desk, in the Hospital's Long Term Children's Ward. This is where I think, I must have waited for several minutes which felt like forever to me—as the transport male nurse was talking to the secretary staff and signing something on a clipboard while they laughed and chatted a while longer—eventually checking me in, I think.

I had been in the Intensive Care Unit for a really, really long time... actually, for my entire life, in-between surgeries that is! So, I will honestly say that this change, had seemed so scary for me—if you can understand, my nervousness? My butterflies were I think um...nope, I am pretty sure that they were puking, actually! Yeah, pretty gross, right? The movement of turns and changes of hospital scenery flashing passed my eyeballs, had made me feel pretty nauseous...and I was feeling a tad on the hungry side as well...

Pencil Artwork drawing of Kipper, laying awake in his hospital bed, in the ICU entitled, "Fragile, Yet Hopeful" by Kipper

We then started moving again, I had no idea where I would end up next—I have never been to this part of the hospital before. I could feel the bed rolling along and could see that the surroundings around me, had continued to change and proceed along—even passing by other people, as they either walked on by, were wheeled in a wheelchair, or were pushed in a hospital bed as well, like I was—staring at me, with what had felt like a judging yet curious concern, or so I had thought. We then made a sudden turn, went down a hallway and through large double doors that had opened automatically. I then noticed that the nurse had waved his lanyard-attached ID badge, across something near the doors and then all of a sudden, both doors actually, opened and at the same time! Now that, was unexpected!

Okay, so for the record, I have to talk about, that! Now, that was pretty cool if you ask me—the nurse was like, this special top secret agent, with the rite of passage, or like a special VIP access and only he, had the special, very important person passage, access—for only the exceptionally brave and purple heart-heroic people that which, have been through the most unfathomably, horrible events. This passage way, was not like any other before, indeed.

Yet, after surviving a great number of ordeals, to make it this far—to now, I, 'Kipper the Brave' …am nobly being carried in, on their special, transport VIP mode. I was being cordially escorted, by special ops security guards, whom were equipped with these VIP badges that would automatically summon doors, left, right and centre, to just completely obey and open on demand—without having to even, say a single word. Outstanding!

Lookout world! Here, here, now enters a highly decorated, wounded soldier with whom has collected, a boxful of purple hearts, for his honorary, new corridor passage way…to discover and explore, new unchartered, territory that is yet, to be unearthed by 'Kipper the Brave'. It was truly, a most hypnotizing experience! Ha, ha!

We then, went into this large room that had a lot of patients in it. We have arrived, I guess…it was the hospital's Long Term Children's Ward…a final destination, for children whom have failed to recover, indefinitely. I then over heard the nurses talking…that this is where I would end up, for my 'final extended medical care'…now that, had made me cringe, just hearing it… What it actually meant, was that they had given up hope and decided that from here on out, I would not recover…

The transportation had come to a halt, I was now next to another hospital bed. The nurses each took a side of the sheet I lay on and I was then lifted off of my transport bed and onto a more high tech, hospital bed. It had a lot more buttons and features, than I at first, had even realized before. It was also, hmm… Actually, it was really comfortable which I definitely, did not at all, even expect that. I was positioned in the middle of the room, with many other patients. Now that the transportation had finally stopped moving, the room's spinning had slowed and finally came to a motionless stop, which met up with my nausea's stance, as that too had finally slowed too.

It really was, a very big room but thankfully, each patient had a sectioned off space above them and there were some carts and end tables that had divided up our spaces a little. We each had, moveable curtains that were attached to tracks up on the ceiling as well but seemed open for the most part—but for when we wanted, or needed privacy that is, they could be closed...

You remember that I couldn't get out of bed, right? So, they had to help me get bathed and washed and also go to the...well, you know...while Kipper quieted his voice in his head—to go to the bathroom but in a bag thingy... I know, gross-me-out, right? Ha, ha! Oh the joys of life—catered to indefinitely, in being very dependant upon others, completely... It is a little embarrassing to say the least. The joys of life? Oh, I say that with utter sarcasm, obviously, as I roll my eyes...

I tried to look around the room, to get a good view of what I was dealing with here by my surroundings... but my observation was blocked by nurses, busily astir—setting up my new space, for me. I knew they were just trying to do their job and help take care of me but what I really, really wanted, was for them to honestly just please, please just move out of the way, so that I could look to see if there was a window, ha, ha!

Finally, people had begun to clear the way and like a slow-motioned movie scene while watching people move on by—they unveiled the mystery that which I was longing for. I was able to allow for my eyes to wander even further, with such a longing gaze that I had not felt for so long—it was now that my eyes could then finally maneuver in unison with my imagination now, beyond my hospital bed. I looked over at a great distance and there where it stood boldly, was a big, tall window, off to the left of me but it was so many feet away—I was still very grateful though that I just couldn't help but begin my efforts, to try and catch a cloud, as quickly as possible.

The room was filled with children of all sizes and ages, each ill with something that needed the extended care that this special ward supposedly offered—for the fortunate to recover, or for just plain forever long term, for those who could not—hence the meaning, terminal—the forever exit, to no return. Terminal means that they are just beyond very sick, with something that is out of their reach for rehabilitation, that humans, can no longer help them—just as I was now there for, too…

I without a doubt, felt that the only way for me, was to, well… to have even thrived for this long and still have any shred of sanity left—especially now more than ever—it was and will always be, whenever I have a window that I can look out of, from my hospital bed. I would then instantly daydream and let my wild imagination break free, taking me on amazing adventures—as they helped me get by and then time, didn't seem to matter much to me at all. Drawing was just all fine and dandy but I drew of my adventures on my clouds, as they were my ultimate inspirations to record on paper, so that I could remember them.

Although, I stared as hard as I could, passed all of the other patients and new-to-me staff while trying to get a glimpse of a cloud… everyone seemed to look at me strange but it didn't bother me. I just stared passed all of the funny, strange and curiously judging looks—with all opened eyes, they were undoubtedly, focused on me for sure.

My neck was soar from just staring in the distance—straining to get the right glimpse through the window, as best as I possibly could but again I didn't care, as by that time, the pain didn't even phase me much. Nurses even tried to move my head away at one point—trying to tell me that it was not healthy for my posture and that it could cause knotted up muscles and painful cramps or worse. Okay, so they were not far off, as they were right, it did… but I just had to keep trying. Each time lately when I would try to stare and await for a cloud to arrive, something or someone would interfere my efforts. If it was a clear blue sky, then it was a nurse, patient, doctor or visitor in the way. If it were not any of those, then it was one of the patient's privacy curtains that had been closed, which blocked my view. There seemed to always be some sort of a blockade in the way.

Please know that I right away, would forgive them within my heart and ask God to forgive them, because I knew that they just, didn't understand my reasons. One nurse got frustrated and shook me once a bit, not harshly, but she was just trying to get my attention and gently grabbed my head in her hands, to get me to look at her—to see if I would listen. I didn't listen very well, I guess that I was just really stubborn. Perhaps, at first they had thought that I was a little out of it, you know, like a bit dumb in the mind and unable to discern their attempts and then respond accordingly... In time, they would adapt to my routine, just as the ICU staff had to. I was still very new here and to them all, even after a few weeks now that had passed on by, without a single chance of a cloud adventure.

    I wanted my window, my clouds—my world with one sky, through whatever window I was blessed to look out of...so with each time after any nurse had struggled to turn my head towards them, I continued to look the other way towards the window's direction. Eventually, the nurses just finally gave up and shook their head, as they would then leave the room or go tend to another patient, more willing than I... but it was okay, they didn't have to understand, nor did anyone else. I honestly didn't do it to deliberately make them or anyone else, mad or frustrated—I just wanted my window. I felt a little alone without it, as I had no family to call my own, no picture frame of me in it, with a mom or a dad...so I continued to try again, for moment after moment, I would not budge.

    So, I decided that I would just suck it up, like a buttercup, ha, ha...and I took in the aches and pains as bravely so—with all of my inner might. In doing this, like so, when I could take off on a cloud—I truly would feel free on my adventures. It didn't have to make any sense to anyone else, but me. Some time had passed and after what seemed like months that had gone by, without there being not one single cloud for me to be able to see—I painfully but slowly, turned my head back to centre for a bit once again and stared up at the ceiling above me. I was laying in an upright sitting position in my hospital bed, so it wasn't completely flat that I thankfully, could see more than just ceiling.

Pencil Artwork drawing of Chunhua, holding her treasured stuffed bunny rabbit toy, entitled "One Of Papa's Angels" by Kipper

After while, upon eventually resting my neck, I decided to study the room around me, as I glanced across the way. There were so many different faces, none of which I had ever seen before—no one that I had known any how... I felt a little timid at first while I looked about the room, but I couldn't help but continue to study what was around me... I had nothing else to do. Ha, ha...

There was a little Chinese girl off to my right, reading a picture book rather quietly to herself but just loud enough that I could hear her, just a little bit. I could see that she had a blanket on her bed, which, it must have been from home, I am guessing—as it looked nothing like a hospital blanket. They let patients, do that here? I had wondered. That was pretty cool, I had thought to myself. Not that I could have that kind of an option, as I don't have a home outside of this hospital, let alone, family to bring me stuff.... Her blanket was a dusty blue colour, which was covered in different coloured daisies all over it—even her pillow case had matched. I'm guessing that daisies were her favourite flower, perhaps?

She also had many drawings that hung throughout, all over the wall and behind her bed, in her 'room space' that maybe were signed by herself, as the writing was not English, but more drawing-like, in Chinese—from what I had read in books to compare. She must have had a really good imagination too, as she drew about a bunny rabbit which I could see, was the stuffy that was cradled in her right arm, on her hospital bed. From what I could read at an angle, her name was written in Chinese.

She suddenly paused her reading and looked over my way—catching my glimpse, she saw that I was looking at her drawings that hung all about. She then started talking and it caught me off guard and I kind of shook my head suddenly, as my eyes were drawn toward where the sound was coming from and away from the art on her wall. "Ha-woh" she said as she continued… "I Chunhua. It means, spring flower. I five, I from China," She added. It was as though I had swallowed a frog when I tried to speak, as I had not actually, spoke out loud to anyone for sometime now, that my voice was really croaky and hoarse. "Uh, he-hello. Um, m-my n-name is, Kipper. M-my name, is Kipper." I repeated with a stutter and then pushed myself to continue. "I-I think it m-means s-something about, wear-wearing a crown." I continued, while I tried to push through my stuttering that is often brought on by either shyness or fear… "I-I think I am s-seven and I am fr-from, this ho-hospital." I replied. "Oh okay that uh, it very, how you say, very cool!" She replied. "It nice to meet you, Kipper." She said with a smile. Her English was broken up too, so to me, it felt like we could relate when talking and I began to no longer feel, so terribly shy anymore. "I-it is ni-nice to meet you too, Chunhua," I added, as I replied with a smile and relieved that I had stuttered less, that time around.

"Chunhua…" I continued "w-why do you always k-keep smiling, if you are not f-feeling well?" I asked. "Oh I happy because I have Jesus, in my heart." She responded. It puzzled me a little, while I had thought about what she had just told me, so I asked another question, to add to what I had already requested to know about her. "But, w-what does that m-mean, Chunhua? To have, Jesus in y-your, heart?" I asked her another question, as I was really curious, in what she had meant by that comment.

"I, I Christian… I have, Jesus Christ, inside my heart. How can people not be filled with smile, when He live in me, or in you?" Chunhua smiled again, as she continued to try and explain this further to me—to a very confused, yet just as equally intrigued, young boy—to me, Kipper. The look upon my face must have been quite something, as I sure felt really dazed and confused but so eager to know more about this mystery that left my heart, wanting so badly to discover, so desperately to be aware of what and whom this man, Jesus is. "I tell you what this means, if you would like that?" Chunhua had asked me, as she pointed to a bracelet on her left wrist. "S-sure, yes, th-thank you Chunhua." I replied.

Looking at Chunhua's left wrist, I then responded, "What is that on y-your wrist? What is, W.W.J.D?" I asked her. "It means, What Would Jesus Do? See, I Christian, right?" She continued "When you and I know truth and choose to embrace it, we no more, are sad or lost. We joyful and love more—we free. Those who know they are, forgiven much, will love much. You see?" She added. "That mean, I believe in Jesus and I remember in my heart and in my mind and in my spirit, that God sent His only Son who is, Jesus Christ, to die for all my sin, so I not have to, try to earn my way to God's Kingdom…not just for me but for all the world, who choose to believe, will have forever through Jesus, real life…" She added. This seemed like the deepest of all secrets that the world never knew, yet, she knew and now I do too. A mysterious gift yet to be unwrapped and passed around for all of the world to see, this, truth… I was fascinated by this new discovery, indeed!

Chunhua paused for a moment and then looked up towards the ceiling for about three or more seconds and then she looked back at me and continued to speak to me, as she motioned with her hands while she spoke. "See, I look to Jesus. I ask Him, what I am to ask you. He, um is right, there. He here, with us" she had said, very confidently, as she pointed towards the ceiling, just above her and then to her heart…. "He, all around us, everywhere" she finished. "Oh… um, wow okay…" I then responded, looking rather surprised and unsure but yet, curious enough that I wanted to know even more.

I tried to soak up the information overload but despite the fact that it was confusing at first, it was beginning to make sense to me—the more that I had thought about it and accepted it, as truth. "Do you too believe?"

IF I COULD FLOAT ON A CLOUD, WHERE WOULD I GO?

Chunhua had then asked me, with a smile. I had to think about it but then as I opened my mouth to speak, I found myself replying with a, "Y-yes, I-I think I do." My face lit up with a realization upon my face. "I don't know, er or I guess I don't really know, Him. W-why do you ask?" I asked her. "Well, do you, believe, in all your heart, that Jesus die for you? So you be free and live forever with Him, in Heaven?" She asked me once again. I could tell that Chunhua, was trying to make sure that I understood what she was trying to convey to me—to tell me—that it must have been, very important to her to do so.

I thought about it and then replied, "Um…I suppose um—w-well, I think I want to." I continued "What do I need to do, to be happy as you are in life—even, while sick?" I asked her. "Well, all you do, is believe. That's it, no need to do any thing or chore or anything else because, Jesus did everything—to give us hope, to put our faith in Him forever, when He die to cut off the devil from Heaven once and for all time. Jesus Christ, He forgave us and freed us from our sin, forever. Pretty cool, hey?" Chunhua remarked. "That d-definitively sounds pr-pretty cool… really amazing, actually…wow, He loves me that much? Wow…" I responded, as I had pondered further in deep thought and felt a greatness of emotion, of sadness for Jesus but also a relief and thankfulness for Him, all at the same time—for what all He had done, for me. "But, I don't even kn-know Him." I stated. "He know, ALL, Kipper… He know all and He love us anyway." Chunhua replied. I began to tear up, in shock and amazement.

"Kipper, do you want to invite, Jesus to live in your heart?" Chunhua asked me, as she continued. "Okay, so do you Kipper, want to know Jesus? You want Jesus, in your heart?" Chunhua asked me, with a great interest to help me, know Jesus more. "Um…I don't kn-know this Jesus but I th-think that I wa-want to." I remarked. "Yes, I think I-I w-would like that." I added, as I began to open up my heart and with a curious mind, I smiled back in return, through tears.

Chunhua smiled and continued, "Okay, fold your hands like dis, okay, now close eyes, think with your mind of Jesus in Heaven, like you are talking, right to Him." She continued. "Then repeat after me okay, Kipper?" She explained. I then nodded my head in agreement and listened intently, to what she had to say, with a purposefully intrigued and open mind and hungry heart, as she continued, to teach me more about Jesus.

"Dear Papa in Heaven," she had started to lead me with words. "Dear Papa in Heaven," I had copied her words but from my heart, to Him. She continued... "Thank you Jesus, for your love and I want, for my life, to be yours, Papa." "Th-thank you Jesus, f-for your love and I-I want, for my life t-to be y-yours, Papa." I echoed her words, as I felt a warming enter my once, impenetrably confused, rigid heart and cold body—now, feeling a warming sensation, go through me that I had never felt before.

Chunhua then continued and I continued to echo her words. "Dear Big Brother Jesus, I ask for you, to now enter and live in me and I ask, for your Holy Spirit, to show me your Way. Please, be my Saviour forever and ever, Amen." Chunhua finished, as she awaited for me, to repeat all of what she had just said. "Dear B-big Broth-brother Jesus...I-I ask f-for you, to n-now enter and l-live, in me". In trying to speak, it at first felt like I was trying to walk through a pool of tar but with my tongue, like someone or something was trying to prevent me from speaking such words...but then, as soon as I asked for Jesus to live in me, I could feel my stuttering beginning to disappear now, as though my words became easier to speak out loud, while I continued to talk to Him... "And I ask, for your Holy Spirit, to show me your, Way." This feeling, was amazing and I felt an inner confidence, I had never felt before in all of my life. I then confidently continued and finished with the remaining words... "Please, be my Saviour, forever and ever, Amen."

As I finished repeating her words, I felt something I had never felt before. It was hard to describe it but I felt, like a warm love, embracing me but from within me. It was like a hug, someone's arms that had wrapped all around my very own soul—my spirit! Whoa! Something seriously had just taken place here and happened to me. Even though I did not really know as to what, I felt that that did not really matter so... I also noticed that the pain in my neck had completely gone and that was a first, for me! Amazing, I had thought to myself. Just, amazing!

I must have had quite the expression on my face, as I lay there in my hospital bed because I then looked up at Chunhua and saw her in a showering of tears, streaming down her little, rounded face—but she was not sad, she was smiling so brightly, with joyful tears! "I so happy for you, Kipper! Welcome to the Kingdom, big brother!" She exclaimed with joy! "Why, wait—what?" I had asked her and in exactly that way. Ha, ha...

IF I COULD FLOAT ON A CLOUD, WHERE WOULD I GO?

"You now saved Kipper and no matter what, happen here…we now go to Heaven and you, now my big brother too!" She smiled endlessly as she wiped away tears, for me. "Let Jesus lead you, with His Holy Spirit, that inner voice that speak to you—encourage for you, to do the right thing." She added as she cried with joy and held out her little arms up towards the ceiling and spoke, "Jesus, you now have another little brother! I so happy for you!" She finished and then hugged herself and placed her hands on her heart, as she closed her eyes, while happy tears streamed down her innocent and sweet, little face.

I will admit that, I also felt an incredible joy, deep inside of me—it was like nothing else I have ever had before, nor knew that could possibly even exist—even for a sick boy, like me. I don't really know fully of what actually had happened or how to explain it, but, it did feel good and truthfully, it felt, very meaningful. Wow…the more I thought about it, I then thought about this little girl that I never met before, whom didn't even know me and yet, she wanted to help me. Chunhua was like a little angel that God must have sent from above, to share this special gift… and with me. I was overwhelmed with emotion suddenly, as I chocked up inside and began to cry, grateful tears—humbling, grateful tears. I was so, incredibly touched, that someone, even so small, could even possibly think to care, about me—and then to find out, that there is this Jesus, whom so loves me, more than even a mother could love their own child, to die for all of mankind, just to forgive us of our sins and love us so deeply, so, so hard and want us to reign in Heaven with Him… Just incredible! Wow! "Thank you, Jesus—for being, my everything…" I whispered to my heart while I looked upward to the ceiling, as I placed my hand on my chest—I then closed my eyes and fell asleep.

Later on, upon opening my eyes, as my head was slightly to the side—I had noticed that there was an older looking boy, maybe he was in a coma, laying next to the window… I didn't say anything out loud. I often talked to myself in my head or quietly under my breath but in a whisper. I don't understand why he was there, I had thought to myself—when I could have had the window, to look out of for myself. I had thoughts that raged through my head…they did not agree with one another at all…. I would hear negative thoughts that were so discouraging and actually, kind of mean—even, self-pitying in a way. I then realized that those really negative thoughts, could not possibly be my own, so why would I want to entertain them, as my own thoughts? I also heard another voice but it was reasoning and sound—positive and encouraging, putting that put first, ahead of my own desires or wants. So I decided not to let myself, become jealous or greedy, or anything bad about the situation—for the mean thoughts were pushing on me to accept. I wasn't going to give in. I did not like the ugly feelings that came from those mean thoughts, at all.

Why would I want to emulate, what I do not like? Oh yeah, the word 'emulate', it means to match or imitate. I wanted to be happy, not sad—such thoughts battled within my mind, waging war against one another. Then I remembered that I had asked that Man, Jesus into my heart—and so upon remembering Him, I had begun to feel something positive inside, speaking to me. I had felt encouraged, to ask for His help and so I did. "Jesus, please, I cannot but, you can… please help me." I whispered quietly and without even, a single stutter—and just as I had sent this request out to the Heavenly realm, but to the Man whom now lived within my heart—the raging voices stopped. A peaceful calm had now overcome my mind and then soothed my heart and then filled within soul. Wow, I had thought quietly to myself—this, or rather, He, really does help.… I whispered to Him again and said, "Thank you" and I then heard, "You're welcome."

I undeniably wondered, thinking to myself and whispering to the nice voice whom stilled my very own soul—as others who were between the window and I, were able to get out of bed, yet I was not able to… well okay, maybe not everyone—but there were others, who could. One thought had whispered to me that I must feel that I was being punished—wait, why would I want to believe in, that? I asked it, why would I feel that way and it just repeated itself using the word, "I" but it continued to just sound like to me, as though it was very much, like a lie—I was learning that it was, just something the enemy whom is the devil—that that is what he would do. Another thought had told me, to feel pity on myself, to ask myself, what had I done to be here, away from my safe place, away from my clouds? Do you see the distraction now, from the truth? I sure do, now… A clarity had bestowed within me. Before, I would not have ever guessed it. How can I explain this feeling I have? Um…this, this feeling, it is like I have a new set of eyes—like I am looking through a brand new pair of eyes but physically, mentally, and spiritually—it was hard to explain but it was truly, amazing!

I then suddenly caught myself and realized that I was not being very grateful, now was I? I needed to tell those pushy voices to stop, to stop with the help of Jesus and so once again, I did. As the voice of truth in my mind, had now said, to say it but in His Name. "In Jesus Name, evil spirits, leave me, in Jesus Name. You are not welcome here, so leave, in Jesus Name." I had then said this with a brave and bold new drive, right from my heart. It was now, just above a whisper, at this time. I was not going to allow my mind, to give way to the darkness—to give into the enemy's deception! This was a matter of good versus evil and I chose not to play the devil's game, no more! No evil doer invader, was going to take me down! Ha, ha! No, sir!

I closed my eyes and relaxed my fists to open, as rested hands and I then just focused on peaceful thoughts, like a cloud in the heavens and then I imagined, a man, sitting on a log in the middle of it all. He smiled and even glowed. I imagined that it was Jesus because clouds help make me calm, so it must be Him, whom helps me on my adventures too.

Thinking a lot more heavily now, about this and as to why did this have to happen to me and the thoughts of feeling lonely—they felt so depressing…so I had to force my mind, to be quiet, to be still. I then remembered what Chunhua had helped do, for me…what God does and will for me. I then took in a deep breath and slowly closed my eyes while I focused my thoughts to be quiet, focusing on anything good while avoiding the very thoughts from the deepest depths of the dark side. Instead, I pictured what Jesus would look like, if I ever met Him, I focused on His eyes, and His smile and love for me in this life—then I eventually had fallen, fast asleep.

Pencil Artwork drawing of a child praying to Jesus entitled, "Faithful Prayer" by Kipper

The next morning, I was eating my creamy porridge with blueberries on top, when I was suddenly startled by a flash of lightning, just outside of the big, tall window. Then I heard a loud crackling bang which followed, not long after and had frightened just about everyone in the room. I quickly voiced, just above a whisper, "God has us, in Jesus Name, Amen" I could then see Chunhua doing the same thing and then all of the other children in the room, no longer were jumpy to each thunder strike that had crackled, following each lightning flash after that. It began raining a lot outside. Like a torrential downpour, of a thousand faucets that were way up high in the sky—they had just been, simultaneously activated and opened up, to pour down on all of the earth, or just the city perhaps but onto everything below. Whoa, that was sure loud! The sky had flashed and crackled a lot more frequently, like a planned out musical play like the opera and its' orchestra! It bellowed and flashed, singing its' Italian melodies at the very top of its mighty lungs!

IF I COULD FLOAT ON A CLOUD, WHERE WOULD I GO?

There was a lot of dark clouds that had filled the sky, from what I could see. A nurse that just walked by, had voiced that she thought that the day would be a long one, because this storm was forecasted to settle in and just rain all day long. But believe it or not, as much as I do love the clear blue skies, when they are blanketed by those amazing, fluffy white clouds—I also love a good old rainstorm! Ha, ha! I really love watching the amazing lightning bolts and strike veins, and as they flash and rippled right across the sky—cleaning the air and giving it that sweet, fresh smell of clean air, during and following a thunderstorm. They didn't scare me. It's one of my favourite weather systems! Okay, okay, anything with clouds is! Ha, ha!

I absolutely know, just how to wield those spectacular, dark and blue-grey clouds, for my adventures too because who doesn't love a rocky boat on the ocean—laden with skilled sailors and an adventure, for sunken and lost treasure! Eh? Arrrrrr! Ha, ha! Of course you don't have to be a pirate, to be on a big ship out on the great, big sea—a good ol' sailor boy, why that's me, can have plenty of wild, amazing adventures! Ha, ha! Just you watch and see! Ha, ha!

I stared long and hard at the dark grey clouds that had blanketed the skies—completely engulfing every last speck of clear sky that there was, through that window within my view, in the Children's Long Term Ward. As I stared really hard, I reached for my most, thirst-quenching glass of icy, cold white milk and took my final gulp—making the sound effects, as I swallowed and felt refreshed, with a great satisfaction upon my face, as it cooled my airways and washed down my breakfast. A determined look, of an adventurer was now upon my face. It was so refreshing! Hmmm…yum! I then got right to work. The nurse just looked at me for a brief moment and then chuckled and continued on her way, shaking her head with a smile as always, as I drifted off to wonderland, once again. I was off!

I tightly closed my eyes and took a deep breath in and then let it out slowly—and as my imagination took over from there and then, opened them! Rain whipped in the wind, as it fell everywhere. Looking up, I could see that the winds were blowing the massive, white sails up above me, on my floating cloud ship. My vessel floated across the glistening, golden yellow sea that was all around us, it was quite a marvellous sight to behold. The boat rocked back and forth, along with the high tides, as the waves pushed it back and forth, and then onward. Guiding the sails to where I needed for my ship to embark, on such a rocky voyage such as this—there was a trusted crew among us onboard, whom skills were of many and dreams for adventure were of plenty, just as I. Secure the becket mates! Ha, ha, er tie the rope here, there and up to and throw—hold onto your hats, don't lose your grip boys, for this here ship, she sails honourably, steadily and true! Ha, ha!

Then the storm clouds up above had calmed, as the heavens filled with a most spectacular sight yet! The skyline above me, had then opened up and immediately then radiated a captivatingly, bright and mighty explosive, eye-popping rainbow in the sky! "Whoa!" We all had shouted! It was made up with such a heavenly blending of colours such as blues, golden-yellows, pinks, reds, greens and violets—all of the colours of the rainbow that which God had created, following the days of Noah and the great flood—as His promise to mankind that He would never again, destroy the earth with another flood…and so, He shoots bows of rainbow ribbon, right across the many skies! It was amazing! This is so that the world may bear witness to, until the end of earth's time, following each and every rain storm and any such movement of water in the right light, to that of His great promise—with the truth on display, for all to see!

Just then, there was suddenly a massively huge, flock of Canadian Geese that had sprung up from out of no where, from below our ship as we sailed onward! They flew up and then across the waters ahead of the ship's bow! For the numbers were so great, that there must have been, at least thousands and thousands and yet, even thousands more! Wow, was there ever, a real crazy amount of them! This was stupendous! The determined and very cool looking birds began to make the ship rock, just by their movement as a one moving body, like all of the parts of an engine that need to work together, in order for it to function properly. This, was incredibly impressive, just to witness! There were far too many, to even count! All for what we could see here, was that there was just an amazing sight, one right after the other! Ha, ha! Amazing! Our eyes were wide and reflected the atmosphere's colourful display.

IF I COULD FLOAT ON A CLOUD, WHERE WOULD I GO?

Pencil Artwork drawing of a huge flock of Canadian Geese in flight, beginning their migration South entitled, "Bird Convention" by Kipper

The story about how rainbows came to be, is really quite amazing! It comes from the Bible and not actually from how the 'way of the world' has disgustingly made it out to be—as it does not have a thing to do, with the 'gender option confusion issue'. In the beginning, God created Man and Woman. In His image, He created them. What's confusing about that? Pretty simple, don't you think? Ha, ha!

Not confusing at all—though sadly, the enemy fed the world his lies and took something, so beautiful that God made and then mutated it into an ugly and very misleading symbolism, to confuse people of their God-given gender—from instead of whom they truly are, to imitate whom they are truly, not. God made, man and woman, period. No such thing as them being 'born mixed up' that's another lie from the enemy. People can take it or leave it, but that's the truth. Oh but the real truth of why we have rainbows as God's promise…it is so beautiful! Wow! Don't you think it is such a sight to behold? It is so heavenly angelic! It is all there, in that book, called the bible…I read a lot. Ha, ha! Oh and no need to ever let anyone tell you, that praying in the Spirit, is only for certain individuals—it says right in the bible that God wants everyone to seek His gifts and to use them for His glory! So cool! So much to learn! Ha, ha!

Pencil Artwork drawing of a prismatic double rainbow
debut entitled, "Radiant Wonder" by Kipper

The air was then filled, with the most wonderful and glorious Heavenly music that I ever heard! I could not make out the words—they were I think, in the Spirit, like a thousand angels are singing in a beautiful, heavenly choir, whom were praising and thanking God, our Papa up in Heaven—with the singing and humming in a most breathtaking and rhythmic, harmonic way…it was just so, moving and heartfelt that I immediately felt overwhelmed with an excitement and I then began to be filled with a real burst of joyful laughter and even, had happy tears, fall down my face! Wow, I had thought! It was as though, I could FEEL their words, and touch their rhythm from within my heart. Just, wow…

I yelled out "Yo, ho, ho! Hold onto your hats, mateees! She may be a rough rollin' sail, you knooow but it be, worth the ride! Ha, ha!" The skies then rumbled with an awakening of both enchanting and colourful northern and southern lights that were just a dancing around, as the clouds above began to disappear. Across the night's now, crystal clear sky, the blueish-grey clouds would part, just enough to allow the dancing flow of the brilliantly bright greens, pinks, and even blues that shimmered the sky like no other, to put on a show! Wow!

My loyal crew and fellow comrades, which I had mentioned before, were with me on this voyage above! Many of my dear friends, from a wide range of my many cloud adventures had joined me. Many you had met, and many you have yet to meet—they, the skilled and the courageous, manned the decks below and raised the sails to the yonder above, higher and wider—to catch an eye of the winds abound, the winds

IF I COULD FLOAT ON A CLOUD, WHERE WOULD I GO?

to our fortune. "Oh dear mates be patient, for ye treasure, it awaits yet ahead!! Err! Ha, ha! Hear ye whistle blooow! The ship, be sailin' late, tonight! Ha, ha!" I cried out and laughed out loud!

It was a little rocky but it really was a riveting trip filled with adventure! Then I heard a horn bellow, with a faded echo, in the distance! BONG-G-G-G!... With a gap of, maybe five Mississippi's in-between each horn. ...BONG-G-G-G!... My mates and I, we continued to hear it again and again...BONG-G-G-G!... What was it, that bellowed a mysterious bong, across the seas of gold? ...BONG-G-G-G!... "What was it?" I had wondered, whispering below my breath. BONG-G-G-G!... For the mysterious sound, continued to sound its alarm... BONG-G-G-G...

"What there you be, Captain Kipper?" Called out one of my crew mates, Andy which you had met, not so long ago—back in the green meadows, racing sailboats. "What be you thinks, comrade Andy?" I replied. "Captain, dare I say, look! What be comin' over our way? Look, beyond the horizon, over there!" He replied, as he had pointed towards the sound, suddenly.

My eyes followed suit of his pointed arm...for there was a mysterious fog, misting in the distance which grew as we continued our approach. Yet, this was no ordinary misty fog, no, for it was, it, wait—it was, glowing! It came closer and closer! Then all of a sudden, we were surrounded by a glowing mass, by the millions! It was a swarm of fireflies! It glowed so brightly, as the flying butt glowers had surrounded our cloud ship while they had passed us! Ha, ha! Wow! Well, it was their butts that glowed! Ha, ha, ha! Different hues of blues, greens and yellows, to golden yellows—there, did they ever, glow! Our eyes grew, as they took in the brilliance of hues, across our widened and glossy eyeballs—taking on such colours aglow by the mass! Such radiance, beauty and wonder, it was! Oh my g-gosh! It was truly wondrous!

Then the ...BONG-G-G-G sound had alarmed again, as it came closer and closer, approaching us, with something that I had never even seen before... Could my eyes, be deceiving me? Everyone was stunned and filled with wonder, wide-eyed—like a child on Christmas morning, that I have read in books sometime, once before... "Look at that!" Alarmed the crew mates, on the decks below. For they had oooohed and aaaahed in amazement! An angelic looking woman had approached us, on her flying white horse! Her hair was long and wavy, with a golden-yellow blond, shimmery colouring, and had a few unique and intricately small but long braids, that were weaved throughout her long, flowing hair—adorned with, out of this world, incredibly unique small flowers of many colours. Everyone on board my cloud ship, was mesmerized, with jaws dropped in utter bewilderment. Wow! Oh and her horse, was majestic in appearance, of a pure white, like fresh snow, in colour. Wooow… who was she? I had wondered, as I stared in an utter, shock and wonder.

The beautiful, mysterious woman had then opened her mouth and for a moment, the scene slowed to a mesmerizing, slow like a molasses flow in winter…as though I had suddenly dozed out, as everything came to an abrupt pause. I then looked back up at her and the motion then regained its normal pace and she began to speak to me.

"To what adventure, are you going, dear young man?" She asked me, with her voice sounding angelic and pure, yet gentle as an angel's breath. Words failed me, as my jaw hung wide open, with no sound. I was just in a complete awe-like wonder, and of her beauty that I found myself, still standing there, with my jaw hanging wide open for a moment longer, for what seemed like an eternity. Then I finally, had noticed that I needed to close it. "I…I…" …my words, they just wouldn't leave my voice box. She then giggled, as she awaited through my ridiculously, very short, stuttered reply. "What my dear, is your name child?" She then asked me, in anticipation and still smiling with that radiating glow, about her. Then I responded, "Kipper…m-my name, i-it is, Kipper." I finally, managed to say something, besides just stuttering a single syllable, strained sound.

"Kipper, what a marvellous ship that you sail up here, on these glorious, Heavenly golden waters!" She continued. "You are indeed a special, brave young boy, aren't you…Kipper?" She asked me. "I—I am?" I responded. Her blue eyes had a glistening twinkle in the corner of them, as she smiled with her perfectly formed and bright white teeth. "Oh dear child, but of course you are, dear young Kipper. You see, we hear your many prayers and requests for others. Very few, even for yourself." She remarked. "Y-you do?" I replied. "Of course" the angel had answered.

"W-who, are you, m-might I ask?" I asked the angel, most curiously. "There are many, many angels among you, dear Kipper." She continued. "You always have been a humble and very brave, young boy. Continue to grow in your passion for adventure and don't let others change that in you…" She stated. "The Holy Trinity—your God the Father, your Papa, your big brother, Jesus Christ, and His Holy Spirit, whom lives within you and flows through you now—He dearly loves you dear Kipper. And He dearly loves your many and very creative adventures, dear Kipper. Never let them go, for this is one of your many gifts that He holds dear to His own heart, with great joy. For it is truly a way, for Him to help you, in your immobility." The alluringly beautiful angel had added.

Pencil Artwork drawing of the angelic sky opening up entitled, "Heaven's Visit" by Kipper

I was mesmerized and a little in shock…okay, okay, so I was actually, completely in shock! Was she, a real angel, like a messenger, sent from God, Himself? Just as I asked myself that in my mind, she actually answered me, out loud! "I am." She responded and smiled. Much to my amazement, I wanted to know more. I then asked her another question, which then exploded into more questions, right after that! "Do you w-work with God, with Papa? H-how, how is Papa? Does He s-see me? Is He, h-here?" I asked, with stuttering excited butterflies. She smiled and continued to address my many, endless questions. "For your Papa in Heaven, is always with you. His Spirit now lives within you forever, dear young Kipper." She added. "Always remember that, He will never leave you, nor forsake you. Even when the world will try to deceive you from this truth, when times become difficult to handle—He is always with you. Remember that." She finished.

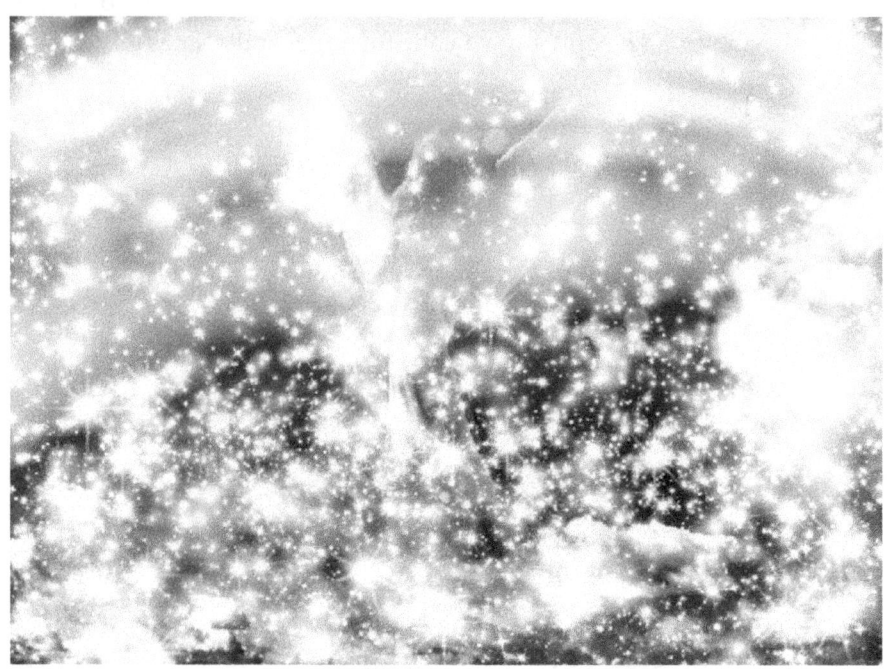

Pencil Artwork drawing of the women angel entitled,
"God's Beautiful Angels" by Kipper

Her angelic beauty, was glowing all around the ship and its young and adventurous crew. "Our Heavenly Father is always here with you, Kipper, He is your Father, your Papa in Heaven. Lean on Him often. He has never left, nor will He ever leave you." She continued. "Fear not and earnestly seek Him, with all your heart and lean on Him, always—for the evil that has created 'the way of the world's' destructive ways, tries anything to stop it—even in trying to distract you, from your Papa's heart. Keep your eyes always fixed on Jesus and He will lead you, home." She continued. "He is, in you Kipper because you chose to believe." She added.

IF I COULD FLOAT ON A CLOUD, WHERE WOULD I GO?

I was just in awe and was filled with a feeling of a real comfort and that calmed me. Is this, what peace feels like? I had wondered. "It is, Kipper." The angel had replied to my thoughts, once again! "Thank you, m-miss." I said. "Wait, w-what name, m-may I c-call, you?" I asked her. The angel giggled. "You may call me, Angel" she then replied, with her pearly shimmering, pure white glowing smile.

Pencil Artwork drawing featuring a morning sunrise entitled, "God Is With You" by Kipper

"Kipper, do you love yourself for you and who you are, even with the troubles in your life and your health that of which you have so, patiently endured?" Angel had asked me. I had to think on her question, before answering.... "I-I think I do...w-why do you ask?" "That is very good to hear, dear young Kipper. It is very important, Kipper, because Papa, lives in you and loving you, also makes Papa proud. You are valued and loved beyond measure. Our Heavenly Papa, loves when you are happy and are grateful for what you have, even in tough times—thanking Him always and trying hard not to give in to the enemy's scheming lies that go against Papa's goodness and His Word." I asked her.

Life is short, I choose to appreciate every moment, even in the storm—thanking Papa, regardless of how long or how little that those moments may be... this I know that I try my best at, now more than ever. "That is wonderful to hear, Kipper." Angel replied to my thoughts and then continued to speak. "He also admires, when you call on Him, for His help. He loves that." Angel added. "He wants to care for you and raise you up, as His child!" Angel finished. Wow! I had thought to myself, as I looked down towards my bare feet, while standing on the boat's cloud surface. Papa, wants me? I asked in my heart and then my eyes began to tear up, with a great overwhelming feeling of, hope.

"You have Him eternally, and that my dear little Kipper, makes you and to anyone else, whom chooses to do the same—regardless of age or walk in life—to be the richest in all of life that this world, cannot offer. Believe with Papa's heart and in what His Son did for every one of us, and you will change the world." She smiled so breathlessly and beautifully, as she spoke with such soothing and incredibly encouraging words, to me and my crew. It really was, truly amazing.

I could feel the magic in the air but it wasn't actually magic, I guess, now was it? It was Papa. I could just tell because everything was just so above and beyond beautiful and colourful, and was just so enchanting beyond my own understanding—both rich in joy and peace and hopeful, in heart and in Spirit. That, was Papa's Spirit. I just knew it! It was hard to fully explain but I just knew that it was Him! This place, felt like Heaven to me. It was just soooo beautiful and soooo welcoming! We didn't honestly feel any fear, or even any pain at all, whatsoever. It was amazing! Oh what a feeling it was, for it just took my breath away and with it, my words too. Do you know the feeling?

"Angel?" I asked. "Yes, dear Kipper?" she replied. "Is this place, Heaven? Angel then tilted her head slight to the right and then she humbly replied, with a slight bow and a warming smile. "Kipper, you are precious, this is, a little piece of Heaven, and this is, Papa." She continued. "He is all around you children, up here, down on earth—even in your own hospital rooms. Papa lives and He lives, inside of you Kipper. And inside any of you whom choose to believe in His Son." Angel remarked and then continued. "You need not be afraid of dying, when each of your time comes. With Jesus in your heart, there is eternal life. But treasure every moment given, for life is a gift. Do not give up living. For when it is your time, to come home to Papa in Heaven—He will come for you, with wide open, loving arms, to welcome you home." She added. "Here, you get a new and perfect body, one without its flaws, scrapes, cuts or bruises—no pain at all, no suffering. For you will dine as sons and daughters, of the true King, forever more." Angel paused and then continued to speak some more, to the young crew of children. "When it is your time children, you will return here, to live a very, purposeful eternal life. You will finally be, home." She finished.

Kipper was astonished, for his eyes grew wide at everything that the angel had said to him and his crew. They too, were in utter bliss and their hearts were filled with wonder. The Angel continued to give her message from Papa and explained it, even further. "Now, I will explain to you children, on what Free-will means, as the enemy has confused the world, from what it actually is. Free-will comes into play, by privileging you with the power of, choice. Choosing between good or bad, has always been a struggle for mankind, since the fall of man, dating back to when Adam and Eve, ate the forbidden fruit. There is power in choice, always, from the smallest of things, to the biggest of decisions that will alter your life." The Angel exclaimed. The children listened intently, as she continued to speak.

"Another example," she continued "...is whether or not, your name will be written in our Father's book of Life—as everyone gets older and can choose for themselves, with a mind of their own while still on earth—it is a matter of Eternal Life, versus Eternal Death or Damnation. And all it takes, is whether or not the person chooses, to ask Jesus to live inside of them and believe in the greatest sacrifice, of all time that God so loved the world that He gave His only begotten Son, Jesus Christ, whom died for everyone's sins and forgave, all—making a perfect, sacrifice for mankind, in finishing our debt at the cross. So that we may live and have Everlasting Life, with Him in Heaven.

Mankind may either, willingly progress through their journey of faith and choose to believe, in the Son of God and in what He has done for them—letting our Heavenly Father teach and help them, to grow. Or, they end up in chaos, faltering and fall out away from Papa...taking much longer, or avoid completely to learn, to trust in the Lord our God… while patiently enduring, through both the hardships and the blessings that will follow." Angel stated.

"As everything happens for many, different reasons and will of course be, beyond your own understanding, for not all things are meant to be understood by man, or he would not bother trusting the Father—this too, is a part of each of your own personal growth, to want a relationship with our Heavenly Papa and to allow for Him to grow within you—so that as Jesus is, so are we in this world… He wants to get to know you and you of Him, through a relationship. Talk to Him, lean on Him, call upon Him at all times.

Depending on what choices each and everyone chooses in life, good or bad—Papa always loves everyone, as His child and will not ever leave their side. He wants everyone to make it. For Papa is always chasing after all of you, to rescue and pursue you, as each and every one of His own children—with an unconditional love, that will never fade. It is not about what we do but about what Jesus has done, for us all. Just when you think you know something or think that you know it all—you do not. For even a teacher never graduates from the school of learning, called life, until it is gone…

We cannot earn, our way to our Father, as it is not about us, but about His Son, Jesus. The enemy will confuse and twist the truth in however way he can, but that does not change the truth, that God is eternally endless and that He is love and has already, forgiven you, COMPLETELY— through His Son's death and resurrection so that we may have, eternal life, after this life…" She remarked.

IF I COULD FLOAT ON A CLOUD, WHERE WOULD I GO?

Pencil Artwork drawing of a window with a cloud view
entitled, "Adventurous Wonder" by Kipper

"So, now do you see? People must choose, to where they wish to end up, because this is not decided for you, for you have the gift of Free-will. We do hope and want for everyone to make it here and live life with Papa and all of His beautiful and amazing creations up here in Heaven!" The angel smiled and continued to explain. "You see, Papa is a gentleman. If one chooses a life without Him, in it, He will give them a life, without Him, in it—however, if they choose a life with Him, in it, then He gives them a life, with Him, in it. Papa never forces His hand, on anyone to follow Him. He gives us many, many opportunities to make the right choices throughout our lives, but it is up to mankind, to pay attention, to seek Him out, and to pursue His goodness and want to be His sons and daughters, through accepting His Son. Only the enemy forces a wicked hand on mankind. The battle is not against flesh and blood, it is against the evil one and his demons that want to kill, steal and destroy, what is good.

Remember, Papa has you in His hands, just ask and always, with all of your heart—believe." She added. "The enemy will then of course pursue harder, with lies fed to one's own mind by filtering true thoughts with lies and deceptions, to distract you from your journey and from keeping your eyes on Papa—but with Papa's guidance through His Holy Spirit and always trying to remain faithful to Him—trusting and believing that God has you, in His powerfully mighty and loving hands. No matter what, you will move mountains dear Kipper, more than you may ever be able, to truly understand—but that, you will. We can do all things in Him, when we believe. All you have to do, is believe." She closed in encouragement, with a smile. She then waved gently with a nod and was off. I waved back, as she continued on her way.

My crew mates, were all bewildered in amazement and an awe-inspiring wonder, as the angel on her horse had now continued onward, passed our cloud ship—following the swarm of glowing fireflies by whom, lit the way ahead of her. Everything and everyone in this life, has a purpose, the key is, being willing to seek Papa out—to find that purpose and then, to pursue Him, with all of your heart. I will definitely keep that in my mind and remember what the angel had said.

Maybe one day, I can help someone, want to live. I think that that would feel really amazing and fulfilling, to help someone else, in need. I smiled and closed my eyes, as we sailed across the golden sea—a treasure I had felt in my heart that we had been blessed with already, and we didn't even really know it, until now. Real treasure did not come in gold nor silver, but rather, in heart, in spirit and in the mind—to know and have Jesus in my heart and be gifted with Eternal Life. "Wow! Now that, was very, very cool!" I had thought to myself.

I could feel the warm sunlight, touching my cheeks and the breeze flowing through my hair. Even my clothes were blowing in the wind, as we disappeared beyond the horizon. What an adventure! Ha, ha! I had happy tears, now streaming down my face, as I laughed with a real joy that had warmed my heart, forever.

The adventure faded, as I began to drift off while I was back, in my hospital bed. I strained a little, in trying to open my eyes, just enough to see the storm had passed on by—but as I closed my heavy eyelids once again, the stars glowed in the dark night sky, through the big, tall window. As I finally began to fall asleep, I whispered to the starry night sky, "Goodnight, daydream world... Hello, nighttime dreamworld"... and again, I was off!

"Jesus answered, I am the way and the truth and the life. No one comes to the Father except through me." —John 14:6

"If love is not given and nurtured, it can indeed be lost by man but God's Love never fails and reigns forever. And truth be told—everyone needs to hear and know that they are truly loved and forgiven, by the Father."
— Unknown

"Lift up your eyes and look to the heavens: Who created all these? He who brings out the starry host one by one and calls forth each of them by name. Because of His great power and mighty strength, not one of them is missing."
— Isaiah 40:26

JENNIFER DAWN DECONINCK SMITH

Various Pencil Artwork drawings of life entitled, "And God Said, It Is Good" by Kipper

IF I COULD FLOAT ON A CLOUD, WHERE WOULD I GO?

Abstract Paint Artwork drawing entitled, "Blow Away In The Wind Like Chaff" by Kipper

Pencil Artwork drawing of a field of daisies entitled, "Wild And Free" by Kipper

CHAPTER THREE

WAS THIS A MIRACLE?

Every night, it is pretty dark in the Children's Long Term Ward. room—minus the dimmed lights, on some of the patients' machine panels and monitor screens, which hummed and beeped, throughout the night of course.

Laying here, I started to feel a little bit cold again…but just as I was realizing this, I remembered that a nurse, would actually come in a couple extra times during each shift, just to come in and check on me. I was very thankful, as he or she would always come in to see, if my blanket was no longer warm or if I needed, or wanted another one. I thought that was really thoughtful of them, even when their tasks were already, always piled up so high, as it was….

The lady and guy nurses were really nice and would then bring me another toasty warm, heated blanket which was so comforting for me. There was a lot of staff here. The guy nurses were the ones that would help give me new IV's and needles, and come to check on my fluid and nutritional intake levels and such, perform blood-work, etc., that sort of thing. I really did like the feeling of a freshly warmed blanket from the dryer—it was toasty warm, like sitting next to a campfire—or at least that is what I would imagine each time, of what it might be like. They really do try to help me feel comfortable here, in the Children's Long Term Ward. So, I am definitely grateful for the kindness bestowed upon me.

I guess that I don't really talk much to the nurses but when I do, it is usually about me asking questions, about how the machines work, which button to press to turn on the blood pressure sleeve—things like that. I guess it is probably because I really don't know what more to say, most of the time. But I do say, 'Thank you' every time that they tend to me, even after I get needles, ha, ha... Yep, they must think that I am, pretty weird, maybe—but they do return a gratifying, "You're very welcome" as they carry on with their duties, even if they smile or seem rushed and even forget to respond at times. Over time, I would grow to be less shy, to everyone there…

Generally, I do hear all kinds of sounds throughout the nighttime, when I cannot sleep and I then, end up laying wide awake with sleepy eyes…hearing sounds of, ringing, squeaking, coughing—even banging, if there is some light construction happening, or children being unsettled in their beds and they kind of, hang one leg over the edge—banging it on the side of their bed, or against their side table, from out of boredom or the inability to fall asleep right way.

There are sometimes whispering voices, beeping, hollering, and even crying—well, that's kind of expected in a hospital, right? At times, I do wonder to myself, why won't these sounds stop? But, I guess it does mean that there is life happening and efforts being made, in trying to help soothe whatever is troubling each and every patient that is here… some complaining maybe more than others, or being more difficult than others, towards the staff at times—but that is probably, pretty normal for hospitals and for the staff who do go through a lot, on a daily basis as well.

Sometimes, I do see some really sad things happen at night and if I dwell on it, I start to wonder if this will ever become less of a burden to endure—because it is hard to hear the crying and struggling happening by other children in the room. Could this possibly ever be, less of a worrisome burden in a way, I would wonder to myself at times…do you know the feeling? …Things like that sometimes, I do think about. I just try not to let it bother me too much, or it can become overwhelming for me. I tend to cry if I think too much about something that is really sad but it is because I care, that I show emotion.

I guess I don't cry as much about my situation, as I am just sort of, used to it and I would much rather try and be positive and encourage others because it will then, also help me feel better—you know, in knowing that

I was trying to at least make some sort of effort—to help someone else feel better about their days. Everyone has rough days. I know I do and it can be hard, to get back up from them…figuratively speaking.

If I just thought about the things that I did for others or just about my problems all of the time—then I would only be thinking about myself and I know that I am definitely, not the centre of the universe! So, I would much rather prefer, to try and focus on others and to try to help them out, instead. I don't want to be selfish, I would rather eat them! Sell, fish, get it? Ha, ha, ha!

Oh, uh, ouch… Cramping and aches had begun to creep all throughout my little frail body, like a serge of electrical waves, suddenly trying to burst through a thin wire, but then melting it, by the unbearable heat that was too much for it to handle… Oh but I just can't push the call button—I am too afraid. Oh no, no, no…I don't dare say a word, or they will come and find me! I can't…I will not! 'They' are scary at night or so it seems, more than during the daytime—I just can't say a word. My imagination took over, as I sank a little further beneath the covers, trying to avoid, direct contact. I then slowly peeled back the covers just enough to catch a peek of the creatures, lurking about—just above the top of the blanket, I stared long enough beyond my hospital bed, to catch a look at the night shift nurses, whom were now on their prowl. They won't take me as prisoner…I whispered to myself, very quietly…

Some come in to poke and prod and on a timely schedule—like clockwork. There are times when I cannot feel the slightest bit of warmth, from some of them. Wait, what is that? I sank back down into my covers once again…peeking only, if I must—for if I get caught, it is game over, folks! Okay…so, here it is…lean in closer, that's right—no, over here… okay, the coast is clear…"fewf" I sighed. They seem like they don't like me, or that they don't even look like they want to be here. I try to avoid the grumpy looking ones, as they tend to not deliver a smile and that's like, a ground zero level, people!

There are sometimes, really short ones and they creep in very quickly and are kind of wobbly, the older they are—checking this and checking that and never seemingly able, to slow down long enough to notice, that I am watching their every move, from the tops of my sneakingly peering eyes… Some are super tall and make these crazy, wild tree-like shadows on the walls, that look like a freaky special on the television during a creep fest, blowing in the wind—reaching out to grab me. It puzzles me for sure which one it is or why, I wish I could read minds but sometimes, I am sure glad that I cannot! Ha, ha! I mean, who would really want to actually know about, what a slug is thinking, or a dung beetle? Ewwww! Ha, ha, ha!

Then something else had caught my attention, as I peered further above my covers. One little girl, in a bed off to my right, was whimpering quietly. I could tell by the dim light, glaring off steady tears on her face—her eyes were closed. She was even skinnier than me. She couldn't speak, as there was a huge tube in her mouth, to help her breathe. Sometimes, she would moan something in her sleep while in her drug-induced light coma...but all that seemed to come out though, was a small, strange choking cry. She didn't move much either and her bald little head, had wires taped on it. I wish I could help her. I don't really know what was wrong with her, or what had happened to her—but I am glad that she had visitors each day and that the nurses, would check on her often.

Daybreak had finally arrived, as the night had turned into a morning hello world sort of sunshine that went from a varied arrangement of glorious hues, of morphing vibrant colourings of yellows, pinks and purples, early in the morning. A few hours had passed on by, as the day's daily routines had arrived and then passed onwardly—along with breakfast and into the lunch hour, then now finally, leaked into the early, afternoon hours of the day.

There was a new roommate, whom was wheeled in on a wheelchair and then helped onto a hospital bed, not far from mine. It was one older girl whom I eventually met, over the next few days following her arrival—as she was busy with a lot of tests and stuff like that, upon her arrival, to now. Her name was Hope and she was sixteen years old. I guess her parents had high hopes for her, remaining in and winning many nationwide, top league beauty pageants—but there was something that really bothered her about her mom, as when she would talk about Hope to others, she had developed the habit of calling her daughter, "One of God's New Ugly Ducklings"—that she was no longer beautiful, as if she had lost her beauty because of her unfortunate hair loss, during the beginning radiation treatments, during the gruelling stages of the cancer, which had plagued Hope's body. But that was not her fault. That was really harsh, don't you think? It was because she had lost all of her hair, only a month after they had found her collapsed on the floor at school, right in front of everyone—which I guess had really freaked everyone out and even cost her, her so-called 'friends'.... I sure felt for her.

After months of tests and many hospital visits in what seemed like endless, painstakingly long appointments and lots of waiting—doctors discovered that Hope was very sick with an aggressive cancer, where her own immune system was deliberately, attacking her own body from within. She was told that it was terminal and that she would then, have to be moved into here, the Children's Long Term Ward—for the remainder of her life. She was so devastated and wouldn't come out of her bedroom for weeks at a time prior, except to use the bathroom. Her story was so sad that I couldn't help but cry alongside with her, feeling her pain too.

Hope didn't have any friends who stuck with her, until now. I would often, talk to her and tell her jokes—anything to make her smile and I figured that if I could at the very least, make her smile, even laugh—then I was doing something good. I would also talk to her about Jesus and encourage her often. I even managed to help her, ask Jesus into her heart! Now I know exactly how Chunhua had felt, when she had helped me, become a Christian, as I was crying and was so happy for Hope, too! Weeks went by, and I was able to get to know more about Hope. We had become really good friends, her and I. I was really grateful for her visits and for giving me, her time.

Hope was so kind and had a big heart. When we would then visit, she would wheel over in a wheelchair to visit me, since I couldn't go and visit her. She was actually, a very kind person. I even drew a portrait picture of her but with her hair. I could feel that it was from, this loving Jesus who lives in me that encourages, for me to try and help her feel better, at any moment that I had the opportunity to do so. I would call her beautiful, whenever she smiled. She would lean over and give me a tight hug and whisper in my ear, "Thank you" I would always respond with, "You're very welcome" in return. She deserved to know of her beauty that God gave her because God made her beautiful and so in telling her that out loud, so that she could hear it for herself and from someone who really cared about her—that brightened her day and calmed her nervousness about her condition.

IF I COULD FLOAT ON A CLOUD, WHERE WOULD I GO?

I really hope that she doesn't have to go too soon, to Heaven to be with Papa. I am going to miss her, very much…but, I knew that I didn't want to be selfish or greedy, so I prayed with her that night. It had been, about eight or so weeks since she had first arrived here, in the hospital's Children's Long Term Ward. Something had urged me to pray for her that night. Though I made it the habit to do it every night, this time had felt different. So I did and I prayed that if it were time for Papa to heal her, so that she could go home to her earthly home, to heal her and take all of her pain away. But if it were her time to go home to be with Papa, that even still, knowing that I will miss her a lot—I added, that I was grateful to get to know her and be her friend and that she was mine. What a gift, she is, I thought to myself… I knew, that either way, she would suffer no more, for God had her in His loving hands, too. By the time the next morning had arrived, Hope had gone home, to Papa…

Hope's 'Before Cancer' Pencil Portrait Artwork
Drawing entitled, "Joy" by Kipper

Days went by, since Hope had parted from this place. My days had felt a little bit more sad, since she had gone but I knew that she was not suffering any longer. She would I'm sure, even tell me to smile, which made me smile, just thinking about her. I think that it was Papa reminding me, just to cheer me up. I would then thank Papa, quietly as I smiled.

One night, in the dimmed lights of the room, I suddenly saw something go wrong. Even though with each night, there seems to be something that sometimes does go wrong, it would be foolish to ever feel used to, numb or even immune to it. I began to pray for him. That boy in the coma next to the big, tall window—he had begun shaking terribly. The bed shook with him too and the machine, was beeping really fast and loud. Readily in came running about five or so nurses, six or maybe even seven, this time. They spoke so loud and quickly, as they huddled around his hospital bed, to see what more to try and fix, from going wrong. Then suddenly, without a word from the nurses—the boy was still. The machine went from beeping to a long and eerie hum sound... It must have been his time—God must have decided to take him home, too.

Pencil Artwork drawling of a starry night sky entitled, "God's Art" by Kipper

IF I COULD FLOAT ON A CLOUD, WHERE WOULD I GO?

Morning broke and I slowly, opened my eyes. Turning left towards the window, I noticed that something just wasn't right—there was no boy in a coma, lying next to the big, tall window, anymore. Nurses scrambled throughout the room—moving around the beds. Not one nurse, even looked into my eyes as they moved about, they just pulled a different child's hospital bed, next to the window instead. I sunk down into my bed even more, but with my eyes still glued to the outside world, trying my best, not to grow with anger or be jealous…so instead, I was just dreaming, praying and hoping for a cloud to come on by—hopefully, it would be very soon.

At last, a cloud had floated by and wasting no time, I was on it! It was time to head back, to my safe place of peace! Oh Papa, it had been so long! I teared up with gratitude, as I darted through the sky, across the valleys and meadow greens—through the mountain pass and down to the creek below, where the sailboat race, was in much need to be completed! I was so excited to have returned! Ha, ha, ha!

Finally, I had reunited once again, with all of my friends from here—many different boys and girls of all ages. It was as if, the sailboat race had paused in time, while it awaited my very, very long awaited return. Everyone was jumping around in the meadow, playing and laughing out loud, chanting and singing to the bird's many songs that sounded again, so heavenly! This is our safe place, not even the nurses, doctors, priests, pastors, or any other kinds of older visitors in our other world, would ever appear, to be in any of my adventures…only children were ever present—and so it seemed. I never really understood that, but it didn't really matter anyway, as we just enjoyed our time here, for however long that it lasted.

It was about time that we got back to the creek and continued the most spectacular, biggest sailboat race of all time! Ha, ha! "Let's finish, the race!" Woohoo! We all chanted, shouting at the top of our lungs! The race morphed from its halted pause, then as each child took their place by the creek, alongside where each of their sailboats were afloat in a pause—the scene then shifted, right into an active motion for a moment and then, backwards with a suddenly slight rewind—by a few minutes of the actual race. It then paused and took on a new height, now bolting into a fast forward motion into the current time. And we were off!

It was now a live, action thriller quest and everyone continued, with excitement and cheered his or her boat on! Actually, everyone cheered for all of the sailboats, because it was just a fun competition among many friends! Woohoo! Ha, ha! Of course if any interruptions happen, we have been able to always come back here, to continue. I bet you're wondering who is winning? Well, I can't let a good story go untold! Ha, ha! Now pay attention, this is a mouthful adventure to tell, ha, ha! Here we go!

Where were we? All yeah, right…okay, here we go people, the game is on! The race is now back into full swing, as we chased down our sailboats, trying to keep up with them, as they plow through the fast surging current, down the creek. It looks like Andy's Silly Ship is still sailing strong—most impressively firm, I'd say and in first place! Ha, ha! Great job, Andy! I shouted!

Oh no, yikes! Sandy's Saint Peers is officially, now out of the race! I can't believe my eyes, ha, ha! "Oh good grief! Sorry buddy!" I called out. As a giant bullfrog had literally, finished swallowing it whole! GULP! Instead of hearing a ribbit sound, this crazy sounding croaking bullfrog, sounded like a cow with a bad case of gas, ha, ha! It cracked its funny sound, as it hopped away with a full belly! Ha, ha, ha! Sandy laughed so hard, he rolled around the ground, just having a blast! Ha, ha! Everyone pointed at the silly bullfrog, as it just demolished Sandy's sailboat for lunch! We all laughed so hard at it, for it really was such a surprise to witness—that no one could possibly had imagined for that to happen. Ha, ha, ha! We all just couldn't help but laugh out loud at that silly, sailboat snatching, bullfrog! Ha, ha, ha! Fortunately, Sandy was still laughing too and didn't feel too bad about his loss.

Pete's Slick Frogger had suddenly sprung a leak and oh boy, his sailboat had begun to take on water! "Down it goes!" Pete yelled amusingly, while he watched his sailboat completely go down, sinking to the very bottom, of the fast moving creek. This was right after it had plowed straight into a big rock and crashed. "Yikes, awe sorry man!" I blurted. My facial expression, showing a funny but concerned looked now, as we watched it go down. This was turning out to be a tough one, indeed!

Although bumped by Marcy's Princess Missy into fifth spot, Sally's Rainbow Puff was gliding steadily and was now holding strong in the race, at the sixth spot. Great job, girls! I yelled. They were definitely close in the race and doing really great!

IF I COULD FLOAT ON A CLOUD, WHERE WOULD I GO?

My Golden Eye is looking real good and just slips smoothly, right passed Marco's Bumbo! "Woohoo!" I hollered out loud, as that shift now put him back to forth place—making me now in third! Oh but wait, hang on! We are now heading towards Billy's Liberty, which is now, in second place! The excitement, was most definitely back on! Ha, ha!

Everyone was cheering and hollering loudly, as if telling the boats what to do, would make them obey and go even faster, somehow. Ha, ha, ha! That was too funny! But hey, we're kids, ha, ha! This is so much fun! "Hey Andy, I'm a comin' for ya, buddy!" I had hollered. Ha, ha!

Andy's Silly Ship is still strong in first place—he is a tough boy to catch up to, that's for sure! Ha, ha! Billy's Liberty is now next to mine! Woohoo! We are now, just nose to nose—our hearts are pounding in our chests, with great anticipation of what could happen next!

It's now Billy's Liberty and my Golden Eye well ahead—we are now racing mightily, for the first spot, to win the race! "C'mon, Golden Eye! Go get it done!" I urged my sailboat onward, whilst I call out loud, to hurry it along. "Ha, ha, no not today, Buddy Boy! Ha, ha!" Billy returns his retort, as we both laugh and jokingly exchange some good old, friendly banter. Ha, ha! Wow—is this race, ever intense, or what? Ha, ha! It was so much fun! Ha, ha!

Everyone's remaining sailboat continued to cruise right along, with the help of the creeks very unpredictable swift current of course, as it continued to carry them towards the end. "Woohoo!" We all shouted, in playful excitement! Ha, ha, ha! You really cannot know for sure, of who will win, when the race is out of our hands! Oh but that is the thrill, don't you see? What is so cool about this, is that no one can control it, nor fix it to one's own advantage—making it nice to have a natural and fair race! It's the perfect setting! Ha, ha! You ought to try it! This is so exciting! Ha, ha, ha!

"Woot-woot! Here I come!" I shouted to Andy's Silly Ship, with a hunger for adventure! Ha, ha! Andy was just jumping up and down laughing in sheer excitement—it was so funny, it was awesome! Ha, ha! Along with the crowd of dozens of other children, whom had come to watch and followed the racers as well—everyone was chasing the sailboats down the creek, trying to keep up with them, along either side of the creek—just running, cheering and laughing, all along the way!

Ha, ha! I, along with everyone else, could hardly contain my excitement, as the race went on! Ha, ha! This race was epic and so much fun! What a wild ride of an adventure, this sure was indeed! Woohoo! Ha, ha, ha!

"This experience, is just so epic!" One child exclaimed! "Ha, ha! C'mon!" Replied another. "Go, go, GO! You can do it! Hurry! Ha, ha! Glide!" Shouted others. "Yay! Woohoo! Ha, ha!" The crowd bellowed in cheers of laughter, as they watched with great delight! The many children both onlookers and the sailors, had chattered back and forth, while they shouted their cries out loud, to cheer the remaining sailboats on!

Marcy's Princess Missy suddenly traded places with Marco's Bumbo, shifting its gear and gliding so swiftly whom was now at fifth place! "Wow, amazing, Marcy!" I shouted! This then placed her ship now in forth spot! Wow, what a rush! I was so excited for her! Ha, ha, ha!

"Oh my goodness, ha, ha!" Cried out Sally, as she giggled watching her sailboat, while a breeze then swiftly picked up and then suddenly began to blow over her Rainbow Puff! "Down I go!" She yelled out loud, with a humble, giggling laugh! Ha, ha! This was quite the event! What a race! What a rush! Anything can happen! Ha, ha! All thoughts from within me, were just bursting out everywhere, like fireworks! I was hysterically floored for everyone! Ha, ha, ha, ha!

Kelly's Commando, was now approaching Marco's Bumbo but as he began to pass him, his sailboat started to spring a leak at the edge of the bow, of his sailboat! Good golly! Oh no! Thankfully, Kelly's Commando manages, not to sink! Wow, incredible! Ha, ha! "Jumping, Jehoshaphat! Ooh, she may be it, boys and girls! Ha, ha!" Roared Kelly, as he watched his sailboat take on water but amazingly, it doesn't actually sink to the bottom of the creek, just yet and still holds on in the race! "Fewf!" He exclaimed! Ha, ha!

Swoosh! From high up above the epic sailboat race, a pelican took a nosedive, straight down towards Nicolas' Racer and his sailboat nearly escapes, from being taken hostage! The determined diving pilot from the sky, fortunately misses his sailboat and only skims the water's surface and then swoops back up to the sky, into the tree tops! "Whoa! That was so close! Ha, ha, ha!" Nicolas yells! All of a sudden, coming out as if from out of nowhere, Nicolas's Racer begins to go faster and even faster, from the added wake, thanks to the bird's missed dive which then ended

IF I COULD FLOAT ON A CLOUD, WHERE WOULD I GO?

up sending massive ripples, right through the water! "Whoa!" He cries out loud, as his sailboat was now hightailing hastily, as it is suddenly then launched directly towards Kelly's Commando! "Oh noooo! Ha, ha! Kelly, look out!" He alerts Kelly, up ahead! Then...BOOM! Both sailboats collide, knocking Kelly's Commando, right over! "MAYDAY! I'm going down!" Kelly yells, with absolute shock but still manages to keep a smile on his face and laughs out loud, at the sight of the crash! Ha, ha, ha! Incredibly, Nicolas' Racer remains afloat and was now, believe it or not, in forth place! "Ha, ha! Oh my gosh! This is crazy! Ha, ha!" Nicolas stated. "This is mega cool! Ha, ha!" Cries out another.

There was a major hustle and bustle among the crowd now! Everyone's excitement had just taken to a new higher level, that's for sure! Ha, ha! The chatter among everyone, had grown much louder and was must more intense! What was about to happen? But to no avail, would we be able to know for sure! Ha, ha! We just all had to wait! Woohoo!

My Golden Eye now awesomely, glides smoothly, passed Billy's Liberty and was now racing Andy's Silly Ship for the win, for first place! "Woot-woot! Ha, ha, ha!" I cried out. Then I heard an angel's voice from behind me. I turned my head to follow the sound, as the motion slowed down a little, causing everything else to become a blur but not, Marcy... The scene slowed to a slow motion all round me, as I looked back to see her. Marcy was as pretty as a spring cherry blossom on a cherry tree, opening on the first day of Springtime, as her dusty rose pink lips harmoniously moved, when that angelic voice came from them, as she spoke.

Dying to catch a glimpse of her big, deep blue eyes, looking my way...oh and her smile, how it made my heart completely flutter with butterflies. "Such an angel..." I caught myself saying, just above a whisper. Oops, I had thought, but I don't think anyone had noticed, nor heard me. The scene had then gone back into a steady onward swing. "Here I come," calls out Marcy calmly, as her Princess Missy now battles Nicolas' Racer, mightily for the forth spot! "Whoa! Yay, that's great M-mar-see and um, sweet! Wow, check it out! You can do it, Marcy!" I babbled, stumbling my words in front of her, yet again. Ha, ha...yikes!

Oh boy, I was sure in trouble now! Ha, ha! Oh but she was sure amazing, wasn't she? I couldn't help but keep looking back to check on how her sailboat was doing, throughout the race—oh, uh, yeah and to try and catch a glimpse of Marcy, too... my face was blushing, yet again. Ha, ha...

Maybe, Marcy was looking at me too—I mean, you never know, right? I shook my head then suddenly, as if to wake myself up quickly. Right, where was I? Back to the race, I had to get my head back in the game, I had thought. Others watched the race while in shock and wonder but were thrilled for the progress that everyone was making—of whom, who were still in the race but especially to see that Marcy, was picking up her lead! "What was happening? Wait, huh? How is she...?" Every boy was so impressed that their minds were so, totally blown out of the water—figuratively speaking of course! Ha, ha! I think, uh um, no I am pretty sure that even my own jaw was hanging wide open, for a while too at times...ha, ha, ha! "Great job, Marcy!" Everyone cheered for her! Ha, ha! Wow! I was so proud of her!

We now could see the finish line ahead, as we continued to cheer on, with our very best for the sailboats—that were still in the race while they persevered and blew in the wind, down the creek. Marcy's Princess Missy suddenly has a near hit, with Nicolas' Racer but manages to steer clear from hitting him and passes right into forth place. "Fewf! Awesome Marcy!" I shouted. Ha, ha! My heart skipped a beat, when she had almost crashed! Yikes! I took a sudden deep breath in and then let it out, just the same. "Thank you Jesus, that she was safe!" I had prayed quietly, from within my heart. I really did want to see her at least, make it to the finish line! I couldn't help it—I cared about her.

The stats were in! Who is going to win this race? Let us take a quick recap of the sailboat race, as it quickly was approaching the finish line! Now, with Andy's Silly Ship still in first place and my Golden Eye, was now at second. Then followed in closely, was Billy's Liberty at third, and then beautiful Marcy, I mean Marcy's Princess Missy was strikingly now, in the forth spot! And last but not least, finishing up the rear, were Nicolas's Racer and Marco's Bumbo at fifth and sixth. Wow! Whoa, was that a mouthful or what? Ha, ha! "That's amazing, guys and girls!" Children had shouted from the crowd. "Woot-woot! Woohoo!" Children had shouted.

The finish line is near, and the race is almost done but with hesitation, no wait, with sheer exhilaration, look! Who is that coming our way! It's Marcy's Princess Missy, now obliterating the boys ahead, as she passed Billy's Liberty and was now racing to beat my Golden Eye and Andy's Silly Ship, for the win! "Whoa, ha, ha! Oh my gosh! Great job, Marcy! Woot-woot!" I was nearly freaking out in excitement for her! Ha, ha! I was so worked up and jumped up and down a few times and marvelled at Marcy's Princess Missy's advancement in the race! "Go Marcy!" Everyone had yelled! Marcy's Princess Missy abruptly swerved in the wind, gliding with a new high-speed now—it was record breaking! A breeze picks up and even stronger now, slipping her sailboat right by my Golden Eye and then passed Andy's Silly Ship, just like that! "Whoa! Oh my, oh my, oh my! Ha, ha!" I babbled! It is over! The race is done and who would have guessed who would have won? "Ha, ha, ha! Incredible! Wow!" Everyone had shouted! "Great job, Marcy!" They added.

It was the beautiful, Marcy's Princess Missy in first place, Andy's Silly Ship in second, and my Golden Eye at third—then Billy's Liberty was in forth, Nicolas' Racer in fifth, and followed in closely was Marco's Bumbo, at sixth. Sandy's Saint Peers, was bullfrog lunch and Pete's Slick Frogger had sunk...as well as, Sally's Rainbow Puff and Kelly's Commando too—so they were each awarded an honourable tie, for seventh place!

I hollered to the crowed that had now surrounded Marcy. "Three cheers for everyone's sailboat! Hip hip, hooray! Hip hip, hooray! Hip hip, hooray!" Everyone chanted. Now three cheers for Marcy's win! Hip hip, hooray! Hip hip, hooray! Hip hip, hooray!" Everyone chanted. Great job Marcy!" Everyone had happily exclaimed. That was so much fun! "Amazing, everyone! Great job, to all of the sailors and their handcrafted ships!" I shouted! And to think that the girl of my dreams would win it all...wow, I was definitely impressed. What a girl, I had thought to myself. I couldn't stop smiling. "Congratulations Marcy, for your win!" Every child that had crowded around Marcy, had continued to cheer for her again and again. The crowd slowly dwindled down and everyone eventually had parted ways.

My cheeks were a rouge red by now while my cheeks hurt from a continuous, ginormous smiling grin. Ha, ha, ha! I just smiled at her and was so happy, that it didn't matter that I did not win.... And do you know what the best part of it all, was for me? Among the crowd of hyper glee that was excitedly shared, it had finally happened to me... I managed to catch a glimpse, of those big, deep blue eyes whom had then, miraculously, eye locked with mine—and we both then smiled, in return. What a day...

Pencil Artwork drawing of children in the meadow greens, congratulating Marcy on her epic sailboat race win entitled, "One of God's Beautiful Daughters" by skipper

My heart was completely putty and soft as goo, by then. Ha, ha! "Thanks for the game!" we all chanted and then headed off towards the meadow greens. What an epic sailboat race that was, indeed! I definitely will remember this, with or without a drawing that I will hand draw myself, to help remind me, of this most perfect, memory.

IF I COULD FLOAT ON A CLOUD, WHERE WOULD I GO?

From around a tree, walked a new taller boy, he looked a little older than I. He wore dark blue denim overalls in colour and had a white t-shirt on. His hair was black and kind of shaggy in length and his eyes were brown. The skin colour in his complexion, was a very light pink to whitish tone. I found that eyes often told a deep story, if one pays attention, just long enough to hear their truths. This tall boy's eyes seemed leery and shy but most definitely curious, at the same time. He seemed interested with this place and then braved up enough courage, to speak.

"Hello. My n-name is Bobby," he had stated. "C-can, I play h-here too?" He asked. I felt a sudden connection to him, as his stuttered wording had sounded kind of like mine. He was shy, yet proved to be brave and took risk to introduce himself to us strangers, regardless of whom we were. "Sure Bobby, that sounds great!" We all happily uttered. "Welcome, Bobby!" We all greeted him and it did not take long, even in that very moment, for a new friendship, to begin.

Hours went by as children played, all across this place of peace. Time did not seem to matter much here, for it was as though that time was limitless and it had no bound here. Children played in the hills and valleys below—up in the huge trees and their branches and such. They swam in the creek and ponds, and floated on rafts across it—laughing and playing and having a genuinely fun time. Everyone was just busily occupied playing, his and her various activity—enjoying and taking in nature's wondrous and breathtaking splendour.

Then I heard something—we all heard it. I began to feel something, rather strange. It seemed, that the others could feel it too. Everyone paused where they were standing, sitting, laying, floating, kneeling, climbing and or running—and looked about them to try and learn more. What was it? They were ever so curious of the sound and of that, rather strange feeling as well. For, how is it that they too, knew of it, heard it and felt it, just as I had? This was rather profound.

Then one by one now, they all listened and peered across the meadow greens—too simultaneously with growing concern, they all had then darted their eyes my way. Not knowing what it was, as I looked around at them and then at myself but then while looking downward, I had squinted my eyes, with confusion. Everything around me before my very eyes, suddenly began to fade out of colour and shape, blurring at a steady pace until finally, turning into a complete darkness and… I was then back, in my hospital bed. White coats by the many—both male and female, had surrounded me. I wasn't feeling too well, as something was happening to me but what, in this troubling place? I did not know. All I did know, was that I was not feeling too well.

In the flash of a moment, I slowly had opened my eyes but was abruptly blinded, by this bright, round yellowish-white light that was glaring right at me. Hooked up to various tubes and tons of wires and sticky things that were connected by these wires, to machines—I lay in my hospital bed, now strapped to the sides and unable to move out from such restraints. I was unable to move my arms or legs, in fact, I found that I could not really move anything at all. What was going on? I had thought. What happened? I had nothing on but equipment and hands working on me. I could hear voices and panic, though all of a sudden, in the blink of an eye, wait… how is it that, I didn't at all, feel anything any further?

Then while looking back up at the blinding round, yellowish-white light just above me, it began to get bigger and brighter—that the longer that I peered into it, the more the brightness did not hurt my eyes. I had become mesmerized by the enticing glow that radiated from it, so much so that the many frantic voices that had surrounded me, had begun to even fade away, from my own ears' awareness. "What, who…are…you?" My voice strained to say, just above a whisper. And then it happened, this mysteriously beautiful and warm glowing phenomena, it had begun to dance around a little. It shape shifted from round, to a star-like shape, and then back again. What, or whom was it? I then felt as though it were speaking to me, trying to communicate with me and even wanting for me to reach out to touch it, to go with it. I then reached out my right hand in wonder and as I pushed to extend my right arm to touch it, while forgetting about my restraints, something miraculous then happened. My view had suddenly changed on me, for it was no longer facing upward, but now downward…wait, what? I could now look down upon my own body and all that had surrounded it. I was no longer tied down to the bed's railings, no longer in any such pain at all. What? I had thought, as I now floated from above. This was amazing…

I was now afloat, as though I was truly on a cloud but still within the walls of this hospital. I was weightless. I could see and hear everything, yet my senses were no longer, the same. I gathered that I had left my body, wait...is this what it feels like, when we leave this humanly place, to go home to our Heavenly home? I had wondered. I had watched the doctors and nurses, as I observed all of which, was going on right before me, below me. But, I still could look down at my still body...how could this be? Amazingly enough, I was not worried by what I had seen, for there was no second-guessing, there was no hesitation at all. I did not even feel, any fear. I felt compassion for the people in the room, yet a separated connection from them all.

Then, I felt a radiating warmth coming from the light from above me and I felt drawn to it once again as I turned to see it once more. My feelings about it were now in afresh, something amazing was transpiring right before me, to me... I was fascinated by how it glowed, danced and was warm and inviting. It was so bright but the longer I stared at it, the more vividly colourful and beautiful that it had become. It grew brighter and more brilliant, than a rainbow after a glorious spring rain, but through a window. I felt that I was no longer in the room, no longer stranded in my bed...I was, free?

Engaged by the light, I began to float towards it. I wanted to touch it, to embrace it. I no longer had any such interest to refrain from it, but rather to proceed towards it. Somehow, I sensed that I knew it, and that it knew me. "Could, this be possible?" I asked myself in the wake of a whisper. I felt a healing warmth that was whispering, a hope to me. It was...I sighed, I was gobsmacked—and utterly lost in its trance. It was such a wonderful feeling that came over me. I could feel, a Divine love from it. My decision was now solidified, I wanted to go with it, period. I became overwhelmed by emotion, choked up a little, as this ever growing hope was now leading me to unveil this true mystery that which I now seek. Its' colours were so bright and beautiful that I can't even describe their names. It was like I could taste, their colours with my very own soul. I wanted to reach out and touch them. I wanted it so much, that I could almost touch it. I could feel, its voice, calling out to me. I know that that sounds very odd but who am I to consider even the least bit strange, when there is an all-knowing and all-powerful and almighty God, whom is a God of the impossible? And so, who am I, to decide such mindful restrictions, on life itself? That, is not my place, nor is it yours.

The body on the bed began to shake... the nurses and doctors began to scramble about even more, as frantic voices grew faster and louder. But as for myself, or rather, as for my spirit, I began to float towards the light. I wanted to touch it, to accept its Divine loving invitation, to seek it earnestly, with all of my heart, mind, body and soul. I began to reach out with my full intent to be transformed by this gleaming portal aura phenomena.

Suddenly, I felt a pull, as though something was grabbing me, like a strong force was trying to hold me down and keep me away, from going towards the light. I did not understand this, why would the earth want to pull me down? I wanted, no, I needed to go to the light! "No! Let, me, GO!" I had shouted with a strained voice, as though I was wearing a mask and my voice was muffled. "I have to go to the light! Let me, go!" I stated, as I began to cry. I tried to advance once again, but I struggled again, trying with all that I had, to reach my hand out to touch the light. The sight of my fingertips, reaching out—being so close, as I nearly was touching it, as it too tried to reach out to me, in a way as well. The force from below me, was pulling me back harder and harder, pulling me downward towards my earthly body, towards the hospital bed's surface. I was now, just above my body on the hospital bed, but still facing the light up above, as I tried yet again and again—reaching upward, as if to grab it, or even catch it. Then, I felt a burst of might, an inner driving force that refused to give up the fight! It felt like a last chance. Taking a deep breath, as I tried to pull myself towards the beacon of hope, among this curious ambiance about the room—towards the light that was opposing this other force that pulled me back, a battle for my spirit, so it may seem. At the top of my lungs, I yelled with all of my might as I cried tears of fight within my strained voice, "NOOOO!" Everything around me then, went black...

I had awoken with tears in my eyes, with not even a word to say. My mouth was covered with a breathing mask but this time, my body was strapped down and hooked up to, even more machines. I was restrained to the bed, preventing my escape, yet again. I felt devastated, my heart sunk further into my pounding chest. I was back in my hospital bed and once again the daily routine, began for me. The nurses checked my vitals, poked and prodded me, took my temperature, listened to my heart… the same ol' same ol'…

The voice of the head doctor then appeared off to my left, as it faded in. He was talking, medical talk…nothing of much interest that ever enticed me to fully pay attention to. And then he grabbed my attention, as he said to me "Kipper, you are a lucky boy to be alive." My eyes were groggy, as I strained to hear his words, while I could hear my heavy breathing through the oxygen mask. He added. "We almost lost you, again. You are a stubborn patient but fortuitously, we managed to save you from dying, again. You are a tough kid, hang in there and we will take care of you." The doctor had continued further. "Don't be alarmed by the straps around your wrists and ankles. It was a precautionary measure that we had to take. We had to restrain you, as during the surgery, you began to move around and yell frantically." He paused. I was confused, for I was sure that I had left my body, that my spirit had been trying to go home but that the doctors, they would not let me go. But why? I wondered. I felt a little perturbed and grief-stricken. While holding back from bursting out crying, I had choked up. Unable to hold back tears, they began to well up in my eyes. I am sure that the doctor must have thought, that I was grateful that they had 'saved me' but I was not… I wanted to go home. It felt like I had sunk down so much, into the hospital bed that was slightly propped upward, for me to sit up—feeling like the weight of a cannon ball… My heart, as so detrimentally felt, had sunk deep into my chest, as I was at complete loss for words.

"Now…*cough, cough*…" the doctor had cleared his throat and then continued to speak to me, once again—however, my focus had been withdrawn from his utterance, any further… "Kipper, you will need to be here in the ICU, for a few more days. Now, after the heavy anesthesia and other, medications, have settled in your stomach, probably say, maybe after a few hours, as food right now will, most likely feel unwanted and hard to take in, so you will remain on a hefty dose of IV fluids instead… So, when you are up for it, perhaps, after a day or two, you may eat all of your porridge, when you feel up to it and drink up all of your milk, once I permit the staff to provide those to you. In the meantime, the nurses will continue to monitor your recovery." He then walked away into a blur, from my sight. All I know was that I definitely, was not feeling too well, that's for sure...

Lying here, I looked around, feeling so defeated and down—plagued with a heartache for freedom and independence, of sorts. I was no longer near a window but was in a recovery room...I don't understand why they don't have windows, in a recovery room. I always have thought, well, I believe that a window should be in every room because I KNOW that they are helpful for patients, as they try to recover. Take me for an example... I, am a prime example of exactly, that! What about, me? I thought quietly to myself, as a huge frown came upon my face, while I looked down slowly and then around the room, with teared-up eyes and a glossy, long stare into nothingness. By being able to look outside, to imagine and dream... people, children especially, can more than just visualize, breathing in that fresh air and feeling that warmth from the sun—that they can jump on a cloud and explore and be free from this place that has us restricted and bound by rules and restraints. They can run around and play with other children.... Th-they can... I choked up once again with emotion. With each additional time that I go into an operating room, and then return back to my current circumstances, although elevated with more further health, complications—well, they only just get harder for me to bear and I just feel less encouraged and weakened, by each additional doctored procedure and ordered restrictions. I need my window... I had thought to myself. Why don't they understand that? I began to cry—but I kept it as quietly and as hidden from the nurses, as I possibly could, to myself...

They say that I am lucky to be alive... Some even say that it was a miracle. But, I often think about that light. That colourful, mesmerizing and warm, Divinely loving light... What was it? Where did it come from? Who, was it...or why, why it not yet, my time? No matter how many times a nurse or doctor, tells me that I should be 'THANKFUL' that I survived any of my surgeries or attack episodes—I just cannot help it, to keep from wondering, from thinking, at the rate that my body was depreciating... Was this a miracle?

IF I COULD FLOAT ON A CLOUD, WHERE WOULD I GO?

Pencil Artwork drawing entitled, "White As Snow" by Kipper

Various Pencil Artwork drawings of nature's captivating beauty entitled, "Glorious Daze" by Kipper (square shape collage of pictures)

JENNIFER DAWN DECONINCK SMITH

Pencil Artwork drawing of a unique cloud for entitled, "Angel's Wing" by Kipper

"Those who hope in the Lord, will renew their strength, they will sore on wings like eagles." —Isaiah 40:31

IF I COULD FLOAT ON A CLOUD, WHERE WOULD I GO?

Abstract Paint Artwork drawing entitled, "Depth" by Kipper

Pencil Artwork drawing of wispy, dancing clouds entitled, "God's Breath" by Kipper

CHAPTER FOUR

HEAD IN THE CLOUDS

Have you ever wondered, about how clouds catch light? From dusk to dawn, the sun slowly rises up into the atmosphere which surrounds the earth that which we live on. The clouds begin to capture the sunlight rays, taking them in layers of very bold yet, breathtaking and mesmerizing beautiful vibrant colours, as they gradually fold one, over the other—changing as if metamorphic in appearance while the earth rotates. Like a rare diamond that is formed, from out of the rough of an ugly looking rock. From a strange looking thing, comes a beautifully and wonderfully made creation—such as we are as Christians, through Jesus Christ. It is an amazing transformation that we are forged, so that God of the impossible, can wield us for His glory. Amazing!

Across the atmosphere, during a sunrise and sunset, sunlight is cast across the sky between the clouds and the ground's surface, which then creates an orchestrated cue of reds, oranges and pinks among the clouds that you will see. If you see yellow, these are caused by the presence of nitrogen dioxide—generally, from high air pollution caused by mankind's greed to over produce, things and stuff in their factories that scatter the earth's globe. When you see the orange to blood red coloured moon, or any colouring for that manner, other than white—you are actually looking through multiple layers of pollution that have been trapped within our atmosphere, standing between you and your view of the moon's debut while at night.

However, I want for you, to further open up your mind for a moment. There is something incredibly unique about this, especially rivetingly beautiful. No, I am being honest here, hear me out, please? When you think of it, there is actually something, pretty cool about this process—no, no, not about the pollution part caused by mankind's evil-led nature, for more…but about what actually happens in the process through it all—a transformation, to unify that. As humans, we do not have the power to decide when this world ends, nor in 'how to save it' from its final days—regardless what anyone else tells you. We, do not have that kind of power—for we are not God.

So remember that. Jesus already saved the world, mankind, by His sacrifice—people's spirits, whom are of the utmost importance, to our Heavenly Father. Not stuff, not nature, not pets, nor careers or money. This planet will die at its predetermined timeline, when God says it is finished. Unfortunately, the majority of mankind, have lost focus on what actually matters in this life—but many, do not yet even know. It is up to us Christ-followers, to speak of God's truth to inform them, not to control them—for we have, Free-will, as a gift. So, we must realize, where the priorities of life, truly are while we are still here. Everything, good and bad, happens for a reason, beyond our own understanding through life. Mistakes are a part of our learning process, for if we did not make any mistakes, how would we learn? Parents, if you are so afraid of your children from making mistakes, in trying to prevent them from making them—you haven't that kind of control, so let go. Instead of embracing fear, encourage God's Light of Hope, within your children. We are, to try to earnestly, seek God and believe, at all costs. The pollution indeed, has become a human problem, however, it is not a problem for God, He cannot be stopped from anything evil. A transformation from the night sky being flooded by the visibility of the pollution in the air, it forms into a beauty at each and every sunrise and sunset. Even during a storm, God brings us the rainbow, even in doubles at times—shining their beauty and enlightening the world with such a friendly and most breathtakingly beautiful reminder, of His promise. How beautiful, is that? It makes my heart, smile.

You see, God makes good from out of any bad situation, right? He is God and He has all power to straighten our paths of ruin, into triumph and victory, shall we choose it. The enemy constantly will take the truth and twist it, for his own personal evil gain—to cause harm to people's lives and to separate us from God. But God then takes the ugliness from something and He transforms that, into something beyond, beautiful. When it comes to a person, God does the same from within them, when we earnestly seek Him, wanting that for our lives and let Him lead us, with all of our heart, mind and spirit. Pretty cool, hey? I would like to think so. Even in a storm, there is Light.

"God promises to make something good out of the storms that bring devastation to your life." — Romans 8:28

"I will praise you in the storm." — 1 Thessalonians 5:18

"I will praise the Lord all my life; I will sing praise to my God as long as I live." — Psalm 146:2

"He made the storm be still." — Psalm 107:29

So, why are clouds a fluffy white colour during the day? We know that clouds help cool the earth by reflecting sunlight—giving us shade and protection from the sun, that is pretty cool and obviously yet another, gift from above, of protection. What do you think causes this? Clouds are made up of billions of tiny little water droplets which science calls them ice particles and they help scatter sunlight that hits them—which then gives them their bright, white colour in appearance. Even from space, these white clouds can be seen! Ha, ha! Pretty amazing! Right? I think it is! God is amazing in what all He has created for mankind. I was told that in the last book of the Bible, it talks about that Jesus will return in the clouds. The good news is, no one shall miss His return. The thing is however, will we be ready for Him? That, is up to each one of you, to prepare as God wants us prepared for such a day as that. I am grateful to say, that I am, ready…

"Behold, He cometh with clouds; and every eye shall see Him." — Romans 1:7

Sometimes, when I am at the green meadows at my place of peace, instead of joining up with friends, I will go on my own for some quiet time, with God's many creations and creativity that I know, comes from Him and not mankind. I go to seek and find a restful and comfortable place, in the meadow. I like to lay down on the ground while facing upward, so that I may gaze deeply up into the heavens, letting my imagination, read the many clouds' stories to me. This is also fun to do with friends, as well!

Pencil Artwork drawings of thunderstorms entitled, "Thy Will Be Done On Earth, As It Is In Heaven" by Kipper

To most people, clouds are just clouds, as they hardly slow down long enough to even notice them and witness their many, unique characteristics. During the daytime, these clouds are usually white and fluffy and casually float across the vault of the above heavens, to even below tree level at times. But in moments of severe weather, they change and vigorously scatter, as they march onward while they take over the skies! Amounting to very loud and ferocious, raging weather systems that can be shockingly devastating, even to nature and life itself.

Have you ever really though wondered, just how the clouds change colours, at all? They become mesmerizing and ever so dreamy! Taking you off into a daydream world and before you even can realize it, your mind is already surrendered—by the captivating transformations that they offer, as they move and morph from one shape, into another! Just amazing! There is so much wonder in the world, for us to explore!

I would look up at the many, wondrous clouds which floated on by, so effortlessly. It was as if, they were inviting me to a grand assembly, where a masterly skilled raconteur, awaits! The skies' stage was set and had bloomed with such a consistent, cloud formation lineup, for the show! The raconteur would amazingly put on, nothing short of its very best performance, each and every time! The clouds came in randomly, each one with their very own story—you see. They took their time, telling their dramatic special number, no two were alike. I truly had felt like a most top, noteworthy VIP, indeed! Ha, ha! I loved it!

Pencil Artwork drawing of a uniquely shaped cloud entitled, "Majestic, In All Of His Ways" by Kipper

They presented such a tranquil impression, as they glided across the wide, spanned sky. Yet, all of which in how this was done, they did it while

IF I COULD FLOAT ON A CLOUD, WHERE WOULD I GO?

on the move—not one paused, not even for a second at all! Just, wow! They shaped and shifted into their many creatively designed forms—showing me at times, a real captivating action thriller! It was always just so, amazing! There were always so many shapes up in the clouds and if you looked closely and were patient—you could begin to see them, as they danced, morphed and put on an epic show, just for you!

Oh the shapes, where shall I even begin? There were shapes like a pirate ship, that shifted into a mighty, roaring lion—then there was a big, fluffy white rabbit, just captured in a leaping action pose, right before your very eyes! And then before it departed, it faded into a wizards' hat and then disappeared, just like that! Ha, ha! Whoa, this was so cool! Papa surely has the biggest imagination, indeed! I have seen dinosaurs, rocket ships, and dragons that soared in cloud formations, right through the sky!

Pencil Artwork drawings of funny shaped clouds each entitled, "Go-Go Rabbit", "Flipped Over Diving Humpback Whale", and "Moo Cow" by Kipper

I had witnessed the most funniest of mystifying cloud guise, ever! From funny shapes like a big, ginormous head of broccoli, oh my goodness! Ha, ha! To a perfectly shaped boomerang, hovering right along as it glides just above the tree tops and then as it passes by, it suddenly turns into a flying fish or even as a sailboat! Err! Ha, ha! Even I, could't have even thought about that combination! Ha, ha! Nice one, Papa! Ha, ha! So cool! You truly have the sheer, undeniably highest imagination out there! I even saw different kinds of food—you know, like a pizza slice that was getting stretched really far and really wide cross the sky—and then it got shorter and shorter and was squished into a fat muffin top that had then eventually, shifted into a big blob. Ha, ha! Wow!

One cloud, even looked like a mountain and there was a cave on one side, with a man on the other, just over the rise of the mountain top. He was climbing over it, chasing a bear towards the cave below! It really looked like it! Ha, ha! I'm not kidding! I actually saw it! It was so cool and it had me entirely captivated, literally watching it, right to the very end! Ha, ha! And do you want to know, what the most amazing part, was? It really did look like it was moving, as if I was watching a moving action scene in a movie, right before my very own eyes! It was so cool! You would have to be there, to see it but it was really, very cool! Ha, ha! I was so grateful to have been bestowed upon, of such a storytelling moment that was indeed, Heaven-sent. I am shaking my head, as I was just so very much, impressed! Ha, ha!

I read once that when you see a cloud shaped like a heart, an angel, a feather or even an exclamation point, that you may have been sent a message, from Heaven itself. I like that one. I was told that the Lord, does work in mysterious ways! Ha, ha! So I think that means, that He works in ways, that are absolutely, beyond our own understanding—that we even the brightest among us, cannot truly fathom, Papa's process. If we knew of it all, then we would not lean on Him, therefore, we would not grow, at all. Good comes from Him, period. So, you never know! Ha, ha! Pretty cool! Anything is possible, when you believe! What cloud story shapes, have you seen?

Or when you find yourself feeling low and you miss someone, that has left this world and so you're thinking of that loved one whom you hold dear to your own heart—you then decide to say a prayer that you are thinking of them and miss them and as you look out of a window, you find with astonishment—a perfectly, detailed angelic wing cloud formation, or even a bird cloud form, in flight! Now that, I would like to think of, is a confirmation, just for you! You may have just received, an affirmation, like a kiss from God, gently upon your forehead—to remind you that He is touched, as He loves you beyond measure and that your loved one, is thanking you and is thinking of you, as well and blesses you, to carry onward.

I like hearing stories and telling stories—when in using my imagination, it helps take away any pains I am having, for the most part… like a distraction from it all, you know? I cannot possibly, even imagine my life while living on a hospital bed and not being able to use, my own imagination—a gift that God has given me. Can you? I can't even imagine life not having any clouds in it, now that would be, just crazy! Ha, ha!

Just dare to allow, for your mind to dream such possibilities, of whom you could potentially be. For if you draw your dream and allow for God to build it, then you will begin to see, just how life is so worth living and you will find yourself living it, with unique creativity! Also it is important for us, to come to realize that no matter how big and how extravagant that your personal dreams and goals may be in this humanly life, God knows what is best for you and He will supersede those dreams and goals, tenfold—when we allow Him to! You will learn to live at peace despite the chaos—through His boundless goodness and merciful, loving grace. You will even, finally experience a truthful life by living in His truth and you will then finally be, set free. For nothing can take you from the Father, when Jesus lives inside of your heart—this promise, is forever.

Like the rays of the golden sun that shines so brightly, cascading its many colours across the horizon—each cloud-present morning and evening, so too, can you shine brightly in this world that has been torn apart. The imagination is a powerful thing, both light and darkness battle it out day and night—for you know that there is good and bad, whom dwell here. When used well and hopefully used for good, we too all must be aware of, to whom we belong, that we came from the Father. It is for each of us to decide our end result, to whom we wish to die to ourselves and then eternally serve and dine with our Father in Heaven—or to eternally die and burn for the devil. A truth much of the world refuses to admit, even among believers.

I can imagine that everyone, really could use a pick-me-up piece of encouragement and on a most regular, daily basis too—and during such rough and unpredictable times, at best. So then, I must inform you for real, of great news that I have now for you, my friend! Papa wanted for me, to share with you, a Letter of Love, directly from Him—for this was written, *especially for you*! Please do share it and may you be Blessed, *abundantly*!

A LETTER OF LOVE

"To You, My dear children, whom is reading this direct and paramount message of my pure and clean, unadulterated Love for you, that no human can truly give:

No matter what in your life that you have done, to no matter whom you may think that you are—for this message, is sent directly from your God, your Papa and Heavenly Father—Himself, of that of Heaven.

For I want for you, to remember this and know—whom in Me, your Father, that you are! You are forgiven, My dear, precious child—of any lifespan, of all mistake, sin and evil-led humanly ruin. Come to me, as you are.

For my Son's Sacrifice, was PERFECT. Believe in Jesus' Name and come to Me, seek refuge and find rest under my wings. You need only, be still. You are worth it, more than you will ever know. You are precious, in your Papa's Loving heart, My child. You are valued, beyond any given measure.

You are always thought of, for this you need to know—you are never forgotten, nor forsaken, for I, your Lord God, am with you, always. Come to me, through my Son, and I will come for you upon your return home. You are Loved unconditionally and Eternally. You are a child, of the Great and Awesome, Almighty, Living God! It is I, the God of the impossible, in whom you are skillfully and wonderfully made! Remember this, for I am, always with you, my child! For I accept you, as you are.

— Love, Papa"

IF I COULD FLOAT ON A CLOUD, WHERE WOULD I GO?

Even on a human level of thinking, it is believed that dreaming about clouds may symbolize, an inner mix of feelings of the dreamer, to whom may be in need of a greater faith, in his or her waking life. It is said however that because of ones' anxiety or fears which it stems from the same thing, fear—the person is unable to have or maintain and keep that faith, strong. It is through, perseverance and holding onto your faith, a gift that which God had given you, when Jesus's work was finished, at Calvary.

It has also been said that they can represent many different kinds of emotion, all depending upon your current status of mood—but who knows? It is far too easy as well for mankind to, overthink, into things—you know of this? That we must also heed with caution, and be aware of where our thoughts are coming from, of what is backing their motive. I think that is another reason, as to why I find clouds to be, so enticing and I just cannot help but want to see more of them and let them take me away, on as many more adventures that I may have—that are yet to come!

The many clouds—they tell a story… If you just take the time to stop whatever you are doing, or wherever you are—I assure you, that you will learn something new, even about yourself. There is wonder found in the clouds, in the skies, in life—in the many wildflowers across the grounds and in the songs of the wild birds in nature, that fly on by. To the many gorgeous mountain ranges and peek tops and countless trails that wind around emerald green and blue pools of glacier waters of many—that which offer such beauty and the calling to a variety in adventure. When is the last time that you took a break from the busyness of life, to appreciate what God has made? 'Stop to smell the roses' they say, have you noticed, just how much more the enemy has busied you along, instead—with the many distractions, from what is right there, before you?

You must remember that you are no robot—that you are not even required, to reach as so high that you will fall. That my friend, is 'the way of the world'…it is not of God's desire nor requirement of you. In all of the rushing around through life, acting like a headless chicken that forgets to use their very own, God-given brain. This fear causes one to act from out of fear only, being too afraid to slow down just enough, for fear of getting to know, the truth about life—to even come to learn, of whom you actually are, or to whom you are meant to become.

Even the fear for God, to get to know you, as you truly are—that the enemy's fed-lies try to instil, such a fear filled of excuses, within you—a seed, had been planted deep within your mind, from the beginning of the devil's deceptive timeline which had begun since the time, of **Genesis Three**... Well my friend, you need not the filters, the masks, nor the gloves—take them off. God already knows, you. For even before life began, He knew you and yet, He still created you, because He loves you. And even He, wants for you to make it. And so, as He sacrificed Himself as a Man, to die for you, it was so that you could bear the gift of Freewill to choose, to be with Him in Heaven, forever—or to go and be with the devil in hell, where love clearly does not exist. The choice, is your to make. Is that not, the most beautiful love story, that the Holy Trinity, has bestowed upon mankind? That just baffles my mind even still and yet, it still fills my heart with delight. Shaking my head while in an utmost respectful amazement, for Jesus and for the Father... I am truly grateful. Hmm, wow, He is truly amazing...

Then you won't find yourself any further, as literally running around for nothing—quite like a headless chicken, with your head cut clean off. Your brain is so, especially wired for true love and for the understanding of things, of life—to the yearning to know more, to understand, to seek out, something bigger than oneself—desiring such an acceptance of oneself by someone and to receive some sort of a healing grace, like no other. There is only One, in whom we can find this.

Life was never meant to be numbly, to be obsolete, crowded and overwhelmed—nor loaded with too many to-do performance and earn it, to prove-it, sort of lists—unnecessary priorities, you must by now, admit it to yourself? Hmm? The sneaky enemy, well he just ends up messing with your mind, in his relentless scheming to do you harm and bring ruin into your life—wounding your heart and making your brain feel like goo—that you are unable to utilize what God has given you, which is not healthy for you at all. For you are meant to be in the knowing, don't you know? To be aware and to not be blindsided, away from the truth. Perhaps, you are not yet asking, the right questions? Quite possibly, seeking the answers, from the wrong source, even? Something to think about, any how, is it not?

> He Died For YOU, take up your cross and follow Him. Sisters and Brothers--For the TIME has come.

Pencil Artwork drawing entitled, "My God, Oh How You Love ME!" by Kipper

"O Lord, my heart is not proud, nor my eyes haughty; Nor do I involve myself in great matters, or in things too difficult for me. Surely I have composed and quieted my soul; Like a weaned child rests against his mother, My soul is like a weaned child within me." — Psalm 131:1-2

Allow for yourself time, to slow down and even pause for a moment each day—taking one day at a time. For every now and then, try to look up—let your mind embrace the unimaginable, as much as possible, to the end. The sky is not the limit, the mind is. So you see, there is no need to fear. Be brave and allow for yourself, time within your life—to cast your cares upon the Father, in whom you will surely find rest and be able to, finally dream. God is good. Remember that.

Opening my eyes, as they slowly adjusted from a faded fogginess, to the light in the room—I looked down at my light green hospital gown. White looking at the white plastic snap buttons that were along both of the sides of my gown, I would look up at other children's hospital clothing and see that they were not all of the same style, nor colour. I have been told that this gown style that I have to wear, is helpful for nurses when they change my clothes daily, making it easier to take off and put a new one on, when I cannot sit up myself. I get it, it makes sense to me. After all, who am I to be picky, right? I have to be grateful that I have the help and everything that goes with it—regardless of the discomforts that go along, such a journey as mine.

A nurse was helping unbutton my hospital gown, for my daily sponge bath time, yeah nothing manly about that one, ha, ha! It was time to get washed up, before the doctor would arrive, prior to breakfast, early in the morning. It was time to wash me but with a cloth…it's called a sponge bath, which I think is funny because they don't even use a sponge, ha, ha! What is up with that? Such a strange term to use, I had thought. Ha, ha! Makes me smile and laugh every time a nurse says, "It is time for your 'sponge bath' Kipper" and then they come at me but with a cloth! Ha, ha! Silly adults! Ha, ha!

IF I COULD FLOAT ON A CLOUD, WHERE WOULD I GO?

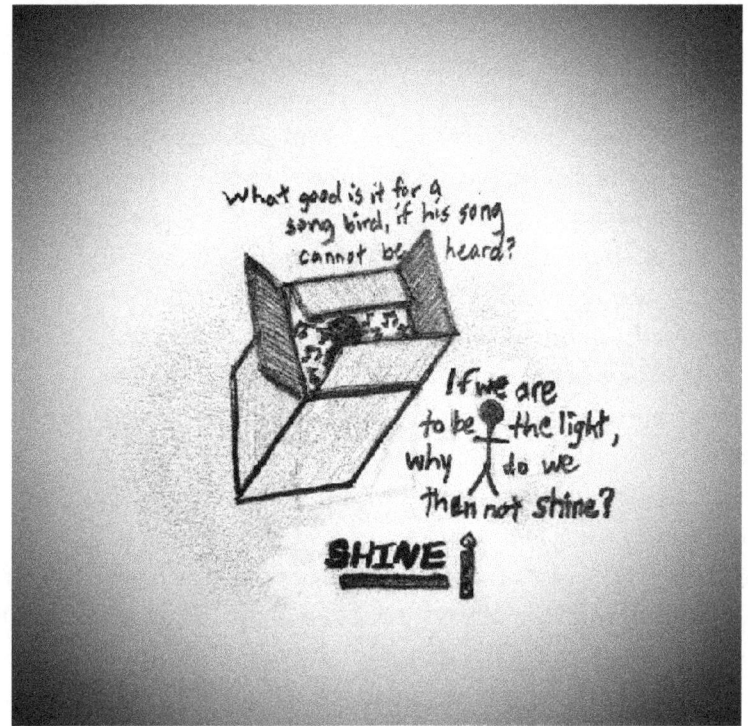

Pencil Artwork drawling of a song bird in a box unable to be heard and a Christian, Child of God unwilling to shine entitled, "Spiritual Bondage" by Kipper

Well, I am kind of, useless, as far as being able to help move things and lift things up and like, feed myself and stuff, right? But even still, I have learned to be grateful for the care that I do receive, despite my depreciating condition. I use to draw a lot, but this past year, well, things have changed once again for me, in my health condition that is... I have not gained strength, nor muscle mass you see—as I only seem to have lost more, as time has continued on. I find it rather, exhausting to hold my hand up, just long enough to draw much of anything, anymore. Kind of sad I know but what options, do I really have?

I am pretty tired during waking hours—to try and stay focused long enough to read, just feels a little to much for me, to handle these days. Now, I really aim for my adventures on the clouds, more than ever! I don't waste that kind of time, that's for sure! Ha, ha! I seem to look a little skinnier too, I wouldn't really know for sure—I don't exactly have a mirror, nor desire to stare into and gaze at this handsomeness, for too long of a time. Ha, ha! It takes a lot, to look this good... Ha, ha! I'm just kidding, but you get the picture.

The children who were mobile and able to move around the hospital, actually would wear a different kind of hospital outfit, than me. They had on a shirt with a collar, with long sleeves and buttons that were like snaps, that were in the front, all the way down from the top. And I liked the colour because my favourite colour is light blue, to I guess medium blue—well and white too because of the clouds, but I really like the blue because the sky is blue and endless. Their shirts have a nice vertical light to medium-like blue colour and white stripes on them, with matching drawstring pants and then just their bare feet for walking—though, sometimes they had hospital slippers on for walking about, too.

As the nurse washed me, I tended to not pay much attention and my mind would often, okay, always wonder a lot of the time but hey, I can't even sit up myself, so I think that it is fair game for me, to be allowed to daydream and pretty much, all of the time now! Ha, ha! Wouldn't you agree? Ha, ha! I would like to think so. Ha, ha!

Anyway, I tend to let my mind wonder a lot, obviously. Ha, ha! I think our imaginations are limited too much these days, because if we are not allowed to let them just daydream from time to time, perhaps even daily—then what good are they for? For we cannot really, truly then be ourselves, if we don't dare to dream, right? I think that it is also important, to make sure that we know the difference between reality and fantasy, of course but it is okay to dream—just as long as it is happy and encouraging, and shared with others, not just kept to oneself, nor harmful to ourselves, or to others. We are to learn to be selfless in this world, when the opposition deems another plan of its own evil desires, to take that from us. Do you know what I mean?

IF I COULD FLOAT ON A CLOUD, WHERE WOULD I GO?

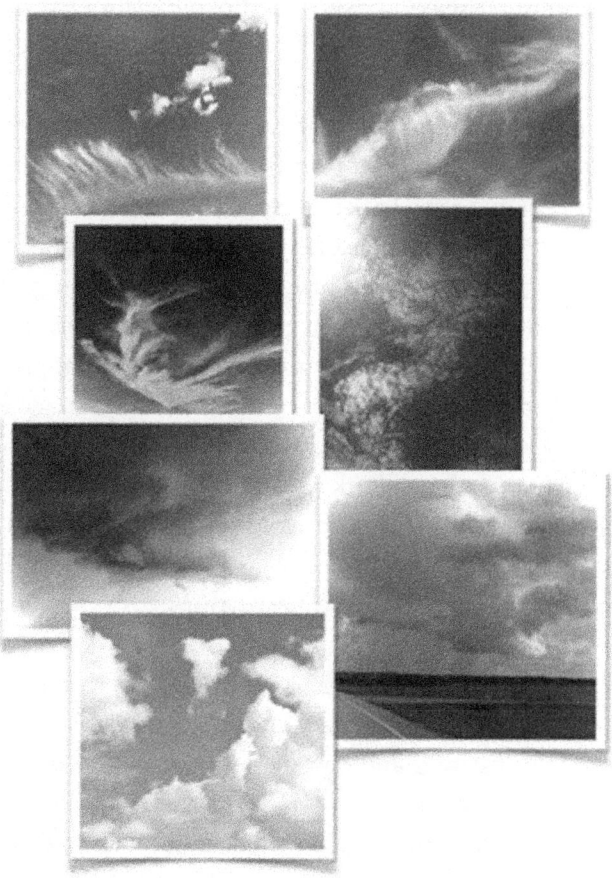

Various Pencil Artwork drawings of uniquely shaped clouds entitled, "Flight" by Kipper

As the now in session, 'sponge bath' was in session...ha, ha, so silly—as I was being tended to, I looked down at my toes while wiggling them. I sometimes imagined myself, wearing what other children in the hospital had on. I would look over and imagine myself across the room, in a different hospital bed—imagining watching myself, actually sitting up after waking up from a big, awesome slumber—stretching my arms out, as I yawned, the most glorious yawn ever and then turned to the side of my bed, to hang my legs over the edge.

I then pictured myself, climbing down out of that hospital bed—all deep within my mind of course—I imagined, hopping down out of my hospital bed, feeling the coolness of the hospital floor's surface, against the bottom of my bare feet. Legs that would actually hold me upright, so that they could literally, take me places! Oh the places I would go! Ha, ha! What would I even do, if it were my very first time? Hmm... where would I go, what would I do first? I had wondered to myself... Hey, I could even, go to the bathroom on my own, like a normal child's routine! That would be awesome! Hey, it's the small things, man, it's the small things... Ha, ha! You got it pretty good, if you can go and do that! Ha, ha, ha! So many blessings that people are given in life yet, many haven't even a clue about them, and don't learn to appreciate them, until they are gone.

So sad...please tell me, that you are grateful? The saying, 'count your blessings' wasn't created, just for kicks—it means to realize, that we don't have to be running around so much and try too hard in this life. It does not mean to do nothing but it means to pay attention to the little things, to not sweat the small stuff and to keep your eyes on Jesus because we cannot do anything good, without Him. We are meant to take advantage of the goodness that is available to us. For what good is a song bird, if it is kept in a closed box? If its' song, cannot be heard?

I began, thinking long and hard, on what I would do, if I had been blessed with, mobility...hmm... My mind then got so overwhelmed, with so many ideas that I just couldn't decide on what to do. Then a light bulb went off and I eventually decided that I would maybe dance around the room, like I had just received a miracle and my body was completely healed, in Jesus' Name! Wouldn't that be...so cool! Yep, I would definitely dance around a little and then I would run, right up to the window! Ha, ha! I would run right up to it and lean forward, looking outside of it... hmm, wow. Now, wouldn't that be wonderful? Oh, the things that I would do...

Sometimes, I would kind of, sink back down and feel a little bit of an envious feeling creep up inside my mind but I knew that it was not right, you know? To desperately want what other children have, that I do not have—that's not right. I would look at them and then look down and kind of feel sorry for myself but then, that would just make me feel even worse. So what good was that doing for my own self esteem, right? No good, at all! Nope!

IF I COULD FLOAT ON A CLOUD, WHERE WOULD I GO?

Then, I finally would just say to myself, no, that's enough of that! I have to be grateful. I have to humble myself and be thankful for everything that I have in my life, even if it is not much, or of what the other children may have. Even a child in a third world country, can find happiness in the simplest of things... It is because I don't want to be jealous or greedy, you know? That would then make me not very grateful, for what I have and that is not right either, by thinking only of myself. This is the trap that the enemy wants for us—to only, think of ourselves and to allow his lies to wage war within our mind, against the knowledge of God. I was not going to play that game. So why be or act like, what you don't like, right? I choose to put others first because that is what Jesus did for me, so why would I not follow, the best example of all time?

I understand that to you, I may look like I don't have much or look like much either but I am alive and breathing, and I like to make others smile and laugh—to encourage them, you know? I always try to remember, to wish only the very best for others and hope that they will enjoy life, even if it is short and can be so, unbearably hard at times. I would not ever wish a bad thing on anyone, there is no need to curse others, not ever. For what good would one gain, of such a cruelty? Nothing good, that I know of.

I know that God wants for all of us to make it, so why can't I wish the same for others? Even though, I am labeled 'TERMINALLY ILL' and yes, stuck in this hospital bed, for possibly my entire mortal life. I choose to believe and put my hope in Jesus. I find that it helps get me through my days. The other children in the hospital and their families and other visitors that would come to visit—always seemed to, well, honestly some are a little awkward and shy when they are around me and they have actually at times, avoided me...but I forgive them and I ask Papa to forgive them. I don't blame them at all. It is not their fault, the devil makes them feel that way towards me. I don't even think that they realize that they are even doing it, nor understand fully as to why they are even doing it, if they knew of their actions, when around me.

In fact, there has been some, who are so nice and even bring me encouragement cards with quotes and scripture on them, and even activity colouring books, stuff like that. They will talk to me and ask what adventure I was on that day, or yesterday and so on... it was actually pretty cool of them! I would also show them the drawings that I had hand drawn, over the years. Like I said, I haven't really been drawing nearly as much lately, but I do still try to do a little—to try and keep track of my adventures. I have to be grateful regardless, there's no other way to really be, I think anyway.

I truly want everyone to feel joy in their lives, no matter what they are going through. Everyone needs encouragement from time to time, we just tend to forget too much, as life gets busy and takes people in different directions through their own personal lives and encountered struggles—not realizing that they too, can "stop and smell the roses" as they say... That they, actually do have the ability to just say, "NO, busy schedule, not today!" Learning to just say no from time to time, to their busy sport, or to their one or multiple after school extra-curricular activities—to driving around everyone everywhere which is preventing them from experiencing genuine, "family time"... Or even to the additional "wanting to get a few more extra hours of work, just to make a few extra bucks" excuse, or whatever and just be—spending time with family for a day, going out on a date at least, once a week with your loved one or companion in life... Learning to take a break, just to let yourselves breathe and to try to allow for yourself to actually, enjoy life while it lasts.

I mean, we kind of need to learn to be honest here. People have allowed for their lives to spin out of control, or rather, into too much of a controlled atmospheric distraction from actually, living—into the overly busy lifestyle, which just ends up causing them more and more stress in anything. Tell me, this is healthy? I bet you can't even do that? Ha, ha... Go hiking, take a walk with a friend or loved one—explore the world around you that for now, we call home, in this camping trip we call life. I mean, why not, right? If you can and have been blessed with mobility and have access to go out there and try it, please try it! I would love to be able to myself but I obviously, cannot. Use those blessed feet that God gave you and explore! Write about your story, because chances are, there are others whom are in need of a connection that is familiar and similar in nature to that of their own lives. Everyone, needs encouragement. What is your story?

IF I COULD FLOAT ON A CLOUD, WHERE WOULD I GO?

"Fix your eyes on what is true, and honourable, and right, and pure, and lovely, and admirable. Think about things that are excellent and worthy of praise." — Philippians 4:8

"For what you may see, I am not strong nor do I have the physical strength of the strongest man, nor that of the weakest. Oh but for what you do not see, is much fiercer—that I have my Father right here standing with me, whom gives me such a sheer, high pain endurance—that of an army. He is my strength whom comforts me. My rock that which helps me stand the tests of time. My God will carry me through, for He fights for me and I praise Him—for even in this storm, I praise Him. For this storm too, shall pass." — Kipper

Pencil Artwork drawing entitled, "Stop And Smell The Roses" by Kipper

Life is really quite precious and very short, and we do have freewill to choose—but us humans tend to always make things seem, so much harder than it really has to be. It is just a matter of how much of 'the way of the world' are you allowing to hold you back in life, or cause you stresses that really just, aren't needed. There is power in the word, 'no' and there is also power in the word, 'yes'... we just have to learn, in how to use each one the right way, however way it works in your life.

Want to know something else? We are not supposed to be the 'hero' of our own story, did you know that? Maybe that does sound weird, but it is true. No really, it is true and you know what? It is a relief and is very nice to know that—I think that it takes the pressure off, don't you? I am so glad, that I don't have to handle everything in my life, or have to do that for everyone else. I mean, that is really, a lot of work! Ha, ha! So, about the hero thing, it really is helpful to understand it. Do you know what that is all about? Have you heard about the story of Grace? I heard about the story of Grace one day, from a kind, nondenominational pastor whom had visited one of my roommates, one day.

There was this young girl that was maybe about, six years old at the time. She was really scared about dying and I mean, she was terrified! This poor little girl, would actually literally, tremble in fear of the unknown—I really felt for her and would even pray quietly for her, whenever I was awake enough and remembered to. She would completely break out in tears, anytime the doctors or nurses, even mentioned a timeframe on her health battle, that she broke out in tears. It was often when they talked to her parents and unfortunately, ended up talking about it, right in front of her usually.

Anytime that the topic was about her health situation, she would overhear snippets...which was really stressing her out and making her feel so afraid, to do anything. She practically, cried all of the time, day and night. So, she hardly slept either, obviously.

So the doctor suggested to her parents, whom were not at all believers in the highest, most supernatural powerful God, whom created the Universe and all living things in it. Anyway, the little girl's parents, well, they were more into science and evolution stuff—'the way of the world' beliefs, that sort of thing—you know the difference, right?

Truthfully, I must be honest and ask myself—who am I, to judge them or anyone for that matter? I am not God, only He is. It's not my place to judge, persecute, nor execute people either. How wonderful it is, that God knows everything and I don't have to try and explain myself to Him! Ha, ha! He just knows all!

Anyway, the doctor had suggested to the little girl's parents that if, they were willing to allow for a nondenominational Pastor to come in to see her, that this would basically be leaving all pressure off the table of 'specific religious beliefs' and by only speaking of the truth about Jesus' Loving Grace, about the Gospel of truth—that it would really help their daughter, overcome her fears. The parents were then open to hear it and from a loving Christian man of the faith, whom didn't pressure any views whatsoever on anyone—to come in and speak with their daughter, in hopes to find out why she was so afraid but most of all, to hopefully help her, no longer be afraid.

To the little girl's parents, this felt as a last resorted hope, as they were willing to try anything at this point, to try and help out their baby girl and to try and calm her nerves—especially because this stress would always provoke health attacks, which further progressed her illness, even more. So you can imagine the growing fear in this child's heart, when after each additional attack, doctors would say that her time would get shorter and shorter. Yikes! I cannot even imagine! Poor little girl!

The following morning, in walked the nondenominational pastor, into the Children's Long Term Ward at the hospital. He was dressed in casual wear—no suit, just blue jeans, a 3D elk image carved belt buckle that looked pretty cool actually, as it was made from an antler and was mounted on a brown belt that he had worn on a regular basis. It must have been his favourite, a gift from someone perhaps…

He also had on, a deep cherry red and white small plaid-style, checkered button up, long sleeve shirt—top neck button undone, to be relaxed and he was really tall. His hair was kind of like, a blondish-grey-blended, silvery hair colour and he had a clean cut moustache and an average shortish-length, trimmed beard. He had the most wonderful and friendliest, kind face that you ever did see. He was very approachable and and an endearing soul.

JENNIFER DAWN DECONINCK SMITH

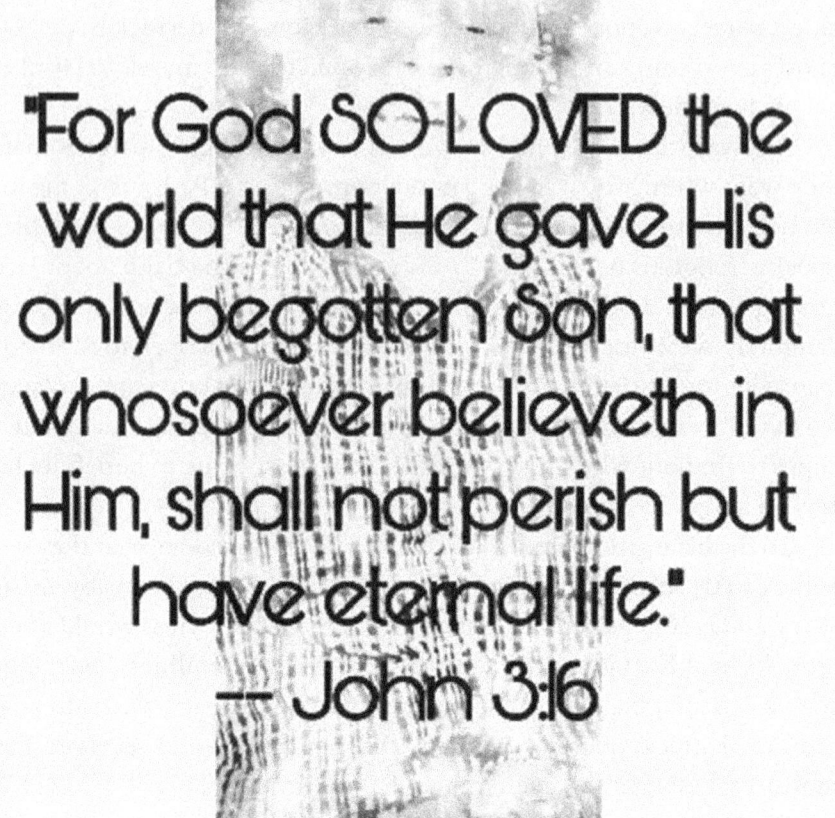

"For God SO LOVED the world that He gave His only begotten Son, that whosoever believeth in Him, shall not perish but have eternal life."
-- John 3:16

Pencil Artwork drawing with Scripture—just one of many wonderful verses shared by this kind and loving Paster who is a blessed gift from the Father; entitled, "A Child Of God" by Kipper

This pastor's smile was engaging and you could just very much see, the Jesus in him, in how he spoke and talked about God's love for everyone! His love for God was just so, well, it was very easily felt, just by his presence in both his smile and when he began to speak about God and life itself, through his own trials testimony. He kept it real—didn't butter up the truth or anything, and he didn't condemn, nor judge her, nor her parents, nor the doctors, not anyone, at all. His voice was a kind and gentle, yet majestic loving persona. He had such an encouraging voice that it just soothed me, as I listened intently, from my hospital bed, several hospital beds away—while he spoke to that girl, across the room from me.

You could just tell that he was a really, genuinely kind soul. It is kind of hard to explain it, but it was a feeling that I just felt, as I had felt so touched by his words and kindness towards this troubled young child, as he spoke of God like his Papa in Heaven, whom was wanting to hold her, in His mighty loving arms. It was just, just so wonderful! Other than reading the bible, which I found a little difficult to understand at times and only heard a wide, mixed interpretation from each denominational church out there—as there had been so many different kinds of people representing such belief systems, that had previously visited patients in the hospital. I had not heard about the true gospel quite like this other way before from anyone, until I had heard it from this man.

I could feel, a Divine inner warmth that would just fill me right up from inside my heart that I would actually become overwhelmed with a heartfelt joyful, sobbing! I felt so happy for her, as this word of wisdom and encouragement, was even touching me! That God knew her, even before He made her; He knew her name, her smile, her purpose in life, her special gifts and talents, her struggles, her pain, her life lessons, even her favourite things and her deepest of secrets…. It was just, amazing to witness and hear about this Papa in Heaven. Just, wow!

It was so engaging, to hear about how Jesus, in how He saw the fall of man by the enemy's hands, and yet instead of letting His own creation take up the cross, to suffer the consequences and die an eternal death… Jesus instead, took our place! Wow! My, God, Papa, you, DO LOVE ME! I sobbed in a humbling gratitude, with my hands on my chest, as I shook my head in total surrender. It was so mind-blowing! He was so incredibly willing to pay mankind's ransom, by humbling Himself and coming to earth, as a man. He knows all and He truly knows how we feel, in every emotion, good or bad—yet, He was never a victim of sin, but rather a true conquerer, our hero—the Saviour of the world, instead! Wow!

Pencil Artwork drawing with scripture about what Grace looks like, to Kipper entitled, "Grace Abounds Forever" by Kipper

"Then He said to them all, if anyone desires to come after Me, let him deny himself and take up his cross daily and follow me." — Luke 9:23

To live among the troubled and the broken, the sinners, the murderers and the poor… To encourage and teach us and love us unconditionally, so very much that we too, would have the choice of freedom, to live the most beautiful life beyond, what we can't even possibly, humanly fathom—should we choose to let Jesus into our hearts and live inside of us to help us, so that we are not, alone… Just, wow… I shook my head in a bewildered shock and yet, I tear up in humble admiration now, for

IF I COULD FLOAT ON A CLOUD, WHERE WOULD I GO?

my King's sacrifice that He made for me and for you. His sacrifice, was perfect. There is not one thing that we can do to try and earn His Love—it is not about what we can do, good or bad, or what we will try to earn up to do, for Him. No, it is about what He has already done, for all of us! Just, amazing...

Pencil Artwork drawing about the power of our Freewill of Choice between Heaven or Hell entitled, "Do You Know Where You Will Go?" By Kipper

To actually know, that we DON'T, have to struggle alone, that made me feel so incredibly special, and really, who am I? I had thought that I was a, nobody, an accident in life, a coincidence of science molecules and such... but now I know that I am a somebody because Jesus sees me as a somebody and He also sees you and each and everyone of you, as a somebody whom is actually, very, very special to Him and for Him to have died on the cross, for all of the sins of man, to purchase our pain, our guilt and shame and even death—to suffer on our behalf, as the greatest sacrifice of all time because God so loved the world, that He gave His only Son, so that we may live. Wow! He did it, for me...so that I may live! He did it for me... he did it for you... I am dumbfounded. If that is not pure Love, then I don't know what is... Tell me, is that not mind blowing, or what? God made us and He wants us even still. Just, wow...

Just, incredible...to think that all has been forgiven and all the wrongs, past, present and even future, have passed away on the cross, and I can just be, and live happy, and be grateful for all that I have, because I get to live with Jesus in my heart and in my life. Why would I want to waste that privilege, that would just be crazy! Ha, ha! Would it not? I cannot even imagine now, a life without Him in it. I wouldn't want it, any other way.

Okay, I can sense that you may be wondering, how could a boy like me, be as joyful and grateful for my life, when granted, yes—I am not mobile like you, nor do I have the same things or stuff that you may have but you see, that stuff doesn't matter to me, or to God Himself. I have what I have and I want to tell you, that with all of my heart, I want for you to know something so cool and important—that you are a blessing and that God loves you and that He genuinely, values you…even if you don't love, Him back. He is always there, waiting for you. I hope that you choose to trust in Him.

I am still learning too. I really don't think that we are ever done learning, until it is our time to go home and be with Papa. It is not an easy road but, I am learning that it is important to be prepared and know where we are going, when our body's clock stops ticking—to know before our time arrives to depart comes and to learn to appreciate, enjoy and live in the process while it lasts. Everyone keeps saying that life is so short, yet will they walk their talk? Many will give excuses for not doing, exactly that. Instead, you end up seeing, that so many people end up just wasting the time complaining and doing harmful things to others or to themselves and don't seem to learn to help others and love on others in good ways, rather than selfish ways.

I am still learning to try and not complain anymore about what I don't have and about being sick and stuck in this hospital bed. I use to complain a lot, when I was younger but I have grown out of that, thankfully. What choice do I have? I know that I may look terrible to others, but it is not about what others think of me that is important—what is important, is what my Papa in Heaven thinks of me and that my friend, is what truly matters most.

The goodness of and from Him, just follows and flows when we allow it to. We humans end up just complicating it up so much when it, ha, ha, is actually, so simple. It's amazing, how us humans like to try and make things harder on ourselves, when we choose to be selfish instead of, selfless. Ah huh, you now see what I am saying? Ha, ha, it's worth it, trust Jesus… Hey, you don't have to believe me nor trust me—believe in and trust Him. Then just watch what He will do. I can't help but just keep on smiling a big grin now, ha, ha! Your mind will be blown away, by His miracles…just watch…

I now call God my Papa too, because I don't have a dad or a mom but Papa, is always there and He loves me amazingly, unconditionally. Wow… I can't see Him, in how you would describe a face, but I see Him in everything He has made in my life—in everything that is around me, do you know what I mean by that? I see Him in the smiles upon other's faces. I see Him in the laughter, from the people around me, from day to day. I even see Him in the miracles that I have witnessed which makes me happy for the other patients, whom have completely healed from whoever had ailed them, to bring them to this place. I see Him in the sunshine and the moving life that I see, outside the many windows with one sky… and in those white fluffy clouds that float by, for me to explore on! OH! OH! And in the flowers and the meadows and the creeks and the sailboat races and the excitement and joy and peace and hope and the faith and… in everything that is good, I see Papa! Do you see Him?

It makes me smile and as I smile, I can't help but begin to cry with humbling, grateful tears down my face, as I thank Papa, for helping me get through, all that I have gone through… it has been so hard… but I am just, I am just so grateful. I won't ever boast of what I have to others, I will only praise Him—thanking Him for what He has done and loving Him and will share with others, my smiles and encourage others, whenever I possibly can while I am still here. I see Him in the food I am blessed to eat—yes, even hospital food, ha, ha! There are so many people in this world that I have read about whom don't even have food or clean water to drink, remember? And in the care that I receive… I know what I am blessed.

It is amazing to think, of the unfathomable potential we could have, if we just let go of our fears—those pesky lies that the enemy tells us again and again and just…let Papa lead and love and show what miraculous desires that He really truly has in store, for our own lives. It brings me to my adventures on the clouds, so freeing and filled with hope and joy. God really does create, with such a wild imagination, even beyond our own understanding! I mean, look at my eyeball! Ha, ha! It is the most complex part of the human body, no such human could have ever created, let alone a big bang—especially, when things that go boom, are destructive, they do not create life, nor are they organized! Ha, ha, ha! That is just crazy talk! Ha, ha! Where do you think our creativity came from? Ha, ha! All from Him!

Anything good, comes from the Father. I just know that my Papa has been right here with me, the entire time. He has never left my side. He helps me on these adventures, to see life's beauty and feel His peace, when I physically cannot even get up. It helps me I think, value life on a much different spectrum, than had I been granted an entirely different life, than my own. Everyone learns differently and please know, that it is okay—if the learning takes longer than others, don't let the enemy make you feel bad about it. Everyone learns at a different pace. Do fish climb trees? Nope! No regrets! Papa has it!

Want to know a dream that I have had, since I was I think, four years old? Ha, ha, yeah that's pretty young I know, ha, ha. Okay…I have dreamed of changing the world one day… you know, like, making a positive difference somehow, in some way… I know that I have no control over my life, so I won't worry about it because worrying is like sitting in a rocking chair, going back and forth, back and forth, back and forth—we are not actually going anywhere or making any progress by worrying, so why then do we bother, even worrying? It sure wastes a lot of time though, doesn't it? Ha, ha! Just as, we cannot worry and have faith at the same time. It does not work. We have to choose one.

"Just imagine, what the world would look like, if our Father's children were not divided by denominations and if we all just prayed and believed—how much different the world could be." — JDDS

You are SO LOVED. *Remember that!*

> We cannot worry and have faith at the same time--it does not work. So instead, with all of your heart, mind, body and spirit--Put Your Trust in God's Hands, in His Way and in His Timing.

Pencil Artwork drawing of God's Hand entitled, "Believe" by Kipper

Pencil Artwork drawing of the Holy Trinity entitled, "Father, Brother and Holy Spirit, Come" by Kipper

CHAPTER FIVE

FRIENDSHIP IS FOREVER

A penny for your thoughts? Since God created us, in His own image and loved us so much that He chose to send His Son to become sin and defeat death for all of mankind, by His sacrifice of pure and holy love, to die for us on the cross, so that we may live—would you not want that? I want that. I want to be a light in the world, to shine for others—to show them, that they are not alone. For all of us—you, me and everyone to come into the knowing and the readying for what is underway—that there is hope and that that Hope, is Jesus.

To you and anyone else who reads this, perhaps it may be after I have gone from this life—I want to tell you dear friend whom reads this now, that Jesus loves you! He loves you, as His own family! Hey, that smile looks, great on you! Smiles are contagious and I want the world to be consumed, with His peace and His real love, like no other that this world cannot provide! This joyful laughter, radiates from Papa's Joy for His children in Jesus, through those who choose to believe. It just excites me and I cannot help but feel so motivated and cry out to Him, in everything in my life! I was told that we can either be a bucket filler, or a bucket dumper. I want to be a bucket filler and that makes me smile. Don't you think? Ask yourself—Are you a bucket filler? If not, what are you going to do about it?

As time went on, I would have so many different roommates come and go, as you can imagine while living in a hospital bed, since I was born.

There was this girl named Sara, she had cancer. She didn't have much hair, as it was so thin and short on her head but she always had a smile on her face. She loved making mini pumpkin pies, in the children's activity centre. She had a kind smile. I tried one once, it was soooo gooood! She could be a baker one day! Some patients were in the hospital for only a one night stay, while others a week maybe, to a few months at a time or longer—while many came and left after different lengths of stay, many also just never got to, check-out.

Patients would get rotated often however, as many of them did not end up having to stay for very long. So I really didn't have the same roommates for very long but that's okay, I got to meet a lot more, newcomers. I think I was fairly sociable, if people wanted to be around me, but there were definitely times when I didn't want to be around anyone myself and I just wanted to be alone, near a window, with my clouds and explore, as much as possible…

One roommate that I had a few years ago, his name was Jordan and he would come climb up on the end of my bed to visit with me and we would colour in a colouring book, together. He had cool, fat colourful markers! They were even scented markers! I had never seen these before, wow! They had like, different fruit and berry scents that you can't even imagine how new this was, for a guy like me—they smelt so real and so good! They often made me hungry! Ha, ha! I always liked the purple grape and the berry scented ones, but the green lime and yellow lemon ones, were pretty good too. I didn't really like the black liquorice one but that's okay, I liked the other ones more, oh and the blue blueberry one, was also one of my favourites!

Another cool thing was that Jordan's Dad would come and visit and when he did, he would include me in his visits with his son too! I was really grateful! Ha, ha! He would entertain us to try and lift our spirits every time, by loosening his upper and lower dentures in his mouth, those are called fake teeth. Anyway, he would clang them together, really funny-like, making funny sounds and making us laugh so hard that our belly ached from laughing, ha, ha, ha! It was so funny! I won't ever forget those visits, nor of the other kind people who had included me. They are remembered in my mind and my heart, forever.

Being included, well, I felt special and blessed—and I wasn't even their biological family. But I was told that it takes love to be family, not DNA. So that was really nice of him to say that and to include me. It makes me smile just thinking about that and also so grateful, at the same time.

It seemed as though time had stood still and it was relentlessly punishing me, as hours went by—one after the other while I lay in my hospital bed. I had undergone, yet another surgery that I didn't know the why's or the for what's reasonings that they were about—which also means that I was back in the recovery room for an uncertain amount of time, yet again. I so missed the window and the sky and the clouds—my adventures…but it was what it was, I began to eventually get used to this, 'rocky unknownness'. I use to feel very alone and empty in a hospital room, without a window but now that I have Papa in my heart, He helps me get through the process, in how to pass the time—I talk to Him and He talks to me.

There are times, well, actually a lot of times when I am caught, 'talking to myself' by others but they don't understand that I am actually just talking with my Papa, you know, to His Holy Spirit. Granted, much of 'the way of the world' would send someone who did that, to the 'loony bin ward' but they just clearly, did not understand, nor have such a relationship with God, themselves, to know any different. It is kinda funny when I am doing this and I catch people staring at me, from the corner of my eye and the looks on their faces, are so funny that I just start bursting out laughing while I am having this full out conversation, with Papa and they have like, zero clue! Ha, ha! It's awesome! Ha, ha!

I do very much still, desire a window with a sky view. The desire just burns inside of me, wanting to see the many clouds that pass by, so they can take me away on another adventure! I really have always been this way, since as young as I can remember—wanting to just go and explore the wonders of the world, on my cloud. I try to remain patient but that is definitely no joking matter, it is not easy! Ha, ha! Do you ever get impatient when you have to wait, even for a short while? I sure do! Ha, ha! I really need to practice that one myself…ha, ha!

What other things could I do as well, you ask? Hmm, let me think for a second… Well, I suppose I could try to draw a picture or colour in a colouring book—but I tend to tire quite easily these days, remember—while trying to hold up either one of my hands or arms. Even if I do, it is just for a few minutes of holding a crayon or marker firmly enough in my hand, that I have to stop and rest my arms for a while. My hand grip is rather, pretty weak for me now as it is, in the real world these days…it is definitely, not as easy for me anymore…

In other words, I don't last very long, as I get even more exhausted—so I personally, have not been drawing or colouring quite as often anymore. Which is kind of sad I know, because I really do love to draw and as many details about my adventures, as much as possible, much like all of the time, ha, ha! And of course more so, than colouring but I enjoyed all of it. I could also read, I loved to read all kinds of books on adventure, fiction and true stories and just basic stuff about life and our world! I do still read a lot, when my eyelids can stay open long enough, to go through a few pages… ha, ha. I guess that is not very uplifting, now is it? I use to do it a little bit more a while back, when I was maybe, under six years old.

Um… you know, I have been thinking and I do often wonder, where do the patients go, you know…when their loved ones or visitors, would come to wheel them out for the day? I believe that there are places where patients can go and do fun things, either inside of the hospital or even outside—perhaps, on the grounds, where they have parks or maybe nice trails to walk along, maybe? I am just guessing. I don't actually even know about that sort of stuff. I can imagine that there are really fun places like that though. You can't teach, what you don't know, right?

I think that they must have a place like that somewhere in the hospital, where they have really cool and fun play centres, or visitation rooms. Oh and even gift shops and cafeterias, right? I would definitely not know of that personally. However, a little while ago, maybe a few days or weeks ago, I don't really know time frames or anything, everything just kind of mushes together these days, ha, ha! Anyway, I am sure that I had overheard that there was a playroom, just a floor away but no one would invite me, nor wheel me down there. No, no, it's not what you may think.

You see, I cannot blame anyone for that, as I was unable to even sit up in bed, ever—so, being in a wheelchair unfortunately, was never an option for me. Of course, I was never the type of spirit that would give up but as troubling as it was, about certain things, I still wondered why… and why me…

It was sometime later in the day but before suppertime in the evening, when I was starting to doze off. I was feeling a little sleepy, when a nurse came into the recovery room and began packing up my things. I vaguely noticed much detail, but I did see that she had then put the bag on the foot of my hospital bed, on my legs. I recalled what that usually meant, another relocation but I was still a little groggy yet, to think much of it. Then I noticed that she disconnected wires and cords and reconnected them to portables on a transport hospital bed that was off to my left. So I was pretty darn sure, that it was time that I got to go back to a room, maybe even with a window! Ha, ha! Yay! Woohoo! The more I came to, as I woke further, I would get even more excited inside about the possibilities but kept it quiet yet, to myself.

The nurse had caught a glimpse of my huge grin and I am pretty sure, that she could so tell that I was trying to contain my laughter and excitement and just smiled back at me, as she continued with her tasks. her tasks. Another nurse had come into the recovery room and they hoisted me up on my hospital bed sheet and onto the transport bed. She then wheeled my bed out of the recovery room, down a hallway, into an elevator, out of an elevator and down the long corridor and back, into the Children's Long Term Ward, check-in zone! I was back! I had thought. Woohoo!

After a brief pause, I was wheeled back into the same room where I had been before, except, I was wheeled right beside the big, tall window! The very first thing that had left my mouth was a huge scream, mixed with both laughing and crying—I totally lost it! Ha, ha, ha! I was so happy and I could not contain this and just went, completely, hysterical! Ha, ha! I had noticed that the space that was on the other side of the window was empty.

There was my hospital bed on the right side from the beautiful window, well from my point of view with my head to the wall that is, ha, ha! I had never been able to be right next to a window before! Ha, ha! The window was in the middle, between my hospital bed and another hospital bed, which appeared as currently empty. I don't know if there was supposed to be another patient arriving, or had just left but it was empty—for now.

Truthfully, It didn't really matter much to me though, as I was just so stoked that I was finally next to a window that I just vibrated with joy! Ha, ha! I even voiced, "I, have my very own window! Ha, ha!" I had called out! I was so excited and felt like jumping out of bed and dancing all around that room! Even though that I couldn't, I still pictured myself, just dancing back and forth, from one corner of the room, to the other and then, right up to the big window! Imagining deeply, with the very depths of my heart, I would then picture myself leaning over the windowsill and while looking through it—I would be able to feel, the warmth of the sun, on my very pale-looking, white face. Yep, I definitely needed to soak up some of those, sunny rays and vitamin D! Ha, ha!

It had been quite sometime, since I was in a room with a window! A very, very long time! Now, looking outside, I could see that everything was white—well, I guess it was wintertime and it must have snowed for a long time, as there seemed to be a lot of that white stuff, which had blanketed every surface that it could possibly reach. I was told that it is cold and can melt in your warm hands. I was shown one time by a roommate, a genuine picture of real, life-like snowflakes! Amazing! Now I know where movies and books get their ideas of a detailed snowflake, God made them!

IF I COULD FLOAT ON A CLOUD, WHERE WOULD I GO?

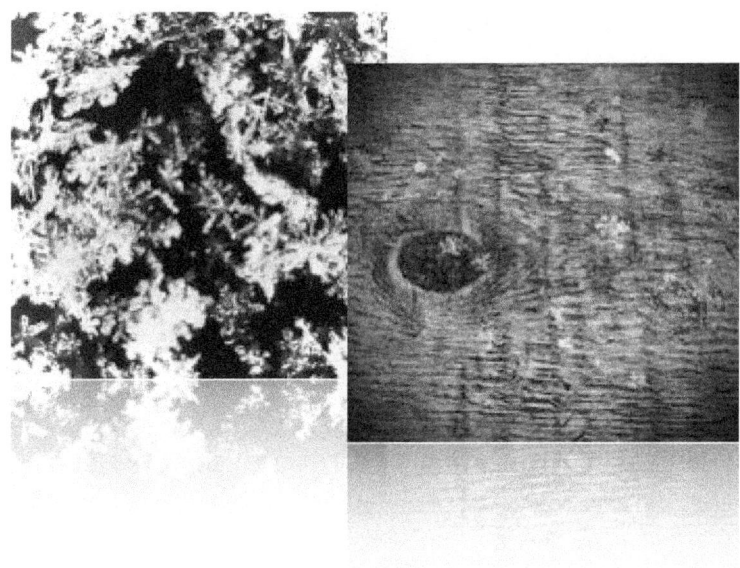

Pencil Artwork drawings of real snowflakes
entitled, "God's Handiwork" by Kipper

I mean, these were so spectacular and so cool that I now see how the world came up with such detailed little fellas because someone one day, was inspired by seeing the real deal that Papa had made! So cool! Right? I sometimes would dream of jumping in it, that white fluffy, cold stuff. I often hear people complain about it during the wintertime months. Actually, they would complain a lot about it even before, during and after it, ha, ha! People are too funny! That's a lot of complaining! Yikes! There is always something one does not like—yet, do they realize that there is always something, to like and be thankful for? Ha, ha! Think on that one, for a change! Ha, ha!

    I imagined making snow angels, with my body laying on the snow and then moving my arms and legs back and forth, as I have seen in books—even about catching the falling snowflakes onto my tongue, as they would fall during an evening snowfall's night—while buildings, fences and trees were decorated with many twinkle lights aglow. That sounds amazing to see! Or to even have a Christmas tree, as they call it—all decorated with strands of hand strung popcorn, and many other ornaments that adorned the tree and not to forget about the colourful lights that lit it all up, to finish it off. What would that be like, I would wonder to myself? I have heard many people complain about the snow, about the various pagan and other excuses about trees decorated but it always just seemed to be, just another thing to complain about, rather than appreciate something beautiful. Would people rather be outside in the snow, as it fell and make the most of things, than stuck in here, in a hospital bed, forever? Ha, ha! Yeah, makes you think, doesn't it? Count your blessings, I was told—count your blessings and remind yourself that things could be, a lot more worse off for you. So, count your blessings—I know that I sure am.

The next morning upon waking, I gave out a big yawn, as I tried to rub the sleepiness from out of my eyes. I then remembered the window—oh and the snow! Looking over towards the window, I could see that the sky was a beautiful, bright blue—with the sun shining everywhere. It took a bit of a wait before I finally managed to catch a glimpse of some very fluffy, white clouds.

Thinking out loud, I couldn't help myself but to say, "Clouds, where have you been, what did I miss...no, where can we go?" I got emotional, deep down inside! I began to choke up a little. I sure missed those clouds—I quickly wiped away tears that fell from my eyes. I was not going to delay this any longer, for it was time to catch up with them and explore!

Off I was, to my safe place! Woohoo! I shouted! I could see trees and ponds down below that seemed so small, like ants below me. As I approached the meadow greens where my friends and I had often met and played so many times, including the sailboat race, that was quite some time ago now—the scene then began to morph and change into something else... "Wait, what was happening?" I whispered to myself. I had then noticed that it was very different. A revelation had come over me and the scene transformed, right before my very eyes!

I then, upon hopping off the cloud—from an outdoor, nature's paradise, formed a solid floor beneath me, as I landed with my own two bare feet, onto a floor! The mountainous hills, forests and valleys transformed into walls and loaded with shelves, they were just packed with stuff! Whoa! This was amazing! What had just happened? I looked at my feet and felt a very different surface beneath me... As I looked up slowly from down at my feet, to my surroundings around me, I could clearly see that where I was, was not that green meadow that I was at before—but rather, a room that was so full of colour and so filled with so many things, instead! Wow! It was then that I had noticed that there were many other children there too! It was just so enlivening, yet a little terrifying at the same time—but only for a moment. I stood there rather stunned. Wow...

What had happened? Did I, time travel or get lost along the way somehow, in the space time continuum? Or did I, you know...pass away? Where was I? I was honestly, a little more leery than brave, at this point with this, sudden shocker. I had never been...to well, here before. Where had I gone? I saw new faces but only children. There never seemed to be any nurses, doctors, or parents—there was no adult to be seen. Where was I? I kept asking Papa while I was filled with a deep, inner concern and feeling a little—okay, I was feeling rather afraid, as I was definitely out of my own comfort zone. Where did you take me, Papa? What was I to do, here? I would ask Him quietly, as I slowly walked further into this mysterious and very colourful room. I was a little afraid yet, really starstruck—and that's affirmative! Ha, ha!

I took a turn about the room and as I looked from my original position and then slowly turned to catch a three hundred and sixty degree view of the entire room, as if in slow motion—I could see that all around the room, there were many large, white shelves that were just loaded with oodles of different board games, puzzles, blocks, storybooks and a huge array of colourful toys! I could see a television centre with large pillows on the floor in front of it, as well. I noticed a dress up centre where kids could dress up to be a Firefighter or a Policeman, a Zoo Keeper or a Chef, a Nurse or a Doctor, a Dentist or a Train Conductor, a Mechanic or a Construction Worker, a Princess or a Prince, you name it, they had so many dress up clothes and toys to go with that! It was so cool!

There was a baking centre with children making food, wow...my mouth watered at the amazing aromas. It smelt so good! There was a lot of different play centre areas that were just so colourful and full of children. Wow, I had thought. Is this, real? It sure felt real! Cool! Ha, ha! My face began to light up a little, as I took it all in.

I could also see a big blue water table and a matching blue sand table, each packed with really fun looking toys and children at play there. I could see a storybook area, filled with tons and tons of books! I love books! There was a crafting centre. It was just so overwhelming with an overflow of life and stuff and colour, that I just didn't know where to fix my eyes on exactly. I sort of glared outward, as my eyes just glazed over the busyness of the room's packed chatter. Ha, ha! Wow!

In the middle of the room, stood a long, blue rectangular child's-height table. It had rounded edges and a smooth texture on the top and had matching chairs all around it. On top of the table, in the centre of it, was covered with a huge variety of colourful art things! There were so many colourful felt markers with different sized tips. I could see gel markers, chalk, glittery drawing things and glitter—pencil and wax crayons, scissors and rulers, fun shaped erasers, glue sticks and white liquid glues, pastels, tacky stuff and putty, newspaper and a huge, thick stack of different types of paper, in different colours. There were many different paints and a lot of crafty stuff like bendy-wire things that were fuzzy, bins filled with stickers and fluffy cotton balls, beads and popsicle sticks for craft making. There were several, great big, huge stacks, of colourful patterned paper as well! I saw google-eyes, different sized and shaped tongue depressor sticks, tons of colourful yarn and string, sewing stuff like big headed-plastic needles and knitting and crochet needles and so much more! Wow, wow, wow! Ha, ha! It was pretty overwhelming that my eyes couldn't really capture it all at once! Ha, ha! Yikes! Papa just keeps knocking my socks off! Ha, ha! He's so awesome!

IF I COULD FLOAT ON A CLOUD, WHERE WOULD I GO?

Pencil Artwork drawing of the Playroom on Kipper's cloud adventure entitled, "God Is With Me" by Kipper

There were so many crafty things—that it nearly made my head spin! Ha, ha! I have never seen, such a huge variety of well, everything I had just seen, before, ever! Wow-wee! Ha, ha! I started to tear up and weep a little, as I was just so shocked and happy and grateful! "Thank you, Papa!" I had said in a rather sobbing way, just below my breath. Ha, ha! "Thank you…"

Around the large, rectangular table, sat many children and no child was strapped to a chair, nor hooked up to wires, or machines. Everyone including myself, could walk freely around the room, to wherever we wished. I had never been in such a room. I wondered to myself, what is this place? Seriously, I was in such shock that I just couldn't grasp where I could have been, as I had never seen such a place before, in a room, in person. It was just so wild, beyond my own imagination, yet God had captured this, just for me and these other children! Wow!

"Hello, my name is Kimmie, what is your name?" A small voice had called out, from behind me. "Oh…um…h-hi, Kimmie. I-I am, K-Kipper. I am Kipper." I repeated myself in response, after I had stuttered initially. "Where are we?" I asked. "Hello, Kipper. You are standing in the Playroom. Don't worry, you don't have to be scared. You are safe here and we are not sick today." She finished saying, as she smiled and then hop skipped away, over to plop onto a floor pillow, to watch a classic cartoon on the television, in the tv room. I watched her, as she skipped away over there and went about her own business. I slowly looked around, glancing at the different play centres, or we can call them, 'zones' that were all throughout the room.

While standing there, I was just so puzzled—though I felt that this place was, well, while thinking on what that Kimmie girl had just told me, it did feel welcoming and even, safe. I looked back at the really big and blue rectangular table, which was obviously the crafty, or crafting centre zone. I then looked about the room again, trying to figure out where it was that I wanted to try out first. But my eyes were then drawn to the blue, rectangular table, once again.

So, I then looked to find a chair by the table and saw one available seat that was left. Perhaps it was meant to be, I had thought—so I walked over, being aware while feeling the floor's surface beneath my own two feet and being conscious about it a lot more than that of the grassy meadow greens— as it felt so real and noteworthy, as I walked on my own, two feet on such a hard surface! I just never had this experience before… Whoa! This was really cool! I pulled out the chair and sat down. I was so dazed at what I had been seeing that my thinking felt a little foggy, ha, ha! I then looked down at the craft materials that were all along the middle of this huge table and I reached over for a blank, white sheet of paper. I then dug my hand into the big box of wax crayons and surprisingly, I had pulled out my favourite colour, sky blue! Ha, ha! Yay!

I had a very, satisfactory smile upon my face and then I put my sky

IF I COULD FLOAT ON A CLOUD, WHERE WOULD I GO?

blue wax crayon to the white paper in front of me, and was about to start drawing a picture…oh but wait, what should I draw? I thought to myself, as I had paused. So I asked Papa and waited for a reply! Ha, ha! Then, not even a minute later, I heard inside of me, "Draw a cloud". Cool, I had thought. So I nodded a bit and smiled in agreement, as I began to draw the outline of a white cloud, with the sky blue crayon, as the sky around it—which would help the fluffy white cloud, pop out from the empty white sheet of paper.

It felt like it had been some time, hmm…I had not done anything like this, in a very long time, now that I was thinking about it. I actually do not remember how old I was, the last time that I had even held a crayon in my hand and drew a picture—it was too exhausting for me to do lately, in the real world. There were a lot of things that began rolling through my mind.

I really don't know how old I am now, but others have claimed that I was at least or almost, eleven or twelve? I have never been to school, but have lived in the hospital, for all of my life. So learning different things, was always really interesting to me, even though, it was often at times, difficult to do. I re-adjusted my grip, on the sky blue crayon, again in my hand and continued to draw the cloud on my white sheet of paper.

Pencil Artwork drawing of Kipper's hand drawn cloud with the sky blue crayon entitled, "Wondrous Cloud" by Kipper

Then, I couldn't help myself but to become distracted once again, stopping before even finishing the connecting of the start, to the end of my lines that I had started. I sat and looked around me, at all of the different centre zones once again and then at the different children, whom were sitting at the same table as I. From what I had noticed, I did not know anyone here at all.

I had noticed that I could not recognize, any of the other children that were in this playroom, in any of the other play zones, from what I could see. Where were my friends Pete, Nicolas, or Kelly? Where were Sandy, Sally, or awwww, I felt disheartened and choked up a little, as I continued to list out the names of my friends in my head...where was that really kind, sweet girl, Marcy? I paused for a brief moment, to try and take a breath and calm myself for a second, trying to avoid balling out loud with tears to keep, from just flying off my face.

Where had they all gone off to? And why wasn't Marco, Andy or Billy, and that tall boy Bobby, not here too? Where were the other children from the meadow greens? I just, couldn't figure it out. They should be here too. I was really concerned by this time. We had been long time friends—most of them and I. With them not here, I began feeling a little bit scared, even empty and shy...and I am hardly, ever truly shy, around other children.

The very thought of losing them, caused me to take a deep gulp and have to brace myself with my hands on the table, to keep from passing out from the stress shock that I thought I might have to brace to absorb. I then heard, "Breathe" from within me... "I've got you..." the voice reassured me once again... so I began to take a few slow, deep breaths and told myself in encouragement "Papa has me, Papa has me, Papa has it... I am not alone, I am not alone. It is okay..." and I then began to calm down. "Thank you Papa" I stated.

Instead, there were so many other children—of so many different colours and sizes but still, no sign of my friends, my buddies, my comrades. "Go say hello"...I heard Papa's Spirit tell me. I thought about it for a few minutes, as I slowly but surely had regained my confidence once again. Truthfully, of course—it never hurts anyone to try and make new friends, right? Papa was right, even though it didn't feel like I wanted to do it—I knew He was still right though. I can at least give it a try, I had thought to myself and I told Him "Okay, I will"...

IF I COULD FLOAT ON A CLOUD, WHERE WOULD I GO?

So I had decided then that I would try and begin by speaking with the children that were sitting beside me first, at the big, rectangular blue table. To my left sat a boy named Jake, whom was five years old and he had just began treatments. For what I don't know but that's all he had said. He had short black hair, tan coloured skin and wore a short sleeved, royal blue t-shirt and light brown corduroy pants.

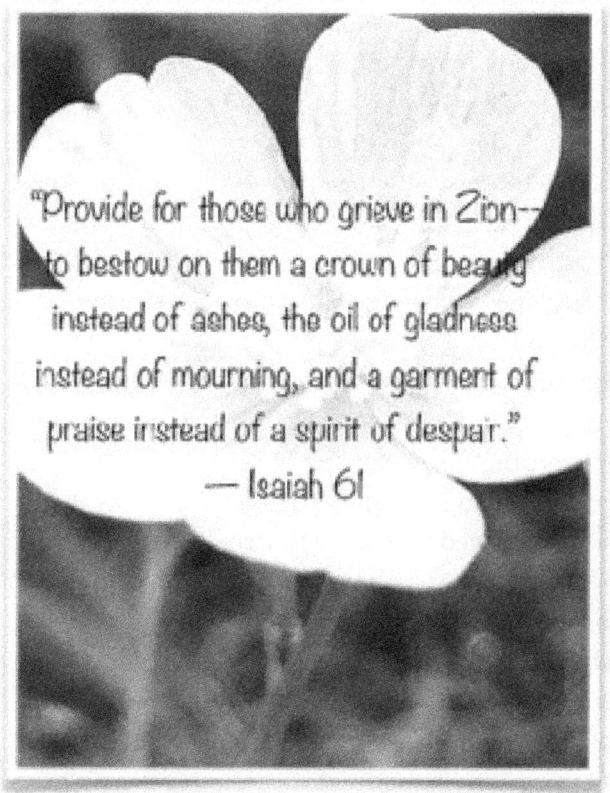

Pencil Artwork drawing with Scripture on beauty, gladness, and praise entitled, "LOVE" by Kipper

Next to him, sat eight year old Mary-Lou, whom was I think Vietnamese, with very dark brown eyes and shoulder-length black hair. She had burn marks all over her head, face and arms. She said that she was in a house fire recently and so that is why her skin and hair, were all burnt up like that. She did not feel pretty at all, she was really quite shy but I had said to her, "What burns? You're beautiful, just the way God made you." She smiled and completely came out of her shell after that and even started to colour her picture, of a garden of flowers and she smiled the entire time. That was pretty awesome, I had thought to myself with a smile.

Across from me, sat nine year old twins, Tyrell and Cheyenne. They sure looked identical! Wow! They had a very pail-white complexion, with a strawberry, reddish-blond hair colouring that was really curly and they each had freckles across their noses, each with a green or blue mix eye colouring—I couldn't really tell which colour it actually was, it was that close! Ha, ha! The twins were actually, unable to talk with their voices but what I had found really interesting, was that they still found ways to communicate in another way. They were using what others had called, 'sign language'. Wow, I had thought. It was kind of interesting, I don't think that I had ever met anyone else, who spoke that way, before. Pretty amazing! I only knew of their names, because they each had name tag stickers on their hospital shirts.

To the left of the twins, was eight year old Babel. He was really dark skinned, nearly black as a piece of burnt toast and his eyes were just as black in colour. Although, I am sure his eye colour was just a very, dark brown. He was missing his left arm—he didn't say too much but he seemed nice, as he played with a toy firetruck on top of the table, with his right hand. I am guessing he had been in the hospital for losing his arm or something like that. I really don't know.

To the right of the twins, sat five year old Betsy-Ann. She was covered with cancerous spots and lumps that were all over her face and neck. Some sort of issue with her own body's immune system, attacking itself and growing things on her body. She wasn't in any pain here though, she had said. She seemed really nice and wasn't at all shy to talk with.

There were more children in the room, each playing in the different play zones, which had surrounded the table, all around us. I surveyed the room again, as my eyes wondered around at all of the different things and bustle happening, all around me. It was rather fascinating, if I do say so myself. Ha, ha! I would go into a bit of a stare while watching many of the children partake in their different activities, that were available to everyone in the many play zones here.

I honestly, had never even thought about getting up from this chair

IF I COULD FLOAT ON A CLOUD, WHERE WOULD I GO?

and walking over to try out any of the other play zones. It had never even dawned on me. I was just so content sitting here and watching everyone that I think I even lost track of time, or so it had felt. I was just so distracted as I sat there, I had felt a little confusion and yet, a little excitement—at the same time. I'd watch a child play something and react funny and then it would make me chuckle a little. It was actually pretty nice to see other children, using their own imaginations too.

I then turned back towards the table and looked down at my rather bare, white sheet of paper and then continued to colour some more. My puffy white cloud grew bigger and bigger, as I swirled and curved my lines with the blue wax crayon, to form into a nearly finished, cloud drawing—but then I paused yet again and I spoke more with the other children. As I talked more, I began to feel a lot more back in my own element—socializing with other children once again and after so long. It was a real joy for me and even though we had just met, I had a feeling that this would be worth it!

So, I tried to get to know each of them a little more and as I did interact with them, I began to feel more at ease, to completely at ease now—even my heart rate, was back to normal and I was a lot more chill and calm. Cool and collected, ha, ha! It was awesome!

Later that day, maybe a few hours into visiting with other children and colouring—one little boy had walked up to me and tapped me on my left shoulder. What or whom was that? I had thought, as I was rather surprised and caught off guard and then I quickly turned around, to see what had tapped me on my left shoulder and to find out what was up. There was a little boy standing there, wearing a blue and red horizontally striped, long sleeve shirt and blue pants whom was, maybe about four or five years old—he was just standing there, just off from the left side of my chair. He had short-medium length, dark brownish-black hair colour, with brown eyes.

I looked at him with curious eyes but he then seemed, to even look a lot more curious than I was! He didn't say a word at first and just stared at me and then poked my left shoulder again. "Hi, what did you want?" I had asked him. He then asked something quietly—directed at me but I didn't quite understand him. "W-what, what did you say?" I responded. I then asked for him, if he could please repeat what he had said and he did, asking me once again—only this time, it was loud enough for me to hear him better.

Not that I understood him fully, as he seemed to have had an accent of sorts but I did hear him this time. From what he asked however, wow, it had most definitely startled me suddenly—by his question. He had asked me, "Why are you here, what is wrong with you?" It rather blew me away, as I sat back in my seat and found that I was, completely without words. "Uh, um, I don't know." I told him and then he turned around and walked away. I just felt that difficult to answer, as I thought harder on it—I didn't really have an answer, myself. I couldn't really answer him, which as he walked away, it had left me to heavily ponder more on the topic that which he had presented to me. But I still did not know the answer.

After a few minutes of being in deep thought and staring at the floor, I then turned back towards the table and glanced back down at my white sheet of paper, with the one cloud I had drawn, with the sky blue wax crayon—just pondering quietly to myself—while I was very much, still in deep thought for a little while longer…

Then, as I looked back up to take another gander around the room, I could hear the different thoughts that just suddenly started coming in like a wrecking ball—just a swingin' back and forth, destroying what good thoughts and feelings that I had felt, even before the boy had asked me his curious and very upsetting question. This wrecking ball swung and slammed around through my head, affecting my heart in how I was feeling at the same time. Hmm…but which one to believe? Well, I honestly had no idea as to which one, as not one genuinely, made any sense at all—to me.

So to cut through the confused chaos and to stop this simmering frustration that had entered me—I then remembered something and then immediately whispered below my breath, "Papa, I can't but you can, Papa"…and just like that, it stopped. See, Papa, God, Jesus, or whichever one of His names that you choose to call Him by, to call on Him—He is all about clarity. Papa does not cause confusion, period. Only the evil spirit enemy, does that. When I find that it becomes nearly to even completely, unbearable to stand, I kneel, in both my mind and my heart and pray in the Spirit to His—I let God take it all and He holds me, as I rest while I wait beneath His wings. It works every time! The key is learning to call on Him, much sooner though. We don't have to struggle. This I have yet to learn more to do, obviously. Ha, ha! So, I am grateful for this discovery, indeed and happy to be able to share about it with you too.

Looking around the room, I couldn't help but feel so happy to be on my cloud, in this room—wherever I was, I was happy. Maybe it wasn't the Playroom a floor away, but it was a place that felt fun and safe. As I thought about this, the scene moved to a bit of a blurred, slow motion now, everyone around me moving at a slower rate than I, as they walked on by and I sat there, just watching and thanking Papa, for this chance to be here and everything.

I then closed my eyes tightly, sending a prayer up to Heaven, asking just above a whisper now, as I motioned my head slowly from side to side, as though time slowed right down except my lips in saying, "I don't ever want to leave this place, let no one ever take it away from me, please?" Then the room faded out and I fell asleep...

I slowly opened my eyes, feeling as though I was awakening from a vividly, lucid dream or a really, deep sleep. For a moment, I didn't know where I was, but I finally came to and realized that I was back in my hospital bed—surrounded by the beeping and humming of machines in the room. I leaned over to my right—wiping my tired eyes, I looked to see that there was just an empty bed, across from mine. There were no others in the room that were awake yet but I was more interested in that window which was next to me, instead. Hey, can you blame a kid for wanting to play, again? Ha, ha!

A nurse walked in and ignored me, as she just checked the machines and wrote down stuff on her clipboard—her focus and speed, were astonishing. Maybe, well...hmm, do you think it, could be possible? Hmm...maybe, she was one of those advanced, high tech robots, with the artificial intelligence that was skillfully built-in so cleverly, that she was not actually, human, but was very much of a clone but in a robotic form... And somehow, many of those nurses actually, look so alike! Ha, ha! Could they be AI Robots? You know, the Artificial Intelligence kind? Whoa! I wonder, could they be clones? Yet, she didn't even notice that I was staring right, straight smack at her, while wide awake and watching her every move. I peeked just above my hospital bed blanket while covering my nose and the rest of my face below it—keeping as non-conspicuously sneaky, as can be. Ha, ha, ha! "Oh, she'll never take me alive!" I had suddenly whispered very quietly, to myself! Muwahahahahahaaaaaa… ha, ha! As quickly as she entered the room, she left just the same. I, sneaky…he, he, he!

Whenever a nurse or doctor walked in, all I could feel from them was a coldness—like a crisp chill in the air, on a fall damp morn, I read about in a book some time ago… I did not feel any comfort from them when they came near me, unless they gave me a warm and toasty heated blanket that is…ha, ha! I had thought to myself while I smiled with a huge grin and laughed! Ha, ha! No, they were all actually pretty nice, they just had a lot on their plate, mind, plateful minded, or is it plates? Hmm…anyway, and to add to that mind of plates, she probably had a lot more things on that mind of plates, than she had very little room left, for even more plates. Ha, ha! They are human after all… or, are they? Ha, ha!

Pencil Artwork drawing of a stack of plates entitled, "Too Much On One's Plate or Too Many Plates On One's Stack, In Life" by Kipper

Later that day, in wheeled a hospital bed, with a boy fast asleep. Along with him came in four nurses, several machines, bags of blood—even bags filled with that cloudy clear stuff that they feed you with, through a tube. That is when you cannot eat on your own and they have to help you

IF I COULD FLOAT ON A CLOUD, WHERE WOULD I GO?

with that sort of stuff. He had IV's hooked up to him, along with stickies that were attached to wires and then attached to several machines which most likely, monitored his heart and stuff.

The nurses had evenly positioned themselves, two on each side and then grabbed ahold of the sheet he was laying on and then counted on three, two, one and then lifted him up quickly and onto the hospital bed that was empty, on the other side of the window that had separated us.

The boy appeared to be older and taller too. He didn't open his eyes or move his arms, or legs. I don't know what was wrong with him but then as staff moved about, I had over heard a nurse say something about major surgery that the boy had gone through…and that they didn't know, if he would even wake up. Gulp! "Oh Papa, please help him…" I asked, whispering below my breath. Blah! Ooh, boy, I got shivers down my spine, the second that the nurses said that he might not, wake up. That never gets easy to hear, not ever.

I had always wished the very best for others—for great things for all of the patients in this place but it seemed to me that this wasn't maybe, a place where God, always answered prayers. The only place I would ever feel comfort of course, was on my clouds, so I had thought, rather sternly.

As I dove into my imaginary world, floating through the lush green valleys and meadows, over creeks and of course to the playroom that I had recently been to—it was in those places that I knew that God must exist, for I felt that He would never completely leave me. I have learned however, that God my Papa, never leaves us—He is always constant.. it is us, who are the ones who continue to change. "Oops…" I suddenly blurted out, just above a whisper while I made quite a look upon my face—lowering my bottom lip, exposing my lower set of teeth and raising my eyebrows to indicate an 'oops' response…

I continued to stare across the room and then through that big, tall window beside me. I could see the clear blue sky which was almost Heavenly except, I did not see any clouds just yet. I continued to stare through it and as I waited, as patiently as humanly possible for a young kid, of my spry young buck age, ha, ha—this young knight awaited for my royal, majestic stallion cloud, to come by hopefully, very, very soon.

Then all of a sudden, a dark coloured curtain had covered the window which had startled me! For a second, it felt like someone had turned off the light, even the sky—everything! Because my eyes could not adjust immediately as it was, given the circumstances. It then also felt as though, someone had grabbed ahold of my head and quickly shook it, rattling what was inside, for a moment—in the attempt, to steal all of my marbles that held the many wondrous and creative thoughts and dreams that I held dear to my existence…giving me a bit of a dizzy feeling, after all of the staring into the brightness outside, had been abruptly cut off from me—from light, now into darkness, I lay.

"What happened!" I cried out in quite a very choked up, and raspy whisper, as if a cat had caught my tongue and tried to feed me a frog! Ha, ha…yikes… I must say, that I did not approve of such a message! Or rather, this motion! I had a most alarmed concern, just screaming from my facial expression! If you saw it live, right here in the room, you would feel it too! I am tellin' ya! Ye-ouch!

My eyes had finally adjusted and as I had noticed a nurse that was standing between my bed and that boy in the coma's bed, it suddenly dawned on me! It turned out that it was the nurse whom had closed the dark curtain, over the window! I'm a master detective, don't ya know! Ha, ha! No, okay, so I overheard her talking, as she was busy scolding out loud and saying, "It's too bright in here!" She huffed and then she puffed and then she, just continued to talk… "This sick boy just had major surgery and must, get decent rest!" She gave me an icy stare, as she left the room… Oh my gosh, she could have, froze me into the ice man! I sunk further beneath my covers with a grave despair.

IF I COULD FLOAT ON A CLOUD, WHERE WOULD I GO?

Pencil Artwork drawing of a darkened stormy sky entitled, "Cloak Of Despair" by Kipper

I could feel the palms of my hands sweat and my cheeks heated up all of a sudden. I felt flush in the face though no colour came about—oh man, this felt humiliating, to say the least! I had definitely felt, a little bit sick to my stomach, as well. I had felt so defeated, as my smile turned all the way, upside-down into a frown that I did not expect, to have had that day!

I just couldn't understand it, why me? Why now? I was angry. If my face had colour, it would have turned a deep red—I tell you! Why did this have to happen again, to me! Why can't it happen to someone else instead of me, and like, it feels like it happens almost, all of the time to me, why? I was so mad, as I cried my eyes out in tears. I lost my temper, I had lost control of my emotions. I couldn't calm down, I began to shake and was so infuriated inside that I had completely forgotten about calling on, Papa.

I began losing all hope just like that when I began losing consciousness, suddenly. My eyes rolled up and then closed and I completely went motionless, sinking into my pillow behind me—every part of my body went limp. The machines which I was hooked up to, had suddenly began to beep and hum, and whistle. Alarm lights flashed which had summoned nurses and doctors running through the doors, scrambling to my side.

I opened my eyes and my initial thought was about everyone else around me. I looked at everyone and was puzzled even more—what was the matter, I had thought to myself? Why, did they worry so? I then closed my eyes for a moment and then reopened them and I was suddenly looking downward at my legs, on the hospital bed. Just as I had some time before. I looked about the room and at the nurses and doctors whom were in a panic mode at this point. As I looked back down at myself, I then found that my spirit, was now actually sitting upright and watching everyone, as they were mad dashing to rescue me and yet—I could not even understand as to why. What were they so worried about? Was I, dead? Did I die? I was not even, concerned…what? That was rather strange, that I did not even really feel a connection with my body, lying there on the hospital bed, or so I had thought.

I then looked up and saw that most beautiful and endearing, bright light again. It was right up above me, behind the bright yellow hospital surgery light, or passed it—like it was beyond this room, as though it were a portal from one world, to another…it was that dancing, colourful and exceptionally beautiful and breathtakingly, very warm and welcoming light again and I just couldn't help but feel so intrigued and curious by it. It was the most engaging light that I had only seen once more, for the first time, quite a long time ago…it really was a long time since I had last experienced its' presence. It was so vibrantly colourful—I just could not take my eyes off of it!

Curious now more than ever, without even a drop of hesitation—I reached my arms up towards the light and as soon as I had, I began floating up off of my hospital bed, towards the light fearlessly. Nothing was pulling me back, I was determined to go to it, no matter what! Glancing back down, leaving the still body on the hospital bed behind me— I could see the many doctors and nurses below, whom were still trying to do their work, by only the humanly skills that they knew best, to try and revive me. I turned back to look at the light above me, as I approached it and then suddenly—a flash of light surrounded me and everything that I had just witnessed, immediately vanished and was gone!

I squinted my eyes, as I slowly opened them, for the view was ever-so, intensely bright and glowing like nothing that I have ever seen before! My arms were up high and covering the way ahead of my sight, trying to block out the brightness at first. But as I had opened my eyes even further, they began to adjust with a soothing warmth which seemed to have come from the light, that which was surrounding all around me. I walked forward a step and then took a second, to straighten up my stance. I then paused, as I looked down upon my feet, wiggling my toes a little and found myself standing, in what appeared to be the clouds, or wait… was this, Heaven? It felt so incredibly real, much more real than anything I had ever come to know.

I straightened myself up, as much as I could upright and then I had noticed that I was, actually a lot taller than I had thought! Ha, ha! Whoa! Not only that, while I stood there taller than I had ever before, in all of my imagination, cloud adventures—I was not at all what I had pictured myself to be, as this tall, as so healthy-looking. I stood there, with no aches and no pains at all. I had not even one mark, nor scar on me, from the many years of IV's and surgeries—I-I was, I was healed! Tears of both relief and joy then vigorously pooled in my eyes! What had just happened?

Amazed by my appearance, I noticed that I was wearing brightly clean, white linen as a shirt and pants for garments—no hospital gown at all. In fact, it did not even look, human tailored, there wasn't even a stitch, nor seam to be found on them. And my body, I wasn't thin anymore—just an average-sized, handsome looking guy, I was! Wow! Ha, ha! I guess you could say that I looked, healthy! And on my own two feet, and get this—it felt, so very, very real! Whoa! I could hardly believe my very own eyes! Ha, ha, ha!

There was this sovereign looking man, just sitting on a log in front of me—something about Him had drawn my attention, immediately towards Him. He was wearing what looked like, a radiantly glowing, white robe and the man had long, wavy brown hair and a moustache and beard. Wait, what? He actually looked—familiar, I had thought to myself. Like the Man in a dream of mine that I had, a long time ago. Was it Him? I had thought.

While I began to walk to towards Him, I caught a glimpse of our surroundings and oh my good, sweet Lord—just, wow! There were dozens of angels in my midst and golden glowing clouds, and a most intense and glorious rainbow that had filled the Heavenly skies above me—to a dazzling perfection that were even in the streets that were made of gold. There was plenty of lush and thriving green and colourful gardens of life, massive trees and amazing plant life and fountains of flowing waters and, and... oh wow...

Yet, beyond all of that, as my stare was fixed upon this Holy looking Man, whom was right in front of me now—all of that which was beyond that locked view that we shared, I hardly entirely noticed it all, not more than, Him. I felt that I knew Him and that He knew me.

There was an, all-knowing and majestic, golden-white glow about Him. Now I really felt that I knew Him and that He, really did know me. It felt familiar and being here, whoa, well it literally felt as though, I had—returned, home? I continued to stare at Him, despite the bold brightness that radiated from Him and impeccably, illuminated all around Him.

I suddenly felt so ambitiously eager, to meet Him, that I began to run to Him! As soon as I had felt this tug on my heart strings, I heard the Man speak to me. With a big, yet gentle voice, the Man motioned His right hand towards me, as He said, "Come closer, My son". An instantaneous warmth then impacted my heart and grew extremely fast, overtaking my entirety but deep from within. I had then been reminded that the Man, Jesus whom I had asked to live within my heart some time ago—this Man, was Him! Eager with anticipation, I continued to run towards Him—it was as though, it was a dreamlike slow motion, in a way.

Slowly but surely, I began to advance towards the Man sitting on the log and as I approached this mysteriously engaging and very wise, Holy looking Man—I finally quickly walked right up to Him and we were now, face to face. I felt that I knew Him, already. It was hard to explain. But I knew that it was genuine and true.

What a feeling it sure was, that had instantly come over me! I had just realized what it was like, to not be weighed down by 'the ways of the world'—by the enemy's lies, by anything! This was well—I couldn't find the right words as it was just so, Jesus! So above and beyond awesome! I could feel no more pain, doubt, anger, regret, hate, envy, no more lies—you name it...absolutely, no suffering of any kind and I was healed! I had not even one scar, on me! It was awesome! I did not even have any sense of loss, in leaving the world behind—none of it stood up to hinder me. No

IF I COULD FLOAT ON A CLOUD, WHERE WOULD I GO?

turning back, this was the new me, I had thought. Not even fear, would ever hold me back, ever again. This, was Heaven, wasn't it? Why yes, how could it not be! Oh, wow…it was just so, incredible! I felt, free!

The very, easily approachable, kind Man had held out His right hand once again and with an absolute sublime voice, He had said, "Kipper my son, do you know, who I Am?" I realized that, it was Jesus! I choked up with tears of joy! I guess my facial expression with widened eyes, must have said it all! Ha, ha! I nodded my head, yes, as I teared up. Tears of joy had fallen from my eyes. I just knew that Jesus heard my every thought and felt my every emotion—without me even needing to say, a single word. The Man then replied, "I am, I Am."

I smiled with great admiration and was humbled, to bow before Him and kneel with my head bowed down, in respect of Him. The setting was no doubt, inconceivably beautiful and so bright! I just loved clouds so much and Heaven was like, on the most ginormous and most amazing cloud of all clouds! Ha, ha, ha! Wow! You could just feel how tender, His heart is! I felt embraced by Jesus' pure and undying love, for me, as a child of God.

Jesus then gently lifted my chin up, with His right hand and said, "You need not bow, my son. You are a child of God. Rise." He voiced. I lifted my head slowly in respect, as I arose before the great King. I felt so humbled and honoured, to be in His presence. There was this awe-inspiring glowing aura that which had surrounded Jesus. It was mesmerizing to say the least. His beauty radiated a joy, like none other that I have ever seen nor felt on earth! And when He spoke, even the frequencies of sound and air, obeyed Him. It was so amazing, I could hardly find the right words that would truly honour Him, for which I could speak from my small voice—yet, together, we carried on, in the Father's house and spoke with one another.

He then continued to speak once again, as I listened ever-so intently. "Dear Kipper, I am your friend. You have nothing to fear. Kipper my son, know that you are never alone—for I, your Lord God, am always with you. It is not yet your time, to come home. Though my child, you may ask one question—for this which you have time. What would you like to know?" He asked me and awaited my answer, lovingly and patiently.

As I had thought really hard to myself, in what to say, I was suddenly overcome with so many questions, that I found it so difficult to pick, just one. I felt exhausted for a moment while faced with this inner dilemma, as you could probably imagine! Then from the bottom of my heart, I just knew what to ask Him but as I spoke, my eyes began to water up again and I then became overwhelmed with tears that streamed, down my face.

I looked down at myself, my legs, the God-tailored cloth that I wore… and then slowly, I looked back up, to look into Jesus' gentle and life-giving eyes. I began to choke up and I really then, began to cry and dropped my head once again. Jesus lifted up my chin yet again, in His gentle and mighty right hand and wiped away my tears with his white sleeve. After only a couple minutes, of gazing into His eyes, He gazed straight into my heart and spirit—and then smiled, which suddenly had calmed me, just like that. Both of my eyes still pooled with tears, Jesus then wiped them away gently again and again, as they fell down my face, nearly simultaneously, one after the other—catching each one, as they fell towards my feet. His heart was touched, I could feel it—as was mine… I then asked Him, "Papa, when can I come, home?" Jesus had wrapped His loving arms around me, it felt so healing and comforting. With His kind and warm smile, all at once, embracing me like the loving Father that He is—embracing His own child—He then replied and said, "Soon My son, soon."

Abstract Paint Artwork drawing entitled, "Third Degree" by Kipper

IF I COULD FLOAT ON A CLOUD, WHERE WOULD I GO?

Pencil Artwork drawing of Kipper's visit to Heaven, embraced in Jesus's arms entitled, "Friendship Is Forever" by Kipper

Then, just as quickly as I had arrived here, in Heaven—a very warm and bright flash of light, instantaneously engulfed everything that was all around me! Everything had suddenly disappeared, as if someone, had just quickly blew out a candle, in the dark.

I very, slowly opened my eyes, to see where I now was. Hopeful in heart as always and praying that I didn't leave Heaven just yet—though it was inevitable, as I was now realizing of the truth—for it had set in rather quickly, as I had discovered that I was once again, back in my hospital bed, in the Children's Long Term Ward, in the hospital.

I was completely overwhelmed with emotion but with a real sense of a genuine, heartfelt hope—something I hadn't felt in quite some time, if at all. I didn't know what exactly had happened to me or how...but as to where exactly that I had gone—I was quite sure, that it was Heaven... my home.

Deep down in my heart, I just knew that something very important, even special—had happened to me. I had a new hope that was fiercely burning like a fire, deep from within my spirit. Jesus lives in there and so,

He radiated through and through, more and more. This wildly burning flame will no longer be allowed to go out while I am still here, in the real world. For I will make every effort now more than ever, to not to complain, nor to give up living, while I have the privilege to witness and share laughter and stories with others—in hopes, to help lead them to Jesus, so that they too, will be able to return home, when it is their time as well.

To me, what meant more than anything in this world, was not about what I had originally thought of, at all. You see, I would always end up, putting my clouds first in my life, as they comforted me and would never let me down—distracting me from this real world, my real life. The adventures I took on the clouds, were always so freeing for me—but they now fell to second place, in my heart. Jesus is now, my number one and I choose Him.

So, as for what now means more, than anything else in all of my life—was that I had a true friend, for eternity…and to me, a true friendship is forever. So, for as soon as, Fatherly promised, I will someday, be able to leave this hospital bed and then finally, go home.

Pencil Artwork drawing of Bobby with his parents entitled, "Family" by Kipper

CHAPTER SIX

SOMETHING TO SMILE ABOUT

From out of all of the experiences, pleasant and undesirable, to the really unpleasant seasons of life that I have had, while lying in this hospital bed—I have always believed, that no matter how small my chances—someday, one will be hopeful for me.

I just knew that my Heavenly Father was encouraging me, one day at a time—to wait and hang in there and to continue to trust in Him, that He has me and will carry me through and in each and every situation, no matter what.

When we say that we are going to do something and then tell others to then let God do the rest, I think that is actually the wrong way to think of it. What I mean is, we are to give everything up to Him, letting Him take on, EVERYTHING—so that we may grow in Him and Him in us and together, we will move mountains, regardless of the challenges. What do you think? We are to lean on Him, completely, this I have learned, after much strife had passed but now I realize that I need not have to wait, to call on Him, at all. Nor do you. It's so cool, isn't it? Ha, ha!

In fact, as I think of it, there is no challenge in this life, or on this planet, that is too big for the Living God! So why not, completely surrender? I cannot help but to keep smiling, as such a peace is now taking hold of me—and so, with a humbled heart, I whisper a prayer to Him saying, "Father, I ask of you, to please embrace all of my life, into Your hands and lead me, through Your eyes and not my own. Help me see, what You see and show me, Your Way, dear Lord. I trust You with my life, completely. You have me, in Your Hands, in Your Way and in Your Timing, Father. I cannot, but God can. I pray this, in Jesus' Name, Amen." I know this to be true. I just know it...

This morning, in walked a man and a woman through the entrance doors, of the Children's Long Term Ward. They seemed as though they were oblivious to their surroundings, as they must have known, just exactly where to go—in a determined bustle, as they trekked in, in a brisk walk way. They certainly drew my attention, I could not help but to watch them—that is, as inconspicuously and non-creepy, as possible of course, ha, ha!

Maybe they have been here before, I had thought and maybe, I just didn't notice them before, perhaps? I don't know. No, I think they were guided here and oh, Papa's Spirit just told me that He showed them the way. Hmm...interesting, I had thought. I don't know but from what I could see, they seemed as though, they were most definitely in a rush to get here.

I could sense that the Father's Spirit, was giving me a preparedness, a readying for something big which was coming my way, very shortly. Though I did not understand it, or as to what it could be, nor even of when, it seemed that those details did not matter much because we are to go by faith and not by human sight. So I responded to His Spirit and said, "Okay" and chose to trust Him anyway.

Their faces definitely showed signs of stress and perhaps, many sleepless nights. As their clothes were quite wrinkled, which by the many visitors that I have witnessed—that was a sign of sleeping in the same clothes, for an extended period of time and in discomfort, causing tossing and turning, instead of a restful sleep. Given that this is a hospital and the human's 'way of the world's' place to 'come and get well' ...then that also most likely meant that they suffered night after night, while painfully awaiting to hear of any kind of good news... I had then wondered for a second—if or of what 'good news' and from whom, it had come to them?

The Lord works in mysterious ways indeed, as His ways were never meant for us to understand it all, just to trust and have complete faith, in His process and in His timing, no matter what... "no matter what..." I had then said just below a whisper, with a smile pasted on my face.

IF I COULD FLOAT ON A CLOUD, WHERE WOULD I GO?

The man and woman's eyes spoke, of a deeply rattled pain or a hurting, that they were possibly feeling…something rather big, had happened to cause their distress—from what I could see, it seemed to me that was for certain and obviously, it was of a child because they ended up here, in the Children's Long Term Ward.

I would tend to pay a fair bit of attention, to whomever would walk in and out of those hospital doors. So to really emphasize that point, while through the many other hospital room doors that I had lived through while here, on multiple hospital beds throughout the years—that is a lot of people, that which I had read faces, throughout the many years, when you think of it!

The distressed looking man and woman, walked over towards my way, pulled up chairs and sat by the boy, whom was fast asleep next to the big, tall and covered window. I had not yet seen visitors by his side, until now. They spoke loving and caring words to him while trying their best to hold back tears, from gushing from their troubled eyes. They even spoke of God, blessing their lives with their son and that they, truly were not ready for his departure, just yet—asking for God, to please help their son come back to them. Words of encouragement, love, happy memories and so forth, had flowed from the quivering of their mouths. They were definitely hurting inside.

They continued for what seemed to me, like hours had gone by—telling him that everything will be okay, even asking for him to try and please open up his eyes, so that he could see, both of his Momma and Pa, again. Well, that sure made sense once they had said that…my heart had then suddenly, gotten a little heavier and I sure felt for them. "Please Papa, please help them, please wake up their son." I had asked Papa, in a very quiet, whispered request.

They began to sob as they spoke to him, looking torn by their son's situation. I wanted to say something nice but grasped that silence, was best on my part. However, I decided to say a quiet prayer to myself this time but for the boy and for both of his parents, once again—repeating the first prayer… "Please Papa, please help them, please wake up their son." I always press in to try and remember to pray, for anyone who comes and goes from here…you never know, you may have been the only person whom even cared enough, to do something like that for them, in their life. For I know that prayer changes lives in a good way—so might as well try, right? What do you have to lose any way, by trying?

Then all of a sudden, I felt a gifting come through me, from my Papa in Heaven. I was told to pray in the Spirit for them and so I did. I could not understand the words but that was because it was God's perfect prayer—that no man nor enemy foe, could manipulate the prayer, that only God would understand its words, prayers and requests made. We need not, have to understand, even a single word, for the prayer then is carried out, not by man's wants, nor words but only, by God's Hand, Way and Timing. It is pretty powerful stuff.

I have learned that, if you just speak to the Father this way, He will always answer you. I felt a different, Heavenly foreign language, hang off the tip of my tongue, as I went to make a sound and then it happened! I spoke but it was not my own thought-created words speaking it—I followed Papa's lead. To others, it would sound like gibberish but that did not truthfully even matter, now did it? It was amazing!

I continued to press inward and as I placed my focus unto Papa, unto Jesus—I let His words flow through my mouth, as it was just below a whisper now. I felt His comforting warmth and pure love, just radiate through my spirit, from His. For our Spirits were talking! It was wonderful! I felt no longer heavy laden by burden in my heart for them, but rather, peace, encouragement and even excitement for them, instead! Whoa! "Thank you Papa!" I had thanked Him and for His purposefully constant and solid, never failing true love.

Then, not more than maybe five minutes later, the mother had stood up, all of a sudden. I will admit that at first, I felt a tad startled by her swift action, as her movement just seemed so randomly unexpected and sudden—but then I remembered, nothing is random in this world. Everything happens for a reason, everything and everyone has a purpose and that God always makes good, from out of any bad situation that the enemy spirit tries to force his deceiving hand in where it does not belong. Even beyond the shadow of a doubt, God is still BIGGER! He never changes which makes His Love, always pure and always constant and true.

I then heard Papa say, "Just watch"…I could sense that He was smiling when He had said that. Ha, ha…I laughed slightly but quietly to myself

IF I COULD FLOAT ON A CLOUD, WHERE WOULD I GO?

and told Him in agreement, replying, "Okay" as I awaited His lead. I had sense within my heart, that God was about to do something, amazing, I just knew it! Ha, ha! I felt excited butterflies at this time, as I awaited God's unfolding plan.

As I watched intently, but as inconspicuously and non-intrusively as possible, the woman then took a studied-look around the room and of her son's surroundings—peering at the covered window and then at all of the children that lay in their hospital beds, in the Children's Long Term Ward. Then suddenly, the woman had then briefly looked at me, for like two or three split seconds, which felt like several minutes long! She then returned her head back down towards the floor, for a moment in silence. I watched her in curiosity...

Studying her every move, as I did not know yet, as to what God was planning, I had then noticed that her lips were moving—that she was speaking, to someone. "Wait, was it to, Papa?" I had whispered to myself and just as quick as a whip, Papa whispered back, "Yes". My eyes lit up! I felt excited, as though there were a thousand brand new and very excited little butterflies, that were flying erratically, within my stomach, in the anticipation for something very good, that was about to happen!

And before anyone could count one Mississippi, two Mississippi, the lady suddenly turned towards the big, tall window and then quickly walked right over to it and she immediately, uncovered it! As she unveiled the big, tall and beautiful window, she cried out loud with a caring compassion, in her voice, "This room is too dreary, in a dimmed lighting, filled with darkness. It brings no light, on a dark day for my, (*sniffled*)... my boy." The lady had choked up with emotion and paused for a moment, just before, as she had mentioned her son—she then continued to speak... "How can chil-children get better, when th-they can-cannot f-feel the light and th-through such a clo-closed covering, from the world?" she had then paused to take a breath from sobbing and continued "if their sur-surroundings are darkened, on-on purpose? So...(*sniffled*)...let there then, be Light". She commanded, and the curtain was drawn completely open finally, once again!

Whoa! Wow, wow, wow! I could hardly believe my eyes! I squinted as the brightness from the sunlight, was sure a sight for sore eyes, indeed! Ha, ha, ha! Ooh Papa! I cried out loud inside my heart, choking up with tears of joyful excitement! I could see the window again! I could see the window again! I bounced a little in my hospital bed, but only a very slightness of course... I could see outside again! I wiped tears from my eyes with the right sleeve of my hospital gown. Thank you! Thank you! Th-thank you, P-P-Papa... I had begun to choke up a bit more and even cried—sobbing a little at first but then, I flat out began to cry harder and harder, though I did it as quietly to myself, as best as one, humanly could. I had definitely broken out in tears, for there was no more hiding it—not at all! Ha, ha!

My heart had felt as though it grew ten times the size, into a complete and utter, humbling surrender. I tried so hard to hold it all inside, as quietly as I could, so as not to disrupt that family—I was so touched and relieved by what had just happened but tried to show respect, at the same time—often biting my bottom lip sometimes, just to try and keep from bursting out, as I wept.

I nearly, could not believe my own eyes! The brightness that beamed through that big, tall window, was oh so bright but I was just so happy to see the uncovered window that the near blinding brightness, did not last long at all, nor did it really bother me! It had been days, no more like weeks—since I last had a chance, to see a cloud. It has been such, a long wait...I sighed with such relief and a real pure joy, at this blessing that was unwrapped, right before my eyes.

Right away, as I gazed through the awesome window, with reddened sore eyes from the bright sun's radiance—I urgently stared through it, in hopes to catch a glimpse of a cloud. Not long after it's unveiling, along came a perfectly formed, fluffy-shaped cloud, just in time for me! Ha! Ha! "FINALLY!" I screamed with a whisper, though silently to myself—with great excitement! "Woohoo!" I had whispered quietly to myself, just above a whisper.

Closing my eyes tightly, I jumped on that cloud and I floated on it immediately, as it darted through the sky! Around and around I went and I yelled out loud, as hard and as high, as I could fly! "Woohoo! Ha, ha, ha, ha!" I yelled and laughed out so loud, with tears of joy, just streaming backwards off my face, while I moved so fast on my cloud, sent from above! "Ooh Papa, thank youuuu!" I called out to Him, with my arms reaching right out, as I cried out, in thankfulness! "Papa...Thank you for Your love!" I shouted! I had not felt this good—as I gave out a long sigh—in as long as I can remember. I was just so, entirely very grateful...

I flew as far as the eye could see! I even flew as far away from the hospital and even beyond the city limits, as I possibly could! Why would I even want to hold back, ha, ha, ha! I wanted to go as far away from this place, as possible! I must have flown so far from the hospital, that it was at least—maybe, one thousand miles away! Ha, ha, ha! Books say that if you drive at about one hundred and ten kilometres per hour, for one thousand kilometres, it would be roughly nine hours, five minutes and twenty-seven seconds of travel by vehicle! That is far! Ha, ha!

I raced and dashed right on through, across the heavens! I was bobbing and weaving around and through tall, bushy trees while hearing the many birds sing, the songs that which their hearts would speak from—I even spun around on my cloud and even did summersaults, through other clouds again and again! "Woohoo! Ha, ha!" I laughed again and again! It was epic!

Playfully, I disrupted the calm floating clouds up ahead and on purpose! You bet I did! "Ha, ha, ha!" Roaring with laughter, again and again, I dashed through multiple clouds—disappearing through one and then bursting out, through another—I had appeared! "Ha, ha, ha, ha!" I cheerfully laughed!

I literally, burst right through every cloud that was in sight! I then dove straight down through the treetop canopy and then right down towards the massive green meadows below—and as I soared so low now, just above the grassy and wildflower blanketed fields, I reached down with my right hand and brushed the tops of the wildflowers, sending petals, pollen and seeds afloat up into the air, just by the brushing sweep motion of my fingers. Ha, ha! This way amazing!

I then glided just low enough, across small streams and ponds that were teamed with life—dipping my fingertips into their bodies of water, breaking the water's calm surface, now causing ripples across them, as I flew on by! "Hallelujah!" I shouted! "Ha, ha!" I laughed out loud! Thanking my Creator for this, as I had shouted with glee! It felt so heavenly, I could hardly believe my own two eyes—it was so real in my heart! Ha, ha! Nothing could ever take this away from me. What a wondrous and most eventful day, of my entire, yet very short earthly life! "Thank you Papa!" I yelled! "Ha, ha! Thank you!"

While soaring through the breathtaking countryside for what had seemed like hours and hours of well, absolutely awesomeness! Ha, ha! I was suddenly drawn to look for something or someone—I did not know of what or whom but I agreed from within my heart, that I would.

While looking around below my cloud, I suddenly spotted a bare hill near by and I'm sure that it was the Holy Spirit, spurring me on, to check it out—so I did. I quickly changed my bearings and flew onward, turning more slightly to the right like those vehicles that drive down a circle overpass as it winds downward in a circle, connecting with another highway as it goes around and around until the circle-like highway lane, then joins the other.

I had begun my rather, steep decent and went down towards this curiously mysterious and even cryptic-looking bare hill—as it had, only continued to draw me closer and closer. I then realized that there was a person down there! "W-whom, was that?" I had thought and said just above a whisper. So now, I just had to check it out and I picked up my pace even more.

As I came closer, I at first, was not so sure if my eyes were telling a tale, or if they were even seeing a mirage. Then as I was now hovering close enough, to see details of the person—I then had noticed that it was a boy, just sitting alone. So I quickly landed and then hopped down, off of the cloud and I almost immediately, recognized him right away! "Wait, what? Was that, Bobby? Is that you?" I asked myself but only in a whisper once again, as if I had suddenly forgotten how to use my own words, through my mouth from my voice box! Ha, ha! I could not believe it, for it was him! "But, w-why? Why was he, here?" I again, had whispered to myself.

I then ran up to him! It WAS, Bobby! Remember, Bobby? He was that tall, older boy that I had met some time ago, in the green meadow—after the great, epic sailboat race! Oh my goodness, he was back! I had missed him, he had been a great, new friend! Wow, has it ever been that long? Hmm, with as many years that had passed, it sure felt like it was forever ago! My eyes really, could hardly believe it! My heartbeat was pounding in my chest, along with excited butterflies that just couldn't help but crash against the inner walls of my ribcage, as they did summersaults and just went crazy wild! Ha, ha, ha!

IF I COULD FLOAT ON A CLOUD, WHERE WOULD I GO?

Pencil Artwork drawing of Bobby, sitting alone on a bare hill entitled, "Rescue Me" by Kipper

I then picked up my pace, as I walked right up to him, which was now only about maybe, ten feet or so away. I had finally met up with him once again and I was now standing next to him, just off from his right side, by a couple feet. Leaning forward a bit, so that I could catch a glimpse of his face up close, I then had noticed that he actually looked sad, sitting there—holding his knees to his chin and staring beyond the valley. His appearance looked as though, he had even been crying for a while, actually. But, why? I had thought to myself…

He was wearing brown cargo pants, a white t-shirt and no footwear—just his bare feet. "Bobby? Are you okay?" I approached diligently, with great concern—for my friend… "I haven't seen you in a long time, Bobby"

I continued, "Where have you been, my friend? Are-are, you okay?" I had asked him, once again.

I must admit…that in all of my years of floating on the clouds, spent through my many, amazing and most wondrous adventures, through a variety of hospital windows—never and I mean never, have I ever encountered, someone, feeling sad. This had really started to trouble me. Why was Bobby so sad and even crying? I did not want to pry and be pushy, or annoying…but, he was my friend and I did not want to make him feel, like I did not care either.

Bobby then, through the tears, had taken a deep breath in and slowly let it out, as he looked up at me, to see that it was really, me—and as he wiped tears from his eyes, he then said with a great, big heart, "I miss my Momma and Pa" he responded while choked up and sniffling, he then continued, as he looked back down across the valley… "I-I can't wake up and I m-miss them, s-s-so much." He began to continue to cry.

Like a swarm of trumpeting loons on the water's surface, bellowing their cries in the late hours of the eve—Bobby sobbed so effortlessly, with such heartache. He then began to, slightly hyperventilate, as he tried to talk while pushing through the crying and the many falling tears. "I don't c-care, if I will then f-feel all of the pain and suff-suffering, in the real world." He cried even deeper and louder, and it really, broke my heart—now bringing even me, to tears. "I wou-would, much rather" Bobby repeated, as he continued to completely surrender, pouring out his big heart to me, "I-I, w-would much rather tra-trade in, th-this pain-fr-free w-world…t-to have them, b-back—again." He stated. My heart ached for him, terribly!

Wow, that was so powerful! I could feel his pain, his tears—I felt his words and his cry! It was so heart wrenching, but I got it—I understood, exactly what he was trying to say. Oh man, oh dear Papa, how my heart just broke for him and for his parents! Like a huge glass vase, falling down in slow motion. Its weight now caught in earth's gravity, as it fell downward, destined to meet its opponent head on and then, impacts the floors' surface—shattering into a million pieces, sending sharp glass shards absolutely, everywhere! It was like an explosion that had set it off and forced the brokenness, as it slightly flew up and then blasted outward, in every direction!

IF I COULD FLOAT ON A CLOUD, WHERE WOULD I GO?

I sniffled a couple times while I was definitely by now, choked up too. Then taking a deep breath in as I swallowed rather loudly, I wiped tears from my eyes. I was now too, sharing his suffering and tears. While looking around us a bit, I then looked back at Bobby. I felt that Papa wanted for me to join him. So I sat down quietly, beside Bobby and crossed my legs, while I brushed the grass blades with my fingers—as I glanced at him for a moment. I then looked back down at the ground and then beyond the valley—while I became in deep thought. I began praying in the Spirit and then in English, asking Papa what I should say to Bobby... I awaited His lead.

I was rather still at loss, for the right words... So I waited patiently, as we both sat there, the both of us—just sniffling and crying away, together—as we each wiped each of our own tears away, yet said nothing at all, for a little while longer. As I sat there, my mind raced through reasoning between fantasy and reality...the pros and the cons—you know, that sort of thing...discerning the differences of what was worth more or less and which place was actually, far more valuable in truth and not by human wants. It was like I was watching my life flash by, as it sifted through, all of the many memories that I have had throughout my entire, short life.

Suddenly, as though a light bulb had flicked on and changed the dynamics of my heart's life song of, well, everything—I finally, right then and there, realized who he is! "No, way?" I had thought and slightly whispered to myself quietly...I then realized strongly, letting my heart win over my mind—Bobby, is the boy who is fast asleep in a coma, in the Children's Long Term Ward—right next to the big, tall window, in my hospital room! Oh, oh and, that those, very kind and caring people, the man and woman which are sitting right next to him, are his parents! His Momma and Pa! I choked up and began to cry even more! Yet, I got more and more excited the more the details had begun to unravel! This is what Papa was preparing me for, this was it!

It had all became clear to me—no one even had to say much more. Papa's Spirit had then encouraged for me to say something further, to Bobby. It was he, who was laying in a coma, unable to awaken, as of yet... Papa had sent me, to help him! I just know it! Wow... I had thought to myself, in amazement. God really does want for everyone to make it! I nodded in agreement as Papa had spoke to me from His Spirit, into my heart—I heard His wisdom flow through me, just wanting to burst out and comfort Bobby! It felt so, so powerful, to say the least! Then, I suddenly knew that I had to encourage Bobby somehow, so I had asked for Papa, to give me the right words. "I can't, but you can God..." I voiced in a whisper.

I felt such a sadness from the depths of my very own soul, for Bobby and about his situation...and for his parents too. Yet, I began to feel a soothing warming come over me, a compassion filled with a radiating peace that had then completely then captured, my mind, body and spirit! I felt, encouraged! Even, motivated! Something, was definitely happening! Wow! Papa was really doing something amazing, here. He was really hard at work, I just knew it! He was about to do something, really big... I could just feel it!

So I then moved in a bit closer, to sit in front of Bobby but at an angle—within a couple feet from him, so that we were now a little more, face to face. I paused as I looked passed the ground's grassy surface, as though I was picturing Jesus' face, awaiting for His words to guide me. I awaited for Papa's Holy Spirit to lead me, with Papa's words to exit through me... and then I began to speak what was asked of me, word by word, they flowed from Jesus in my heart... "Bobby?" I said, as I leaned my head down to get his attention, to point his eyes to look up at me—out from being buried within his folded knees to his chin. He then looked up a little with his eyes.

I also tried to motion for him to look up at me with my right hand, in a slight wave down to the ground in front of him—in hopes to get his attention once again, as he cried. He finally noticed and lifted his head slightly and looked over at me. "Now" I could hear Papa commanding me to begin again! It felt powerful! And so it flowed... "Bobby, I am your roommate in the hospital...in the Children's Long Term Ward—we are roommates, Bobby, you and I—we are roommates." Bobby sniffled, as he lifted his head up more, to look up at me a little better—now, partially wide-eyed, as he wiped more streaming tears from his face, with his white t-shirt—we got his attention!

I continued... "I seen your parents Bobby, they are sitting RIGHT next to you! Right now, in the hospital." He looked shocked but curious

IF I COULD FLOAT ON A CLOUD, WHERE WOULD I GO?

at the same time, raising his head a little bit more... "You can't give up Bobby—you just can't quit now, on life, Bobby." I continued. "Your parents Bobby, they really m-miss you, so much!" I began to get a bit choked up again myself, as I talked more to Bobby. I could feel the Holy Spirit getting emotional, as that sure showed that He is with me because I too, get emotional but with tears of joy. "Bobby" I carried on... "They want you back, Bobby! They want for you to come back, into their lives, Bobby. To be with them again." I added.

Then with a curiosity-lit look upon Bobby's face, something had begun to brighten, deep from within him. "Th-they, they m-miss, miss m-me, too?" Bobby struggled to ask me, while pushing through the choked up crying, sniffling and the tears, once again—as he had looked up at me, with tears streaming down from his incredibly anxious and very stressed out face.

"Of course, they do!" I continued. "Bobby, I don't have any" I choked up then proceeded as best as I could. "I don't, I don't have any par-parents..." I began to choke even more but pressed on, in my attempts, to encourage him instead of discourage while trying to help him... "I hardly have m-many visitors, Bobby—of p-people, whom...who on a daily basis just-just don't come to vi-visit me. People who could even, p-possibly care for me in, ah, such a, l-loving way—like, your parents, care for you, Bobby."

I quickly swiped away, a heavily falling tear from my face—trying not to make this, about me... And so I continued and swallowed my tears, as best as I could. "Bobby, you see, I don't get many v-visitors by m-my side—but Bobby, you get your parents! That's awesome, Bobby! And now, you can go back to them! Th-they love y-you, B-Bobby!" I was weeping under my breath. "They really, uh, they really, really m-miss y-you, they w-want you back." I tried to catch my breath in the middle of it. "Bobby, y-you can go back, you have to go back. You can go back to them, Bobby. Just try. Th-they won't leave you, they c-care so much ab-about you. Th-they won't leave you." I barely managed to finish.

Bobby's face had then lit up, with a warm glimmer of hope that had shone for the first time, since I had arrived. His tears had slowed for the moment, as he thought about all that I had said. About his parents, truly still missing him and sitting by his side right now, at this very moment and even, wanting for him to return to them, in the real world… I can only imagine in how much it felt, how heavy laden this must have been for him—for him to have to take it all in. I have never really been in his situation before. Something like this was definitely, very new to me.

Then Bobby's warm glimmer of hope upon his face, had begun to fade. He did not look the least bit happy, nor excited at all, anymore. Bobby then said something most alarming and very sad to me, as he choked up again and pushed to talk through the tears and sobbing—which I will never forget. "Kip-per-r, you h-have been a good-g-good f-friend, to m-me… b-but I d-don't th-think that I-I, I don't th-think that I c-can, can do it." He shockingly remarked and then tried to continue. "I-I don't, I don't think that I, that I—that I ha-have, an-ny strength l-left in-in me." He paused for a second and then looked down to say, "I-I, c-can, f-f-feel, it."

I suddenly swallowed in a big, gulp-like motion. I felt so concerned for him and was completely, at loss for words. "I-I kn-know that deep down insi-inside of me" Bobby continued to push onward, despite the heart wrenching sadness that filled us with overwhelming tears. "th-that even if I-I ca-can, go b-back, that I migh-might, n-not have, mu-much t-time, with m-my p-parents… And that scare-scares m-me, very mu-much!"

I shared his sorrow, all across my face and throughout the depths of my heart, mind and spirit. He surprisingly, continued with more to say, pressing on, voicing his deeply felt, hurt. "I-I'm torn K-Kipper." Bobby had said, as he continued. "I-I don't, I d-don't know wha-what t-to, d-do. I don't kn-know, what I-I sh-should do." Bobby had finished talking, as he continued to wipe away more tears with his t-shirt. He was in such turmoil—utterly overwhelmed and with such a tormenting fear that was practically, eating him alive, crippling him with fear from trying, as he drown in sorrowful tears—figuratively speaking that is.

Thinking hard with all of my heart, I pressed in again but even harder this time, focusing in on Papa in my heart and asking Him, of what I should tell Bobby, I waited for His guidance, after the pause. How could a scrawny, sick, little kid like me, possibly have much of any help to offer him—in such a time, as this? I did not feel, even nearly adequate enough, for the task at hand. "Papa" I said, "Papa, I ca-can't, b-but you c-can". I had told Him, while I wept, from the deepest parts, of the insides of my own

IF I COULD FLOAT ON A CLOUD, WHERE WOULD I GO?

heart—where He lives. Even though I did not feel like "enough"...just as soon as I had thought this—Papa had told me, that I was. I choked up and cried inside, wiping away more tears. So, from there on, I just knew and felt so deeply, that to Bobby, I had to say more. I had to encourage him to try...to not give up the fight. Papa had sent me, for a reason.

I could feel the painful distress that Bobby was in and that of both of his parents as well, it was very heavy laden for sure—I felt the connection between both worlds like I honestly, never have before. I too felt the distressing hurt that they all had shared, even before I had left on my cloud, from my hospital bed. Such wounds that waited in limbo, for a rescue to come help pull them out of this quick sand sorrow, that was quickly dragging everyone further down into despair, maybe even into depression. Which is a scary place to be! It was time to take a stand.

The enemy brings all of his baggage-loaded luggage, moves in and stays there—as a VERY unwanted guest! Raise the rent and kick him out! He acts like your thoughts are now his and schemes all the time, in spreading lies into your mind while using words like "I" or "me" or "my" to make you think, that his thoughts are now yours and he condemns you over and over, making you own those lies, as your very own! Don't do it! Don't go there! He is evil and wants to steal, kill and destroy! For he knows, no love. Only God is Love.

So I waited, to hear from Papa on what I should say but it didn't actually end up, taking very long for Papa's Spirit to respond. "Bobby" I said, as Papa's words just rolled off my tongue, as He spoke through me, with not even another stuttering sound. This message came as a bold, stance, for my Heavenly Father, was now answering the door for me, as He stomped on the devil's lying schemes! Wow! We continued. "It's not over yet. Bobby, you HAD major surgery—and all they need for you, is to wake up! Bobby, you can heal from this, from whatever it is, that is ailing your body. You can do it, Bobby! Please, please don't give up now—there is still hope, there is so much life, left inside of you. Just watch. You will see!" I balled as tears ran down my face, as I spoke to him from Papa's heart, through mine. Oh my gosh, I was overwhelmed with such an anticipating, hope! "Think of the happy memories Bobby. Let yourself dream with hope, for new ones that are yet to come. Picture it,

Bobby. Picture it! You must keep trying Bobby, you mustn't give up hope, Bobby…" I exclaimed.

I persistently kept trying to cheer him on, to encourage him as positively—as I was able. "Bobby" I continued. "Bobby, and when you need to get away from the pain, from the stresses of the real world, you have hope to lean on, you have Jesus. If you want to escape from anything that feels like it is trapping you in a corner and making you feel like giving up—all I do is look out of the big, tall window…look out of any window, and find a cloud! I focus in on something intrepid, something wonderful!"… "What i-is, in-tr-trep-pid?" Bobby interrupted while tears still rolled on through. "Adventurous" I replied, with an encouraged, satisfied smile on my face.

I had felt that maybe, just maybe, Bobby was beginning to hear me—to hear Papa. "Bobby—you can ask Papa, to take you anywhere, with your imagination and as fast, or as leisurely as desired—you can float on a cloud to anywhere you wish that brings you, serenity, that gives you, His Peace, like no other." I responded. Realizing in my own mind that I am of course, no saviour at all—I continued to ramble on, in my attempt to help another life, with mine. However way, that Papa saw fit, I was willing. I chose to just let Him take it and lead me.

Together, we continued, "You can go visit with your old pals, or catch up with newer friends—even make new ones, any time that you like!" I exclaimed. "No one and I mean, no one—has to be trapped here Bobby, not, one. This is not a place to feel trapped, nor lost my friend—but rather, to be found and even restored." I continued to try and explain what Papa's heart was telling me, to tell him. "Bobby, listen—you CAN, go home. You don't have to stay here. You have nothing to fear. You have the strength, to go back home. To go back home to your Momma and Pa, now wouldn't that be worth the effort?" I asked him. I believe in you, Bobby. You have nothing to fear. For God says, Fear not, I think about three hundred and sixty-five times in the bible, or so I've heard, and if that is true, then that is one, for every day of the year! That's pretty cool!" I exclaimed. "Bobby listen, you don't have to be afraid. I am your friend and remember, that friendship is forever, Bobby. Please? Don't give up Bobby. Don't give up, the fight!"

I insisted and decided to hard-press this matter into the moment, as I had suddenly felt the end nearing now, for his life—and so there was very little time to waste, for much longer. I had to continue to try and help get Papa's message through! There was no more time to wait! No more time to pause any longer... Then lastly, Papa spoke within me, "NOW!"

Well, I must tell you something about that! The feeling from Papa's 'Jumpstart NOW' while he tugged on my heart strings to rise up, was WOW! It had felt like, well I would describe it, as you would like in trying to start a dead battery in an engine, and having to jumpstart it. Then with electrical booster cables, from one lively machine to a dead one—then cranking the power source to the max and sending about twenty-four volts of bolting power, right through those cables to bring the dead battery back to life! Except in this case, you have an excelling death, at a fast rate, in a dying boy, whom needs the most mightiest and most authoritative and commanding, powerful strength, for him to be jumpstarted back to life!

It was time! Just do it, Bobby! I thought to myself! Say it Kipper! I said in my head, while I could sense the enemy was scheming lies now to try and prevent me, from speaking any further! They kept telling me to be quiet and not speak anymore. Trying to bite my tongue, so that I could no longer even make a sound! He tried EVERYTHING except, he and his scheming lies, were NOT my everything, PAPA WAS AND IS MY EVERYTHING! I told the devil, NOT TODAY! And I burst out the cry from my heart, from Papa's to Bobby's! NOW! "No more time to lose, it is time Bobby! Bobby, looked at me. Wake up buddy! Bobby, we are calling for you. God has you! We are here for you Bobby! We wait for you! Now, Bobby, wake up! Wake up Bobby! Wake up!" I shouted while I pressed in hard, in the believing, on Papa's healing for him!

Then all of a sudden, without any further words from either one of us—Bobby, immediately then lay down completely on the ground, behind him and then he just literally, disappeared—right in front of me! Whoa! What? Do my eyes fail me, I had thought? Wow! What, what had just happened? I was instantly startled but I was not at all, scared! Where did he go? "Where are you, Bobby?" I said out loud, no longer in a whisper, as I looked around to see where he may have gone.

It was really a different feeling that had seriously overtaken me—despite my extremely, impatient curiosity! Ha, ha! I was so fascinated by what just happened while I honestly had no clue, as to what really took place—that I almost thought for a split second that I had possibly, maybe even lost him for good. But I didn't want to entertain any fearful thoughts, for I knew that they were not my own, nor were they from the Father! I had to press in to believing Papa's truth. So, while I mentally pushed in while blocking the negative voices that had begun to pound on the door of my mind, by the master schemer enemy himself—I pressed inwardly, resting my mind in the promise of Papa's peace, I then said out loud with a reassured faithful hope, "Nope, I am not going there! I can't but Papa can! Ha, ha! Papa will answer the door for me, instead! So evil enemy, you WILL GO where JESUS tells you, to go! In Jesus Name, Amen!"

Pencil Artwork drawing of a set of, full double rainbows entitled, "A Promise from Papa" by Kipper

Then from across the valley and over the horizon which was sandwiched between the land and the cloud-filled sky—I noticed a set of very, vibrantly colourful and full double rainbows that had opened up, right across the heavens just above me! Their very bold beams of colour, had shone so brightly that it was so breathtaking… lighting the sky and then they pierced right through me—hitting me with a ray of a supernaturally renewing and a most compelling, get-up-and-go motivating hope! Ha, ha! Wow! This was it! I felt the Holy Spirit grab hold and lift me up and pull me towards the sky, to summon a cloud!

IF I COULD FLOAT ON A CLOUD, WHERE WOULD I GO?

When Papa says, "Now" He means, NOW! For when something is meant to be and the time has arrived, nothing will stand in its way! Ha, ha! All I had to do was think of a cloud and boom, there it came as it descended downward towards me! For what didn't even take very long, this was beyond amazing—it was only a matter of a couple minutes, maybe not even that!

The soft fluffy white cloud was like a cotton candy-like fluff, with its overtones of blues and grey edge-detailed appearance, as I watched it approach where I had stood. I stood firmly in my Papa's arms, as He protected me from the persistent yet, nonsensical enemy's flaming arrows. "Thank you Papa!" I thanked Him, graciously!

Finally the cloud had arrived! It was now majestically floating above the ground, where I had stood—no more than a little over a foot, in front of me. I immediately jumped onto it and knelt down, as I was now leaning forward and was told by Papa to, "HOLD ONE!" "Yes, sir! Ha, ha!" I yelled, in excitement! Let's go, hurry! I thought in my mind, with a great anticipation to find Bobby! I needed to investigate this myself. I just had to try. So I was so beyond ready, to fly as fast as Papa took me! We were beginning to accelerate now up into the sky and then I, like the snap of a finger duo and a thumb, I began to go faster and then even faster—I flew like a rocket ship, shooting straight for the stars! BOOM! Ha, ha! Whoa, it was so fast!

I knew where I was now going! Believe it or not but to where I was aimed to inquire—to seek where Bobby may have gone, well it was not to where you would normally think that I would actually intend to be willing to go to, either—nope! Ha, ha, ha! This was going to blow your mind! Ha, ha! Papa whispered to me, of where I would find Bobby! I could hardly contain myself! I knew but I couldn't voice it! I had sensed a new horizon, was underway!

I actually hurried so swiftly that my surroundings had a blurring appearance to them, as I sped up so fast, that the trip seemed fleeting—lasting for only maybe, no longer than five to six, or maybe even seven minutes, max! I had arrived, back to the city and you guessed it—all the way back to the hospital! I just had to find out where my friend Bobby had gone, I could not wait a second longer, than necessary.

I had to go back to my hospital bed! No really, that is where I was headed! I just had to! I wanted to see for myself, the sense that I had felt of what had just happened to Bobby, in where Papa had whispered to me, to "go find a new horizon"! When those outstandingly, brilliant double rainbows had shone, right after Bobby had lay down and disappeared, Papa had then spoken to me of this and to a place, where I did not want to originally be—I now wanted to be! Ha, ha! Wow!

It was something special, I just knew it! I was so curious, and yet so excited and filled with a most endearing, anticipated hope—I couldn't help myself but to return back to the hospital, just to find out where Bobby had gone. I was hoping and praying that he didn't die and go to Heaven quite yet—that he didn't leave us, just yet...

I arrived at last—I had travelled such a long ways and finally, came to the city's largest hospital building, in the country! Swerving and dodging around towers galore and building roof peeks and so much more! I now flew a little slower, as I got closer and closer—though at first, I went speedily just to make up some time. God's timing is always perfect, He is always, just right, on time! I was now close enough to the hospital's joint buildings that I had to slow down now, in my approach.

As I came around this massive medical building of many buildings, which were joined with multiple other tall and huge buildings as well—you could see each had its own unique shape and different purpose, for their own profession. I had to get to the Children's Long Term Ward Building and fast! It was another attached building, yet to come into view—connected with long corridors and was several floors high. Yes, exactly, that is a lot of Long Term people, living in there!

I was now finally within a birds-eye-view of it, but as it became bigger, and bigger the closer I got to it—I finally had spotted the Children's Long Term Ward—it was now finally, within my view! Flying lower and lower now, I could see the many windows of this building and people that stood inside. As they were going about their typical yet generally, unpredictable day at the hospital, I could see so many of them, as I descended even more. "Wooow, cool!" I yelled.

"So this, is what it actually looks like but from the outside world?" I had said, just above a whisper. There were so many windows and I even saw people, even children peering out from some windows of those, whom could get right up and look out of them. I smiled as I passed on by

IF I COULD FLOAT ON A CLOUD, WHERE WOULD I GO?

and they could actually, see me? Wait, what? Wow...each one returning a smile and waved to me, as I passed on by. As if they knew what my mission was, from Papa. I felt emotionally touched, and just, happy—Papa was working hard, diligently as always. I felt it. It felt gratifying to see joy in other's faces, as always and not just always focusing inwards—you know?

I could now see the Children's Long Term Ward building in sight—the side of where that big, tall and recently unveiled window was drawing near, where my hospital bed was. As soon as my hospital window was within view, it was as though my cloud had instantly picked up its pace, displaying a determined direction, now more than ever and I was now going faster and faster—accelerating, as everything around me now, had gotten blurry once again, due to the velocity that I was now currently in.

As I came around to my hospital window, the cloud began to slow while I descended ever so near—to my highly desired destination. Oh, wow, I had thought! I was just so close that I had butterflies now that were going just absolutely, crazy inside! It was as though they were plagued with an astonishing expectation—like you wouldn't believe! Ha, ha! I could just tell that Papa's Spirit, was just so, overwhelmingly excited for me! I felt emotional but incredibly driven, with a passion for life and for whatever it was, that Papa was about to bring on that which, I was about to acquire!

A whole new level of blessing, was currently underway, by my Heavenly Papa! Ha, ha! Wow! Oh my! The adrenaline sure had become very intense by now! I had certainly teared up like crazy and my heart took on a warming, deeply from within. Papa has this, I just know it! I could feel His powerful Love, drawing me near.

My mind, body and spirit's focus were all working together in unison—focused on my Father's Love and I only wanted, what He wanted for me. I hadn't a complaint, nor not even a single excuse left, inside of me. I was in complete surrender! Hallelujah! Ha, ha! This Heavenly peace, was awesome! I highly recommend that you let yourself soak up such a living and life altering peace, like no other! Should you choose, to accept it. You won't regret it!

I was now approaching the big, tall window—I only had maybe, three or so feet to go, as I had gotten closer and closer! My heart was pounding in my chest. Then, all of a sudden, the scene turned into a gloriously bright white fade in glow—instead of fading out, into a blackness. Wow! I then woke up and opened my eyes.

I had finally, arrived! "Thank you" I whispered in my heart and through my lips—to Papa. I was back in my hospital bed again but for the very first time, probably the only time that I have ever experienced, in all of my life—I did not at all, feel sad. Wow! I was now, just so emotional but I did not forget what I had aimed to find out, just yet. So I gathered myself up. Quickly wiping away staggering tears falling from my eyes, so they could not blur my vision—so that I could look beyond them, in hopes to see what was awaiting for my discovery, on the other side.

Rubbing my eyes rather quickly, to get rid of the initial blurred vision and grogginess I had gained from my recent adventure and deep, deep sleep—I then turned my head towards the big, tall window and then looked passed it, to where Bobby's hospital bed was—to where he lay. I was still fairly groggy even still, but I remembered why I was in such a hurry—that I so very much wanted to know, where Bobby had gone.

I then suddenly heard shrieks of crying but with, laughter? There was a heaviness feeling in the Children's Long Term Ward that instead, was being reversed and had become weightless and uplifting! It was loaded with tearful crying and heartfelt excitement! The man and woman began to sob deeply and outwardly—I had felt a mixed pile of emotion! Did he make it, or didn't he? I had wondered and so desperately, wanted to know! They were crying out loud and hysterically, that they now roared with great gratitude—so loudly within their hearts but outwardly! What did that mean? No one was saying anything, they just made a lot of noise.

Immediately, now in ran doctors and nurses in mass—to come to try and discern the situation that was now, so loudly amplified at hand, within the hospital's Children's Long Term Ward. The room had gotten lively and was busy all of a sudden, by people—both medical, patients and visitors! Wow! What was going on? I could not see passed them, the parents especially, were still in the way of Bobby's hospital bed. Did he, make it? Or did he, go to Heaven and they were praising Jesus, for taking him home but were in mourning, at the same time? I wanted to know!

IF I COULD FLOAT ON A CLOUD, WHERE WOULD I GO?

Oh man... I tried to practice patience but really was struggling in that, that's for sure! Oops...

The atmosphere and the growing crowd, was wild! Everyone was so hysterical! I was shocked by the amount of attention that was being drawn to this room! I just had to find out the truth of the situation, but too many people were still, blocking the way—and so, I was unable to find that out, just yet.

Did he wake up? I had asked myself, while with a great anticipation to know, already by now! "Bobby!" I had heard the man and woman suddenly announce out loud! It startled me so, they roared out loud, with humbling cries of, of JOY! And to Papa in Heaven, as they rejoiced and praised Him, resoundingly! Wait, what? Those butterflies had returned! An anticipation so great, had taken over me—it humbled me! I felt like a little child on Christmas morning, wide awake and so excited as an intricately wrapped gift had just been presented to me—now wide eyed and soaking in the curiosity and thrill, of the unknown! That is what I had imagined that it could possibly be like! Wow, wow, wow! I wanted to see Bobby! I wanted to see his face, to be sure.

Crayon Artwork sketch drawing entitled, "Grateful" by Kipper

My heart, just jumped out of my chest! Okay, that was figuratively speaking but it sure felt like it! Ha, ha! My eyes welled up with tears that were ready to begin their impending descent and then, I could hear Papa say to me—as the loving Father that He is, he whispered His breath into their child's ear. Then saying to me, "He made it." I began to sob like a baby but with a moved, humbling joy! He made it! He made it! I cried inside! Sobbing like a tiny child wanting his daddy to pick him up and embrace him so tightly... I imagined myself kneel down to the ground and then falling forward with a great humbling surrender, to Papa—I pictured laying my arms and head down on the floor and praised Him, over and over!

The parents and others had cleared just then, in a slow motion-like view now—as I began now, to manage to catch a glimpse of Bobby laying in his hospital bed and saw that his eyes had actually opened! He was even crying too! With heavy eyelids, red and puffy eyes and tears streaming steadily down his cheeks, I could tell that he was still, very happy to have returned! He got to return to his Momma and Pa. What a miracle! His tearful joy was heartfelt to say the least and it was incredibly overwhelming for sure! I could see him looking up at his parents, trying to smile but while sobbing, at the same time, just as they were too.

Everything around me—the movement, the mixed emotional commotion, it was now in slow motion as I watched people interact with Bobby—the doctors giving him a high five, the nurses were even choked up and smiling, while some even were hugging Bobby's Momma from the side, with a congratulating excitement for them all. Wow...just wow...

The parents continued talking to their son and thanking the staff and Papa—especially Papa... "My Bobby...our boy—praise the Lord! Thank you so much everyone, for everything—for all of your constant prayers and support! Thank you! Thank God, you are back, Bobby!" Expressed, Bobby's parents. They were so overwhelmed with such emotion, through all of the sniffling, the sobbing and the tears—the pleading and the desperate praying and begging for a miracle...but at last, Bobby had returned to his parents and had awoken.

Bobby's parents had both tightly embraced their son in their arms, where he lay there, looking up at them with tears of a new, yearning and hopeful love. They continued to talk to him and encouraged their son, again and again. "You're awake! Thank you God! Th-Thank you s-so mu-ch for waking up our boy, th-thank you!" His parents had locked sight on the One whom saved their son, from an early death yet, even in their own hearts, they now knew that their son needed Jesus—that they all did. They were so grateful. "We missed you s-so m-much, Bobby! We love you s-so, so much baby! Th-thank you God…thank God that you are awake!" They cried out loud! Bobby's eyes had opened! He made it! Amazing! Our God, is an awesome God! He is a good, good Father!

Papa told me just now that previous to this visit, the man and woman, were not believers at all—not at all! In fact, they didn't want a thing to do with God, before this. Yet, all along the way, in all of the parent's suffering and anger, and frustrations that they had endured, as they hungered for this God whom people had claimed to perform miracles—they just demanded for Him to please come and just save their son, right now, promptly and to just do it!

After what had seemed like an eternity of time passing by, and the parents despising on and off in the appearances by very religious, preachy people who claimed to be Christians or Christ-followers but just ended up being very skeptical of them—as those people tended to fall back on 'the ways of the world' beliefs anyway, failing to actually, live the life and walk the talk. Such people would basically come right up to them, telling them what they did wrong in a past lifetime, or claimed that it was a family curse that had passed down through the generations, to their son—as if this was something they should accept. Well, all of that was ridiculous, it was nonsense. All they really needed, was Jesus. Period!

Some, had even tried to convince the parents that they needed to be delivered by the casting out of demons—or some rubbish nonsense, like that…. They just couldn't stop, in the 'verbal hitting them over the head' approach, what with all of their different versions of the bible in scripture nowadays and the many split denominations of God's children across the globe, by only believing and using certain parts of scripture and then completely overlooking, even denying other parts. That is a dangerous business to be doing! If the bible is the Word of God, then, it should ALL be true and be taken very seriously and read as a whole, not in pieces for one's own personal agenda, or evil-led gain. Should it not? That's what Papa has told me any how, and I don't think that He would ever lie. Now that would just be completely foolish, to ever think that He would! Ha, ha! Fortunately, God is bigger and none of that phases even Him.

Anyway, the couple were practically hammered in condemnation from one denomination to another—being told that they were just not "performing" up to God's standards yet, not "earning" His righteousness and blessings, or anything that they supposedly by God, felt led by. It sure sounded more like they believed more in 'the demonic ways of the world' and not really believed in God at all. The list went on…it drove the man and woman as far away from wanting a thing to do with God, or so-called Christians and any other labeled types out there and their pushy religions. Christianity is not a religion, it is a lifestyle. Just ask Him. If you are listening to Him without your own expectations, then you will hear Him. I will pray for them, for Papa to make Himself known to them and open their eyes up, to His truth one day.

In all honesty, the 'help' that those people—God Bless them anyway—that they had pushed on them, thinking that they were doing their religious duty and pounding their religious nails into the man and the woman's hands and feet, in their attempts in order to try and 'help the man and woman, get closer to God,' …who were they kidding? Well, it was just not helping, plain and simple.

All they did was literally, make it even worse and so much harder on the man and woman, during their distress and sensitive time of need. What good was that? I do not think that was pleasing to Papa either, in the least bit. But thankfully, Papa is so much bigger than even that and He will and always makes good out of any bad situation, when we choose to believe and let Him take it out of our hands and onward into His. He is amazing!

Religion is not Christianity, it is so much different, than that and I would never want to be religious ever again. Unfortunately, many people, even churches will behave religiously, making it about the building, the money, the 'To Do List, To Be Good', that they forget the very purpose that they are even there. People need Jesus. We cannot even say that enough. Times are getting tougher and people are dying, whom could have had a chance to enter Heaven and live, instead. What are we doing, my friends? One of my favourite songs that I have had for some time now says, "They will know that we are Christians, by our love". People need to know that they are loved and that Jesus loves them so much more that He died, for them too.

I am a believer and I believe that Jesus died for me and loves me, so much—that is why He did, what He has done. That is the most important thing that anyone could ever tell someone—is that, not amazing? There is no 'ritual' nor list that you must do, to earn a thing. Just tell them about the true gospel, in what Jesus did. It is just, so simple! That makes me smile, every time! I even weep over it. Just thinking about "Papa LOVES US SO MUCH, that He gave His only Son, to take our place on the cross and die, so that we may live—it is really, a beautiful story…but many, even church-goers, and Christian-claimed people, don't even seem to get it, nor understand it—let alone accept, that it has been, finished.

As for the man and woman, they couldn't possibly feel loved by such people, because they did not know the truth. Papa's truth that He Loves unconditionally—not the way that mankind, 'love'. Being preached to by others, it only just made them feel worse, sadly. But it was only until one day, when there was someone very different, than the many, very religious people out there, who showed such character and truly lived with belief in all that he did or said.

In fact, this person was not at all giving off that persona which many religious people do, even though most of them, don't even realize that they do it and by what and how they do, what they do—their actions are often spoken louder than their words and rejected for condemnation, instead of being interpreted as encouragement. This, well, I'm sorry to say but it literally just ends up pushing away non-believers, and even struggling believers—further away, from a desired relationship with God, which God ultimately wants, with everyone.

This person was not religious-looking, at all. It was a man whom wasn't even trimmed up like a businessman-looking, suited up, buttoned up, pristinely ironed dress-shirt and tie, oh and those polished shiny shoes—a stiff church-goer, you know the type…you can find them every Saturday or Sunday, following their specific denomination church service, at restaurants or in the grocery store—dressed to impress but not smiling hardly at all, if at all, looking just so condemned and unhappy… I feel for them, and so I pray for them too, to know Jesus for whom He really is. The church is not a building, it is the people. The Holy Spirit came, to move into and within our hearts, through us and actually, LIVE. I am so grateful, that being able to praise God, is not defined within confined walls. We can praise Him, anywhere! Hallelujah! Ha, ha!

As for this mysterious man—well, he had on a Christians lifestyle themed t-shirt, with a lion head on it. It definitely looked like nothing fancy nor business-like at all—and he was also wearing what looked like to be, comfortable-looking blue jeans. He was pretty chill, cool like but so friendly and like an average joe that you could feel comfortable to approach. He was laid back, walking in a relaxed, non-arrogant sort of way.

Oh but another interesting characteristic about him, was his hair! He reminded me of a lion, the lion picture that was on his short sleeved t-shirt, that he had on. He had this really long ponytail but it was no ordinary ponytail, it got noticed! Ha, ha! His ponytail had very long, blond with brown roots, mixed-coloured dreadlocks. Yes, dreadlocks! He at first seemed intimidating but when he approached you or walked on by, he would turn to say hey man, Jesus loves you! Smiling as he continued on. He didn't even behave like, nor speak like those religious folk, which had to others, especially towards the man and woman. Some people only know how to talk the talk but many don't yet know how to even, walk the walk AND in faith. Yikes, what a scary place to be in life...

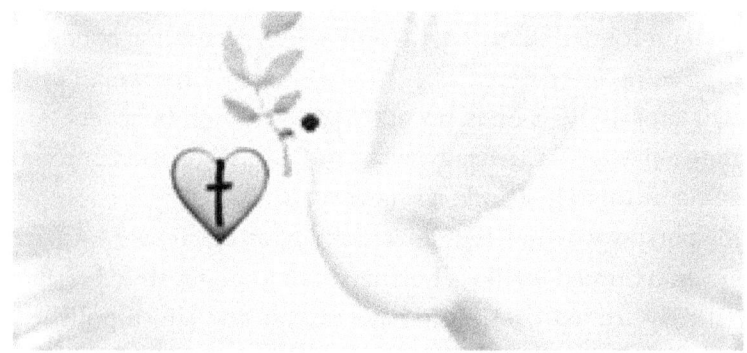

Pencil Artwork drawing of what Peaceful Hope looks like to Kipper entitled, "Peace" by Kipper

As a matter of fact, he was so kind and polite and fortunately, for the distressed man and woman in their faithless, time of need—this man had approached them that very day. In fact, it was on the day, just before they had entered the hospital, when they had arrived in the parking lot, to visit their son.

They had noticed this man and saw that he was certainly not like your typical, average looking joe. Anywhere and everywhere that he went, he got noticed—at first in a judging way but by the way he approached others and in the way he would speak, it often blew socks off. Figuratively speaking, well of course! Ha, ha! Anyhow, it was in what and how he said it—this kindness and generosity, was greatly received, by many who had encountered this man.

Remember, while keeping in mind that he had these long dreadlocks, tied up like a ponytail and wore blue jeans, with a t-shirt that said Christian on it—a very intriguing and eye-catching combo! Ha, ha! It sounded amazing! He would always, quickly catch people's eye.

Another thing to keep in mind was that he most likely got easily misjudged by his appearance and ensemble—in how he dressed and his choice of hairstyle—possibly even misjudged, as someone you don't want to approach? We are human and we have the tendency to mistakenly judge a book by its cover, before ever actually, reading the story first. Many people pre-judge others before they even meet people, that they sometimes don't even get to know the person for whom they are, at all. Which is really quite sad… They miss out, often ending up then, unfortunately robbing themselves blind, from getting to know who they really are—with all judgements removed. Sadly, it is a very rare opportunity, indeed.

The strange looking man, well he was just so kind and compassionate about both his love for God and God's love for him, and especially for everyone else in whom God has created on earth. That means you too! God sure is amazing, to have to be as patient with us humans, ha, ha!

As this interesting character, walked among the public, he witnessed his life's testimony of hardship and how God's Grace had saved his life—getting emotional every time. He would always make the point to ask others, if he could pray on them—complete strangers, while sharing God's love for them, faithfully. Wow, I had thought. God was doing something really amazing through this man's life. I asked Papa, to tell me more of this story.... It was like a good book that I could not put down. Ha, ha!

This man worked his job, God's work, with strangers on the street—even going to restaurants to eat a meal, he spoke to waitresses and waiters/servers, managers and to customers. He would always pay back tenfold in tips, giving money to anyone God told him whom had needed it and never tipping less, than the full bill's value. Wow...

Pencil Artwork drawing of many lit candles entitled, "Be The Light Of The World!" by Kipper

He would go to any kind of store, going about his business you know, doing some normal shopping, or to the grocery store, in malls, at clothing and footwear outlets, at markets or gatherings, on the street etc, you name it. He would get a word from Papa about someone and he would then go up to them—not in a judging way but only sharing from Papa's love. People need to hear that God, loves them and why. They don't need to be judged by man, condemned, nor preached to about what they did wrong, or should be doing. The denominational churches have got some of that wrong. We all share a commonality and that is Jesus! So, just share Jesus with others and with one another, and you will see miracles happen! I have!

Papa says that Christians have a mission to do—to stand up for what we believe and show the world Him because Papa wants a relationship with each and every person, on this planet. Fellow sisters and brothers, where are you? Lend me your ears, ha, ha, no, no please do not toss me your ears—that would be just nasty! Ha, ha, ha! Okay, okay, back to the matter—it is true, that people are dying and going to hell but because many of them, did not even know of the Gospel which they could have, then been saved and given the gift to go to Heaven instead…do you believe in Jesus? If not, no worries, you are welcome into Papa's growing family! The more the merrier! All you have to do, is believe what Jesus did for you, that He died for your sins and then ask for Him, to live inside of your heart. That's it! Ha, ha! Pretty simple, huh? As for those whom are already saved and are actually, sharing God's love without judgement—to actually be doing it daily, both in public and at home, I am so excited and happy for you! Great Work! It really is so rewarding!

I mean, there is someone standing or sitting right next to you, or near you right now, who wants to know if they are loved and not alone. It's okay, go ahead and take a look around you. The Fatherless whom are among us, have been deeply hurt, growing up one way or another. Some have unhealthy life-altering 'addictions' that are used intentionally, to numb their pain—to try to avoid the hurt that is inside. They need to know, that they do not have to, any longer because God already did that for us at the cross and said that it was, finished! He loves all! Is it not yet time, to give back? I know that I cannot go do all of the mobile stuff that I had mentioned but oh wow, I can just imagine it… But in my dreams, I most certainly do. I'm just trying to understand it myself. This is all very new to me, as well. I don't think that anyone has perfected anything until they have gone home. Wouldn't you agree? We have much learning yet to do.

I am wondering, that if speaking to people on the street, or at the grocery till, to strangers, who don't even know that they are loved by God or why or even to a neighbour—it sure sounds mind blowing, doesn't it? Yeah, I know, right? Imagine, if every believer actually chose to, actively believe—especially when they prayed. To every believer, what have we to lose anyway, by giving? And on the other hand, what do they have to gain? Well, to gain, would be nothing short of God's love and to be transformed and grow in this life. Deep thoughts, I know…

Here ye, here ye, Lady and Sir Warrior Knights, both of brand new and the ancients, in whom are filled with the Holy Spirit—speaking in the Spirit, as the Word of God has commanded. Now, I seek you out, I span the globe in search of His hidden Warriors—both, from within the deepest of the deep of waters, through the farthest and most treacherous wooded of the woods—to the utmost of barren, hot and dry of the desert lands, and from the many dying villages, to the vastly growing cities from all around the world! Dear Christian Soldiers, I call upon you now. I plea the song of the Father's undying and most lovingly, patient heart! Join the great cause! Come as you are!

The enemy continues to snare our brethren from eternity, let us throw off his scheming plans and actively pursue, our unsaved family! Believers, believe with me and unite in Jesus' Name! Be strong in the Lord, my friends, my sisters and my brothers! To His many peoples of the many nations, He who lives in you, we are called upon, as the time is now! Oh dear family—to go out and into the world, we must—be His light and save the unbelief! So, let us as one, while believing in the One and rise up, from out of the masked darkness and into the great Light. Come, dear ol' souls and BELIEVE!

To the inactively, timidly Christ-like living people out there—all I ask of you, is this…why, are we so afraid, to be who we have been called upon, to become? No matter where anyone is, nor what anyone has done—all that the people of this battered, enemy's war-torn, fallen world needs, is that they just need Jesus. That's it! Go, now and tell them! Tell them, so that they may know the truth, teach them why and Papa will show them in and through their own lives. Share Papa's love and watch their eyes light up, their hearts grow, and their lives will change, forever. Hallelujah! So excited! Be brave, dear sisters and brothers, be brave and stand in the Father, through the Son and with His Holy Spirit! Put on the full armour of God and stand firm!

Back to this crazy looking, yet gentle soul of a man. He was just so, genuinely kind and always smiling from his heart through his posture and attitude for life, towards complete strangers and yet, going out of his way, just to tell them, the truth that, "Hey Miss, or Man, Jesus loves you… God Bless you, man. No really, God Bless you!" Even asking them, if he could pray for their family members or on them if they had any sort of

IF I COULD FLOAT ON A CLOUD, WHERE WOULD I GO?

ailment or bodily disfigurement. And get this, limbs would grow, backs would straighten, pains would be of no more because of Jesus' Name! AMAZING! "Hey, can I pray for you?...God Bless you..." And for many people, they would respond surprised and many would want it. Wow! God Bless that man and everyone whom lives on this planet!

He even helped random strangers at a food counter, offering to pay for their food and does actually pay for them. That, is from Papa's heart! Amazing! He even shared his money, claiming it's not his money, that God provides it for him so that he can share it and pay it forward for someone else in need. Amazing! He also helped clothe, an entire family, who were not even saved and were struggling in life, both financially and with 'addictions'. I say it like that because there's actually no such thing as, an addiction. No really, I mean what I say. There is choice, remember? Free-will…

We have the power to choose between good versus evil. To say Yes or to say No. An addiction is just another word for 'excuse' simply put… in choosing not to change it. So, you see, there are no addictions, only choices in life and we must learn to wield the power of 'yes' and of the power of 'no'. Even if you think your life is too chaotic and too busy for this or for that. That is another excuse! Ha, ha! Just say, 'no' then and change it. Life is short, my friend. Might as well make the most of it while it lasts, and enjoy every moment of God's many blessings!

Crayon Artwork sketch drawing entitled, "Free-will" by Kipper

There was this young boy who was close to my age, who had asked for this man to pray for his eyes—he was legally blind and couldn't read anything, without his special glasses and instantly this boy could see! It was a miracle! He was blind and now he can see! That is powerful! Wow! How can one, stand there and honestly try to deny, the power and love of God, when they witness, that? Ha, ha! Total, awesomeness! Ha, ha!

Then, if that's not cool enough, the young boy tells many others shortly after, in a clothing department store of his testimony of what had happened to him and even they could not deny such a miracle that they too, chose to become saved and this was just one child, whom touched by the hands of God and by witnessing God's goodness and loving grace to others, helped save others. Wow! I wanted to know more, I asked for more of this story, for it soothed and energized me! I just was riveted with excitement and suspense, every time a good story was being told! Ha, ha!

These people, were transformed by the renewing of their minds and by seeing the truth of God's genuine and unconditional love for them, in wanting to heal them too—wanting to save them from a very unforgiving and unloving hell and to provide for them, as the loving Father that, HE IS! So cool! Wow…

I overheard the nurses chatting about a real life story. "There was this little girl, about six years old. She had bright red curly hair and bright green eyes. She use to walk down the hallways of the hospital." The nurse was talking about it one day. She continued. "During a car crash that the little girl was in, she was not even, the least bit afraid! The little girl had talked about a Man, a white and rainbow glowing Man, holding her in His arms, as the car rolled over and over and over. Her parents were not believers, they actually did not want to believe in Jesus and so they sadly had perished in the crash. But the little girl whom sat buckled in the back seat, she was being held by the very arms of God! They said that when the ambulance had her with them on the way to the hospital, she kept repeating, "Jesus was with me, Jesus was with me. He saved me. The Man was holding me in the car."

One of the paramedics was an atheist, whom was completely against the belief of the very God whom had made him. He kept denying her claim and ordered for the Psychological Ward, to take her in and keep her until they got her well. What a misconception and sad truth! The poor little girl, hadn't a single human person left in her life, to stand up for her. She spent years in the Psych Ward, loaded on doctor ordered drugs and was repeatedly, refused departure because she would not recant what had happened to her, on that day of the car crash. She refused to deny what had happened to her and whom had saved her. For years, every single day, in her tiny little padded white room, she continued daily for years, singing "Jesus, loves me this I know..." She would even be caught, talking to a corner of the room, or as if someone was sitting next to her, on the tiny bed where she had been restrained, daily. She however, did not give up on Jesus, because Jesus did not give up on her. She died while living in there...that was fourteen years ago... she would have been about twenty years old, exactly on that very day, fourteen years ago since her car crash." The nurse had stated and paused for a bit.

"And get this" The nurse then added. "Her name was, Faith. So, whatever that Man had told her, whom she claimed had stayed with her, during the car crash... And seriously, there is no logical possible way, that she could have otherwise, survived it on her own! I think that she really was, telling the truth. Jesus really did, save her life that day, and helped her keep her faith, strong, for fourteen years straight! Wow, just imagine! She even lived up to her name. But get this, the paramedic whom was an atheist and had ordered for her to be sent to the loony bin ward, following her car crash...he just recanted his own faith and turned to Jesus, the day that young girl had passed away! It took him, fourteen years, before he could see the truth but through that child's faith—a faith, he had never known before, until now. Wow! Just amazing... He had even attended her funeral, and months later, created a Faith Charity Fund, for disaster caused orphaned children, due to car crashes or disasters of any kind—in honour of her life. Wow..." The nurses had finished and went about their tasks.

I wonder how many more people, God used this situation and made good out of it, saving more lives, in the long run? Wow, just amazing... I had thought to myself. What a sad story, that's for sure! But I was so thankful to hear that she always had Jesus by her side throughout it, even though the world was harsh—she never gave up on her faith in Him. Good for her! I felt so emotional but also, I was so very proud of her. I wonder, just how many people, have been held against their will in such places, when it turned out to be that the enemy was just withholding them because of their faith? Makes you wonder, huh?

I hear of horrible stories that are happening even now, across the world—stories of evil actively trying to take down true believers for their faith, in trying to instil fear into their hearts, so sadly, some then renounce their faith from out of fear...but many thankfully refuse and continue to hold fast and prove their faith true—some unfortunately even are then killed, even publicly. But they are with the Lord now, and I thank Him every time that I wake and know that He has me, no matter what happens to this body of mine, while still here in the land of the fallen. If we have Jesus in our hearts, nothing can take that away from us. Our body is just a shell, that will be replaced by a perfect one, when it is our time to go home to the Father. We have not a thing to fear, not even fear itself. God is bigger.

These are hard times and it is of utmost importance, by choice, that we unite as one in the Spirit, to be the Light in this messed up world and to help save, as many of God's unsaved children in this world, as possible—of all ages, from zero, to one-thousand years old! The time, is now.

For even to think of that little girl, whom had been saved by Jesus but tormented by the evil enemy's lies, through his evil ways in the world, by using unbelievers—it is truly a miracle and a gift of faith from God, that she felt Jesus' love and His protection, fully—how could she not help but call out His name with joy, even in hard times? She learned to praise Him in the storms and at such an early age! Wow! Is that not what we are to do, when we are weak and He is strong? It was beautiful, just beautiful... actually, it was beyond awesome! Emerging as the Light, like a submarine ascends up from the deep and breaks through that water's surface, with a mighty roar—I too, want to break through like a mighty roaring child of Papa! Ha, ha! I am learning and Papa told me, "Fear not of death—for you already know, as believers—of where you shall go live, with Me in Heaven." So I say unto you, dear friends out there! Stand firm and don't look back—keep the faith and steady yourself and hold, your, position, in Jesus' Name!

That awesome guy with the interesting dreadlocks that I had mentioned earlier on, he would ask if others were believers and if they were not, he would just say, "Cool, that's okay. Can I pray for you?" Or Papa would tell him of some pain that they were having and so he would ask that person about it, always blowing their mind, of how could he know and so on. They would be in shock and wonder if he was just kidding around or could read their mind, ha, ha—but he would just be honest and say no, God was telling him about it just now, and pointed it out that He wants to heal them. He explained that is why God had revealed it to this man, so that he could share about it with those people... He would then ask that person, if he could pray for them and they would either agree or disagree but he never gave up, asking if he could just pray for them—many finally would agree and then through the power of Jesus' Name, they were healed, even giving their life to Jesus! Absolutely amazing! God is a good, good Father!

Can I tell you that Jesus loves you, too? Jesus loves you. I smile every time I say that, because I believe it, too. Christianity is to live a Christ-like life—it is a lifestyle which means that everything we do and everything that we say or even think, We must do it unto the Lord, and not unto people, whether of word or deed.

Papa had then whispered into this man's heart to speak to the man and woman, whom had just gotten out of their car, in the hospital parking lot. He had received a message from Papa's Spirit and became driven in love, to deliver on Papa's behalf. He was not even a believer for something like more than fifteen years and he didn't believe in God, nor even want to have anything to do with Religion or Christians or church—none of it but then Papa saved his life and he went through a miraculous transformation, in everything in his life and chose to believe! Now he spends his days just loving on people and sharing his testimony and God's love and why he now truly believes in Jesus—and in the hope, to help others too.

One just needs a little extra patience and a boat load of genuine encouragement, from a caring source, from time to time. You know? I felt so happy for Bobby—for his family. I began to choke up and get so emotional myself, crying and sniffling like a baby, but to myself, as quietly as I possibly could. Ha, ha...

It was just so amazing and to have witnessed it, wow... Thinking about everything, I then realized something...that, had I not spoken to Bobby, encouraging him to try—had his mother not uncovered the window, unknowingly giving me the chance, from out of her prayer to Papa that was answered about their family's torn situation, to turn around for their son... Wow, what an emotional mouthful! To have such an opportunity, to make a difference in Bobby's life—perhaps even his spiritual-self, in possibly speaking to his spirit...Just wow...would, any of this, have happened? Mind blowing, I know! Right? Everything happens for a reason.

I had then thanked Papa, deeply from within my whole heart—whispering, "Thank you" as I pressed my eyelids tightly, closing them for a moment, with folded hands. Amazingly, everything had fallen into place! Now that, was a miracle. Bobby had cried his leap of faith—his parents became believers and too cried their leap of faith, giving the control to Papa to take a hold of their son's own life and with all of the support around him, in refusing to give up on him, or on God—Papa answered. ...I guess God really does answer prayers in this place, too. Now that—was something to smile about.

"I am the Way, the Truth and the Life, no one comes through me except through the Father." —John 14:6

"For I know the plans I have for you." Declares the Lord. "Plans to prosper you and not to harm you, plans to give you hope and a future." —Jeremiah 29:11

But just as He who called you is holy, so be holy in all that you do; for it is written: "Be holy, because I am holy." — 1 Peter 1:15-16

"Dear friends, let us purify ourselves from everything that contaminates body and spirit, perfecting holiness out of reverence for God." — 2 Corinthians 7:1

"Don't let anyone look down on you because you are young, but set an example for the believers in speech, in conduct, in love, in faith and in purity." — 1 Timothy 4:12

"How can a young person stay on the path of purity? By living according to your word." — Psalm 119:9

IF I COULD FLOAT ON A CLOUD, WHERE WOULD I GO?

"Therefore, I urge you, brothers and sisters, in view of God's mercy. To offer your bodies as a living sacrifice, holy and pleasing to God—this is your true and proper worship." — Romans 12:1

"Make every effort to live in peace with everyone and to be holy. Without holiness no one will see the Lord." — Hebrews 12:13

"You are to be holy to me because I, the Lord, am holy, and I have set you apart from the nations to be my own." — Leviticus 20:26

"But now that you have been set free from sin and have become slaves of God, the benefit you reap leads to holiness and the result is eternal life." — Romans 6:22

"Religion that God accepts as pure and faultless is this: to look after orphans and widows in their distress and to keep oneself from being polluted by the world." — James 1:27

"He has saved us and called us to a holy life—not because of anything we have done but because of His own purpose and grace. This grace was given us in Christ Jesus before the beginning of time." — 2 Timothy 1:9

"Therefore there is now no condemnation for those who are in Christ Jesus, for the law of the Spirit of life in Christ Jesus has set you free from the law of sin and death." — Romans 8:1-2

"We who are strong ought to bear with the failings of the weak and not to please ourselves."
— Romans 15:1

"Do not conform to the pattern of this world, but be transformed by the renewing of your mind. Then you will be able to test and approve what God's will is—His good, pleasing and perfect will." — Romans12:2

~So that you will know what is and what is not, the Will of God, and live in His Kingdom.~

Pencil Artwork drawing of Hope's Violin Talent, at her beauty pageants entitled, "Gifted" by Kipper

CHAPTER SEVEN

PAPA'S FORGED LAMB OR INFERNO'S PUPPET

Have you ever dreamt about becoming more than just, another one of 'society's involuntary robotic zombie workers' whom just, live to work for their entire lives—instead, to actually go beyond that overwhelming, stressed-out mechanized, way of life? I mean, to become like a real, Light of the World Christian Warrior, spinning around with your fiery sword of the Spirit, battling and slaying the shadowed demon enemy's henchman, from all clever Shotokan moves, or Muay Thai combative ways and directions and while remaining still as Papa's forged lambs, allowing for your King, to yet again, answer the door on your behalf while you choose to kneel and await on His command.

Meanwhile, you're trying to avoid losing yet another, spiritual jab from the enemy but this time, it is Inferno using another one of his puppets through flesh and blood, by some guy who calls you 'Buddy' whom gains all that he deceptively desires for himself and uses you for his wicked ways but he or she ends up turning out to be, just that, another relentless user—as they really just were not your friend at all and they stab you in the back—taking advantage of your kindness, yet again—then tells you, "It's nothing personal, it's just business..." Yikes! Ouch, now that bites!

These days, I would especially be careful in whom you confide in, if they never actually go out of their way personally, to show care and encouraging support for you or others and literally don't behave and act on, in having your back on things in life—even making time for you, regardless of their schedule—then I would stay away, "Runnn buddyyy, runnn!" Oh boy! But hey, you know what is actually, more sad than that? No really, I'm not kidding…remember, it's not nice to always just think about ourselves, even if we feel that we are the one being under attack, by the flaming arrows of the evil one. I still choose to forgive and love them anyway because I just want to be nice and I ask Papa to forgive them, even if they really have hurt me, I know that it wasn't really, them trying to do it at all. Remember, puppets of the inferno's claws, are not even aware that they are his puppet. You cannot give what you do not have. Nor, can you teach what you do not know. And if they do not have the ability with unfiltered, ears and eyes to interpret your message of help, to shape them up and teach them what they need to know and what they need to see and hear—then it does not matter how many times that you wish, to hammer such reasoning into their heads—they cannot hear nor see you, as you are, for as long as they are still under their evil master's spear…they are fear controlled, rather than love enlisted. For they know not, what they do…. Who knows, you could be the only person in that fella's or gal's life in the flesh, who cared enough to do that for them, even if they ended up turning on you at some point down the road. And if you ever prayed for them, that too, you could possibly have been the only one in their life, whom even cared to do the right thing. May God Bless, them anyway.

Papa, please forgive them, for they know not what they do. That's just the way it is sadly but everyone needs to know that when Papa said everything was finished and all is forgiven, it means, ALL. We all make mistakes but the difference is, do we want to learn from them and of the source behind them and its motive—or do we just toss it to the wind and behave badly, whenever we decide to accept the enemy's lying thoughts that which he will relentlessly feed our minds of such lies, about anything and everything? I sure don't want to listen to him, he's depressing.

Free-will means, Papa is a gentleman and allows choice. That is amazing. I know the enemy does not want to offer any choice, other than only in what he wants, in the causing of endless chaos and destruction—throat jamming his ways onto, everyone. That is not loving. Only Papa, is love. The enemy only cares about himself and what he wants—he does not know love, only lust, hate, lying, anger, doubt, betrayal, greed, envy, jealousy, fear, selfishness, pride, regret, worry, mistrust and anything that is the yucky, and oh yeah you bet I am going to say the word, the negative thoughts. For none of these, come from the Father—surely, you must know this by now?

I choose Papa because Papa first chose me—He knew me and all that I would do, good and bad, before He even made me and yet, He still made me. I feel loved! Ha, ha! That makes me smile and touches my heart more than a big chocolate candy bar treat, or a yummy ice cream sundae, with hot fudge, dripping down the sides of it…yummm! Ha, ha! Makes me hungry just thinking about it! Ha, ha! Nope, nothing compares to what my Papa and His Son have done for me. Yet, the most amazing and beautiful thing ever—is that He did it for, EVERYONE. Wow, isn't He awesome or what?

Come a little closer, so that I can whisper another truth to you that I have learned, for it may be more shocking than from what it may appear… That fella or gal who had just turned on you like that—well, the battle is not actually against flesh and blood… It's in the bible, so it's not actually a secret but the enemy wants to keep it hidden from you. The real sad part is that those people, whom seem to have the 'knack at stabbing backs', and I say this with a heavy heart actually, but for them—the enemy uses them like a puppet. Is that not sad? Consider them, the next time that you decide to kneel and pray, for God loves them too.

Many people, end up treating this life like this is all that there is and so they only live for this life and sadly, they really just don't care much about what good or bad things that they do, let alone actually realizing that what really matters, is knowing where you are going once this, 'temporary camping trip' is done and then it is time to go to the eternal home of our prior choosing…where that home will end up being however—will depend upon whether the individual wants an eternal life in Papa's Kingdom or an eternal death in a not so nice of a place, called hell…

And what is even more shocking, is that all it comes down to, is so simple and easily accessible to everyone in this world, by either choosing to believe in God and accepting His Son into their heart, or not. That is how simple it is and yet, many don't even realize this! I just think that is mind bottling, for even a kid to know about. Adults tend to make a lot of things very complicated, when it just doesn't have to be.

Okay so I have repeated myself a few times, but it is only just to try and convey to you, just how simple of an opportunity that it is, for you to become, so much more in this world and it only takes a few words from the heart. Reminding ourselves that it is not about what 'we have done' or about what 'we do' …**it is about what Jesus has already, done**. You can read it in the bible if you want to learn about it. It is really, very interesting and it changed my life and look at me, I am stuck in this hospital bed, until I get to go home but until then, even I have to try and make the most of it—from this hospital bed. Ha, ha! A task not so easily done by a scrawny, sick kid like me. This hospital bed may be my "physical prison" by the enemy, but my imagination and my faith, which Papa created and has given me, is my escape, my calm and my rest …and for that, I am grateful.

Or what about time travel? What if, you could go back in time, selectively altering your future that suits only you—meaning that you cannot select for others, nor of their outcome but as you manipulated the space time continuum, for your own personal gain—it simultaneously changes the people, their looks, how they communicate, like for example, through their nose instead of their mouth?

Say they happen to have knees that bent backwards instead, so that they could jump and hop really, really fast—like a grasshopper! Or their eye colours alter, so their black pupil becomes their iris eye for the colour and the pupil is now a shimmering candy apple red, or emerald green, or a pinky-purple fuchsia, or even an iron grey, in colour? And the clear cornea would actually be reflective and create a holographic sort of appearance, when they made eye contact with you—now able to scan things and people, just by a single blink of an eye! Weird huh! Ha, ha! Hey, you never know! Ha, ha!

Imagine the colour of the ocean then went from the blues and greens to a blackened colour with an almost gel-like texture but could also be more of a putty sort of thing—being no more of a transparency but also that its buoyancy took on an altered sort of gravity, that would actually cause you, to bounce! Woohoo! Ha, ha! What if, all of your personal self-seeking, life alterations had ended up affecting, literally everything and everyone all around you—would you still do it? Would your curiosity, get the better of you and get out of hand? I would have to say that is most likely what would

IF I COULD FLOAT ON A CLOUD, WHERE WOULD I GO?

happen because since we are just human and the evil enemy is always scheming, to try and ruin our day—it is pretty darn easy, to know that we would not have much control either way, now would we? Or would we?

What if, your current location, had mirrored itself randomly, filling the entire city, repeating itself every couple blocks, making it literally really difficult, to find your way through its mirrored maze mayhem? Even the wildlife then would have to live in reverse to each other, meaning that what use to crawl, now flew, and what use to swim, now slithered, to what use to fly, now then walked and what use to walk, could now swim, with its much needed fins and everything! Wouldn't that be weird! Yet, if we were born into a world such as that, we wouldn't know any other way, right? We conform to our circumstances, so easily when we begin like so. But change, now that has shown proof that mankind, truly has a great difficulty to accept and make the most of it, regardless. We complain, far too much. Even in the bible, it says not to complain… hmm… interesting…. So then, complaining then originates straight from the evil enemies' lying thoughts and we as humans, have come to accept it as, 'normal' …very interesting indeed…

My point is this…just because we are born into what we have or are now whatever it is that we are, have you ever thought about the possibility, that it was faulty to begin with? Like how man had fallen since Adam and Eve, that story—well, it is true. We were born from out of a fallen world, yet we behave like 'the way of the world' as an 'acceptable' chosen behaviour and thus, we fail to break away from that and become who we truly were always meant to be, with our God-given purpose, our destinies! Would you not, like to find out whom, you could be? I sure do!

It is at least, something to think about for sure, I know that Papa has much bigger plans for each and every one of you and for me but the enemy, the evil one and his many lies, have had it in for us from the beginning of time—trying to always force feed us to eat the forbidden fruit, figuratively speaking—each and every day, twenty-four-seven, around the clock! If you have not questioned why you do certain things and then get unpleasant results that you wouldn't wish on your own children to do or behave like—do you think that just maybe, it is time to switch it up for the betterment of all others as well and not just for yourself? To be able to realize that life, it is not about us who must try to be the hero in this world—someone already came and did that for us, remember? Jesus' sacrifice was, perfect. We just keep getting in the way, with this 'way of the world's' evil ways. God is writing your story, may we ought to give back His pen?

"Let no corrupting talk come out of your mouths, but only such is good for building up, as fits the occasion, that it may give grace to those who hear." — *Ephesians 4:29*

"These are grumblers, malcontents, following their own sinful desires; they are loud-mouthed boasters, showing favouritism to gain advantage." —*Jude 1:16*

"Do al things without grumbling or questioning, that you may be blameless and innocent, children of God without blemish in the midst of a crooked and twisted generation, among whom you shine as lights in the world, holding fast to the word of life, so that in the day of Christ I may be proud that I did not run in vain or labor in vain." — *Philippians 2:14-16*

"Therefore if any man be in Christ, he is a new creation; the old things pass away. Behold, all things have become new." — *2 Corinthians 5:17*

"Now that I am speaking of being in need, for I have learned in whatever situation I am to be content. I know how to be brought low, and I know how to abound. In any and every circumstance, I have learned the secret of facing plenty and hunger, abundance and need." — *Philippians 4:11-12*

"Keep your life free from love of money, and be content with what you have, for he has said, "I will never leave you nor forsake you." — *Hebrews 13:5*

"What causes quarrels and what causes fights among you? Is it not this, that your passions are at war within you? You desire and do not have, so you murder. You covet and cannot obtain, so you fight and quarrel. You do not have, because you do not ask. You ask and do not receive, because you ask wrongly, to spend it on your passions." —*James4:1-3*

"May the God of hope fill you with all joy and peace in believing, so that by the power of the Holy Spirit you may abound in hope." — *Romans 15:13*

IF I COULD FLOAT ON A CLOUD, WHERE WOULD I GO?

God is Love.

Crayon Artwork sketch drawing entitled, "My Decree" by Kipper

CHAPTER EIGHT

The Greatest Gifts, Money Cannot Buy

I have wondered at times, what it would be like, to be an astronaut from earth. To move about the vast weightlessness, vacuum of space and its frigid temperatures… But then I remembered that when I get to go home, when it is my turn and Papa comes for me—that I will then, forever be able to actually fly. I will soar with the eagles, gliding in and among the mountainous valleys and hills—no longer in need of the clouds beneath me. To float without any restrictions, without any issues, from malfunctions, to unpredictable dangers of the unknown darkness out there—to the heavy suit which would just, slow me down… I will travel far and wide, as time will be of no significance, being able to travel great distances, all within only a moment's notice! To explore the milky way, to the many far off constellations and galaxies, not yet discovered by man—to dance with each of the northern and southern lights around earth's atmosphere, while in unison to the songs of Papa's amazing grace of His ever so kind, wondrous nature…

You know, it's funny how I had not even imagined that, about being an astronaut, when I was younger until lately, while in taking up such an interest, in going above the clouds and dreaming beyond, into the stars. Just imagine, what would it be like to go, even higher but beyond all of our own, understanding? To truly seek, the beyond and to be able to go there? I'm so excited! Oh, what will it be like, I had wondered to myself…

IF I COULD FLOAT ON A CLOUD, WHERE WOULD I GO?

"Kipper.... Kipper.... You have a visitor." I shook out of my daydreaming daze, opening my eyes and then rubbing my eyeballs a little, trying to wipe the sleepiness away. Then I looked to see who was calling my name. I was still a little out of it, as I had gained very little sleep from the night before this, just from not being able to sleep very well, lately. My sleep patterns have been really all over the place and I don't really know why but I guess if my spirit is unsettled because my heart and my mind are not at rest and feeling at peace, then my body can be greatly affected. My health had taken a further decline as well, taking my energy and slicing it into fractions of what it used to be.

When I began to wake further, I did eventually realize where I was, it had taken me a little time, to get myself sorted out, regardless the time of day. I always knew that I was still in my hospital bed of course and not on one of my cloud adventures, when my energy was sunk—a clear indicator of my reality versus my dreamworld. It was there, where I had an endless about of stamina and vigour. It is funny how when we are 'sleeping', we are not tired and we seem to go, go, go... people do that in the real world too but they eventually burn out or are high on something not cool and bad for their health.

Sometimes when I wake up, I do tend to drift off a bit and daydream, taking me a little longer to pay much attention to the doctors or nurses, whom are performing their daily routines on me. A little groggy and with a mind that is foggy from irregular sleep patterns, or lack there of any pattern at all—I don't really have to worry too much about being that way, as they don't really need for me to have to do a thing. All I can do is just lay there anyway. I am definitely well taken care of, in that regard. I am grateful for that, even if it can be a little or very much of a frustration in my mind—to have to deal with them in having to do, absolutely everything for me, but truthfully, you just get used to it and nothing embarrasses you anymore after a while. I wish I could have some independence in the real world but I guess that is another good reason, why I really enjoy my adventures because I feel free. So, not having it in both worlds, is all right with me...

I sure hope that if you have the privileged ability to be mobile—that you don't waste it, making good use of your much larger range of movement and the places that you could go...wow, I can only imagine, you definitely could do much more than I can, if you are able and choose to try. I won't let myself feel jealous though, that's not right to be that way, for any reason—no matter how much or how little, we think that we have.

A nurse then slowly raised up the top part of my hospital bed for me, just enough so that I could sit up a little more upright, to see forward but without falling forward on my face or out of my hospital bed. Ha, ha! That would be entertainment for ya or a bit of a disaster—just flop over and well, hello there mattress, how's it goin'? As it was then suddenly holding my eyeballs, ha, ha!

I looked to see who came to visit, as I don't always get visitors, whom directly come to visit me. They are usually indirectly, visiting—they first come to see my roommates and then sometimes, not always but the really kind ones do reach out to visit with me, as well, which is really thoughtful of them and we do have good visits too. People like to try and make me laugh and so do I, so it's a fitting match. Ha, ha…

There was a couple, an elderly couple who I recognized, walking over towards my hospital bed… noticing them, once I woke up enough to open my very, very heavy eyelids and see clearly through my once, very foggy sleepy eyeballs. Who would come to visit me, I had wondered? Then I heard their voices as they greeted me. Oh, it was the kind Pastor and his Wife from whom I had met some time ago, who lead that little nondenominational Christian church, whom had talked to that little girl, a long time ago… They were always very kind people and fortunately over time, they had visited me a few times too, when they came in to visit and pray with others. They always made the time to give me a little of theirs, actually. I always felt welcomed and embraced by their presence and for their very generous support, given in prayers.

They came to see me, again? I was really touched and suddenly had a little bit of nervous butterflies fluttering around inside of my stomach, just having a fit and wanting to burst out and say, 'hello' to the world! Ha, ha! I was very happy to see them! I am always so excited to see them come visit me, I love their visits and hearing their stories—they soothed me. Did I mention I was happy to see them, yet? Ha, ha!

"Hello!" I welcomed them with a smile, as they walked up to the side of my hospital bed. "Hello Kipper, how are you doing today?" The man asked me, as I reached my arms out, as best as I could, as I received their hugs. He leaned in and embraced me in his arms, as he said with a gentle kind voice, "God, loves ya Kipper." I smiled with a warmth now radiating through me in hope and contentment. "I am good thank you, how are you?" I replied, as the woman immediately embraced me in her arms too, as I finished asking. "God Bless you" she said to me. "Thank you! God Bless you two, as well." I had replied.

What brings you both to come see me, today?" I asked. They smiled and chuckled a little, as they looked at one another and then back at me to reply. "Well, Kipper, we have something we would like to ask you, if you are interested?" The man asked me. "I awaited eagerly as I smiled with widening eyes. He then continued. "Dear Kipper, you are a precious child of God. He loves you so much, so that we can love you, so much too! We all care about you Kipper. God is our Heavenly Father, whom always loves us, always is with us and protects us. He wants the best for us and it doesn't matter what struggles we go through, or how many times we fall—He is always right there and always looking out for us and loving us no matter what and no matter where we are at, in life. God loves ya." He replied.

I felt starstruck as I sat there, feeling so amazed like a thunderbolt of hopeful energies had begun, blasting through the sky at a thousand miles per second and then all over the room, it sped! I must have looked so silly, as I was smiling so big, from ear to ear that my cheeks actually managed to muster up a little bit of a rosy red colour—they actually began to really blush even more, ha, ha, ha… "Awe, ha, ha, he is blushing…" The woman giggled with delight, as she commented to her husband. As I blushed, my cheeks even started to hurt a bit from the huge, ginormous smiling that I had found myself doing! Ha, ha! I couldn't help it though, ha, ha!

The kind Pastor would often start telling me about some of his adventurous hunting stories that he would have for me, with Papa always a part of his adventures at the heart of them all—they often were so funny that they made me laugh and laugh and smile, just so easily and endlessly! I was comfortable with them. They are awesome people!

To lighten the mood even more, the man would quickly tell me some really funny memories, to make me laugh some more. He was just so funny and so filled with life and of his love for God that I would completely forget that the nurse was even poking and prodding me, during my daily routine...ha, ha, ha, I didn't even notice it! Ha, ha!

Then with a wishful thought, I suddenly blurted out in a jokingly manner, "Maybe you both could be, like my adoptive parents! Like a mom and a dad to me?" I asked them in a sheer excitement child-like voice, as my imagination had clearly taken over! Ha, ha... Yet, to my surprise, they were so excited too! They then both said, "Ha, ha... That's what we wanted to talk to you about! Ha, ha! And Kipper, we would love, to be your adopted parents! We accept your offer!" They replied with pure loving, joyful voices! WOW! Did that just really happen? I was starstruck! Ha, ha! I was at loss for words! They wanted to be my Mom and Dad! I could hardly believe my ears! I, wait, was I dreaming? I pinched myself on my right arm, just to check. "Ouch, ha, ha!" I reacted in bewilderment and real joy! They chuckled at my bounciness of excitement! "YAY! I HAVE PARENTS! I have a MOM and I have a DAD! Yay! THANK YOU!" I bounced up and down for what little that I could, given my lack of mobility of course but nonetheless, I shook myself around a bit, on my hospital bed and I was just so excited, as they hugged me again. I could barely get a word out, I was so speechless! Nothing but a huge smile, from ear to ear, I was! Ha, ha! The Pastor and his wife were so excited as well and laughed with joy, at my reaction and excitement. "Thank you, DAD! Thank you, MOM! Ha, ha!" I thanked them, vibrantly!

Tears began to roll down my one cheek and then the other, I was so overcome and filled with a tearful joy in my heart that I just couldn't help but feel—beyond loved! Just...wow! Is there such a feeling? Well, there sure was today! Ha, ha! Papa really DOES love me! I reached out to my now, adoptive parents, as I spoke the words I never got to before, as I sobbed in complete and utter surrender...saying, "D-dad...M-mom..." ...now burying my head into their arms, as I wrapped my arms as wide open as I could to receive both of them at the same time—as each one, together had endearingly embraced me, with wide open, loving arms... They hugged me tightly, as I hugged them in complete bliss and with a peaceful serenity felt deep within my very own heart and spirit. My mind was at a calming peace, as I cried and cried with tears of joy. I had never in this world, not once, felt this with another human being before, until now.

Deep from within my heart, as we were in such a tight and long embrace that I didn't want to end—I thanked Papa quietly inside, saying, "Th-thank you Papa…" with a sigh of relief and again I repeated my gratitude to Him once again, "Papa, thank you for your love. Thank you…"

After maybe about a couple hours had gone by, staff began to fill the room. Something was different and I slowly lifted my head backwards a bit, to see what all of the commotion was about. It was Christmas time, and the hospital room was now being decorated up, to fit the celebration. The nurses gathered the children whom had the ability to walk and the strength to help out, as they decorated the nicely filled out green evergreen tree, standing in a corner of the room, now adorned with Christmas lights of many colours. It really did look so enchanting, as I watched it come together from my hospital bed, now resting as I lay with my head turned to face it. I had never seen this before. It was really cool, to witness. I really liked the lights, I think that they were my favourite.

Then some children whom were patients, came over and hopped on my bed, a nurse raised the head part so that I could sit up again. They had a roll of string, some big plastic sewing needles, and a large bowl, filled with popcorn that was coloured with a variety of food colouring dyes and some shimmering glitter. "Come on Kipper, would you like to help string the popcorn garland, for the Christmas tree?" I was shocked, I did not expect that.

My eyes widened in surprise as I replied almost immediately "Sure! Thank you!" "Oh you're welcome, we don't want you to feel left out, just because you can't walk up to the tree." It felt so cool to be included, and it was really, a lot of fun! I would string a couple onto my string, and then we took turns, as I took rests in between. It was pretty darn awesome teamwork, if you ask me! Ha, ha…

What a fun experience I thought to myself… Smiling with this newfound joy that grew inside of me a little more every moment that had passed. Being included, just really made me feel…special. Next, there was the lighting of the tree, the children in their light blue and white vertical striped hospital clothes, were joined by other children who had light yellow and white vertical striped clothing from another wing of the hospital. Then there was another crowd of people that entered the Children's Long Term Ward—both parents and visitors, nurses and doctors had now filled the room.

The nurses then handed out these, fuzzy red and white Santa hats, with white fluffy balls at the ends, every patient got one, including me. Even though I knew the truth about Saint Nick, I just wanted to wear the hat because it was festive and I never had a hat before, other than surgery hospital caps. Those, were not very, festive.... I lowered my lower lip, bearing my bottom teeth, in a yikes, sort of way... I knew the real reason for the season, was Jesus's birth. Why else, is the candy cane, in the shape of the letter, 'J' when held upright, as it was meant to be, and not the other way around? Ha, ha, bet you didn't know about that one? Ha, ha...

Mom and Dad had helped about the room and then came over and sat at the sides of my bed, as we took in the wondrous splendour of the room's overflow of visitors, patients, nurses and doctors that had joined all of us, long term sick kids in the room. It was a big room, so it could handle the load of people. Mom put the hat on my head for me, as I couldn't find the strength to reach up to do it myself. They too had festive decor on as well. Mom wore a nice looking brooch that had an angel on it, holding a baby boy, with a glowing halo around his head. It was baby Jesus. It was actually a very pretty pin and it told the tale that took on real life, once upon a time...

This atmosphere, oh my...it was so surreal and almost fantasy, even dreamlike, to be able to experience this and with all of these people. Then the children whom were helping decorate the big tree, had then completed decking it out, all adorned in the many different handmade creations that patients had made, in the Playroom a floor away. The many lights that encapsulated the big, wide evergreen tree, dazzled to our hearts delight. The nurses had then decorated the window frame around the big, tall window, with a shimmery garland, filled with plastic tree greenery as well as bright red poinsettia floral creations that someone had made. They couldn't actually have a real tree or real greenery in here, as there were many allergies and sensitivities that the patients had lacked tolerance to. But that didn't matter anyway, it still looked really nice and festive. They had also put Christmas lights up, all throughout the room, everywhere. It was so cool!

One doctor then started walking over to me. I had for a second, felt a little concerned as to why. For the only reasons that he ever was anywhere near me, was to give orders to send me to other rooms and have surgeries and how or what I should eat, and so on. Then, just as he had come by the side of my bed, I had to look right up to see his face. Then something happened, he had offered me something, that I did not expect! "Kipper, would you like to put the star on top of the tree?" My heart was definitely being embraced a lot more than ever lately, and I couldn't help but choke up and get emotional, again. I was shocked and excited and then I realized, how could I do that? Then the doctor continued to speak. "With the help of your dad, we can lift you up, if you would like?" He asked me with a smile. I had never before, seen him smile. I felt a jolt of hope go through me, as I embraced this moment, dearly to my heart. "O-okay, y-yes please... th-thank you..." I replied, with a shocked look that was now upon my face. He smiled and handed me the golden shimmering star tree topper to hold. It had such details on it like I had not ever come across before—okay, I had never held one nor seen a tree topper, before either. It was no basic looking star, however, for it was intricately carved from wood, it had the Angel of the Lord along the side of it, the Bethlehem manger scene, setting, carved across it. I could see baby Jesus, wrapped in swaddling clothes, laying a manger. There were three wisemen, standing off to the right, and barn animals, off to the left, of where the Saviour lay. I lightly grazed the carved detailing with my fingertips, all along this treasure that I got to hold, in my hands. I thanked the Lord Jesus, as I gazed upon His little face. What a gift, to this world, from Heaven—my hero, I had thought deeply inside... For I love thee, take me dear Lord, in Your most amazingly loving, embrace... I then looked up and readied myself for transport, as Mom moved the blanket off of my lap for me. My Dad caught my Christmas hat swiftly, as it began to slip when I moved my head—he adjusted it as both he and the doctor, one on each side of me, now had picked me up.

The moment had suddenly morphed into a slower motion and all of the people in the room, began to clap, for me? I became emotional, choking up with a humbled heart, beyond belief—for not even a single word could gather, for me to say. I was carried towards the tree in a slow motion, for all that had which surrounded us was moving about, ever so slowly, that it felt, like a dream... My eyes glanced among the crowd and upon the many faces—so many joyfully enriched smiles, and clapping, th-they were cheering, just for me. What have I done, to have deserved, such praise? I was so touched and felt, so loved… I cried with a steady flow of salty, warm tears, as they fell down my face. Stunned I looked, oh most definitely…

Pencil Artwork drawing of a feather cloud formation
entitled, "Papa's Wing Carries Me" by Kipper

The visual before me, was as though I was now watching a movie and that I was some other person, whom the audience, was now captivated to

IF I COULD FLOAT ON A CLOUD, WHERE WOULD I GO?

watch! Everyone in the audience about me, had slightly blurred a bit, as they all appeared in a slow motion, rhythmic gesture—encapsulated in dedication to cheer me on, as some had even jumped up and down, smiling from ear to ear and celebrating, me. It felt as though, I were dreaming. Was I dreaming? Like it, I cleared my throat, as I tried to speak in my heart, yet choked up even more. It c-couldn't possibly, b-be real... could it? I honestly, could not even imagine, such a joy—even, within my own cloud adventures and beyond those many windows traveled by many clouds, with one sky.

As I tried to smile, oh man, I just cried with a humbled heart! I cried probably the hardest that I had ever before, for a child like me. And everyone was filled with such, with such joyful tears and admiration! It was like a grace that was so profound and so surreal, so humbling and dreamy, yet so genuine and from the Father, from my Papa. Oh, what a feeling! Heaven on earth, MY GOD, you DO love me! I balled and many cried with me too. Then I managed to put a smile on my face, as meek as this boy could try to do. I opened my heart and received this blessing! Papa, Thank you...

Dad and the doctor then lifted me up high, onto my dad's shoulders, as the doctor and nurses helped stabilize me upright. He then reached me over to the top of the tree, the staff helped hold my arms up towards the top. I felt like I was taller than everyone else in the room and I wasn't even on my clouds to do this! Ha, ha, ha, ha! Wow, what a feeling!

My Dad gently held onto my right arm and surrounded my star gripped hand in his big yet gentle hands, and lifted my hand above the tree's top branch that stood straight up and helped me, place the star, just right. The slow motion rhythm now transitioned to the now, steady moving wave of people clapping and cheering my name on, "Yay, Kipper, you did it!" One called out. "Good job Kipper!" Cried out another. I smiled so big my cheeks began to hurt...but just a little, I didn't hardly notice it because I was just so happy.

The staff had then, helped my dad lower me back down again. I could see the joy and smiles from my adopted Mom and Dad, as I looked about the room of a sea of shining faces, all looking back at me...I was filled with just a warm and fuzzy-like, toasty warm feeling all over. It was at that very moment, as the lights shined their many colours across the room and caused the decorations...the garland, the tinsel, the shiny ornaments that hung elegantly upon the tree, they all just glistened from the twinkling lights and reflected all around me and on me.

The crowd then began to sing Christmas carols—songs of angels and peace, love, hope and joy—of Jesus. It sounded as though, Heaven had come to visit, me. I could feel the love, I need not even have to say a word… I just took it all in, as I were. I just knew Papa was there with me and holding me tightly encompassed in His loving embrace, by the support I was receiving from everyone in the room. What a feeling! As everyone sang their hearts out to Christmas carols and Christian songs that were being played on a stereo that the staff had brought in, I gazed towards the big, tall window, as I was now held up to look out of it, for the first time…I could see the North Star, shining brightly and promisingly.

Then the hospital staff wheeled my hospital bed closer… As I was choked up with emotion, they placed my hospital bed, right below the windowsill, so that I can look directly out of it, without straining my neck, anymore…could this night get any more emotional or more awesome, I had thought to myself! "Yesss! Thank you!" I humbly thanked them over and over again. The doctor and nurses carefully set me back into my hospital bed, then my Mom had tucked me back in.

Dad then handed me a small package, it was wrapped in a glistening, light sky blue coloured wrapping paper and a natural colour brown looking hemp rope that was tied around, each side. There was a tag on the top, in the centre of it, with a golden and silvery ribbon bow on it. I opened the tag to find it saying, "To our dear son, Kipper, you are the light of our life, the sunshine to our smile, the joy in our hearts, we are so grateful to you, for adopting us, as your Dad and Mom. We love you lots! Love, Dad and Mom and Papa". My eyes welled with tears and I was without words, as I looked at them briefly and then back down at the gift. They smiled and asked me to open it.

They started helping me untie the rope and then we unwrapped the gift, together. Slowly, unwrapping the glistening, light sky blue wrapping paper that was so beautifully wrapped around this gift. There was a white box inside with a lid, snuggly atop. I pulled the lid off and set it down on my lap. In awe and as tears had now completely overwhelmed me, I sat there, staring at the inside of this box, for what maybe seemed like forever to everyone else awaiting with a great anticipation, eagerly waiting and

IF I COULD FLOAT ON A CLOUD, WHERE WOULD I GO?

wanting to know the revealed mysterious contents, of what was inside. I reached inside and pulled out, a picture frame...with a picture in it, of my adopted Mom and Dad, and ME!

That was it for me, I completely lost it, as tears flowed down my face, as I tried cracking a smile but then I just was gone and lost in the moment. I had a picture of my new family... a family of my very own...I cried and cried and balled like a baby, as I buried my head, into Mom's and Dad's arms and just cried... God had just given me, beyond everything that I could not have even imagined possible—He made possible. Th-thank y-you Papa! I cried out from deep within my heart, to His.

Everyone else in the room, were just heart struck with joy and tears too, streaming down their faces! What a blessed day this was! It was the best second gift ever. The first, well that is Jesus... It takes love to be a family, not DNA.

Pencil Artwork drawing of a Christmas Tree entitled, "Jesus Is The Reason" by Kipper

CHAPTER NINE

It is time, to come home

An incredible and truly, rewarding miracle has happened right before my eyes—for the first time, since I began my journey in life, while living on this hospital bed. I have been here since I was born and never have I experienced, such an overwhelming, freeing warmth of emotion, granted to me, to be able to witness and take part in. To be loved, beyond measure, I got to take part and it was, truly amazing! Christmas, was definitely now my most favourite time of year! And I now have a family of my very own! Isn't that so cool! Just, wow...

My dear friend Bobby, whom I first met on one of my cloud adventures to the green meadows, following a most epic sailboat race, of all time—which was now, several years ago and in person for the first time in the real world, I too got to meet him. Well, he had survived his accident, his major surgery and now finally, after a long time—has opened his eyes to see his Momma and Pa, whom were lovingly, by his side. He didn't remember me much in real life but remembered me from his dreams. We have a bond that will never end, regardless where either one of us, go from here...

So much time has passed and I still don't really know how old I am now, however if I were to take a gander—my guess would be maybe, somewhere around thirteen years old, perhaps? That is quite a lot of years while living on a hospital bed, of all places! Ha, ha... Yet, it is also rather a quite young age, and shortened version from that of much of a full life—is it not? Although, whom is to judge, whose life, is a full one or not, regardless of their lifespan? Some will say it was cheated and not a full one at all but then again, who are they to say that, when no one knows just exactly how long our natural lives, are meant to last here—before we can go home…long, short, in the middle, it does not really matter—what really matters the most, is if we made the most of it or not, you know? I cannot really imagine it will last for much longer, for me…why you ask? Well, just being honest here but things have changed a fair bit over the last several years—actually, a lot. As time went on—so too has my condition progressed and in doing so, my health has severely, declined…

Unfortunately, it is with over this past year and especially, since Christmas—that I now, must be fed through a tube, indefinitely… P-please bare with me, as I try to explain this with the attempt of trying not to become overwhelmed by tears and then a loss for words, to follow. Trying to convey in how I feel, about how much further I have atrophied, over a short period of time—well, it has become quite difficult for me, to say the least. You know?

Pencil Artwork drawing entitled, "Rise Up, Rise Up" by Kipper

As try as I might, with a gradual ascending of tearful choked up words and sniffles, here we go… Taking a deep breath in and then slowly letting it out, Kipper began to explain, some more. M-my muscles, well they had all decided to reverse time, on me—rather rapidly in fact, as they excelled in degeneration and now, they have since left me—taking what little strength I had, with them. No, no, it's okay, I can talk about it. Hey, it happens. Life happens…

I am more of a rack of bones in a skin suit these days but my hunger for life and adventure has still not diminished, nor changed. But rather, I divide my time much more evenly these days—between the dreamworld and that of the real world, now more than ever—leaving nothing to chance and learning to really appreciate what little time…what little time I may ha-have here. I need a minute…sorry…

Okay…I am back—I'm okay… You know, quite frankly, for what it is worth, I am grateful to have lived a life of adventure, rather than a life of regrets. And you know what, that is just exactly that…within reason—it does not really matter to me in a way, considering that I have not even been able to sit up at all on my own, since I was born here. And truth be told…from this place—well, it will be where I get to go, home. I can't wait to see Papa, face to face once again when this is all over… then I really will get to stand on my own two feet, for all the rest of my existence. So, with that said, I am going to remain strong in spirit and filled with a heart of hope—for my future is yet to come. Hey, it's all right, this is not the end, true life begins, once I have come to learn all that Papa has wanted for me, in this life—for eternal life begins when Papa is ready, to return for me. And you know what? Even when we make mistake after mistake, Papa patiently sees us as a little child whom when we fall—He picks us back up, dusts us off and lovingly asks for us to climb back up on the bike and try again. Wow…

A nurse was standing next to me, replacing the cloudy clear bag that was hooked up to me. The daily routine began for me, though these days, a little more complex, as the nurses checked my vitals—they tested my blood pressure, poked and prodded me, took my temperature, listened to my heart, replaced the bags that helped me go to the bathroom, replaced my food bag, upped my medications again, through the IV fluids…they washed me, clothed me, covered me with multiple toasty-warm heated blankets which felt so good! This was to keep me from shivering so much and so forth…

IF I COULD FLOAT ON A CLOUD, WHERE WOULD I GO?

But there was no one telling me much these days, who could blame them, right? Who are we kidding, seriously, ha, ha…I looked like a rack of bones, nowadays. Even the nurses avoided looking at me at times, looking embarrassed to see my appearance—my, situation. Believe it or not but I actually, feel sorry for the nurses and doctors now.

I mean, think of it…after all of my years of living right here, everyday, day in and day out, I have had gratefully yet again, had breath in my lungs to see another day and was still, terminally bed-stricken—all of their hard work in trying so hard, to save me, to help me recover in hopes for improvement—it has only gone down hill in full gear. I cannot hardly, fully imagine, how they must be feeling… Can you even fathom just how they must be feeling, deep down inside? They probably feel, like they have failed me…but they haven't… this is my life, welcome to it.

I began to realize, just how hard it must be for them. With all of the patients they see on a daily basis, all throughout their many years of work here—I now understand some of their bitterness and coldness that I thought that I have felt at times, over these last several years. Think of it… They bring you back but only get to see you barely survive, with little improvement—which must feel, so defeating for them. I cannot really blame them though, it is not their fault and it is really no one's fault at all. That is just the way it has been for me, for my life—I do not blame anyone, at all. Not a one… Through everything that I have gone through, regardless of the persistent hardships—they have shaped me into who I am, to this very day. I choose to be thankful.

So truthfully, I give all credit to Papa and I thank Him for giving me this life, for giving me an imagination and a hunger for adventure and in showing me, just how to use that mindset and how to lean unto Him, through faith and patience—for giving me breath… I am truly grateful. I have no regrets. Perhaps, as they say that God won't put us through what He knows, that we cannot handle… well, there is only one me in this world, so it took, me, to be in my own two, bare feet. Ha, ha…

You know, I have been wondering lately… If well, if the doctors and nurses just knew that…*(sigh)*…well, when one of my health attack episodes would happen, if they weren't sooo good at bringing me back, again and again…could I have then been home, long ago?

Pencil Artwork drawing of delicious looking baked cookies entitled, "God has made us, let us let Him finish perfecting us!" by Kipper

However, I do acknowledge that just as the hairs on our head are numbered—so too are our days, are numbered as well. Everything happens for a reason, yes even bad things too…try and hear me out, I will explain further. Although yes, sadly bad things do happen to all of us—but, just as a shadow cannot exist without the presence of light in the midst…so too, our Heavenly Father always, always will make good happen, from out of darkness, in any bad situation—when we learn to believe and let go of control, so that we can let Papa, do His good works. Because we just simply, do, not, have, control. We were never meant to—or we wouldn't need to have faith and trust in Him, now would we?

We humans, constantly forget that we, do not have control in this life. Why? Because the enemy tells us lies of the exact opposite and we then, end up making even more and even bigger, harder mistakes, for us to try and get back up from. Not only does Papa have it in His capable, almighty hands, remember, not us—but He never changes, He is constant and our solid ground, our rock. When we try to control our lives and try to be an 'idol', or the 'provider', or the 'hero' of our own story—ha, ha…I'm sorry for laughing but, you see, it just never works out well in the long run, when we do. Just, try it but you have to have faith in Him, you have to trust Him, taking the biggest leap of daily faith, of your life! It is a daily thing, a daily walk through faith. Faith cannot be selectively used, for when we think it is deemed of any worth for only areas that we maybe think that it is necessary. That is just foolish thinking! We need, Jesus, daily. He is not some imaginary man, that only existed in and for ancient days passed. Ha, ha! Not, at all! Ha, ha…

You can do it, I believe in you! Go ahead, dear friend and let go of the wheel of your life and let God, be God, in all of His Glory! He loves you so, very much! He wants to give you the best life, even beyond your own understanding—yet as our Heavenly Father, He does not force us because He gave us, there's that word again—Free-will. He made us! He is personally and in great detailed writing, perfecting your story and it is filled with, unfathomably, wonderful great plans, for you! Go ahead, He wants His pen back.

I live on a hospital bed! Why? Ha, ha…I don't know but I trust that Papa knew that I was the right person, to handle it as I would learn to push onward and just trust and lean on Him, for strength and perseverance, beyond anyone's own comprehension.

It sure makes me laugh out loud though, funny enough! Ha, ha! Because, as this brings joy to my heart and I honestly cannot stop smiling, whenever I think about it…. You see, I don't even have to understand why I am here, living this way or why or why not someone else could have instead and so on, etc., etc.,—and also because it is not in my hands, so why worry myself sick about it? If I truly want to trust in Papa in Heaven, then I have to do it with all of my heart—like a mighty roaring lion, whom when faced with adversity throughout life, chooses not to starve from the real thing, and be more than just a survivor—but to be fiercely humbled before the King and will go at any length that is asked of us by our Father and be willing to, go into any fiery pit of trials and tribulations throughout life, so that God can use us for the goodness, of His glory.

My life, it never was and nor shall it ever be, mine, nor in my hands. I am so relieved, that I do not have to explain myself to Papa, as He knows everything, ha, ha—I don't have to worry or stress on what must I do tomorrow. Will I make it or will I pass on, during my next attack episode? Or will the sky, even have a single cloud pass by my window? Should I, fret about what will I do, if no one comes to see me? Worrying gets one, nowhere fast. I now have the confidence in Papa, in knowing that I don't have to worry at all, because I trust Papa wholly, that means fully—with all my heart. How does that saying go, now? "Yesterday is history. Tomorrow is a mystery, but today is a gift—that is why it's called the present."

Papa, will provide, period. I need only be still. We cannot worry and have faith at the same time, remember? It does not work. I cannot halfway trust, it does not work. I either must choose to trust fully, or I choose not to, there is no in-between choice, with Papa. When we choose, to completely trust in Him—we become at rest. In His loving arms, He carries us—not only through this life, but into eternity, with Him.

All I have to make sure of, is that I decide where I want to end up when my time here on earth is done—and as for the rest, the rest is history! Ha, ha! I know that my name is written in Papa's book of Life because I believe in what Jesus did for me and so I know where I am going, once my time here has finished and you know what? THAT, is all that Papa requires of me because as I have mentioned before, it does not matter what we have done or do, what matters most, is what Jesus did for us. His sacrifice was PERFECT. It was perfect!

"Come to me, all you who are weary and burdened, and I will give you rest. Take my yoke upon you and learn from me, for I am gentle and humble in heart, and you will find rest for your souls. For my yoke is easy and my burden is light." — Matthew 11:28-30

IF I COULD FLOAT ON A CLOUD, WHERE WOULD I GO?

Pencil Artwork drawing of the Earth's moon entitled, "A New Creation" by Kipper

I am sooo, sooo grateful that I get to be one of Papa's Forged Lambs, in His Flock of billions and no longer, one of Satan's Inferno's Puppets. You can trust in God, you have nothing to lose by trusting Him but rather, everything so, so good in Him, to gain. That, gives me great comfort and puts my mind to rest.

You know, here's a rather interesting, fun fact for you: Papa literally, just told me, that the only book in the entire world—in all of creation that which you cannot get sued legally, by copying or using any of the material in it, for your own personal or public use, is Papa's book, the Bible! Ha, ha... now that is pretty darn cool, if you ask me! The one true book that matters the most for all of the world, in the entire universe—the most important book that you will ever encounter in all of your days—Papa has created through His disciples. Ha, ha, ha! Wow, now that is a pretty cool truth, right there...thank you Papa!

I don't mean to be 'preachy' ...I am only telling you from what I have learned. Does that make some sense? I certainly will not tell you what you should be doing, or whether you are doing things wrong. That is not my job. Only the devil will condemn and do it to us and through people, but it is not from God. God is a loving Father and He very much wants, for all of us to make it! Free-will is a powerful thing, to have in our possession—the key is, how will we decide to utilize it? Time will tell, right? Time will tell...

I know that that day will come for me, when it is time. I know that when something is meant to be, nothing will stand in its way. But sometimes, it isn't fast, sometimes it takes a little longer for that to happen to some of us, whom are still in the waiting.

While lying in this hospital bed for days and nights without end, it is so easy to over hear conversations, between nurses, doctors, patients, visitors, councillors, priests and so on. Over a period of time, I had found out that most of, or all of my old friends from the green meadows, were children that have now since then, passed away. All children, go to Heaven. God knows everyone's heart. I think that they, went home. That could explain why I hadn't seen them in such a long time, on my adventures, or in my hospital room.

By Papa's Grace, Bobby had been in the hospital for no more than three additional months, after he managed to wake up, following his major surgery. He had now since then, been moved to home care, in his own home with his parents now, I guess. Oh and remember Kimmie? She was the little girl, with the green skin? Well, she had recovered following a vital kidney transplant, taking away her yellowish-green skin colouring, making it a healthy whitish-pink.

The twins were not here long, they were sent home only days after we had met. Mary-Lou had plastic surgery and now doesn't look like she was badly burnt, anymore. She was sent home after several plastic surgeries later. Betsy-Ann never made it. I never did find out what had happened to the others but I often think about them, praying for them in hopes that they are well and happy.

Penny for your thoughts? Why is it that when someone dies with an illness, we say that he or she had lost their battle? From the moment they found out they were ill, did they give up? No, they fought and persevered, beyond anyone's comprehension—inspiring those all round them and

IF I COULD FLOAT ON A CLOUD, WHERE WOULD I GO?

then leaving behind a truth to life, a reason to live—a legacy. I believe that we should say, that they won.

And when people of any age or situation in life are referred to as "normal" and others "not normal" ...I'm sorry, whom decides that? What is "normal" anyway? Are we just simply afraid of the unexpected, the gifted, or of a genuine miracle? Let us no longer be afraid, for we belittle what God can do, or in Him, what we can become. Imagine the possibilities, just imagine!

There are always others in worse situations than ourselves, as we try to convince ourselves. But often I wonder, that those who we say that are in worse sorts—are there any others beyond them, whom are worse off than them? Or does it end with those, whom are worse off than us?

I gather that I am one of the others being worse off, than you, perhaps... It does not feel any better to say either way though. It really doesn't feel good to hear that there are others, whom are in worse condition than I, either...really though as yourself this, what is the ultimately, worst scenario? And what knowledge and experience, does such a human, have to even prove that? The only one, that I feel, whom could even fathomably, make such a claim from true, personal experience—is Jesus... through His sacrifice, the greatest sacrifice, of all time, from the horrendously cruelest of cruelty that He had endured being beaten and torn a part prior to being nailed to the cross, and when, He was on the cross and then gave up His life, for all. Only He, can personally testify, to such a truth.

Who decides who is better off and who is the least fortunate? I have never understood that. I don't know whom my biological parents were. I never saw them, from what I can remember. I don't know if I ever had, any sisters or bothers. I do know however that I will not recover, nor improve from this illness that has taken over my body, from day one. I was born here. And I am not afraid to say that I will most likely, die here.

I have learned to embrace my situation by living those journeys, that I have taken on the clouds through my many windows, with one sky. Always wondering, if I could float on a cloud, where would I go? Physically, I have never been out of this hospital bed on my own, ever. It was only through my imagination and dreams that I could escape and connect with other children, all suffering from something, keeping them in this building too. But then Papa blessed my life with people, my adoptive Mom and my adoptive Dad—to the many roommates that I have had the privilege to get to know, while still stuck, in my hospital bed.

I have learned that although many nurses and doctors will appear bitter and cold, they do care and that they too, have struggles. They are dealing with the daily struggle, in trying to save lives of all illnesses, of all ages, cultures, religions, backgrounds, colours, shapes and sizes. And regardless of our differing illnesses, we really are, in good hands. For if there were no one in his or her shoes to help us, if Papa didn't provide for us, then hope would not need to exist—and somebody has to dream.

Lying in bed, I began to feel a pull in my heart. Once again, all of the machines around me, connected to me, had begun to beep and hum and whistle. Warning alarms had sounded, so loudly. All of the lights, blinked quickly to warn medical staff to hurry in. Nurses and doctors ran in one after the other, all to come to my side. I heard so many voices, speaking quickly and loudly, sounding so frantic and extremely, frustrated.

I began to float up, off of my hospital bed, just as I had so long ago before… and then I was suddenly looking down, at my body once again, covered in wires, hands and tubes. Although I've been through this so many times, I always thought it a little strange, knowing that I knew that that body, was mine, but I was not at all, missing it. I was not afraid. I cared for that body but felt that there was no longer, a connection between it and myself.

I found myself looking up and saw that glowing vibrantly bright light, dancing right above me, again! I then began to float towards it, slowly. Gradually, I floated faster and faster, now leaving behind the frantic voices and my small, still body. I was weightless and I had no fear at all, weighing me down—there was not the least bit of hesitation within me. I began to feel warmth from the light that had surrounded me. I did not have to reach out and strain for it, for the Light carried me this time.

Fascinated by how it glowed, danced and was warm and inviting, I reached out towards it, to touch it. Its bright, colourful beauty, became more brilliant than even that rainbow, I had seen some time ago. For I, was no longer in my hospital bed.

Engaged by the light, it began to speak to me. It was again that healing warmth of such a Divine love that pursued me, embracing me like before, a long time ago. And this time, there was nothing pulling me down and grabbing me, from continuing this journey — there was no struggle and no fear, at all.

I came to a powerful beam of light and then I saw, what had appeared to be, glowing golden-white angels by the thousands, floating all around me. The brightly radiating, long and life-filled, floating tunnel, between this Heavenly place and the world that I had left behind, had closed. Standing, yet floating in front of them, was that Man, whom I had met here once before, a long, long time ago.

He was just as I remembered Him. Dressed in a glowing, golden-white robe, with long wavy brown hair, a moustache and beard. The man reached out His large hand gently and said to me, "Kipper, I have come for you. Take my hand." Without hesitation, I took a deep breath and placed my small hand in His, and with that, I had a satisfied smile upon my face and a warmth in my heart—and I asked Him once more, "Is it my time?" And He said, "Yes, my child, it is time, to come home."

I for the first time, during my long awaited return, yet during my very, short life, was not homesick—I was free.

And I was home.

†

Jesus Loves You! God Bless You!

...Oh wait, you ask if this,
Is The End?
Oh, but my dear friend—
In Papa's Heavenly Kingdom,
You are forgetting...

—✝—

<u>*Eternal Life, has just begun!*</u>
See you on the other side! :) I lightly grazed the carved detailing all along this treasure, that

CPSIA information can be obtained
at www.ICGtesting.com
Printed in the USA
BVHW030028181219
567009BV00001B/4/P

Printed in the USA
CPSIA information can be obtained
at www.ICGtesting.com
LVHW010736220524
780462LV00014B/648